A CROWN OF THE GODS

SHADOWS AND CROWNS

A CROWN OF THE GODS

BOOK FOUR

S. M. GAITHER

THE HIERARCHY OF GODS

Rook   ICE   BONE   SERPENT   FIRE

Sun   STAR   MOON   SKY   STORM

Stone   OAK   MTN.   SAND   OCEAN

SHADOWMERE

DAWNSKEEP

STONEBARROW

★ Malgraves

The former Kingdom of
Alnor

GRAYEDGE

The Kingdom of
Melech

BLOODSTONE
MOUNTAINS

FOOTHILLS
VILLAGE

HERRATH

★ Ciridan

VALSHADE
FOREST

FALLENBRIDGE

LOTHERAN
RIVER

OBLIVION
GATEWAY

GREAT
SOUTHERN ROAD

EDGEKEEP

The Wild In-Between

To Amanda—
Thank you for putting up with me.

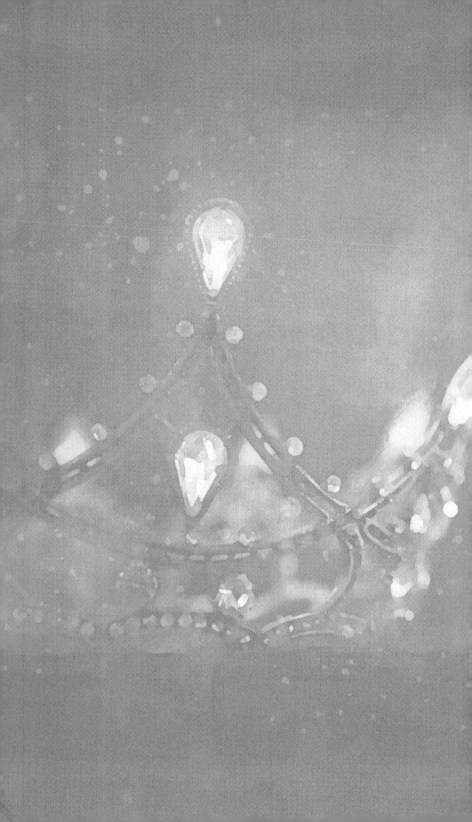

PRELUDE

PRINCE VAREN STOOD OUTSIDE THE LIBRARY WINDOW, balanced on a makeshift stool, his short legs stretched out as far as he dared to stretch them.

He was spying. Trying to keep his eyes on his father, who was talking to a stranger dressed in black leathers. The stranger had his face angled away from Varen. A fire was roaring next to the two figures, its light creating shadows that stretched frighteningly tall against the endless shelves of books that wrapped around the room.

Outside of that room, in the courtyard where the young prince watched from, it was fast becoming cold. The sun was setting. Wind howled from the east. The only part of Varen that *wasn't* cold after standing in that wind for the better part of the last hour was the throbbing patch of red on his cheek.

That stinging brand was his mother's work. She had

been chattering away with one of the ladies of her court when he'd stumbled in to ask her for a bedtime story. When she'd started to summon a servant to do the job, Varen had automatically teared up at the thought of old Nana Faye and her scratchy voice reciting whatever strange stories she remembered from her childhood in the southern empire. Those stories of wild magic and monsters frightened him, and Nana Faye had always seemed to delight in his fear.

The tears had been his mistake, of course.

The queen did not like tears.

He should have known that. He *did* know that. The slap had only been a sharp but necessary reminder. After that, he had left his mother—without another word about stories—and sulked his way toward his room.

But something had caught his attention before he reached it—a seizing coldness, like the nasty shock of having a warm blanket jerked off by someone trying to wake him up.

There's magic afoot, he'd heard one of the servants telling another.

He didn't understand magic.

He only knew Nana Faye's stories about it, and that his mother hated it as much as she hated tears—so he should have avoided it, the way he usually avoided crying.

But curiosity had overcome his fear and led him to

follow the pull of that magic...and this is what had brought him to the library window.

Another shiver of power grabbed at his skin. It seemed to be coming from that man dressed in black, though it was hard to tell where the cold, easterly wind ended and the frigid magic began. That cold—whatever was causing it—made his throat ache.

A small cough escaped him.

The man in black glanced toward the window, and Varen ducked.

Minutes later, when he felt courageous enough to look inside again, his father was alone in the library. But the flames in the fireplace had shifted to a pale shade of blue, and there was a single raven feather floating down through the air, slowly coming to rest where that man in black had only just been standing.

How odd.

Varen heard someone approaching. He shuffled off the upside-down pail he'd been using as a step stool, planted his feet on the hard stone path, and squinted into the darkening twilight.

A young girl with waves of reddish brown hair emerged from the darkness. His big sister. His twin, most people assumed—though he was actually ten months younger.

"What are you doing, Ren?" she asked, head tilting. She had a book tucked under her arm. *The Tiger and the*

Queen. One of his favorites. He sniffed and rubbed away a tear that started to fall.

The only thing worse than Nana Faye reading to him was his *sister* reading to him. It simply didn't feel *right*; she should have been listening to the story alongside him instead.

Her gaze jumped to the red spot on his cheek, and she frowned.

Varen sniffed again. That didn't feel right, either. Like she was concerned about him...and what for? He could take care of himself as well as she could. She acted so much older than she ought to act.

Then again, people said the same about him.

Strange children, the court called them. Sometimes that court whispered, at least sounding sad or worried. Other times they sounded loud and...*cruel*.

But that didn't mean they were wrong, did it?

And maybe if he could find a way to act less strange, his mother would be more interested in reading him bedtime stories.

"Come on," his sister said, grabbing his arm and pulling. "You're s'posed to be in bed."

Despite less than a year between them, she was already much taller—and stronger. He didn't see the point in fighting her. He let her pull him through the palace, back to his room, and then he crawled into his bed and slipped beneath the covers.

His sister stretched out across the foot of the

mattress like she always did, resting on her back with the book extended above her as she read it. He usually complained that he couldn't see the pictures when she held it at this angle. But tonight, he didn't care. He didn't want to see them, her, or anything else.

He closed his eyes so the tears would stay in as he listened to his sister tell the familiar story in her usual, overdramatic reading voice.

Once upon a time, a young queen lived alone in a big castle near the very top of a mountain, surrounded by the tallest trees you could imagine.

And within those trees there lived a family of tigers.

The young queen was captivated by them, and every day, she drew closer and closer to the dark forest, hoping for a glimpse...

Varen fell asleep just as the queen finally gathered enough courage to step into the forest in search of her beloved tigers, only to find herself changing, sprouting claws and stripes and becoming a beast herself.

SOME TIME LATER, Varen jerked awake, shivering. He felt it again. *Magic.*

His sister was gone. The room felt too big—too empty—without her in it. He tried to huddle under his blankets and go back to sleep, but the cold persisted, so he shuffled from his bed and plodded down the hallway to his sister's room.

She wasn't there.

The icy fingers of magic continued to curl around him. Beckoning him. Pulling him down one hallway and then the next, the next, the next, until finally he came to a large set of doors—the entrance to the sitting room his mother had been in earlier. He could hear people moving inside.

His fingers tapped the mark on his cheek.

Still tender.

He didn't want to speak to his mother again tonight...but he wanted to know what was happening in that room.

There was a storage space and a servant's corridor that connected to it. Using that instead of the main doors, he inched along with his back to the wall, and soon he caught sight of his mother, of the sequins of her dress shimmering in the light of a low-burning fire. The ladies of her court were gone. But she wasn't alone. There was a...

His breath caught.

What was that?

As he stared into the room, at the nightmarish...*thing*...before him, he wondered if he was still asleep. He gave his head a shake. Nightmares weren't real. *Monsters* weren't real. His sister told him that all the time.

And yet...

And yet, here a monster seemed to be, taking up an

entire half of the massive room. Its curled ears were pinned back against its monstrous head, and it stared at the queen with eyes that burned bright, flashing between shades of white and pale, frozen blue. It looked like one of the beasts from Nana's stories. Like a wolf—but one surrounded by unnatural ribbons of black that writhed like living shadows around its body.

The queen clutched one of the metal rods from the basket by the fireplace, her fingers white from the strength of her grip.

There was another rod left in that basket. One with a sharper end. *A better weapon.* Varen snuck forward, his gaze locked on that shiny, sharp end.

He came to his senses at the edge of the fire's circle of light. He stumbled to a stop, dropped slowly to his knees, and clenched his small fists into the shaggy carpet.

Why had he come in here?

The queen had not noticed her son; she only had eyes for the wolf.

It stalked closer to her.

Her grip on the metal rod tightened. She stood her ground, and Varen could just barely hear her whisper, "I knew the gods were angry with us. You've come for a sacrifice, haven't you?"

The shadows around the wolf danced, as if excited by the idea.

The queen recoiled slightly, but she still did not flee.

7

Varen curled closer to the floor. A sound escaped him —another soft cry.

Another mistake.

His mother moved to him as she heard it. She took hold of his arm, pulled him to his feet, and held fast. She kept him by her side even as the wolf turned its eyes on him. She forced him to stand up straight even when he tried to cower against her skirts.

A soft growl rumbled through the room.

Varen shivered. His mother's grip on his arm tightened, weakened, tightened again...until finally she seemed to make up her mind, and she shoved her son in front of her.

The monster had started forward, only to pause at the sight of a child with weak knees and shaking hands —almost as if it felt uncertain. Confused, maybe.

But even to Varen's four-year-old mind, the unspoken command his mother had given was clear enough.

Take him instead.

Here is your sacrifice.

Varen closed his eyes and braced himself for the feel of teeth and claws against his skin.

When several moments passed and the sharpness did not come, he cautiously peeked one eye open again.

The shadows around the monster were twisting and reaching toward him.

But they thinned as they passed over Varen, turning

to barely-there vapors that left nothing more than a chill on his skin before they moved on, sweeping back behind him and surrounding his mother instead.

Silently, they swallowed her up—so silently that the queen's final gasp was easily heard. She was cocooned and suspended in the air only long enough to release that gasp, and then she was falling, slumping, crumpling to the floor. No longer moving. Or breathing.

Dazed, Varen crawled away from her. His stomach ached. His hands and feet felt funny. Tingly. He wanted to keep crawling forever—or until he reached someplace far away where no one could find him—but he froze once more, just outside of the firelight, as a wave of cold overtook him. He glanced over his shoulder.

The wolf stared at him.

He stared back.

He should have shouted for help. Instead, he reached out a trembling hand...

But why?

To tell the beast to stop?

Or to beckon it closer, to grab at those shadows around it? They were thick, a shield that hid the true shape of the beast. The only clear things among its darkness were its eyes, which were now the bright red shade of burning coals.

A thought gripped Varen as he watched the shadows dance.

Mine. I want them to be mine.

He was afraid, and he was thinking only of how *strong* those shadows must have been, to do what they'd done to the queen. He wanted to be strong, too. He wanted something to protect him.

Mine. They should be mine.

The beast growled, as if in opposition to this unspoken thought.

Varen staggered to his feet. He looked at the queen's body. Still not moving. Not breathing. It hit him then, all at once, with a force that nearly knocked him back to his hands and knees.

Dead.

His mother was dead.

Anger intertwined with his fear, but he still did not shout. He couldn't make himself loud. He never could, it seemed. The royal court whispered about this too.

Strange child, to be so young yet throw so few tantrums.

His anger had always been quieter—darker—wrapping around him like a weighted security blanket that he carried with him wherever he went.

But in that moment, someone *else* was being loud; someone else had started to shout for him.

His sister.

She appeared in the doorway, clutching a stuffed tiger in her hands. It was his own toy; Nana Faye had been sewing its tail back on. Was that why his sister had left him alone in his room? So she could go and collect it?

His hand was outstretched toward the beast again,

Varen realized. And he couldn't seem to pull it back. Or maybe he didn't *want* to pull it back. He still wanted those shadows. He wanted to control them, to use them to cover up the dead queen so his sister didn't have to see what had happened.

The room grew darker. Colder. Those shadows closed in on him, just as they'd done to his mother. As they encased him, he felt his body slumping just as hers had.

He wanted to lay down and go to sleep.

Before he could, several things happened all at once.

Through the blackness, he saw a flash of white, snapping teeth. He felt an arm wrapping around his waist, pulling him away from the teeth and the shadows, and then he was on the ground with his sister beside him. She kept her arm around him, kept pulling until they were in clearer air. Once there, she straightened and stood in front of him with her arm drawn back, as if readying a sword and preparing to slay that beast before them.

But there was no sword. And there were no guards rushing to protect them either. No other help was coming. There was no way out.

The dark beast stepped forward—

Only to meet a wall of brilliant light.

It washed over the wolf and drove it back. The beast tossed its head, lowered its body and snapped its gaze from side to side, searching for its shadows.

But the light was growing, scattering and chasing those shadows out of sight, out of reach. And it seemed to be drawing out *more* light from everything around them—even pulling it from within the wolf itself—until the entire room was drenched in a blinding glow.

Warmth overtook Varen, sinking deep into his skin. He closed his eyes and let the feeling of it carry him away.

"Ren." His sister's voice, shaky and soft, from somewhere in the distance.

He slowly blinked his eyes open at the sound.

The light was gone.

The beast was gone.

It was only him and his sister now—there was no one else in the entire world, it felt like.

She moved first, crawling over to the stuffed tiger that had fallen nearby. Wordlessly, she gathered it up and handed it to him. He clutched it to his chest, and his sister clutched him to *her* chest, and despite the overwhelming feeling of death and dangerous magic that permeated the air, Varen felt safe enough to close his eyes and fade away again.

The next time he opened his eyes, his sister was nowhere to be found.

Varen could no longer speak. Not to his father, not to Nana Faye, not to the multitude of doctors and nurses that paraded in and out of his room.

Even at his mother's funeral, he neither cried nor spoke.

Weeks passed.

He dreamt about the light that had surrounded him and his sister almost every night. And when he finally found his voice, the first words that came out were quiet and shaking, just as his sister's last word to him had been. "Where did she go?"

"She took ill," his father said without looking at him, "and she's gone away to get better."

So Varen waited for her to get better.

Most days he sat alone in the tallest of the palace's residential towers, accompanied by stacks of books. The books went mostly unread. He was too busy watching the gates for a procession that would herald the Princess's return. She was going to come home. She was going to come home and explain the light that she had conjured from nowhere, and the wolf that had fled from it, and everything that would come next for the two of them. *Together.* Whatever came next, they would face it together.

Soon, little Prince, Nana Faye mumbled distractedly, every time he pestered her about it.

"Soon," he repeated to himself every time he climbed the winding tower steps to start his watch.

But the weeks became an entire month, and another, and then a year had passed.

She still did not come back.

And one day, he decided he had no choice but to stop waiting for her.

CHAPTER 1

Eighteen Years Later

CASIA BALANCED IN THE SHADOWS ATOP ONE OF THE ROYAL Palace of Ciridan's protective walls, trying to keep her focus on the mission before her.

A dead guard lay at her feet.

He had been the sole protector of this secluded, distant corner, and she'd given him the chance to surrender and step aside.

He'd refused.

A crisp wind blew from the east, making her eyes water and burn. She rubbed away the tears and continued to scout out the scene before her, silently counting the people moving along the paths below.

Some were her own allies, disguised and blending in through various methods.

But too many of them were her brother's loyalists—more than they'd expected, it seemed like.

"You okay?"

"Of course." She glanced over at Zev, and she found her best friend looking at her from beneath raised brows. "Why wouldn't I be okay?" she asked.

His mouth quirked at her dry tone. "Fair enough. Stupid question, I guess."

Cas returned to her scouting.

The reasons for her *not okayness* were vast.

Immeasurable, almost.

Three weeks ago, she had gone to battle with her brother. She had watched the man she loved die by Varen's hands...and then watched that man live again, reborn as something she still did not fully understand. She had briefly left the mortal realm herself, just long enough to have a meeting with one of their world's most powerful deities—Solatis, Goddess of the Sun—and then she had been sent back into this realm with a new sword in her hand and a daunting purpose roaring between her ears.

Shadows are falling, that upper-goddess had told her during their meeting, *and it is too late to stop them from coming now. But perhaps you can still drive them out.*

So here Cas stood, looking at a palace that was missing its ruler. Though many of Varen's followers still remained, waiting for his return, she wasn't certain her brother was even aware of those followers anymore. He was now in the process of becoming the middle-god of Death and Destruction—a servant of the dark, terrible upper-god that was hellbent on destroying the mortal world as she knew it. If that upper-god was not stopped—

She gave her head a little shake.

Tonight, she had to focus on a relatively smaller battle.

One she knew she could actually win.

She was using Varen's absence to her advantage. If this particular mission went according to plan, his former palace would become hers instead, and from it she would begin her reign as queen of this kingdom—the necessary first step in collecting allies to wage war against rising gods and falling shadows.

"It was stupid." She tilted her face toward Zev and offered him a small smile. "But thanks for asking, all the same."

"What can I say? Knowing when and how to ask stupid questions is one of my greatest skills."

"At least you're skilled at *something*," Nessa muttered as she reached them. Silverfoot was curled around her shoulders, and the fox's green eyes were alight with a magical glow as he scanned his surroundings and sent back information to Rhea, who waited along with a group of their soldiers in the nearby forest.

Nessa and Zev began a quiet debate about who had the most useful skills between them until Cas brought a finger to her lips and shushed them. She was trying to concentrate on the flicker of light she thought she had just seen.

A moment later, she saw it again—a series of quick, deliberate flashes of white from one of the tower windows.

"There's the signal." She rolled the tension from her shoulders and neck and started for the nearby stairs. "Watch my back?"

"Always," Zev replied, already moving to an opening in the parapet. Nessa knelt at the opening beside him, and they both readied their bows and nocked arrows.

Cas moved swiftly down the steps. She paused at the bottom just long enough to steel herself with a deep breath, and then she started to walk, gripping the handle of her sword with a slightly trembling hand.

Shadowslayer. That was the blade's name. It was the one that had been given to her by the Sun Goddess during their encounter, and she had only just started to unlock its power. There was plenty left to discover—about this sword's magic, not to mention her own, Elander's, and her brother's...

Her thumb traced the talisman nestled in the pommel of the sword. The Heart of the Sun—broken during her last battle with Varen and repaired by Solatis herself. It warmed at Cas's touch, rumbling faintly, like a living thing waking from sleep.

With a whispered plea to the Moon Goddess—one of the four most powerful divine beings within Solatis's court—the soft rumbling swept from the Heart down to the symbols etched along the steel blade.

With the help of the Moon deity herself, Cas had almost perfected at least *one* new trick over the past few weeks. Shadowslayer pulsed briefly with light, the crescent-shaped symbol in the metal burning the brightest. Gossamer strands peeled away from the blade and disappeared just as quickly—quick enough that any onlooker would have thought their eyes were playing tricks on them.

Even as the outward sign of it faded, Cas could feel it surrounding her—a shield of magic that had instantly camouflaged itself, taking on a reflection of her surroundings and making her essentially invisible as she moved through the palace grounds.

Her body shivered from the power of it.

The sword had guided that power, but she was discovering that the weapon was more of a conduit; it helped draw forth the magic that already existed inside of her. Magic that had been transferred from Elander to her when he'd brought her soul back into this mortal world after her death in a previous life.

How deep that inner power went, and how she could work with the sword to more fully draw it out and control it...well, she was still in the process of learning all of that.

She made her way along the route they'd mapped out earlier, taking care not to make any sound that could give her away.

Finally, she came to a plain, unassuming door tucked away at the end of one of the many paths that crisscrossed through the elaborate royal gardens.

The door opened as she reached for its handle. Light spilled from within—alarmingly bright—and Cas held her breath with her hand still wrapped tightly on her sword.

A figure stepped forward, blocking some of that light and taking on a handsome, hazy shape before her. *Elander.*

He must have sensed her magic. He always did; the connection between them—by their magic and other-wise—was such that he could always find her, even if she was invisible to the rest of the world.

She forced a slow exhale and let her shield fall away. She was glad to release it; her skin had started to feel itchy, a bit too tight and too warm—the way it always did when she used that Moon magic—though the onset of that discomfort had taken longer this time. She was getting better.

Elander pushed the door open and welcomed her in with a sweep of his arm. "Your Majesty," he said, his smile a welcome distraction from their otherwise dismal surroundings.

I'm not officially due that honor yet, she wanted to remind him. But she held her tongue. She had to start thinking of herself as *Queen,* or else how could she expect the people of this kingdom—and beyond—to do the same thing?

She stepped inside and quietly closed the door behind her. "We've found Lord Orbryn, I assume?"

"He's being held on the third floor balcony. Secured, as is the path to reach him. Come on." He beckoned, and she followed without question; he knew this palace well from his time spent pretending to serve its previous rulers, which was why he'd gone before her to take the lead on securing things.

As they wound their way through the lesser-used hallways and rooms—avoiding all but the occasional ally who had helped establish their path—she tried not to think about the last time she and Elander had been together in this place. About the blood, the betrayals, or all the things she'd found and lost within these walls. Or the brief bit of childhood that she'd spent here—one that was still mostly a mystery to her.

But despite her best efforts to push these thoughts out, every step she took sent fractured memories and painful questions bursting upward. They swirled around her like dust that made her lungs burn and her heart pound.

She stayed close to Elander and kept her hand on her sword.

The sounds of a skirmish reached them. They paused and pressed into the shadows until it grew quiet again a moment later. A familiar figure rounded the corner just ahead—one of the elven soldiers who had first followed her into the battle at Dawnskeep, weeks ago. Cas didn't know his name, she realized; all of the people caught up in her many wars were blurring together.

"The balcony is through here," he told her. "We'll hold the doors and keep you from being interrupted while you speak to Lord Orbryn."

Cas thanked him, and she and Elander stepped outside.

Laurent was waiting for them on the balcony, flanked on either side by more of their allies. In the center of them was a man on his knees, bound in ropes being held tight by two more elven soldiers.

Cas had known little about this man before this mission, but Elander had been able to fill her in regarding the most important parts. Lord Cedric Orbryn had been a powerful force within the Ciridan Court for longer than Varen himself. He had served the previous king-turned-emperor from a young age, and now, with Varen missing, he was the undisputed head of operations within this palace.

She had glimpsed him a few times during her

previous visit, but she had never truly looked at him the way she did now.

His eyes were dark. Hollow. He seemed perfectly steady despite the awkward position his arms had been wrestled into, and poised in a way that made him look powerful, even as he knelt there with his head bowed. As Cas stared at him, she couldn't help but think of the massive figures—stone likenesses of various divine beings—that presided over the more extravagant graves in the city burial grounds. Those statues had weathered natural disasters, rulers determined to destroy them and all they stood for, and countless other catastrophes. Lord Orbryn looked as if he could have done the same.

"Cedric, is it?" she asked, by way of greeting, as she walked forward and crouched in front of him.

He didn't reply.

Cas didn't care. They could skip the niceties and go straight to the point. "I am told you have been serving as steward in the absence of Varen. I'm here to inform you that, as of tonight, I am relieving you of your duties."

Still no reply.

She took the knife from her ankle sheath and used it to lift his chin up. Moonlight washed over his face and revealed a bit of dried blood that had trickled down from a cut on his temple. "You hold a great amount of power and sway over this palace and its supporters, as I under-stand it," she said. "It would be helpful if we could work together to transition the rule of this kingdom away from my brother."

Lord Orbryn finally lifted his eyes to hers. He cracked his neck from side to side—seemingly oblivious to the way it made the knife skim his skin—and then he asked, "Where is the king?"

The soldiers holding him shuffled anxiously.

Cas kept perfectly still, staring at the blood on his face and guarding herself against the unsettling images that flickered through her head. Images of the dark upper-god, Malaphar, in his black bird form, circling over a hilltop. Over her brother. Images of shadows engulfing Varen, twisting and turning and finally revealing a tiger-like beast. And then her brother rising as the new Middle-God of Death and Destruction, breathing out magic that leveled trees and beasts and people alike...

"Gone," she said, her voice tight. "And he is not coming back to you."

Lord Orbryn stared up at her through those hollow eyes of his. They reminded her of Varen's. Were eyes like that inevitable in this palace? Would hers eventually look the same after she took the crown and started calling herself Queen?

No, she told herself firmly.

Because she was not here for hollow reasons.

She cleared her throat. "There are things in motion now that will crush you and everyone else in this palace and beyond—enemies far greater than anything the royal army could hope to deal with on its own. Varen won't protect you from these things, but *I* will, if you'd only cooperate."

He breathed out a strange, choked noise; it sounded almost like suppressed laughter.

The back of Cas's neck burned. "I would prefer not to have to take this palace by sheer force. We could avoid unnecessary bloodshed."

His reply was mocking. "Such a gracious offer."

"It *is* gracious of her," said Elander, his tone a quiet warning as he stepped closer, reaching for the sword at his side.

Behind him, Laurent had become noticeably more tense as well—but his attention had shifted from Lord Orbryn to the set of double doors that led into the palace. He started slowly toward those barred doors.

Cas narrowed her eyes on the lord before her one last time. "Make your choice, Orbryn."

"You have no business here, child," he said. "You should leave before the supporters of this palace crush you."

"You underestimate how many supporters *I* have. It is not a question of whether or not I can take the crown of this kingdom. The only question is whether or not you get to live to see me wear it."

"You can wear it all you like. That doesn't make you a queen."

Her irritation burned too strongly for her to form an immediate reply.

Elander replied for her.

"Wrong answer," he informed the lord, his voice so dark, so cold, that it even caused Cas to shiver. He didn't bother with his sword, and instead took Orbryn's throat in his grip. The quick, violent motion of it caught the soldiers holding the lord off guard, and they scrambled to secure their captive once more—though this was unnecessary. Elander was strong enough to hold him alone, to lift him partway to his feet and keep him there.

Orbryn looked as though he was trying to laugh again. Then Elander's grip tightened and lifted him higher, choking off any sound that might have escaped.

The amusement in the lord's eyes shifted quickly into alarm.

Cas had no doubt that Elander could—and would—kill this man with his bare hands if given the chance.

The only question was whether or not she should let him do it.

Lord Orbryn had useful knowledge, but the chances of him cooperating appeared slim to none.

Perhaps we should make an example out of him.

Movement distracted her before she could decide either way.

"Trouble," Laurent muttered as he backed toward them, sword drawn and ready.

She turned toward the palace just as the doors began

to shake. Those doors flew open seconds later, and three men wearing the insignia of her brother strode onto the balcony. The one in front carried a sword that was coated in blood. Cas should have been accustomed to such things by this point, but the sight still turned her stomach.

How many of her allies had fallen while trying—and failing—to hold the doors?

She readied her sword, keeping her eyes on the three approaching men. Behind her, she heard the sound of Elander throwing Lord Orbryn away—back into the hold of the two elven soldiers, who caught and restrained him with a few grunts of effort—and then withdrawing his own weapon.

He and Laurent converged on their intruders, and the clashing of swords rang startlingly loud in the icy air.

After several seconds of coughing for breath, Lord Orbryn spoke again. "If you are going to take the throne," Cas heard him say, in a low voice that seemed to be meant only for her, "then it will be by *force*."

Cas slowly turned back to him.

The sickness she'd felt was gone as quickly as it had arrived. A fiery beast had taken its place in her belly— the fires of hurt and loss and resolve that had been building inside of her for months now, fanned fully to life by this last, quiet rebellion from Orbryn.

"Sounds like a plan," she told him, lifting a hand.

Sparks of Storm magic danced over her skin, quickly forming a rope that snaked around her arm and then shot up into the sky. Another signal.

An echoing roar was the response.

Lord Orbryn's eyes widened, and his head jerked toward the sound—

Just as a dragon rose above the trees in the distance.

CHAPTER 2

THE LOOK OF BARELY-RESTRAINED HORROR ON LORD ORBRYN'S face was oddly satisfying. He had clearly underestimated just how much trouble Cas was bringing to his doorstep —assuming she was nothing more than a foolish nuisance.

But she was not a fool.

And she had come prepared.

Over the past months, her supporters had been growing steadily, reaching numbers that had made her confident enough to plan this siege of the Ciridan Palace. They'd come to her from all across the Marrlands; Soryn, the young Queen of Sadira—the fallen kingdom in eastern Kethra—had sent hundreds for this particular mission, as had Soryn's cousin, the High King of the empire that lay to the south. The dragon was courtesy of the High Queen of that southern empire, and upon its back rode the queen's emissary, Lady Sade Ellison. These allies made up the bulk of the army now flooding into the yard below, joining those who had already helped Cas infiltrate the palace itself.

Cas turned her attention back to Lord Orbryn as he attempted to wrestle free of his guards. He was trying to twist so he could see that army swallowing up the grounds below them.

Cas moved with purposeful steps, walking over to stand in front of him, blocking his view. She leaned back against the railing. Folded her arms across her chest.

Just as the dragon in the distance released another roar, Elander's sword speared the last of the intruders' throats. Blood-choked gasps and the unsettling *thump thump thumps* of a dying, writhing body filled the air for several unsettling moments.

The battle below raged louder, a cacophony of clashing swords and shields pierced with the occasional scream of terror and agony.

Cas kept perfectly still through it all, arms still casually folded across her chest.

Lord Orbryn looked as if he'd momentarily forgotten how to breathe.

"I could order them all to stop," Cas said calmly. "Renounce your hold on the throne. Announce *my* ascension to this palace and to the city beyond it, and—"

"Not a chance," he interrupted in a quiet, seething voice.

Cas bristled. There was no time for any other reply; more trouble was coming—another small brigade had just charged out onto the balcony.

Elander met the first soldier, Laurent the second, and Cas herself sprang forward as a third man—and then a fourth—flew out from the dark halls of the palace and nearly managed to impale one of the elves securing Lord Orbryn.

She ripped Shadowslayer free of its casing as she stormed into the path of the attacking men. Her frustration with Orbryn surged into a tangible form as she moved. Lightning uncoiled from her blade and encircled both of the men closest to her, searing through any and all exposed skin and catching into a violent dance upon the metal bits of their weapons and armor.

They dropped to their knees, scrambling wildly across the space and trying to shake free of the magic's embrace—and one after the other, they collided with the balcony railing. As the magic leapt from their bodies to the iron railing, they slumped back and stared at Cas, dazed and unmoving, save for an occasional twitch brought on by lingering static.

Two more soldiers followed those first four.

Cas spun, and the trail of lightning she'd summoned spun with her, circling back into her command and recharging, building into a thick rope of electricity that lashed out, entangling those soldiers and ripping them off their feet.

The first was unconscious before he hit the ground.

The second rolled about for a few seconds—electricity sparking with every movement—before he groggily lifted his head and sought his sword, which had flown from his hand and clattered to the ground a few feet away.

He reached for it, but Cas's boot landed on it first.

He lifted his gaze, saw the dangerous gleam in her eyes, and promptly forgot about his sword as he let his head drop back to the ground.

"The right decision," Cas muttered.

Her eyes found Lord Orbryn next.

His stubborn expression had not changed.

"We'll do this the hard way, then." She looked toward the palace—which had grown loud with the noise of more ensuing battles—and then turned to the elven soldiers holding Orbryn. "Keep a tight grip on him while he reconsiders my words," she commanded. "We'll be back to deal with him shortly."

Lord Orbryn started to speak, but Cas did not hear what he had to say; she was already heading inside, following Laurent and Elander as they moved to help with those battles igniting inside the palace.

She rebalanced Shadowslayer in her grip as she strode down the hallway. She no longer crept through the shadows. She was finished with hiding. Finished with negotiating.

The true Queen of Melech had arrived, and by the end of the night, *everybody* would know—whether Lord Orbryn cooperated with her or not.

She was hard to miss, anyhow; the Storm magic she'd summoned still lingered, crackling in the spaces around her.

Drawing closer to Elander made the sparks burn brighter— another side-effect of his rebirth at the hands of the Sun Goddess. He had once been one of the Vitala— one of twelve warriors of light who had served that goddess. Now, it seemed he had been reborn into that light, and Cas's magic fed off his partially-restored power with an eagerness that sometimes made her dizzy.

She worked to settle her power before she overextended it, breathing it back down until it blinked out of sight with a hiss like raindrops striking a campfire. She focused instead on feeling the solid weight and sharpness of the blade in her hand.

Up one hall and down the next they went, bringing order to the chaos and reminding their allies of the plans they'd made for the inhabitants of this palace.

They swear allegiance to their new queen, or they get brought to the dungeons.

If they resist beyond this, kill them.

If she thought she could have accomplished it

without force and bloodshed, Cas would have. But the past months had proven that violence was the primary language her brother and his followers spoke, so she'd had no choice but to become more fluent in that language herself.

And, as expected, violence and resistance was the first choice of far too many on this night; dead bodies already littered the halls, and the number of them increased with every passing minute. Her brother's hold on the ones within this palace was strong. He was nowhere in sight—not even on this mortal plane, most likely—and yet the soldiers, the servants, and the court folk alike still seemed more willing to die than to be thought a traitor to him.

Did they truly believe in his rule so...*passionately*?

Perhaps the wars he'd started were just something to believe in. Perhaps the same thing could be said of the ones following Cas herself. How much did they truly believe in her cause? How much did they truly understand about what was happening to their world?

They were strange, awful things, these crowns and wars, that rallied people in such unsettling ways.

She had no time to dwell on those thoughts, however. As she rounded a corner, one of Varen's men caught her off-guard, rushing at her with a wild cry.

She ducked his initial swing and spun back to face him.

A quick survey of her surroundings told her he was

alone. But so was she. Laurent and Elander had gotten caught up behind her, dealing with attackers of their own.

The man charged toward her again, sword at the ready.

She didn't think, she simply reacted—a sidestep to the right, a violent twist, a quick crouch followed by a powerful upward thrust, and then Shadowslayer sank into a small slit in the side of the man's leather armor.

The stab was too shallow; he was still able to move too freely. He curled away from her strike and brought his fist forward in the same motion. It struck her shoulder and knocked her off-balance.

He lifted his sword once more, preparing to stab.

With a brief bit of concentration, Cas sent lightning spiraling around his blade.

He dropped the sword before that electricity could make the leap from his weapon to his body.

For a moment he seemed to consider bolting. Then came a flare of courage, and he abruptly turned and punched her stomach, slamming her into the wall with enough force to take her breath away and leave her momentarily stunned.

A glint of steel—a small knife, quickly drawn and angled toward her throat—brought her back to her senses.

She jerked her knee into the man's groin.

He doubled over, and she brought an elbow down

between his shoulders, driving him to the ground. His head struck the decorative pommel of his own fallen sword. Electricity sparked from the pommel upon contact, and his body twitched with it for a moment. Then he went still, save for the occasional ragged breath.

Unconscious.

Cas gripped Shadowslayer's handle more tightly in her sweaty palm, considering how easily it could pierce the back of this man's neck, and the way his blood would blend with the dark, plush carpet beneath them.

Something stayed her hand.

Shadows are falling...

The Sun Goddess's words rang through her mind for the hundredth time since their meeting. She had tasked her with driving said shadows out, and it had seemed an insurmountable task. Here in these halls, with blood and violence waiting around every corner, it seemed even *more* impossible.

But Cas kept her sword lowered, and she took a step back.

A trio of her soldiers caught sight of her from the other end of the hallway. They raced to her when she beckoned, and she instructed them to bind the unconscious man, to add him to the rest of their prisoners.

As they dragged him away, Laurent and Elander finally caught up with her. They both glanced at the unconscious man for only an instant before turning their worried eyes to Cas.

"I'm still in one piece," she informed them, already starting to move again.

They continued through the halls.

An hour passed—perhaps more. She was losing track of time. Of her surroundings. Of the amount of blood spilled and the number of prisoners they saw bound and taken below.

Eventually, they managed to fight their way into the expansive entry hall where Zev and the others had rounded up an audience that included many of the most powerful residents of the palace—advisors and noble courtiers, high-ranking servants—each one a specific target that Elander had given them before they arrived here.

And now, Cas decided, this group would be the one to bear witness to Lord Orbryn's surrender.

She summoned another soldier to act as her messenger, gave her orders, and then sheathed her sword and waited for his return.

Her fingers itched to tap against Shadowslayer's hilt, but she held them steady.

Zev caught her eye. He sauntered her direction, and she could tell from the look on his face—unusually pensive for him—that he was holding back a question. That same, foolish question from earlier, she assumed.

He didn't speak first for once, so she asked the question instead. "Are you okay?"

He sighed, and he gave a slight smile before he repeated her earlier answer. "Why wouldn't I be okay?"

She returned his smile, though hers was shorter-lived.

Minutes later, a tightly bound Lord Orbryn was being escorted—at sword point—into the center of their circle of captives.

Cas stood up a little straighter, but otherwise made her outward appearance deceptively calm and collected.

"I've assembled the ranks for you," she told the lord, gesturing at the rest of her captives as she spoke. "So now you won't have to repeat your declarations of surrender to them individually. That's me being *generous* once more."

He lifted his chin, fixed those hollow-grave eyes on her.

"You're welcome," she added.

He spat at her feet.

"Mistake," she heard Zev growl. In her peripheral vision, she saw both him and Laurent moving to make Lord Orbryn pay for that mistake.

But it was Elander who reached the lord first. Cas suspected he'd been waiting for this opportunity ever since they'd been interrupted on the balcony. He caught the lord's jaw in one hand and wrenched his head upward, exposing his throat before pressing a knife to it.

The circle shifted nervously. A few of their captives

struggled against the ones holding them, but they were quickly wrestled and threatened back into submission.

The edge of Elander's knife pushed more firmly into Orbryn's skin.

"Wait." The word snapped out of Cas, more reflex than anything.

With obvious reluctance, Elander waited.

"If you are a *queen*," Lord Orbryn sneered, "then surely you aren't so squeamish as this. Why not allow punishment of those who seek to spit at your feet?"

Cas continued to keep her voice perfectly level. "You want me to punish you, do you?"

"I would prefer you kill me—it would be the lesser evil, if the alternative really *is* surrender."

Elander tightened his grip, his gaze still livid and fixed on his knife, which still rested lightly against the hollow of Lord Orbryn's throat.

For the second time tonight, it occurred to Cas how easy it would have been to end that lord's life. Elander looked all too eager to do it. She could have turned and walked away, and it would have been finished without any more effort from her.

So why wasn't she walking away?

She knew the answer as soon as she asked the question. Enough had already died here tonight—enough to make their point.

As annoyed as she was with this lord, there had to be lines. If she planned to win people over by arguing that she was not her brother, then she could not act *entirely* like her brother. Particularly not when she was surrounded by so many witnesses.

"Lower your knife, Elander," she said.

"Spare me your pity," Lord Orbryn snarled.

"Oh, I promise you, this is not *pity*," Cas said, coldly. Months ago, it might have been pure pity that stayed her hand. Now it was more than that.

It was *strategic* pity.

"He knows too many useful things about this palace and its inner workings," she reminded Elander. "We planned to keep him alive, if possible—and that remains the plan. For now."

Orbryn sniffed. "You'll get nothing *useful* from me."

Cas's gaze turned as icy as her voice. "We'll see." Her eyes flashed toward Elander, and he finally complied, releasing his grip on the lord and taking a step back.

"Weakling," Lord Orbryn hissed at her.

That fiery beast in her belly—the one that had started to awaken on the balcony—flared to life once more, rearing its head and baring its teeth.

She was tired of being doubted and mocked.

Tired of people calling her *weak*.

She glanced at the knife in Elander's hand. "He can live," she said, "but not without consequences for his insubordinate attitude."

Elander moved even more swiftly than before; he didn't need her to elaborate on what she wanted him to do. He was no stranger to death and blood. And though he had left behind the darker divine powers associated with such things, he could still speak in a tone that would not have seemed out of place in the deepest and most terrifying of their world's hells—

"You know how to read and write, correct, Lord Orbryn?"

Orbryn had clearly noticed the change in Elander's tone, along with the dark feeling that had overtaken the space and turned it from expansive to suffocating. He stiffened, looking truly unnerved for the first time.

"I'll take that as a *yes*," said Elander. "Of course you do."

The lord's eyes narrowed, questioning.

"So you don't need your mouth to tell us what you know, correct?" Elander asked.

Cas was staring at the tiger emblem affixed to Lord Orbryn's coat, but she felt Elander's gaze trail briefly over her, questioning.

She nodded.

It was over in an instant—a series of diagonal strikes over the lord's mouth, ripping it into bloody ribbons.

He did not cry out in pain. Not at first. When a noise finally did escape him, it was quiet, strangled and choked from the blood that had seeped inward.

Gasps echoed through the crowd around them. Most came from Lord Orbryn's supporters, who quickly went silent and still as they watched their leader fold over in pain, choking on blood and heaving for breath.

They're finally paying attention, Cas thought bitterly.

Elander crouched down next to Orbryn, and his voice dropped lower as he said, "Try spitting in her direction again and see what happens."

Orbryn struggled to breathe for another moment before lolling his head upright and expelling blood and spit all over the perfectly polished floor.

He made a point to turn his head away from her when he did this, Cas noticed.

She took a step back. She should have felt something as she stared at the blood splattering the shiny floor, but she felt...nothing.

Nothing at all.

She realized that she hadn't even flinched when Elander's knife had cut its paths across Orbryn's mouth, and she *did* feel something with that realization—a flicker of fear. Not fear of the blood, but of what she was becoming every time she allowed it to be spilled. Or spilled it herself. She couldn't let herself become completely numb to it, she knew...and yet it was cold indifference that kept her moving, that kept her from sinking into a sea of panic.

Such a fine, dangerous line to walk.

She swallowed the fear down. She commanded the ones who had escorted Lord Orbryn into the hall to escort him to the dungeons, and then she left the mess he'd made behind and marched her way onward through the rapidly-quieting palace.

She passed allies who lowered themselves in quick, respectful bows, palace servants who cowered and held up gestures of surrender, and more enemies who were bound and being dragged away—all sights that made her feel equal parts bitter and accomplished.

Their methods might have been messy, but it was beginning to look as though tonight might end in a victory.

Then again, could it really be so simple?

"Doubtful," she muttered to no one.

But she kept walking with purposeful steps all the same—and though she'd had no specific destination in mind when she'd started this march, after a few minutes of walking, she suddenly knew where she needed to go.

CHAPTER 3

THERE WERE FOUR GUARDS STATIONED OUTSIDE OF THE THRONE room, all of them dead, and their killers were nowhere in sight.

Cas avoided looking at their faces. She stepped carefully around them and went into the room, closed the door behind her, and finally released a bit of her false bravado by way of a long, shaky breath.

She'd needed to come in here just to prove to herself that she was capable of doing it. That she could forget about the atrocities that had taken place in this room, and she could rise above the past and turn the throne before her into a force for *good*.

She'd managed the first steps of this plan, at least.

She was actually *here*.

Moonlight streamed through the large windows that

lined the space. Ribbons of it illuminated the tall-backed throne in the center of the room, glinted against gold and silver threads in the cushions, and washed over the polished, curling armrests.

There had been more windows behind that throne the last time she was here—countless ones that she had shattered with her magic during her desperate escape. Now a solid wall had taken their place, and the only interruption was a long, narrow pane of glass close to the ceiling.

There were no other people in the room.

It was strange to see it so empty, and Cas felt oddly small and entirely alone as she stared at that dark, narrow window high above her, like a child who had stumbled into a part of the house that was reserved for her parents and their guests.

She inhaled deeply.

No one else could know she felt this way.

No one else *would* know she felt this way.

A door creaked open behind her. She twisted around, starting to withdraw her sword—but relaxed just as quickly as Zev announced himself with his usual carefree and inappropriately loud voice. His sister, Rhea, followed closely behind him.

"I get to sit on the throne first," Zev declared.

Rhea swatted him in the back of his head, but it didn't stop his pursuit of that throne. He hoisted himself up and flopped down into it in the most un-royal fashion imaginable.

Nessa was next through the door. Silverfoot was still perched on her shoulder, but as soon as the fox caught sight of Rhea, he hopped to the floor with a happy little bark and rushed over to her.

Not entirely alone, after all, Cas thought, a slight smile curving her lips as she watched her friends fill up what suddenly felt like a much smaller, less-imposing space.

Elander arrived a short time later with Laurent and a group of soldiers, informing her that Lord Orbryn was now truly secured—along with nearly one-hundred other prisoners—in the maze of cells beneath the palace. The amount of their enemy's dead was perhaps a third of that number, while the rest had fled into the night—with no plans to return, hopefully.

Twenty-three of our own are dead, they told her—a number that they assured her was a victory, given what they had managed to accomplish tonight.

It could have been much worse.

They had surprised and overwhelmed the palace into a quick surrender, just as they'd hoped to do. The bloodshed had been minimal...

Something had actually gone according to plan.

But she was so used to things *not* going according to plan that she was still bracing herself, waiting for whatever terrible news was lurking just out of sight.

There were various doors along the throne room walls, many of which led to spaces being used to hold ceremonial artifacts and equipment. Useless garbage, mostly—though Cas did find a few supplies with which to clean her sword.

She carried those supplies over to a corner where a twisting staircase led up to a small loft, and she sat cross-legged on the floor with her back against the bottom step.

It proved therapeutic, cleaning the blood from Shadowslayer's blade. She polished that blade until it glistened—and then she kept polishing because she couldn't seem to stop. The rest of the world slipped a little further away with each swipe of cloth against metal.

One, two, three...

She paused and looked up as she felt the weight of someone's gaze upon her. Elander was watching her closely, wearing a slight frown. Her own lips were parted, she realized. Had she been counting out loud?

She pressed her lips back together, but her hand kept moving, her mind still silently counting its motions.

One. Two. Three...

"We did what we had to do, you know," Elander told her, stepping closer.

"I didn't even flinch when your knife cut his face," she said quietly.

"Flinching in the middle of a battle is a good way to get yourself killed. And as long as we are in this palace, surrounded by people with questionable loyalties, we have to consider every move we make as part of our larger battles."

With a great deal of effort, she finally forced her hand to stop its safe, methodical swipes against the blade. Her gaze lifted to more fully meet Elander's, but she didn't speak right away; she couldn't find the words.

Finally, she swallowed away the dryness in her throat and simply said, "You're right."

And then she went back to cleaning her sword.

He sat beside her, holding the hilt of Shadowslayer, keeping it steady as she inspected the symbols etched into the base of the blade.

After a few minutes, more words came tumbling through her lips. "But it isn't just the blood that was on this sword, or all the rest that we spilled tonight. Even if it was necessary, and a *minimal amount* like you all claimed, it's all becoming a..."

He tilted his head toward her, waiting, but her words were stuck once more.

A trigger. It's triggering.

Why was it so hard to admit that out loud, even to him? Even now, after everything they'd gone through together?

She narrowed her gaze on one of those symbols on

her sword—on the wind-swept cloud of the Sky Goddess. "It makes me think of other blood," she finally managed to say. "Of my own, on the floor of Briarfell. Of Asra's, all over the room within this very palace. And of..." Another quick glance at his attentive gaze, and her voice cracked before she could get out the rest of her sentence.

Yours.

The memory of his bloody death was gut-wrenchingly vibrant.

She'd been trying for weeks to erase those images of her brother's sword stabbing into Elander's back. Of the terrible silence and stillness that had followed. Of the way it had felt as if the entire world was collapsing and falling, crashing down and burying her.

But it was not the sort of thing a person simply... *got over.* Rhea kept telling her that. They *all* kept telling her that. And they were right. She needed time to process what had happened.

The problem was that she had no time, because lately every day presented *new* horrors that also demanded her to make sense of them.

She sighed. "It's foolish to get caught up in those things, I suppose."

His reply was quick. "It's not foolish."

"But there are larger battles looming, like you said." She'd put a note of finality in the words, but she could feel him still staring at her, his concern eating into her like an itch that she would *not* allow herself to scratch. "Speaking of which," she continued, trying to change the subject, "have you learned anything else regarding Caden and Tara's whereabouts? Sensed anything?"

Caden had been missing ever since the battle of Dawnskeep. Tara—Elander's other former servant and friend, who had been imprisoned in the Storm Goddess's haven for the past several weeks—had also disappeared without a trace.

"No," he told her. "I've been trying, but...I think the divine bond between us is completely severed."

She frowned, unsure of what to say.

"We did what we had to do," he repeated, more to himself than her this time. "Also, don't think I don't realize you're trying to change the subject."

"I don't know what you mean."

"Casia—"

The entry doors opened, interrupting their conversation. Soldiers flooded in, led by Sade, who wore a grim but accomplished expression.

Cas rose to her feet and went to greet the Sundolian dragonrider, leaving her sword in Elander's care—along with her temptation to keep up her methodical cleaning of it.

Sade bowed slightly as Cas reached her, and Cas noticed that her bold red hair was more disheveled and darker near the crown of her head.

From blood?

Sade quickly lifted her head, preventing a closer look, and a sliver of moonlight caught on one of the strange scars that covered much of her throat. Those faint scars had been caused by Ice magic, Cas had recently learned—which seemed obvious, now that she thought of it. They had always made her think of patterns of frost on glass.

"A perimeter is nearly established around the palace, as planned," said Sade.

"And the city beyond?"

"Calm enough. A few scuffles reported—likely palace dwellers fleeing, trying to impose their will upon the townspeople. Nothing major. Very few deaths...your associates in that city seem to be keeping things under control, as you claimed they would. At least, for now."

"Good," Cas said, though her heartbeat still quickened at the thought of innocent townsfolk getting caught up in these battles.

It was a thought that had haunted her during her entire march to this city...so much so that she'd made a point of spending time in that city—meeting up with old acquaintances, calling in favors and hiring extra hands to maintain order—before coming to the palace itself.

Despite the relatively good news, Sade was frowning, and Cas understood why. 'Associates' was the polite term for the hands she'd hired. She had only sought out the ones she believed to have at least a *few* shreds of morality—but she was not a fool and neither was Sade. They both knew most of the sellswords in this realm cared little about any greater cause.

But Cas *also* knew those swords were loyal to whoever could pay them the most money. And it just so happened that she now had an entire palace's worth of treasures to reward them with. They would help her keep the city under control as long as she kept paying them to do it.

It left a sour taste in her mouth—paying with the tainted riches of this palace—but she would do what she had to do to further secure her hold on things.

Her hand started to reach for the sword that she'd forgotten wasn't on her hip, thinking absently of tracing the talisman set within its pommel. She caught herself and clenched her fingers into a fist at her side.

Her voice was perfectly even as she said, "Let me know when that perimeter is fully secured."

Sade nodded and, after giving curt orders to some of the soldiers who had followed her in, she was gone as quickly as she'd arrived.

Cas said a silent bit of thanks for her, and for the leaders of the southern empire being willing to send her any help at all. Her gaze fell to the bracelet on her wrist as she bowed her head—a gift from Soryn, the rightful queen of the kingdom to their east, who had sent just as much help. Another ally. Another thing to be grateful for.

So it wasn't *all* bloodshed and doom.

She had to keep reminding herself of that.

As the door swung shut behind Sade, Cas glanced at Elander, who hadn't moved from his place by the stairs. He was looking in her direction—at her still-clenched fist, specifically—the worried frown back on his face.

He never misses a thing, does he?

She sighed and unclenched her fist. Avoiding his gaze as best she could, she walked back to him, reclaimed her sword and—after one last inspection—sheathed it.

Their earlier conversation was over with as far as she was concerned. Several of the soldiers who'd followed Sade in still lingered, and there were too many people in this room now. Too many listening ears—and too many other things to deal with, besides. She would just have to bury that conversation down, once more, and keep moving.

Luckily, she had become something of a master at this.

Elander got to his feet and went to one of the windows, apparently not in the mood to dig that conversation up by himself. He focused instead on opening the curtains more fully and securing them in place before peering out at the dark courtyard below.

The additional light this let in drew Cas toward the window like a moth to a flame.

The stars were bright tonight. Unusually so. They made her think of the goddess associated with those stars, and of the rest of Solatis's court—the goddesses of Sky, Storm, and Moon—and how she was relying on that court to stand by her side in her upcoming battles.

An alliance of divine beings and mortals unlike anything the realms have ever known...

That was what Solatis had told her it would take to save this world from the rogue Dark God, which was why Cas had embarked on her current mission—so that she could position herself on a throne that would allow her to rally the ones on the mortal side.

In the meantime, the Court of the Sun was moving on her behalf through the divine realms, trying to find answers to all of the many questions she still had regarding herself, Elander, and all of the messy magic and deities rising and falling around them.

Once the middle-goddesses had answers—and perhaps more allies—they had promised to send her news.

Cas had hoped such news might reach her before they arrived in Ciridan, but there had been no word yet. It made the victory tonight feel somewhat hollow, knowing that she couldn't see the full scope of the war from where she stood.

What was happening among the divine realms?

What had become of her brother?

How long before that divine war spilled into her mortal one?

"It's strange being back here like this," Elander commented. "After everything that's happened, I mean."

In spite of the twisting, unsettled feeling in the pit of her stomach, Cas felt a grin tug at the corners of her mouth. "Shall I start calling you Captain again? For old time's sake?"

"It does bring back fond memories."

"Like that time you tackled me, arrested me, and threw me into the dungeon?"

"Mm, yes—those are some of my fondest memories."

She dropped her voice to a low, teasing tone. "You liked having me in handcuffs, didn't you?"

He leaned one shoulder against the wall beside the window. Considered the memory. Lifted his eyes to the star-dotted sky. Even with his face angled away from her, she could tell he was wearing a smirk to match her own. "I'm sure we could find a pair of those around here somewhere," he told her, "if you'd like to recreate that particular moment of our history."

Her cheeks warmed. "With a happier ending this time, I presume."

"Much happier." He was still wearing that sly smile when he looked back at her, which sent a pleasant shiver racing down her spine.

That warm sensation wrapped around her and settled in her lower belly, replacing the uneasiness as his hand reached for hers.

She reached back. Let him pull her close enough that she could feel the heat from his body. It was briefly disorienting—though only because she wasn't used to feeling it; she had grown accustomed to the cold pulse of Death magic that surrounded him, with only occasional bursts of heat when their skin brushed or their lips touched.

But ever since Solatis had brought him back to life, he had radiated a different kind of power. A warmer kind. And his scent no longer made her think of the dead of winter, but of a frigid day giving way to the promise of spring—crisp and cool, but with a hint of powerful earthiness underneath.

She breathed in that earth and winter scent. Looked up into his eyes and studied the way the starlight caught and shimmered against the seas of pale blue. The world seemed to settle around them. She started to lean against his chest, craving a firm foundation to rest against. But a sudden commotion outside—dangerously close to the window—made her jolt upright and reawakened them both to the reality of the moment.

The feel of his fingertips against her should not have been her focus at the moment, but she couldn't help the disappointment that flared through her as he leaned away. She bit her lip and averted her eyes to keep it from showing.

Elander didn't bother hiding the disappointment in his voice as he said, "We'll have to finish reminiscing later, won't we?" He sighed good-naturedly and brushed a kiss over her knuckles before releasing her hand.

Something struck the window.

Cas instinctively ducked, and Elander threw his arm around her, further shielding her from any potential attack.

The glass rattled for several seconds but didn't crack.

Cas hesitated, then cautiously stepped around Elander and peered out. There were figures moving across the yard below, but she couldn't see them clearly. The air was thick with oddly colored smoke and sparks of energy—magical residue.

Her fingers pressed against the cool glass. After she'd shattered so many of the windows during her last visit, she wondered if Varen had replaced them with something more resistant to magic. Something elvish-made, perhaps.

Elander's reflection appeared next to her hand. The disappointment on his face had sharpened into alarm. "I should make another round and see to it that things are still under control out there."

She nodded and tried to keep her voice light as she said, "I'd expect nothing less from my royal *captain*."

He gave her a quick smile and turned toward the door.

Her heart skipped. That haunting memory of blood and her brother's blade flashed through her mind. She blinked it away. "Be careful, please."

For a moment she considered going with him—but that suggestion was met with objections from everyone within hearing range. She had made enough of an appearance for one night; the important thing now was making certain the soon-to-be queen survived to see the dawn.

So she stayed in the throne room, heavily guarded, as the siege and securing continued. Her soldiers marched in and out of the space, keeping her informed about what was happening. The windows occasionally rattled, shouts and screams echoed around them, and more than once, Cas started to unsheathe her sword and march back into the fray, only to be coaxed—and occasionally dragged—back to safety.

As the hours pressed on, the palace eventually grew calmer.

By the time the sky outside began to lighten with the promise of the new day, the world had taken on an eerie silence.

A new day. A blank canvas. One that we can paint a different future on, Cas tried telling herself.

But truthfully, it felt more like the kind of quiet that lingered over a graveyard—one that felt haunting and full of questions. They were the survivors, but what were they supposed to do now?

She stood in the corridor just outside the throne room as the first rays of sunlight began to sneak through the skylights. She watched those rays illuminate the broken pieces of a statue that had been toppled during the night. She flipped over one of the pieces with the toe of her boot, and she immediately recognized the eye that glared up from beneath a thick brow; it had been a bust of the late Anric de Solasen. Varen's father.

Her father.

Another ripple of unease unfurled inside of her. She stepped back inside her sanctuary and walked over to Zev. She suspected he would be ready with some way to distract her from her anxiety.

And she was right; he had, at some point during the night, located a storage room that contained several bottles of sweet, white wine. Sacred, expensive wine, likely meant to be reserved for special occasions and rituals that took place in this hallowed room.

He'd ignored Rhea's protests to leave it alone. He'd also managed to con Nessa into helping him procure glasses from somewhere, and after a quick glance at Cas's face—and with barely a word spoken between them—he slipped one of the glasses into her hand.

He hooked an arm around her and steered her over to the throne. She sat on the edge of the plush rug that lay before it. Zev resumed his position on the throne itself, but not before filling Cas's glass to the very top.

The full sunrise spilled through the windows, painting the walls in swaths of golden orange. Cas watched it wash over the room as she sipped slowly from the crystal-rimmed glass, allowing herself to savor the wine along with the bittersweet victories the night had brought.

Nessa, Silverfoot, and Rhea soon joined them. Glancing at each of their tired faces in turn, Cas thought of all the late nights they'd spent gathered in one pub or another, relaxing and debriefing at the end of a mission. There was no cozy, roaring fire this time, nor the warm, buzzy feeling of a mission completed...but at least they were still together. And Elander and Laurent had been by only moments ago to check-in with her—so they were safe too.

"I feel like someone should give a victory toast," Zev commented, lifting his empty glass and giving it a shake.

Rhea massaged the space between her eyes. "I feel like you should lower your voice. It's been a long night, and some of us have a headache."

"To headaches, then," he declared, "because they are a small price to pay for victory."

Nessa rolled her eyes.

Rhea muttered something about other prices paid, which made the corners of Nessa's mouth wilt as she gathered Silverfoot up in her arms and hugged him tightly enough to make him let out a little squeak of protest.

Cas leaned over and scratched the fox between his ears.

"But we *did* survive the long night," said Nessa, after a moment of thought. "We came out alive on the other side of things. Again. Somehow."

Cas met this with a slight smile and a raised glass. "To the other side," she offered, and the others joined in, tiredly but earnestly repeating the familiar words.

They lost themselves in quiet, directionless conversation—even managing a few strained laughs—until they were interrupted by the main doors flying open.

All of them were on their feet in the next instant, staring down the man who raced through those doors and headed straight to Cas.

"What is it?" Cas demanded.

He drew back slightly under her fierce gaze, but quickly collected himself. "There's a strange woman here to speak with you. Or a...ah...not a *woman*...but, um, that is..."

"Not a woman? What do you mean?"

"I mean she's strange and...she's not..."

Cas's gaze narrowed toward the door as she held up a hand, silencing him. "Let me guess. She's inhumanly beautiful yet strangely terrifying? Incredibly tall, dark skin, pale blue hair..."

He nodded.

"Surrounded by an unsettling feeling of magic?"

Another nod.

"I've been expecting her," she assured the messenger before taking a deep, bracing breath. "Send her in."

The instant the words left her mouth, the door was already being thrown open once more.

The Goddess of Storms stood on the other side, barely contained in her human form, and she did not look pleased to have been kept waiting.

CHAPTER 4

EVEN IF CAS HAD NOT RECOGNIZED NEPHELE'S DIVINE ENERGY as it flowed into the room, there was no mistaking the goddess for a mortal of this realm.

At a mere glance, she *looked* the part well enough. But a closer inspection revealed eyes that were an unnaturally bright shade of purplish-blue, strands of pale hair that seemed to float around her, as if caught in an isolated updraft, and skin that occasionally lit with lightning-streak patterns created not by the lights over-head, but from the magic within her body.

A slender, white dog trotted at her heels. It was tall enough to look Cas in the eyes as it approached. A warm shiver ran down Cas's spine as their gazes met, and she realized that she recognized the eyes staring back at her. The first time she'd encountered the Moon Goddess, that deity had taken the form of a deer that had stared at her with this same glowing gaze.

The dog gave a slight wag of her tail as recognition passed between them.

"We have much to talk about," the Storm Goddess said, her voice low as she inspected the room and everyone in it. It had grown crowded with soldiers over the course of the night. Too crowded, perhaps.

Cas read the unspoken concern on the goddess's face, and she dismissed all others in the room, aside from her most trusted circle of companions.

Elander and Laurent returned moments later to complete this circle. While they all settled at a table in the back of the room, the Moon Goddess swept her way quickly around the space, a blur of silky fur followed by a trail of sparkling light. She paused briefly at each window, lifted her pointed nose, and breathed out a shimmering spell that formed into a translucent barrier. She did the same thing at each door.

"No interruptions this way," the Storm Goddess explained, "and no eavesdroppers."

Once the windows and doors were secured, the white dog returned to their circle, lifting with surprising grace and balancing on her back paws. With a toss of her head, ribbons of bright light flowed out like a cape from her neck and shoulders, cocooning her body as she straightened and stood taller.

Within seconds, those ribbons fell away to reveal a

woman with the same startlingly blue eyes she'd had as a dog—Inya, Goddess of the Moon, Keeper of Cross-roads and Pathways. Her complexion was as dark as Nephele's, but with stardust-like freckles splashed over her skin rather than hints of lightning dancing upon it. She greeted the circle with a smile, pausing as she reached Cas and pressing a hand to her cheek. Her touch was warm and soft. It made Cas feel oddly sleepy.

"So," Nephele began, her effortlessly thunderous voice jolting Cas back awake. "You've had a busy night, it seems." Her eyes scanned the magic-sealed windows, narrowing on each in turn, as if bracing herself for that magic to be immediately tested by their many enemies.

Knowing this goddess's flair for dramatics and drawing things out, Cas wasted no time with her reply. "And I'm hoping you two have been just as busy over these past weeks. Did you find any sign of the Sun Goddess?"

"Impatiently getting to the point, as usual." Nephele arched a brow, looking mildly amused, before she continued in a solemn voice. "We have scoured nearly every realm—divine and otherwise—to the best of our ability over these last weeks. Solatis is gone. At least in a physical sense. And we don't believe she's ever going to take physical form again."

Cas pressed her fingers to her temples and squeezed. Sometimes it helped keep her negative thoughts from running away with her—as if she was physically pinching them to a stop. *Sometimes.*

"It seems she used what power she had left to activate more of Casia's dormant ability, and to create that sword she now carries." The Storm Goddess's eyes shifted to Elander. "And to bring you back to life, and to restore you to your status as one of her *Vitala*. Or partially restore you, at least."

"Partially?" Laurent repeated, frowning.

"She couldn't give him all the power she originally gave to the divine warriors. Presumably because she didn't have it to give." Nephele extended her hand toward Cas, her eyes on Shadowslayer.

Cas hesitantly handed it over.

"The Heart of the Sun carried and protected parts of her power for so long..." said Nephele, holding the sword up so that the Heart in question was fully illuminated by the lantern burning in the wall behind her.

"Parts that had originally been given to those Vitala warriors, correct?" asked Laurent.

"Correct," said Nephele. "Which is how Elander brought Casia back into this world twenty-something years ago—by tapping into the life-giving elements of that power."

The others nodded knowingly; Cas had already explained this part of her strange past to them.

Or tried to, at least.

She shifted in her seat. Even though she had been

carrying this knowledge around with her for weeks, it still felt like it hadn't properly settled.

"I still don't fully understand exactly what—or *who*—the Vitala even are," said Zev.

"They were guardians, originally," explained Inya. "Divine beings that Solatis created specifically to watch over each of the original most powerful mortal houses—houses that eventually became kingdoms across the three empires."

"But now those guardians are gone...save for Elander?"

"We believed *he* was gone, too, until now. All of them were slain by monsters under Malaphar's control."

"On the shores at Dawnskeep, right?" Cas recalled. "I heard that story when we were in Briarfell; when they were killed, it supposedly triggered the creation of Solatis's Heart."

The Storm Goddess nodded solemnly, and the Moon Goddess's eyes shimmered.

"So don't count on any more of these Vitala fellows showing up to help," Zev said. "Got it."

"At least we have one," said Nessa, ever the optimist.

Nephele's gaze shifted between Cas and Elander, looking considerably less optimistic. "Do you understand the gravity of what I'm telling you? You two are linked by more than just the relationship you shared in Casia's past life. Even if Elander was responsible for giving you the magic that reincarnated you, Casia, we still believe that Solatis had a hand in *who* you were reborn as—which, of course, was one of ancient royal blood."

"Solatis believed in empowering humans," said Inya softly. "They were her ultimate, most precious creation, as far as she was concerned. It's why she guarded those twelve mortal houses so fiercely to begin with." She moved to Cas's side and reached to tuck a strand of hair behind her ear.

Again, that warm, sleepy sensation overtook Cas at the goddess's touch. It reminded her of the way Asra used to smooth her fingers through her hair when she hadn't been able to sleep. Motherly, almost.

"You were perhaps her last attempt to champion the human cause," said Inya.

"And Elander was always meant to be your guardian," added Nephele. "We've seen signs already that his power is connected to yours, haven't we? His ability to awaken more of the Heart's magic when he last fought against Malaphar, for example."

Cas stared at that Heart, repaired and secured in its place in Shadowslayer's handle. Then her gaze lifted, briefly, to Elander. His head was bowed in thought. Sunlight streamed through the window beside him, the decorative screen casting strange patterns over his skin. And, at least in that moment, it was easy to believe all of the things the goddesses were saying about him. He looked ancient and ageless and achingly beautiful...like something that couldn't be contained in any one realm or any single lifetime.

Your guardian.

A sensation Cas couldn't quite name soared through her, making her feel weightless one second, heavy the next. It was both a wondrous and terrifying thing, to be so connected to another soul.

To such a *powerful* soul.

"That magic that awakened was strong enough to drive Malaphar away from Oblivion," Nephele continued, "and that upper-god hasn't shown his full form for weeks now, has he?"

"But he's still perfectly intact," said Elander, frowning. "I only made him a bit wary, and he still attacked us by proxy—and appeared in a shapeshifted form at Dawnskeep. And he was still able to start Varen's ascension."

"Well...*yes*..." Nephele appeared uncharacteristically flustered.

"But you and Casia make each other more powerful," Inya put in. "And you can keep growing together. That's the *good* news."

"How strong could he actually become?" asked Laurent.

"That's my question as well," said Rhea. "Because if Elander isn't truly a full-fledged Vitala, as he was before, then what does that make him?"

"Still a demigod—of sorts." Inya tilted her head

slowly from side to side, as if continuing to puzzle things out even as she spoke. "More divine than Casia, maybe, but less divine than Nephele or myself. He is..." She searched Elander's face as she tried to settle on a word. "A messy, annoying kind of enigma."

"As is Casia, honestly," added Nephele.

"No offense meant," said the Moon Goddess with her gentle smile.

"None taken," Cas said, distractedly. Her mind was racing; she had countless more questions about Elander's semi-divine state—about what it meant for their upcoming battles and any future beyond them—but she pushed them aside, and instead she asked, "How did you learn all of this if Solatis is truly gone, and you weren't able to speak with her?"

Inya's smile drooped a bit. Her eyes shifted to a dull shade of grey. "Another of our court."

Cas was confused, but Elander muttered out what sounded like a sudden realization. "The Star Goddess."

Nephele's expression soured. "Yes. She finally decided to talk to us."

Elander met the perplexed looks around the table with an explanation. "Her magic makes her aware of many things, including the movements of all the different divine bodies. She just isn't usually very forthcoming with anything she knows."

"She has an actual apparatus for keeping track of such things—a gift from Solatis, from long ago. The

Animatir. The *Map of Souls*," Inya said. "With it, she can see both the fully divine and partially divine, along with the occasional exceptionally heavy mortal soul—such as our dear Casia's—and predict their movements and chart their paths. It's not always completely accurate magic, but she is right about things more often than not."

"That sounds useful," Zev mused. "Do you think she'd let us borrow that map?"

Cas's mouth nearly curved upward, and the Moon Goddess's eyes sparkled once more.

The Storm Goddess seemed less amused. "There's something else that map warned of—that Casia's brother is dangerously close to full ascension. In a matter of weeks, he will have finished his transition, and the Dark God's court will be at full strength once more."

Cas could tell that Nephele meant this as bad news, but only one part had truly caught her attention. "A matter of weeks?" she repeated.

"Maybe less."

"But he isn't at the height of his power yet?"

"The full process always takes some time. However—"

"So why are we not attacking him as we speak? Could you not have found him? I would have gone after him myself if I'd known—"

"Then it's good you *didn't* know." The goddess's lip curled in annoyance, and her hand tightened around

Cas's sword. "If I thought you were capable of handling such a thing, I would have given you this information well before now. Obviously."

Cas glanced between the two goddesses, her face growing hot and her temper building. Inya quickly looked away, which left Cas to lock eyes with Nephele's burning, intimidating gaze.

"Your brother now has the entire court of the Dark God potentially on his side. He does not fight alone."

"I am not alone, either."

The curl of Nephele's lip became a full snarl, and Cas braced herself for the verbal lashing she knew was coming.

But to her surprise, the goddess...hesitated.

Several moments passed and Nephele still said nothing.

A begrudging look of acceptance eventually crossed her strangely beautiful face.

"No, you aren't alone," said Inya, her slender hand coming to rest on Cas's shoulder and giving it a squeeze. "And, just as important, you and Elander collectively have perhaps all of the power we could hope to glean from Solatis—all that's left of her."

All that's left of her.

Cas's breath caught at this abrupt reminder of how dark their situation had truly become.

Inya hurriedly offered more of an explanation, before Nephele and Casia could continue their argument. "It's our belief that Solatis knew she would not be able to take physical form—or *any* form—for much longer, and so she decided to put all of her hope into Casia and Elander instead. But neither of them are the goddess she was, that's true; their bodies have limits when it comes to magic. The sword she gave Casia helps carry some of the load, but not all of it. Which means...well..."

"Which means what?" prompted Rhea. "What has happened to the rest?"

Nephele answered before Inya could. "Shattered and spilled into this mortal plane. Can't you all sense it? The death of an upper-goddess—and that's essentially what has happened to Solatis—is proving even more chaotic than we could have imagined. It seems the excess magic could not simply *disappear*, and it couldn't be contained either. So now it's flooding this world, growing tainted and throwing the order of things into chaos. The other divine are absorbing it, and it's giving them the ability to move more freely about. Things that should not be walking in this mortal world are doing precisely that."

Inya nodded. "Varen's ascension is adding to the instability as well. And the slaying of the Stone God set this all into motion some time ago."

"It's all changing," said Nephele, "and now it's easier for us to come to you like this—but it will *also* be easier for less friendly beings to come after you."

"So Malaphar got what he wanted, essentially," said

Zev. "This was always his goal, wasn't it? The Fading Sickness that targeted the non-magical population, the failed bargain he made with the former leader of this kingdom to *increase* that magical population and the energy they created....he wanted divine magic to flood this empire once more, and now it has."

A feeling of impossibility settled like a thick, melancholy fog over the group of them.

Nobody spoke for several moments—not even Zev. Laurent got to his feet and paced the room, his arms folded across his chest and his brows drawn tightly together. Rhea bowed her head while she absently scratched Silverfoot's ears. Elander leaned against the wall, staring out the window, looking lost in thought once more.

"So the battlefield is set," Nessa finally said, very softly.

"Yes. And we would be wise to approach it carefully," said Nephele, her gaze sliding pointedly back to Cas. "Rather than rushing to recklessly attack whatever enemy is currently making us the most furious. The rest of the Dark Court is restless and ready to spring into action. We are standing upon unstable ground—one wrong move, and it could all crack and swallow us up before we even realize what's happened."

Cas exhaled slowly. The Storm Goddess had made her point—and it was a reasonable one. She could admit that. "What of the third upper-god's court?" she asked, taking care to smooth the sharpness from her voice. "Did you speak with them?"

"Some of them."

Neither goddess looked optimistic about whatever conversations they'd had. But Cas was not ready to admit defeat in this as well. "Surely they want to rise against Malaphar, given that he destroyed their higher power? Why wouldn't they be on our side? The Goddess of Healing already helped us once."

"Yes. But she wants nothing to do with our latest... shall we say...*adventures*," said Nephele.

"That still leaves three more, doesn't it? Sand, Mountain, and Ocean," said Laurent, counting them off on his fingers.

"Santi was intrigued by your plans and plights, at least," said Nephele after a slight pause.

"The Sand Goddess?"

"Yes. And she has several spirits in her service that could be of great use to us as well."

"We're going to pay her another visit after we leave here," said Inya, some of the usual lightness returning to her voice.

"And the others?"

It was Elander who answered this time, after Nephele and Inya both hesitated again. "The God of the Mountain has long been close to the deities of Fire and Ice. He'll go with them, if forced to pick a side. The

Goddess of the Ocean could go either direction—or neither direction, most likely."

The fog of impossibility grew thicker.

"It took the power of two of the Moraki—both Sun *and* Stone—to even contain Malaphar in the past," said Nessa after a pause. Her gaze was on her hands as she spoke. They were clenched tightly together—almost as if in prayer. "If we can't gain enough additional support from the divine, and if Cas and Elander only have *part* of Solatis's power within them, then how can we expect to put an end to the Dark God's reign of terror? A mortal army alone isn't going to be enough."

No one had an answer to this.

Cas looked around the room. At the goddesses with their heads bowed and eyes closed. At Elander, who had gone back to staring out the window. At each of her friends and the nearly identical expressions of quiet devastation they each wore. That same devastation threatened to clench her heart and steal her breath, but she couldn't let it.

She had to *do* something.

So she rose to her feet.

"We'll keep searching for answers," she said. "Malaphar has to have weaknesses, right? If the other two upper-gods were able to fall, then so can he." She knelt beside Nessa and laid her hand over hers.

Nessa stared at their hands for a long moment before she managed a deep breath and a nod.

"In the meantime, we'll focus on what we can control here," Cas continued. "We'll unite all the mortal leaders we can, as planned, and we'll keep appealing to the divine to help our mortal army. But whether or not those divine decide to help us, my plans remain the same. We keep going until we reach the other side of this."

She straightened and stepped toward Nephele, her eyes on Shadowslayer. "Solatis entrusted that sword to me." She held out her hand. "I am going to fully unlock whatever powers she infused it—and myself—with. I won't rest until I do."

The goddess stared at her, her face an impenetrable wall and her hand still wrapped securely around the Heart centered in Shadowslayer's handle.

"I am going to keep fighting, sword or no sword," Cas said, more boldly. The fog around them all felt as if it was thinning—if only a little bit—just enough that a chorus of agreement was rising through it, more enthusiastic than before.

She was going to keep fighting, and her friends would be fighting beside her—and for a brief instant, that was all that mattered.

Nephele finally gave a single, slow nod. Her gaze turned approving, almost, as she passed the weapon back to Cas. "Let's just hope it's enough," she said.

CHAPTER 5

ENOUGH.

Nearly four days had passed since the siege of the palace and the visit from the goddesses, and that word had haunted Cas's thoughts throughout every one of those days.

It pounded through her head even now—her silent battle cry as she summoned magic and swung her sword in a dizzying dance that she practiced over and over again.

Hours ago, she had bribed Zev into following her to the training grounds. It was a large, flattened space, hidden from the rest of the world by towering grey walls, with a ceiling made of reinforced glass, allowing for a hazy view of a cloudless, steel-blue sky. It was nearly an entire mile away from the main palace and all the trappings of it, and it felt much farther—which was why this place had become her refuge over the past days, allowing her to briefly get away from the complicated business of overtaking and reforming that palace.

But no matter how far she went—or how hard she tried to focus on other things—she couldn't get away from her own thoughts.

Enough, enough, enough.

Zev was, to his credit, doing his best to help distract her. They had been alternating between magic and physical weapons all day, working their way through the various weapons they'd found in the small armory located in one corner of the grounds.

Cas pulled Shadowslayer from its sheath, and she worked on balancing it in her grip; she was still getting used to how incredibly light it was for a sword of its size.

Zev twisted his own non-magical blade as he moved closer, spinning it this way and that with impressive dexterity. Showing off, as he typically did. He came within mere feet of her, steadied the sword, sized Cas up, and charged.

Cas lifted Shadowslayer and braced herself for impact—

He rolled aside and swept behind her instead.

She whirled after him.

He spun out of reach.

Around and around they went until she finally stumbled, and then an instant later he was behind her again. The tip of his sword pressed against the back of her neck. He gave a series of teasing little taps, and a quiet chuckle rose out of him.

Cas kept perfectly still as he laughed, waiting for the moment she felt his guard falling away.

When that moment struck, so did she.

She twisted to face him. Their blades clanked together. A metallic screech rang out as Zev pulled his up and away from hers. She regained her balance and thrusted forward. He dodged and danced out of reach, still laughing as he went.

"Have you always been this sluggish?" he taunted. "Or are you just slowing down in your old age?"

She narrowed her eyes and squeezed her sword's grip. The blade pulsed with light, pale shades of white, indigo, turquoise, silver—all the different shades of magic derived from Solatis.

One of Zev's eyebrows lifted and fire gathered in his palm in response. He snapped his wrist forward, and the fire snapped with it, a small inferno that expanded as it hurtled through the air.

Cas held her blade straight up in front of her. Pale, bluish-green light overtook it, and then threads of that light peeled away and rapidly formed a cocoon of magic—Sky-kind magic—that caught the hurtling flames. The shield was similar to the ones she created with Moon-kind magic—except this shield absorbed rather than reflected, sucking in the fire and twisting it tightly into the negating strands of turquoise energy.

She swept the blade upward. The twists of magic heaved up through the air with the motion, scattering and harmlessly disintegrating before they reached the tall ceiling.

Zev's expression was a mixture of amusement and awe as he watched the last bits of that magic disappear. "That should be considered cheating."

"Might I remind you that you were the one who taught me how to cheat my way through life? Through fights, during cards, at market negotiations..." She continued listing things off in between swings of her sword, and he laughed as he parried each attack.

They kept this up for several minutes, until Zev drew his sword back to his side and summoned more fire.

Cas's arms were shaking by this point. She couldn't get Shadowslayer lifted in front of her in time to focus on summoning a shield.

Zev launched his magic.

She dropped to the ground, just barely catching herself before painfully planting her face into it. She balanced on the tips of her fingers and toes while the ball of fire soared directly over her; she was fairly certain it singed at least a few stray pieces of her hair as it flew by.

"That was too close." Zev sounded much less amused. "Maybe you need a break?"

Cas took her sword in a tighter grip and bounced back to her feet. "I can keep going."

"Are you sure?"

"I need to practice that Sky-kind magic more...I'm too slow with it."

She swung her sword again before he could protest any further, giving him no choice but to lift his weapon and meet hers.

Her arms were still burning, but she ignored the pain shooting through them and kept attacking. The sky was darkening, the day ending, and that relentless word was in her head once more—

Enough, enough, enough.

She had to do enough. She had to keep working until she got all of this right—until getting it wrong was no longer a possibility.

The minutes passed by in a blur.

She was growing frantic with the need to become stronger, more capable, just...*better.*

It became such an obsession that she soon forgot about everything outside of herself and her magic.

Storm energy billowed to life around her. She worked hard to control each individual branch of electricity, determined not to let it actually *touch* Zev; it simply made a cage around him, instead, pressing closer and limiting his movements.

"Feels like you're cheating again," he remarked, laughing, before launching straight forward.

The lightning flashed brighter. It distracted him for a split second—long enough for Cas to properly adjust her stance and manage one final, finishing strike. She hit his sword with a force that sent him tumbling backward, and the sword flew from his grip as he fell, hitting the dust-swept ground hard enough that the blade spun for several feet before coming to rest.

"Okay." Zev held up his hands. "Okay, I surrender."

The cage of lightning flickered away.

Cas finally lowered her sword, satisfied with what she'd managed to accomplish—at least for the moment. She even felt a smile starting to curve her lips as she sheathed her weapon. "I might be getting old and slow," she said, "but I can still kick your ass. That's all that matters for now, I suppose."

He grinned back. "Go easy on me. I didn't sleep much last night, and I'm a bit off because of it."

"Excuses, excuses." Her voice was light and teasing as she offered him a hand and pulled him back to his feet, but his comment worried her. Was there a tired dullness in his eyes, or was she imagining that?

How had she not noticed it before now?

She averted her gaze, pretending to focus on cleaning a bit of dirt from one of her boots as she casually asked, "Where were you last night, anyway? I didn't see you after dinner."

"Catching up with some of our old friends in the city. They missed me terribly, so I felt like I should treat them to a visit."

"I hope you were careful."

"When am I not?"

She cut her eyes back toward him, frowning.

"It was a routine trip to check in with our associates, Cas. The ones we're paying to help keep the city under control, you know? Just making sure we're getting our money's worth out of them." He picked at a loose thread on his sleeve. "If anything had gone wrong, I would have told you."

She nodded despite the concern still pinching at her insides. What else could she do but believe him? She couldn't be everywhere at once. She couldn't keep up with everything all of her friends and allies were doing at every moment. She needed to trust that they could handle some things on their own.

But the lack of control she had over it all was fast becoming frightening. It constantly felt as if something was going to fall through the cracks, and that she would be too late to catch it before it hit the ground and shattered.

"So nothing went wrong? Nothing to report?"

"Nothing *new* is wrong." He hesitated. "But it seems the cases are still rising."

A lump formed in Cas's throat. Cases of Fading Sickness, he meant. According to their sources in Ciridan and beyond, they had been growing steadily worse over the past month. This was not particularly surprising. Malaphar was growing stronger, so of course those cases were on the rise. And they were still mostly confined to the non-magical population, as before...but would that change? How long until he started targeting even the humans who *did* have some divine magic within them?

A world where humans were essentially being phased out, and only the divine and their monsters remained...that was what they would soon be approaching if they could not find a way to stop that sadistic upper-god.

She unsheathed her sword again.

Zev mirrored her frown. "I thought we were taking a break?"

"Go ahead and take one. I can practice by myself."

He studied her for a moment, but ultimately didn't need to be told twice. He went to one of the wide sets of stairs that led up out of the training ground, stretched out along the bottom step, and closed his eyes.

Cas looked back to her sword, to her own reflection gleaming in its wide blade. Her grey hair, her pale eyes... she used to hate the way these things marked her as one who had been touched by the Fade. Now she had so many other problems that she rarely even thought about the sickness. But could she afford to lose sight of it?

Other people still thought about that terrible sickness whenever they looked at her, she was certain—and it was not a look that was gaining her any support.

But if she could figure out a way to slow its spreading, then it would go a long way toward making the people of this kingdom trust in her ability to lead and protect them.

She'd done it before. Months ago, while on a mission to the city of Belwind alongside Elander, she had expelled the Fade from a young girl on her deathbed. It had been more by accident than conscious effort at the time, but now Cas thought she understood the magic that had been behind it—at least in theory. Moon-kind magic could reflect, redirect, amplify...and that, combined with the life-giving magic of Solatis that she carried, had been enough to overpower the Dark God's cursed sickness.

She had a better command of that magic now. Maybe she should have been trying to cure cases of that sickness this whole time?

When? she wondered, bitterly. *In between all the battles with kings and gods and their monsters?*

An overwhelming feeling of hopelessness started to settle over her. She swung her sword at the air in response, and she forced herself to narrow her focus back to the moment. To one swing. One breath. One thread of magic, one proper sword fighting stance, one problem at time.

Another hour passed. She was getting close to exhaustion—and to finally *admitting* that exhaustion—when her power abruptly surged in strength, catching her off-guard.

She had been in the process of trying to create

another cage of lightning like the one she'd used on Zev earlier; it unraveled quickly as her power overwhelmed her, and balls of electricity soared out of her control.

Something was drawing those balls toward the door in the center of the eastern wall. They struck the space above the door and broke into a shower of falling sparks.

A figure—Elander—walked through that arched doorway in the next instant, ducking and covering his head to avoid the sparks.

"Easy," he said, eyeing the scorch marks she'd left on the wall, and then sidestepping a lingering spark of power that ignited close to his head. "I've gotten fond of this body. I'd like to keep it in one piece."

I've gotten fond of it too, Cas thought, heart fluttering a bit as she walked over to greet him. "Sorry," she said. "I lost control for a moment." She quickly sheathed her sword. Then she held up her hand and clenched it into a tight fist, which caused the last of those showering sparks to disintegrate. Her hand shook slightly from the effort.

Elander's gaze drifted over her shaking hand. His attention didn't linger, but she could tell he'd seen it. "How much time have you spent within these walls today?"

"I haven't really been keeping track." She unclenched her fist, and then walked over to a nearby bench and settled down on it before her tired legs could further give away her exhaustion. "My magic has been building since that meeting with the goddesses; their presence always stirs it up in strange ways, so I've just been trying to work on things as often as I can."

"Anything else fueling that work? Certain antagonizing words by one of those goddesses, perhaps?"

Her cheeks warmed a bit at the knowing look Elander was giving her. She pursed her lips together, trying to keep her frustrations to herself, but the words escaped her anyway. "The Goddess of Storms still doesn't think I'm capable enough to handle things, in spite of all the times I've proven otherwise," she said quietly. "It's annoying. I have enough doubts without her vocalizing more of her own."

"She doubts all humans. I've told you not to take it personally."

"I'm not like all humans. We all know that at this point, don't we?"

He followed her to the bench but didn't sit down. There was a bow on the ground beside it—one that Zev had carelessly tossed aside after a brief bit of practicing with it. Elander grabbed this bow instead of sitting, and he studied the markings along its grip as Cas continued.

"But she was right about some things," she said, "which is why I can't stop thinking about it, I guess. And why I can't stop obsessing during these training opportunities." She gritted her teeth. Briefly closed her eyes against that frustration building inside of her. "Because she was right about Varen, and about how I don't have what it takes to defeat him."

"We don't know that for sure."

"Don't we? We witnessed it. When we were at Dawnskeep, when I tried to drive him back...I was as good as finished. The shield I once had against the gods —thanks to my father's bargain—is obviously undone now. Everything is shifting, unsteady, and when Varen attacked me...well, if you hadn't shown up, I probably wouldn't be standing here right now. And we only drove him away; he's still out there."

Elander reached for the quiver leaning against the bench, wiggled an arrow free, and nocked it.

"And he's only gotten stronger since that moment," said Cas. "*All* of our enemies seem to be getting stronger."

"You're getting stronger as well. As is the rest of your army—and me, too."

She studied him as he took aim at one of the many targets lining the walls around them.

Her guardian.

He *was* stronger than she ever remembered him being. And now his mere presence was enough to change the air around her, to make the strength of her magic swell too. But how strong could their magic become?

Strong enough to kill gods?

"Have you remembered anything else about your time as one of the Vitala?" she asked.

He released the arrow. It struck one of the targets directly in its center. "Just flashes of things that still don't make much sense. And I've searched the libraries here in hopes of finding more information about those guardians in general, but..."

"But that was always a long shot." Most of the literature and legends regarding anything divine had been scrubbed from this city long ago. "Still, there were twelve of those warriors once upon a time, and they were connected to powerful families. There must have been records, and sightings and stories that followed... all of those things can't have disappeared, right? I asked Sade to search Rykarra's libraries, too; maybe she'll have better luck finding something."

"Good thinking."

"She won't be back for a few days though."

She'd left the night before to make the trip back to the palace of Sundolia's High King and Queen, which was only a few hours by dragon flight. She had been overdue for a check in—and, war-related check-ins aside, the Sundolian woman had also been homesick...even if she wouldn't admit it; Cas had overheard her using an Air-kind crystal to send a message to the children of those monarchs she served—a message complete with silly voices that didn't fit her normally serious personality.

Cas had only visited briefly with the royal family of Sundolia, but it was long enough to realize how much those young children adored Sade. She hated the thought of keeping her from them, so she hadn't objected when Sade had brought up the possibility of going home.

"But you don't want to wait until she returns to figure out more about these things, I'm assuming?" Elander lowered the bow and glanced back at her.

"I prefer to learn by doing, anyway." She beckoned him closer.

He seemed dubious, but he put the bow aside and came to settle on the bench beside her.

"I think we need to experiment," she said.

The smile that crossed his face caused another flutter in her chest. "You know I'm always up for experimenting with you."

She punched for his arm, but he caught her fist before it landed.

"With our *magic*, that is," she said as he pried her fingers apart and laced them with his own. "I'm curious about how tightly our power is intertwined. So as long as you're here, I thought maybe we could try something..."

She lifted the hand he wasn't holding and summoned a swirl of Storm magic into it. But she didn't focus on the feel of that magic, as she usually did; she surrendered control of it and instead turned and stared into Elander's eyes.

"See if you can deliberately add to its power," she suggested.

He kept his gaze locked with hers. The concentration that passed over his face was subtle—just the tiniest wrinkle appearing in his brow—but that was all it took. Cas felt the magic swell in her hand. She had been anticipating it, but it happened so quickly that her breath still left her in a little gasp.

Elander's eyes darted to her hand, and his lips parted, his curiosity clearly piqued.

"It's the same magic," Cas said, "just as the goddesses mentioned. You gave some of your power up to bring me back—but it's still linked to you. So if we both concentrate on it together..."

She looked to her hand and focused on the strands of electricity twisting upon it.

Elander did the same.

That storm of magic became even bigger. The air all around them crackled and pulsed. It was such an effortless surge of power that it left Cas breathless again. She clenched her fist, crushing the magic away in the same motion, and then rose abruptly from the bench. "This is..." She couldn't think of a proper word.

"Interesting," Elander finished.

She nodded slowly. "It's been happening naturally for the past week or so—almost every time you come near me, my magic feels like it's swelling, fighting to get out."

He considered her words for a moment. Then he copied what she had done, summoning lightning into his own palm. It was still odd to see him using magic derived from Solatis. But there was no denying he was getting better at it. However far removed he was from his past life and magic, some part of him clearly still remembered certain things.

Cas mirrored his role from before, channeling her energy into that summoned magic. And just as earlier, it made the tiny storm expand in a way that left her dizzy.

"It feels different from when I summon magic alone," she said, voice hushed as she marveled at the solidness of their combined power.

"More powerful when we summon together...but that's not all that surprising, is it?" With some concentration, he flexed that magic even brighter.

She felt his energy moving against her own, similar to a caress over her skin. Except this touch felt deeper than any caress of his fingertips—so deep that her whole body shivered with it.

"You okay?"

"Yes." After a few tries, she managed a somewhat normal breath. "Feeling you like this is just a bit, um... let's say...*invigorating*."

That devilish smile—the one that made her heart skip—was back on his face.

She looked away. Taking a deep breath, she splayed her hands in front of herself, attempting to control her strands of magic and separate them from his.

She couldn't do it.

Not that she really *wanted* to. It was almost overwhelming; a connection unlike anything she'd ever felt with him, so frighteningly deep and exhilarating, and yet...

"I guess it's infinitely preferable to the way my magic was *draining* yours when we were both still carrying the Dark God's mark," she said.

"Agreed."

The air between them continued to throb with their shared power.

Elander stood up. She couldn't help the way her body angled automatically toward his. The way her feet carried her closer. He took her hand, interlacing their fingers once more, and he drew her even closer. Their foreheads pressed together.

Magic hummed between them.

How strong could they become?

Strands of her hair floated up around her, tickling her cheek as they brushed past. A tingling sensation swept up from the tips of her toes to the palm of her hand, so tight against his, and she felt as if she was floating—

"Do you two need to go find a private room?"

Startled, Cas took a step back and glanced to her

right. Zev was still stretched out on the steps nearby, casually propped up on one elbow and twirling a bit of summoned fire around the tips of his fingers.

She took another small step away from Elander, settling her magic and smoothing wrinkles from her shirt as she went.

"Or you could just leave," Elander suggested to Zev, before giving a smile that was somehow simultaneously sharp and cheerful. "Then this space would be private enough."

"Actually, *I* should leave," Cas said, collecting the cloak she'd tossed aside earlier and wrapping it around herself. "We can experiment more later. I need to go meet Rhea." She glanced between Zev and Elander. "You two could keep practicing magic together in the meantime."

Elander scoffed.

Zev made a similar face.

"Get along, you two," she called over her shoulder as she left.

"We always do," Zev yelled back.

Cas choked down a laugh, knowing better.

She picked up her pace as she left the walls of the training ground, letting the memories of those arguments fade into the distance behind her. They could sort out their differences without her. She had been telling the truth about needing to go; she'd gotten so caught up in her practicing that she had almost forgotten about her planned meeting with Rhea.

She'd put both Rhea and Laurent in charge of corresponding with the nobility of the surrounding realms and beyond, and the first task they'd been given was to invite as many of those nobles as possible to this palace.

She had even set a date. In just over two weeks, she planned to hold an official summit in which they all would be on even footing for the first time in a very long time—a point which she planned to emphasize. In the past, this empire had thrived under such arrangements. Cas planned to guide it back to something akin to that... an empire where the power was more evenly distributed, and therefore its burdens and gifts were *also* more equally shared.

It was the same reason she intended to be only a queen, and not an empress, as well. Her predecessors had made the mistake of declaring themselves as both rulers of their kingdom and empire, and it had been the beginning of divisions that had left their lands vulnerable to crises like the ones they were facing now.

She entered the office that Rhea had requisitioned to find her leaning over a table that was covered with countless letters and envelopes, each stamped with a different seal. Silverfoot was draped across one of her shoulders, and Laurent stood by the window adjacent to them, reading yet another letter.

"There you are," Laurent said, glancing briefly up

from that reading.

"Sorry I'm late."

"The training grounds, again?" Rhea asked, a touch of concern in her voice.

Cas brushed the question off with a nod and quickly turned her attention to the mail on the table. "Responses to our summons requests?"

"Yes," said Laurent.

"More than I expected. And they've come quickly—that's a good sign, right?"

Laurent hesitated before answering. "We weren't ignored, true...but we should warn you: Most of these aren't good news."

Cas picked one up to see for herself. She made it less than halfway through reading it before her eyes glazed over from the irritation the words ignited in her.

"Lord Falone of the Windhaven Realm, isn't it?" Laurent asked, peering at the letter's broken, sapphire-colored seal. The dragon on that seal had been torn in half. "I assumed he would be a *no*. He has long been one of Varen's most adamant supporters, from what I've gathered about him. We were warned by some of our cooperating palace staff that he wouldn't recognize your claim to the throne."

"Never mind him," Rhea insisted. "We do have *some* positive replies in this pile. And others will come around in time—once the shock of what you're doing in this palace wears off."

"We don't have much time, unfortunately," Cas pointed out. She resisted the urge to crumple the letter from Lord Falone in her fist, throw it on the floor, and stomp on it for good measure. Throwing a tantrum wouldn't accomplish anything.

"We'll keep trying," Laurent said.

"Perhaps we should send actual messengers, rather than letters?" Rhea suggested. "We could procure Air crystals to make the trips quicker. Not trips to every realm, but some of the leaders of larger territories might be worth a more personal visit..."

"I know who we can reach out to about those crystals," said Laurent.

Cas nodded. "Maybe I could go—"

He stopped her with a pointed look. "Your place is here, at least for the moment," he reminded her.

She bit her lip, and glanced back at the pile of letters, trying to come up with an argument that she thought would sway Laurent, but she couldn't think of one. He was extraordinarily difficult to sway.

"There are plenty of representatives who would speak for you," Rhea assured her. "We'll just have to decide who to send."

"You're both right, of course," Cas finally relented. "We'll send emissaries."

Here it was again, that feeling that she couldn't keep a firm hold on everything she wanted to. She had given this task to someone else—*delegated*, as a queen was supposed to do.

Now she just had to let go and let them do it.

It was a shame that *letting go* had never been her strong suit.

She turned her attention back to that pile of letters. After a brief hesitation, she stacked up several of the opened ones and tucked them under her arm. "Keep me informed about whatever messengers you send," she said. "I'm going to retire to my room to go through these."

Silverfoot let out a low whine.

Rhea's expression softened—she looked like she was searching for words of wisdom. Or comfort.

Cas didn't wait around to hear them. She left before any more of her frustration could surface. Once she made it to an empty hallway, she decided she couldn't wait to reach her room, so she slowed down and slipped one of the letters free. She held her breath as she read it to herself.

THE COUNCIL OF COASTHAVEN, ON BEHALF OF LORD AND LADY ELYON, WOULD LIKE TO TAKE THIS OPPORTUNITY TO DECLARE THEIR NEUTRALITY CONCERNING MATTERS OF THE CROWN OF CIRIDAN AND ALL ITS ASSOCIATED ACTS, AGGRESSIONS, AND GRIEVANCES...

She shoved the letter back into its casing. Pulled out

another—this one from the Silverkeep Realm on the other side of the empire, as far from Coasthaven as it could possibly be in both distance and culture—only to find that it said essentially the same thing.

As did the next.

There *were* a few positive replies, as Rhea had said, but most were neutral, at best...and far more were so positively hostile that Cas worried she'd made more enemies than potential allies with this little exercise. And all because she'd attempted to reach out a hand to them.

"*Politics.*" The word seethed out of her like a curse.

Her blood still simmered with the magic Elander had stirred up at the training grounds. She let it float to the surface, let her concentration drift to it instead. Her skin tingled just at the mere thought of how they'd managed to summon magic in tandem. *That* was comforting, at least. She'd felt so powerful such a short time ago, standing with him...

"The more powerful our magic becomes, the less allies we'll need anyway," she mumbled to the empty hallway.

But as she fought against the urge to read another letter, she secretly didn't *feel* powerful. She felt worried, and full of nothing but questions and that damn, cursed word that wouldn't leave her alone—

Enough, enough, enough.

Would it ever feel like she was doing enough?

CHAPTER 6

Later that evening, Cas stood in a small bathroom off the main chambers she'd taken up residence in, studying her tired reflection.

The space was cramped and dark. It was nowhere near as extravagant as her last accommodations in this palace—but she hadn't been able to stomach the idea of returning to the previous room she'd stayed in. That entire previously-used wing of the palace—which had also contained the room Asra had died in—had been closed off at her orders.

The area they were utilizing instead was one that had originally been reserved for long-term guests. Most of it hadn't been used in some time, and there had been plenty of cobwebs and dust to deal with, but Cas preferred it this way; she could imagine it as a dead space that had only been waiting for her to arrive—to plant something new within it.

She'd put Nessa in charge of much of that planting, and the job suited her well. Within days, Nessa assembled a team that had organized and collected supplies—everything from linens to food—to equip the palace properly for their operations. It was still a shell of what it had been under Varen's ownership—not fancy, and not particularly comfortable—but it was livable, and they had commandeered enough of Varen's former servants to make it functional.

She looked away from the mirror. The dim lighting in this room was doing nothing to improve her exhausted appearance or her mood. She quickly finished stripping off her dirty clothes, washed up, and then reached for the robe draped over the nearest cabinet.

Running her hands over this velvety soft garment cheered her up a bit. It was silly, but Nessa had insisted she needed something luxurious and new in her wardrobe—something that made her feel like a queen—and so she had made a point to purchase this robe from one of the shops in Ciridan. She'd left it in a box on Cas's bed earlier, complete with a perfectly-tied bow. When she'd had time to do all this, in between running the day-to-day operations of the palace, Cas had no idea. Her friends never ceased to amaze her.

She heard a knock on the bedroom door.

Elander was in that adjacent bedroom—he'd been

reading through some of the letters she'd brought up with her—so she didn't worry about rushing to answer the knock.

But when the sound of conversation drifted her way, curiosity got the better of her. She wrapped the robe around herself and peered out of the bathroom just in time to see a servant bidding farewell to Elander and leaving the room.

Elander walked back to the desk by the window. He sifted through the letters upon it, picked one up, and glanced back at the door the servant had left through. He hesitated only a moment before he started to follow that servant.

Cas's heart grew restless—the way it usually did whenever she watched him leave lately. It had been a long, draining day, and she wanted him to stay; she gave it no more thought than that before she took a step into the bedroom and said, "Going somewhere, Captain?"

His body visibly tensed at the word *Captain*. He paused and turned back to her. His eyes drank her in, snagging briefly on the curves of her hips and on the hint of her breasts that the loosely-tied robe left exposed.

"Is everything okay?" she asked.

"Yes. I was just going to go speak with..." He trailed off as his gaze met hers, and it stayed there as he reached for the door, which had been left partially ajar. "Actually...never mind. It can wait."

"It can," she agreed.

A corner of his mouth lifted. "You don't even know what *it* is."

"But it can wait. You have other things to do."

He pushed the door closed, tucked the letter into the inner pocket of his coat, and then walked over to meet her. He brought one hand up to cup her chin. Used the other to tug on the sash cinching her robe together. "Other things, hm?"

Her skin flushed with heat. "Yes."

"Such as?"

"Let's see..." Her pulse thudded in her ears as he continued to play with that sash. "You were going to arrest me again, as I recall," she reminded him. "It's been several days since you suggested recreating this moment of our history, and you've yet to make good on that promise—did you forget about it?"

His thumb stroked a soft path across her lips, parting them. "I didn't forget. Trust me."

She started to shift her stance, but he gripped her robe more tightly and kept her still. The fingers near her mouth slid down, caressing her throat as they went. His gaze was intense. Impossible to look away from.

After swallowing several times, she managed to whisper, "Well?"

Another smile briefly crossed his face. His lips grazed her ear as he leaned in. "Why don't you start by putting your hands behind your back?"

That voice alone would have been enough to undo whatever might have been holding her back. But he didn't stop with this command. He continued to persuade with his mouth—not with words but with teasing strokes of his tongue, nips of teeth, and warm, deliberate breaths across the sensitive skin of her ear.

She moved her hands behind her back, partly so she could brace herself against the wall behind her.

Once they were there, Elander worked his fingers into the knotted sash securing her robe. He untied it slowly. Took hold of one end of it. Twisted it around his hand and gave another little tug, which pulled it free of the loops that held it in place. He left the robe itself draped around her while his fingers trailed along its edges, nudging the cloth open inch by inch, as though taking his time to unwrap a gift. The combination of his touch and the robe's silk trim brushing over her skin made her knees feel like collapsing.

She started to grab for him, reaching upward, intending to rake her fingers through his hair and pull his mouth down to hers.

He caught her wrists and lowered them. "Behind your back," he ordered.

Rebellion briefly crossed her mind. Desire—ignited by that dark, rough edge to his voice—overruled it.

Once she had done as he commanded, he took the robe's sash, slipped around behind her, and used it to bind her wrists. "Not exactly handcuffs," he said, in between brushing kisses along the side of her neck, "but it will do for the moment."

"You're very resourceful."

He moved in front of her again, caught her jaw and lifted her gaze to his. "Yes. And I take my job very seriously." He smoothed a hand down her side, over her hips, and then reached around to take hold of her bound hands. Pressed them against the wall behind her. His other hand slid beneath her robe, gliding across her stomach before sliding lower.

A gasp slipped through her lips.

"Checking for weapons," he informed her with another sly smile. "Standard procedure."

His hand slipped between her legs, and his fingers tapped over her warm center, coaxing more sound from her lips—not quite a gasp this time, but a soft note of pleasure that drew him closer. His mouth claimed hers in a swift, hungry kiss, their tongues tangling briefly before he pulled away.

Her reaction was automatic as he leaned back—she followed as if it was part of a familiar dance. She had forgotten about the grip he still had on her wrists. He pressed them more firmly against the wall, holding her back, and laughed quietly at the pout she gave in response.

"Resisting arrest." He shook his head at her, his lips hovering just outside the reach of her own. "Yet another mark to add to your record."

"How thick do you suppose that record is at this point?"

"I've lost track of all your transgressions, honestly."

"I'm a lost cause, I suppose."

"Afraid so." His hold slipped from her hands and trailed over her arms, across her neck, and down along her curves before coming to rest on the small of her back. "So now the question is...what am I going to do with you?"

"I'm sure you'll think of something."

His eyes seemed to darken with what she could only assume were plenty of creative thoughts on the matter. "Any ideas for me?"

She *had* ideas, but his other hand was still teasing a path between her thighs, and the featherlight touch of his fingertips was making it difficult to focus on forming words. She ran her tongue over her dry lips.

"Tighter bonds?" he suggested, gaze drifting to her hands that were still dutifully braced against the wall— even without him holding them. "Or I could have you on your knees, maybe. And the possible punishments..." His fingers dug into her back, pulling her onto her tiptoes, pressing her hips into his. "Well, the possibilities are endless, really." He brought his mouth back against hers with the final word, roughly parting her lips with his tongue. The hand between her legs became equally rough, massaging and tracing all her most sensitive lines until they were wet; slick enough for his touch to slip easily inside her.

He pushed deeper, his finger curling slightly against her soft inner walls. She arched her back, lifting her hips to answer the beckoning motion. The hand against her back slid lower, cupping her from behind, adding to the fingers stretching and teasing her warmth until her body writhed and her legs buckled from the intense pleasure of it. He caught her as she crumpled, lifted her with ease, and carried her over to the bed.

He briefly loosened her bonds so he could pull her hands above her head as he laid her back against the pillows. Her fingertips brushed the satin-wrapped head-board. The robe fell open completely as she stretched out before him. It framed her body, and for a moment, he studied her bare form as though it were a painting within that casing of velvet and silk.

He removed his shirt and tossed it to the floor. Undid the buckles of his belt and pulled it from his waist. Cas's next inhale was unnaturally loud, and he clearly noticed, because a slight smirk crossed his face. He was breath-taking, and as aware of it as ever. He paused his undressing and leaned forward, bracing a hand on either side of her.

A bruise had formed on the side of her ribcage—one of many she'd earned during their battles while seizing the palace. His lips fell against it first, sweeping gentle kisses before moving on to her stomach. He kissed his way across her navel, then trailed lower, following the line of her hip down to her thigh.

She twisted against the mattress, eager to rise and meet those kisses and all the many, many other things she knew his mouth was capable of.

He responded to her movement by slipping one of his large, strong hands underneath her and clenching it into the plentiful flesh of her backside, digging his fingers in and holding her still. Then his mouth was against her other hip, his lips dragging that same, tortuously good path as before—except now along her opposite thigh. His tongue traced paths that captured her in a way no shackles could have. It made her eyes close and her body feel as though it was floating one moment, crashing toward the edge of everything in the next.

She wanted to leap from that edge.

Every time he touched her, she grew more and more certain that she could fly from it. He kept bringing her to it...only to draw away and let her linger there until she came back down to him and his eager, waiting touches and kisses.

"Is endless teasing the punishment you decided on, then?" she breathed out after a few minutes of this.

His laughter spilled warm breath over her thighs and sent a throbbing need straight to her very core. He lifted his head from between her legs and brought his mouth over hers in a slow, deep kiss.

"I'm not that cruel," he whispered as he pulled away.

"And as long as you comply like a good little fugitive, I don't intend to leave you suffering or needing in any way tonight. Not indefinitely, anyway."

"Compliance is not one of my stronger traits. You know this."

"I know better than most." He huffed out another laugh before he returned to his torture—though only briefly. Then he drew away from her and stood beside the bed, his gaze watching her intently as he finished undressing.

He was no longer touching her, but she still felt that desire to soar, just from staring at his impressive, fully bared figure.

Her stomach flipped several times as he crawled back onto the bed, straddling her legs and reaching for her bound wrists.

He pulled her partway up, then tucked a pillow underneath the small of her back for support. They sat this way for a moment, a tangle of limbs among disheveled sheets, heat and desire pooling between them. He traced the velvet roped around her wrists, twisting the dangling length of that sash around his finger and giving it a little tug, pulling her hands forward until they brushed against his hard arousal.

"You can use your hands now," he said with a wicked little smile.

She already was, cupping them together and slipping them over that hardened length. It was cumbersome, yet strangely arousing, to have her touch limited this way.

His head tipped back slightly as her touch traveled over him, his eyes briefly closing as he fought to keep his composure. After a moment, he lowered his gaze, first to meet her own, and then lower, watching her work. His lips parted and his tongue traced over them. "You're capable of complying after all."

"Only when it's something I wanted to do anyway," she fired back, which made him laugh again—though the sound was cut short by a sharp inhale and a soft curse as she *complied* with more pressure, more precise strokes. His muscles contracted and released at her touch—at her command.

Within minutes she had him completely at her mercy, and she couldn't help herself; she leaned forward and whispered, "You've lost control of your prisoner, it seems."

"Have I?" The challenge in his voice was playful...yet tinged with a darkness, with a hint of ruthless desire that was also burning in his eyes when she pulled back to meet them.

He took hold of her binding. Pulled the slack from it with a clench of his fist, and her hands—still busy caressing him—clenched tighter in automatic response. He kept hold of that binding and used it to guide her next strokes, his strong grip moving her hands up and down until her palms were glistening with the first drops of his seed.

Then she was on her back.

He pushed her hands away from him, guiding them above her head once more.

"You're going to want to put those hands against the headboard again," he told her, "so you can brace yourself against something."

The pillow beneath her back was yanked out and tossed aside as he slid an arm under her and lifted her, angling her hips so he could guide himself inside her in one smooth motion.

As he filled her, she found herself reaching for that headboard as he'd suggested, pressing into the satin cloth that covered it. Her fingers curled, trying to grip the smooth material, trying to brace herself further as Elander took her legs in the crook of each of his arms and rose onto his knees so that he could drive deeper.

The first deep thrust made that headboard rattle and the entire bed creak and moan beneath them.

The next rock of his hips brought him even deeper. She cried out from the pain and pleasure of it, and his mouth was upon hers in the next moment, his tongue pushing in, lashing against hers as his hips moved more furiously against her. She met each of those movements at first. But the pleasure of it soon overwhelmed her senses, and her body relaxed and simply rode each rise and fall of him until her mind turned blissfully blank.

"Seems I've got my prisoner under control again," he mused, tipping his face toward her throat. She quivered as his lips pressed to her throbbing pulse. "Let me know when you want to surrender completely," he added with another slow, deep thrust for emphasis.

She managed a breathy laugh. "Did you really think I would come quietly?"

"No." His tongue flicked against her pulse. "In fact, I was hoping you wouldn't."

The low tone he spoke in made her feel as if she might ignite from the heat rising through her. And suddenly she *did* want to surrender. To his touch, his words—to every part of him that made her burn this way.

She didn't say it out loud, but something told her he already knew.

He kept one arm hooked around one of her legs, keeping her lifted, angled so he could slide deeper. His other hand released its grip on her leg and roamed freely over her skin, massaging and pinching the hard peaks of her breasts before he took one in his mouth and sucked it until a soft cry tumbled through her lips.

His mouth continued to explore her breasts while his hand traveled higher and curved gently around her neck. His thumb stroked the red mark he'd left with his mouth. That dark and ruthless desire flashed in his eyes again. Her legs squeezed together from a sudden jolt of need. As she tightened around him, some of his composure slipped, and his hand fell with it, falling back to roughly reclaim his hold on her other leg.

He wrapped both of her legs around him. His grip slid to her hips next, and he yanked her more completely against him before lowering his face toward hers and taking her mouth with his. His hands reached up, pressed her outstretched arms down into the mattress, securing her while he drove himself into her again and again.

His kiss grew rougher with every one of those drives, and she met him with a ruthlessness of her own—with lips and tongue and teeth.

One of his hands left her arms and slipped between her legs again, pressing against her thigh and pushing it outward. A moan of approval escaped her, and he slowed in mid-thrust, as if to savor the sound while he continued to throb inside of her.

"Not very quietly at all," he whispered, approvingly. "Good."

Her head fell back, her muscles shivering and growing weak with a need that made it nearly impossible to breathe.

And—as promised—he didn't leave her wanting for long. He pressed against her thigh again. Another moan, and this time he didn't slow at the sound of it. He moved faster, and soon she felt herself slipping, becoming lost within the waves of that fire that burned—no longer just inside of her, but in between and all around them, blazing toward a crescendo.

They surrendered together in the end. Release seized —and then collapsed—her body as he spilled into her, as he pressed her wrists firmly against the bed and his mouth muffled her cry in one final, commanding kiss.

They stayed together for several moments after, his forehead pressed to hers and his breath still coming in rasps.

Slowly, she released the grip her legs had claimed around him. He leaned back as her shaking legs came to rest on either side of his body. He wrapped an arm around one of those legs, steadying her, and then simply watched her for a moment. His lips were parted, and he was holding his breath—as if in awe, maybe. His eyes shimmered with an emotion that she couldn't name.

Did such things have names?

She didn't know, but she would never tire of seeing him like this—of that much, she was certain.

She always felt as if the world had evened itself out whenever they reached this sacred moment. As if they had no past lives. They were not gods or queens or something strange and in between. They were nothing important at all—just two more lovers in a world filled with them—and nothing mattered except for the feel of his hands against her skin as they caressed her inch by inch, sending aftershocks of pleasure tingling through her.

"Checking for weapons again?" she asked in a sleepy, content voice.

"You can never be too careful." His roaming ceased as his hand reached her jaw, and he cupped it and gently kissed her lips before rolling over onto his back and draping an arm over his face.

She watched him as she pulled her robe back around her body, smiling to herself, and then she plopped down onto the pillow beside him.

Her heartbeat finally slowed, and her eyes had just started to droop shut when Elander released a soft sigh.

"Damn it," he muttered.

"What's wrong?"

He lifted his arm from his face and peered over at her. "Seems I ended up sleeping with my apprehended fugitive again."

She grinned. "Some captain you turned out to be."

"I should probably just resign at this point."

She poked him playfully in the side. "Nonsense. One day you'll get it right. You just have to keep trying."

"Maybe." He slid an arm around her and pulled her against his chest. "And then I'll properly lock you away."

"Forever?"

"And always."

"Sounds awful."

"Well, you should have thought about that before you committed to a life of crime."

"Maybe. But locking me up forever still seems like an unjustifiably harsh punishment."

"Some part of me thinks you enjoy being punished."

"A fair assessment, I suppose." She pretended to give the matter some serious thought. "Actually, if I'm being honest, your particular brand of *punishment* isn't likely to deter me from any sort of crime. In fact, if it's part of the deal, I'm pleading guilty and turning myself in every time."

Quiet laughter rumbled in his chest, raising bumps along every inch of bare skin she had pressed against him.

"Go ahead and lock me up forever. Please?" She presented her hands to him—which made his laughter grow deeper and richer, and he responded to her plea by locking her in a cage of his arms. She surrendered to this makeshift prison without much of a fight, curling tighter against him and letting his scent envelope her, and his strength keep her.

He kept one arm hooked around her when they eventually pulled apart, and he brought his fingers up and smoothed them through the long waves of her hair. They laid like this for ten minutes, drifting in and out of awareness, until his fingers stilled in her hair and he quietly said, "Can I ask you something?"

His tone had turned serious. She lifted her head from his chest so they were eye-to-eye. "Of course," she said.

But he hesitated.

She sat up straighter, an uncertain little smile tugging at the corners of her lips. "What is it?"

He returned her smile, but it wasn't the same as before; it had taken on the same serious, heavier quality that his tone had. He gathered up one of her hands in his and ran his thumb absently across her knuckles. Took a deep breath.

"I just wanted to—"

Someone knocked on the door.

Neither of them moved right away, still caught up in the weight and uncertainty of whatever he'd been working up the nerve to say. His lips parted, and he took another deep breath.

Cas tried for a deep breath to mirror his, but she didn't quite manage it. That look in his eyes...

What was he going to ask her?

The knock came again, louder this time.

Cas narrowed her gaze toward the door and got to her feet, tying her robe more tightly around herself as she rose. Elander was beside her a moment later, pulling on his pants and belt. She let him answer the door while she found more substantial clothing to put on herself, though she continued to watch that door out of the corner of her eye—and she froze as she heard the voice that floated in from the hallway.

Nessa.

Cas caught a snippet of the conversation. They had a visitor waiting downstairs, apparently.

"Yes, but *who* is here to see her at this hour?" Elander was asking.

Cas drifted closer, peered around Elander, and caught sight of Nessa's face—it was pale with shock.

She dropped the clothing she'd collected, pushed her way past Elander, and took Nessa's hands in hers. "Nessa? What's wrong?"

"There's...there's someone here to speak with you."

"Yes, we've established that." Elander's voice was patient, but he was clearly struggling to keep it that way. "But *who is it?*"

Cas gave Nessa's hands an encouraging squeeze.

Nessa squeezed back, and she kept her eyes locked with hers until finally she managed to say, "Prince Alder."

CHAPTER 7

Elander was certain he had misheard Nessa.

"That's impossible," he said.

"I know, but—"

"Prince Alder is dead." He looked to Casia for confirmation. He hadn't actually witnessed the elven prince's murder in Briarfell, but *she* had. The images of it had been in her nightmares for weeks, alternating with countless other nightmarish things.

She looked just as confused and unsettled as he felt.

"I know he's dead, obviously," said Nessa, frustration mingling with the fear that was making her voice more high-pitched than normal. "But it's *him*. He's here. Come downstairs and see for yourself."

He and Casia exchanged another confused look—but what else was there to do?

"We'll be right down," said Casia, already disappearing back into the room, scooping the pile of fallen clothes from the floor as she went.

They finished dressing quickly, grabbed their weapons, and hurried after Nessa.

"This reeks of magic derived from the Rook God," he told Casia as they made their way down the hall. "It has to be some sort of trick."

"I know," she said. "But I want to try and beat Laurent to this particular trick."

Elander hadn't thought about the effect it might have on the half-elf—to see his brother brought back by what was likely a sick and twisted magic. But it was clear from the concerned look on Casia's face that this was *all* she was currently thinking about. Which was likely what the trickster had been hoping for.

"Of course," he replied, as calmly as he could. "We just need to be careful."

She only picked up her pace in response.

When they reached the main foyer—where several armed guards awaited them—Laurent was nowhere in sight. Nessa stood off to the side, her arms hugged around herself and her face devoid of nearly all color.

Elander didn't note any other specific faces, because his eyes quickly found Prince Alder amongst the guards—and this was where they stayed for a very long time.

Because it *was* him.

In a manner of speaking, anyway.

It looked precisely like him, and it was made of flesh and muscle and sinew...

But this was not a living creature.

Elander tried to roll away the unsettling feeling tensing up his neck and shoulders. It had been a long time since he'd felt this kind of magic at work.

Casia had not stopped walking when he had. She continued toward the Prince in a daze until he caught up to her, took her by the arm, and drew her to a stop. She kept her confused gaze locked on Alder as she whispered, "Is he really...?"

"It's Death magic."

She jerked her gaze to his. "Varen?"

He shook his head. "It doesn't feel powerful enough to have come directly from the middle-god himself."

Casia's gaze lingered on him. She didn't speak, but he could read the unspoken questions in her eyes. The fear of the unknown. And a possible explanation *did* cross his mind, but he kept it to himself. He needed to gather more evidence before he spoke of such things.

He looked back to the Prince, who was smiling, wearing nearly the same obnoxiously carefree expression he'd often donned in his previous, true life.

"How is this possible?" Casia asked under her breath.

"The one responsible likely took something of the dead Prince to use—a bit of bone, or blood, or something similar—and created this double of him. They're controlling it, too. It isn't actual revival, and it doesn't ever last long. Just long enough to glimpse into the dead one's mind and body and learn whatever secrets they were stubbornly keeping, or to use their creation as a puppet...to antagonize their enemies, for example."

"That's disgusting."

Elander nodded, even as personal memories of using similar magic flashed through his mind. It was one of the least disgusting things he'd done while in the service of the Dark God, really.

That was not who he was anymore, and yet, those shadowy slivers of his past were still easier to access than the memories of his time as a guardian of the light —the latter of which he had been actively trying to summon for weeks now.

Casia was stepping forward again, so he broke free of his troubled thoughts and moved after her. They came to a stop directly in front of Prince Alder.

"Once a king-to-be, now reduced to a lowly messenger." The Prince chuckled in a way that was remarkably similar to the sound his living counterpart had once made. "Oh, how the mighty have fallen, hm?"

Elander declined to comment on that fall. "And what message do you have for us?"

The puppet of the Prince lifted a hand at a strange angle. His fingers twitched disturbingly, as if trying and failing to bend properly. But control seemed to return to him after a brief bit of concentration, and then he reached into the pocket of his coat and withdrew a small brown envelope and tossed it at Casia's feet. His movements remained just stilted enough to suggest that something was not completely natural about his existence. Watching them made Elander's skin crawl.

Casia cautiously picked up the envelope and pulled a ripped square of cloth from it. "A tattered flag?" She turned it over in her hands, revealing an insignia that featured a prancing horse with a garland of leaves draped around its neck. "This is the realm of Mistwilde's flag. And these dark splotches on it..."

"Blood," Prince Alder informed her with another of his not-quite-normal smiles.

Casia stiffened. She held the blood-stained scrap at arm's length, her fingers clenching it with obvious effort. Determined not to drop it in spite of how uncomfortable it made her, Elander assumed. Remembering their conversation from the night they'd seized this palace—about the way the sight of such blood made her feel—he reached over and took the flag from her, pretending he wanted to study it as well.

She regained her composure quickly after it left her hands, fixed a glare on the princely puppet, and said, "What is the meaning of this?"

"Her Majesty, Queen Sarith of Briarfell and Moreth, would like to offer you some advice. Your allies have been meddling in the region of Mistwilde, interfering with her business there. You should see to it that those allies step aside, or it will be more than just a bloody *flag* arriving at your doorstep next."

"First of all," Casia began, her voice low and seething, "she has no right to the title of Queen—"

"Neither do you, according to some."

"—and she has no business making any threats against me or my allies," Casia continued. "Those allies went to Mistwilde because they believed that King Talos and his followers would align with our causes. And I will not let that elven *queen* bully them into believing otherwise."

Prince Alder's eyes skipped around the room. His head lolled about in an unsettling way, looking as though it could detach and tumble right off his neck.

Several of the guards took a step back, as though anticipating this, but Casia stayed put.

The Prince's eyes eventually rolled back to her. "Your brother informed her that you would be busy with redefining operations in this palace," he said. "She respects your claim to Melech's crown and doesn't intend to interfere with your wearing of it—she simply requests that you send word of your withdrawal from Mistwilde in exchange for her goodwill."

"She's going to be waiting a long time for that word," Elander muttered.

"She's going to be waiting *forever*," Casia snarled in agreement.

Elander nodded along with her, but there was something bothering him—that mention of her brother. Varen was no longer a mortal king; what did he stand to gain from a continued alliance with Sarith?

What was so important about the Mistwilde Realm that it still interested him, even as a newborn god? And why would he go out of his way to tell Casia not to go there? He had to know that telling Casia *not* to do something was one of the best ways to get her to actually do it.

But maybe that was the point...and this was yet another one of Varen's tricks.

He started to ask his questions, but he was cut off—because the spell holding Alder's body together started to break.

Bits of black energy peeled from his skin and floated up. They extinguished the burning wall sconces as they passed over them, leaving the room in darkness—save for the moonlight shining from the skylight high above.

Elander took hold of Casia's arm once more and pulled her back, and they watched as the moonlit Prince became a sickly being with mottled skin and molting hair, a corpse with empty eyes and twitching, failing muscles, a walking skeleton with flesh dangling from it...

And then finally nothing more than a single bone, splintered and bare, that dropped into the center of the entryway; this was the piece that had been used as part of the reanimation spell, apparently.

The rest of him was gone.

Back to the realm of death and memory...just like that.

No one spoke for several moments after that final piece of Alder spun to a rest on the polished floor.

As the last wisps of the power that had sustained him disappeared, Elander lifted his gaze and saw that Laurent was standing on the other side of the foyer, staring at the splintered bone with a hauntingly blank expression on his face.

Had he been there the whole time?

It was even more difficult to read his emotions than usual. Then again, Elander cared less about his feelings and more about what a mess the entire situation in Moreth—and now Mistwilde—seemed to be turning into.

Laurent was the rightful king of Moreth. So even if they left Kethra's other elven realm alone, as Sarith insisted, it still would not mean the last of their dealings with her.

Then again, he had his own personal matters to settle with that so-called queen, anyway.

His gaze moved of its own accord, sliding over Casia. Her clothing hid the signs of her suffering at the hands of that queen. It had been nearly a month since the beatings that had drawn blood from her arms, her shoulders, her back. And time—along with the extra dose of divine energy Solatis had granted her—meant that the scars Sarith had left on her skin had mostly faded.

But the image of them was still vibrant in Elander's mind.

So no, his business with Sarith was not *finished*.

For the moment, however, he had other, more immediate problems to worry about—such as finding the puppet master responsible for the gruesome show they'd just witnessed.

Because that master was close by.

He could sense them.

His gaze followed Casia as she quickly rushed to Laurent's side. Within moments she was completely absorbed in conversation with him—her hand holding tightly to his and her eyes looking nowhere else but into the half-elf's.

Good.

She was fully distracted, which made it easy for him to turn and slip away without being noticed. To go hunting. A bad idea, perhaps—he was almost certain he wasn't going to like what he found—but he couldn't help himself.

He stole down a side hallway to find a less conspicuous exit—one guarded by fewer soldiers to wonder about what he was doing—and he headed out into the night.

Once he had put some distance between himself and the palace, he closed his eyes. Breathed in deep. Let the hints of magic in the air wash over his senses. He hadn't been mistaken. Alder was gone, but the same energy that had surrounded his corpse was still present—a distant, yet familiar magic. It created a faint but unmistakable path that twisted off to his right, leading into the forest at the edge of the palace grounds.

Elander followed that path until he was deep in the trees, to a place where the light from the palace lanterns no longer reached him. The moon was no help, either, as it had slipped away behind the steadily increasing number of thick clouds. But his eyesight was better than a normal human's—all of his senses were closer to divine than mortal, now—so it was easy enough to navigate through the darkness. He picked and shoved his way through countless overgrown paths, still following that magical energy, until he came to a treeless space dotted with crumbling statues.

It looked like it had been a shrine of sorts, once upon a time. But like most divine-related things in this city, it appeared to have been abandoned long ago. Moss covered the broken statues. The small pond in the center of it was coated in scum. Only a few of the stone walls that surrounded the area remained, and they were all in varying states of advanced decay.

And there, sitting atop one of those crumbling walls, was the very person he'd hoped he *wouldn't* find at the end of his hunt.

"Caden."

His old friend lifted his head at the sound of his name, and a corner of his mouth rose. "Ah. Fancy meeting you here."

Neither of them spoke for a long moment after this, not until Elander glanced back toward the palace. "We have you to thank for our latest messenger, I presume."

"It wasn't my idea; I thought it was rather tasteless, for the record. Of all the dead people to use..." Caden shrugged. "But I suppose it got your attention, didn't it?"

Elander breathed in deeply through his nose, trying—and failing, mostly—to not let his discomfort show. The scent of decay and dust burned his nostrils. "It's been a long time since I've seen you use that power. I didn't think you were capable of it any longer."

"I wasn't." Caden's eyes flashed briefly to a strange, rich shade of red. They were glowing, almost. The air around them turned colder, the grass swayed in a sudden, unnatural wind, and Elander's discomfort shifted into something closer to fear.

Because it was becoming difficult to deny what had happened.

Caden was no longer a *fallen* spirit. His power had been restored, just as the God of Death himself had been restored—or replaced, rather. And this Caden...perhaps he was more of a *replacement* than a restoration too. There was no telling what powers he might possess.

What strength Varen had given him, what he'd done to him, or what he'd commanded him to do.

Elander somehow managed to keep his voice devoid of emotion as he said, "A gift from Varen, I'm guessing."

Caden picked at the loose pieces of stone in the wall. Flicked a bit of gravel from his clawed finger. "He's been quite generous with his new powers."

Elander hesitated, unsure of what else he could possibly say about the matter. The alternative to accepting those powers had been destruction, almost certainly; that was how it usually went when a new middle-god ascended. The new god chose new servants, and the old ones were lost—if they even survived the fall of their former patron god in the first place. Which they typically didn't.

But nothing about Elander's fall, or anything after it, had been *typical*.

So Caden remained, his strange existence continued —and could Elander really be angry at him for surviving it all, however he'd had to do it?

Caden hopped down from the wall and strolled forward. The movement was so casual that it made it feel oddly aggressive, as if he felt he was entirely in control of the situation at hand. It sent a stab of annoyance through Elander that made his next words come out sharper than he'd intended.

"You could have refused to serve him."

"I tried."

The world seemed to contract, and in the newly-shrunken space everything seemed too loud—the falling leaves, the bugs skittering over the pond's surface, the blades of grass brushed together by the breeze.

And Caden's voice rose above it all as he added, "I *did* ask him to let me die, for what it's worth."

Elander stared, a cold sweat breaking over him. This revelation only made it all seem worse somehow.

"I asked at least once, before the transfer of power was completed," Caden continued. "Maybe twice? It's all a bit of a blur. But it doesn't matter. Varen refused. He insisted on keeping me alive—seemed to think I would be more useful to him than any new servant he might be able to ensnare. *We have things to accomplish together,* he told me."

What things? Elander wanted to ask. But his numb lips couldn't form the words.

"And the magic he now carries was hard to resist," said Caden. "I've been a servant of that magic for ages; it was simply reflex to return to it. And it binds more completely than anything—more than the words you and I have spoken, or whatever we've been through together. You know that."

Elander stood his ground as Caden paced closer to him. "Tara as well?" he asked. "She's disappeared from Stormhaven. Was that Varen's doing?"

Caden hesitated, as though he was trying to decide

on the best way to explain what had happened. Or fighting to explain any of it at all...

Could he even speak the truth about these matters?

Elander didn't know. It was impossible to tell how powerful a hold Varen had on Caden and his thoughts.

"I went to see about her," Caden finally said. "The Storm Goddess wasn't home to keep up with her captive, and the humans and spirits that serve her haven are weak. I could have easily stolen Tara away..."

"But?"

"But she was already dead when I arrived. I assume her life-force started to fade as soon as you were killed at Dawnskeep—same as my own life did. The difference between us was that Varen was able to reach me in time, sustain me, and bring me back from the edge of perishing. Much like you did, once upon a time." He exhaled a deep, shuddering sound—part laughter, part sigh. "Lucky me, I suppose."

One dead, one taken.

Elander felt dizzy. He shifted his stance, searching for balance. Guilt clawed at his insides. He still didn't know what to say. Only one thought came to mind, and it didn't feel adequate...but he had to say *something* to interrupt the awful silence.

So he said it. "I'm sorry."

Caden smiled—a sharp twist of his lips without any warmth behind it. "Are you, though?"

He *was*. Desperately so. But there was no point in

arguing; it was obvious that Caden didn't care to hear these apologies.

An oppressive silence started to close in around them, until Elander quietly said, "You should leave this city."

But Caden only shook his head, and his eyes flashed once more to a bright, unsettling shade of red. "I'm afraid I can't do that," he said. "Because I need to see the new queen before I leave."

CHAPTER 8

EVERY NERVE IN ELANDER'S BODY FLARED TO LIFE, EACH FIRING a warning across his skin that rapidly burned away any guilt or sorrow he felt about the situation.

"You will stay away from her," he said in a low, threatening voice.

"You don't command me anymore."

"I'm not commanding you. I'm *warning* you. Stay the fuck away from her."

"I wish I could. But orders are orders."

"Disregard them. You did it with my orders all the time."

"You didn't enforce those orders with the same *enthusiasm* that my new keeper does."

Darkness briefly overtook Elander's vision, blurring the world's edges and reducing everything to black and white. Everything was either a threat, or it wasn't. And Caden had somehow landed on the *threat* side—it was as simple as that, at least for a few brief, heated moments.

"Relax," said Caden. "I just want to talk to her. Those are my only orders. She has questions, I know." He gestured toward the path Elander had taken to find him. "Quite a history within the walls of that palace you all have overtaken, and so much of it has been lost to her for so long...Varen wants to make certain she understands the truth of things, that's all. Things are even more complicated than she realizes, I'm told."

The truth of things.

Ridiculous.

Elander blinked, breathed in deeply, and managed to regain a bit of his usual clarity. His fingers curled around the short sword at his hip. "Stay away from her," he warned again.

"Or else what?" Caden smiled as his gaze fell on that grip Elander had taken on his weapon. "You'll kill me?"

Elander squeezed the sword more tightly. Took another deep breath.

Could he bring himself to do such a thing, if it came down to it?

He didn't know. He didn't want to think about it— and he refused to be provoked into an answer either way.

Caden's taunting smile did not so much as flicker as he took a step closer. "Let's see if you can manage it, just for fun, shall we?"

He gave no more warning than this before darting forward, drawing his own sword as he came.

Elander fought the instinct to withdraw his weapon. He leapt aside, avoiding the upward swing of Caden's blade by mere inches.

Caden laughed as he twisted and lunged into another attack. He made it to within inches of Elander and then abruptly darted to the right—no, now he was going *left*—and then he was somehow behind Elander in the next breath, his boots pushing off a slab of the ruined wall and propelling him into another recklessly powerful attack.

Elander ducked and leaned aside, narrowly missing the falling swing meant for his head. He sensed Caden landing to his left, but when he spun to face him, the space was empty.

Where did he run off to now?

It was more apparent than ever that the limits of Caden's fallen state no longer existed. He moved like he hadn't moved in decades—*he moved like a divine being*.

Elander scanned the darkness, cursing under his breath. Even with all of the evidence directly in front of him, he still didn't want to believe what was happening. Perhaps that was why he was hesitant to fight back—to hunt Caden down the way he might have done with any other target. He *could* have done that. Easily.

But instead he kept still, and he kept his voice perfectly even as he said, "I am not in the mood for games tonight."

Silence was his reply for several long moments.

Then came the same cold, unnatural wind he'd felt earlier, and this time it swirled up dark scraps of energy along with it. Traces of Death-kind magic. Caden wasn't bothering to hide his newfound powers—he was flaunting them.

His voice, quiet and hollow, reached Elander a minute later. "You know I never cared much for games myself."

A falling blade followed the words, materializing from within those swirling shadows.

Elander sensed it too late to avoid it completely. He moved, but it still caught him in the back, ripping through coat and shirt and skin, alike. Reflex summoned magic with his next breath, creating a shield around him that forced Caden to jump back before he could press the edge of his sword in any deeper.

Elander's pulse quickened. That shield had taken no more than a heartbeat of effort from him, and yet it felt more powerful than any he'd managed to summon before. Was this the guardian power they'd discussed with the Sun Court?

It *was*, wasn't it?

Casia had been threatened...and now that magic inside of him was waking up further in response.

His skin warmed and tingled with that rising power. But he still found that he couldn't fully concentrate on it —not when he could feel blood sliding down his back.

Blood.

Caden had actually drawn blood.

"I'm not the only one that was reborn into something new at Dawnskeep, am I?" asked Caden in the familiar, slightly smug drawl that he'd always used when he knew Elander was keeping something from him.

Elander forced the shield—and all his other surfacing power—to flicker away. "Not exactly something new," he muttered. "Things are—what was it you said a moment ago? *More complicated than you know.*"

Caden maneuvered so they were standing face-to-face once more. "But you're perfectly capable of meeting my magic with your own. That much is obvious. So why don't you fight back?"

"Because it's already been a long few days," said Elander drily, "and I'd just rather fucking not."

"Fight back," Caden demanded, closing more of the space between them.

Elander finally drew his sword—though only to catch Caden's as it sliced toward him. "You don't want to fight me," he said through gritted teeth. He shoved hard enough to dislodge their swords and send Caden tripping backward.

Caden regained his balance, narrowed his eyes, and leapt forward, slamming his blade back against Elander's. "On the contrary—" an attempted shove, and then another, and then finally he managed to push hard enough to force Elander to take a step back "—I've wanted to for quite some time now."

Elander dug in his heels and gained enough leverage to dislodge their blades once more. He leapt out of reach as Caden took a predictably wild and quick follow-up swing, and then he continued to back away.

Caden followed him.

Another swing, and Elander finally lost his patience —he swung back.

They were a whirlwind of steel and concentration and curses for several minutes, each familiar enough with the other to anticipate their movements, so that neither had any true advantage—until finally, a mistake; Caden's boot caught one of the many pieces of broken stone scattered across the clearing.

Elander swept a foot against his ankle and finished tripping him.

Caden was on his back in the next moment. His arm struck another wayward boulder as he hit the ground, and his sword was jarred from his grip and landed just out of his reach.

Elander brought the tip of his blade to Caden's

throat, but hesitated. Considered. The stab alone wouldn't kill him—but a stab infused with magic might. If Caden was truly ascended once more, it only meant that he was immortal. Not invincible. Spirits were easier to kill than gods.

The possible outcomes unfolded as cold yet comforting calculations in Elander's mind—like a game of chess. Moraki took Marr. Marr took spirit. The divine world had a hierarchy. It *still* had an order to it—even if so much of it had gone to shit—and he was not a god, but he was likely still high enough in that hierarchy to overcome this enemy beneath him.

Enemy. Caden was an enemy now—

And *yet.*

Elander still hesitated.

Caden reached for a small chunk of stone and flung it toward Elander's face. When Elander jumped to avoid being struck, Caden rolled out from beneath him and leapt back to his feet, drawing a knife from beneath his coat and slashing it upward in one smooth motion.

Elander spun away, but he misjudged the angle Caden struck from and he didn't twist sharply enough. The tip of the knife caught the side of his face.

And that's what you get for thinking instead of stabbing, you fucking idiot.

It had left only a shallow cut. Elander barely felt it. But blood was soon flowing down his jawline and pooling under the collar of his coat. He swiped a hand over his jaw and his fingers came away coated in red.

He should have made Caden pay for that blood. For the blood still trickling down between his shoulder blades. Even if he didn't fully understand his magic yet, he damn well could have tried to use it.

He knew he was being a sentimental fool *not* to use it.

"Fight back," Caden growled again.

Elander squeezed his empty hand into a fist. Felt the blood turning cold and sticky, congealing against his skin. Lifted his other hand, which still held his sword, and shifted his gaze from it to the knife Caden held.

Then he tossed his sword to the dirt.

With a furious snarl, Caden dove for him. Blinded by his temper, his impatience—these things had always been his weaknesses, both as a divine and fallen creature.

Elander moved much more calmly. He caught Caden by the wrist and gave his arm a vicious twist, throwing him off balance before slamming him into the nearest of the crumbling stone walls.

Caden's eyes widened as little chips of rock rained down over him. They opened even farther when Elander's magic sparked to life—not a shield this time, but hot flickers of electricity.

Caden's fingers twitched violently as that magic burned into his wrist. His knife slipped.

Elander caught it as it fell, tossed it aside, and then took an even more punishing grip on Caden's wrist. He settled his magic; he didn't need it. His strength and fury were enough.

"What did Varen tell you to say to Casia?" he demanded. "And why is he still sending messages on Sarith's behalf? What is going on in the Mistwilde Realm? Why draw our attention to it, when we clearly already have our hands full here?"

Caden lifted his head and glared, silent and defiant, his breaths steaming in the cold night air.

"Answer me."

Another silent, icy cloud of breath.

"I have no desire to fight you, but if you do not answer me in the next ten seconds, then *I am going to break your fucking arm.*"

He remained defiant until the grip on his arm tightened and twisted more viciously. "I'm only a messenger," he ground out. "I don't know."

"You must know *some* things."

"Yes. And I'll tell what I know to Casia whenever I speak with her."

Such idiotically stubborn words.

So typical of the Caden that had once served him. A humorless laugh nearly clawed its way out of Elander's throat at the thought.

But there was no humor in this situation.

Nothing particularly *funny* about his once closest

friend and ally making threats against the woman he loved.

His grip tightened subconsciously, squeezing more words out of Caden—drawing them out in between gasping, pained breaths. "You can keep doing that all you want," hissed Caden, "but it doesn't matter. Nothing you could do will be worse than what Varen will do if I return without delivering the things that I am duty-bound to deliver."

Everything went very still. A thought occurred to Elander in the silence—grim and unwanted, but unyielding, as he stared into the agonized face of his once-ally.

What are you going to do, kill me?

It had been a taunt. But perhaps there was something else—something more desperate—lingering below the words. The same quiet anguish was in Caden's eyes now. As if part of him had truly been asking Elander to kill him. *Hoping* he would do it, maybe.

The cold wind of Caden's magic had settled.

The night was entirely silent.

Elander swallowed the frustrated sigh that threatened to escape him. This was wrong—a damn mess. All of it. And how was he supposed to take care of this on top of everything else?

He released his hold on Caden and took a step back.

"Get out of my sight," he ordered. "Or I will break more than just your arm."

Caden stared at his newly-freed wrist. Slowly, he stepped away. He picked up his fallen sword, but he didn't provoke Elander any further.

For whatever reason, he seemed to decide that tonight would not be the night he died, after all.

He sheathed the sword. Brushed the bits of stone dust from his coat. Began to speak several times, changed his mind, and then turned and started to leave.

"One more thing before you go."

Caden stopped and tilted his face just enough to partially meet Elander's glare.

"Tell Varen that if he has a message to send to us, he can stop being a fucking coward and bring it himself next time. Same goes for that bitch of a so-called elven *queen*."

Caden stared at him for several seconds. Then he bowed his head the slightest bit, the gesture borderline mocking.

Hot irritation flared through Elander, but he ignored it. He was done with this fight. For now.

He waited until Caden was out of sight before he reached for his back, for the stinging wound between his shoulder blades. He winced as he felt the blood soaking his shirt. Some of it was still warm. Fresh. He brought his hand away, searching for something else to touch, something else to crush between his fingers.

He settled for a piece of stone resting on the wall he'd slammed Caden into. He took it in his fist. Squeezed it until it fractured into several tiny pieces.

And as he watched the pebbles and dust trail through his fingers, he couldn't help but think of grains of sand in an hourglass, counting down to an ending that he did not want to reach.

CHAPTER 9

ELANDER RETURNED TO THE PALACE BY A DIFFERENT ROUTE, seeking out an even more discreet doorway than the one he'd slipped out of earlier. He eventually found an unlocked entryway that led into the wing of the palace that Casia had ordered closed off.

She'd told anyone who questioned her order to close it that she was simply making it easier on their limited soldiers and staff—condensing the palace to a more manageable size. He knew the real reason behind it, of course, and he understood. He didn't particularly want to relive those memories, either.

But after what had just transpired outside, the things that haunted these empty hallways seemed much more manageable.

He made his way through the empty wing—and then up to the floor where his room was located—

without making prolonged eye contact with anyone. Silently, he slipped into his bedroom. Leaned against the wall. Took the first deep breath he'd taken since he'd watched Caden leave.

He had just made up his mind to lock the door behind him when the knob turned and Casia shoved her way inside before he could stop her.

She fixed him with a hard stare. "You were trying to sneak your way up here."

He gave her a tired smile. "*Sneak* is a strong word. I was merely being discreet."

"Where were you?"

He moved to the wardrobe in the corner of the room without replying.

She closed the door and followed him. "What happened? Where did you go? I sensed your magic earlier, and then I..."

She trailed off with a little gasp as he lit the lantern on the desk next to the wardrobe, slipped free of his coat, and the red staining his shirt became more visible. He could feel her watching him expectantly as he draped the coat over the door of the wardrobe.

But he wasn't sure where to begin, so he simply... didn't.

He sifted through the clothes hanging before him, not really focusing on anything he touched. He grabbed something clean—he wasn't sure what, and it didn't matter—and he turned toward the washroom.

Unsurprisingly, Casia was still staring at him when he turned around.

"You can't just disappear, come back covered in blood, and not tell me what happened." Her voice was calm, but her eyes were still hard and her lips were set in a line that told him she would not drop this until she wrestled the truth out of him. And he didn't plan to keep it from her forever, of course. It was just...

"Elander. Please."

He sighed. "I found Caden."

She opened her mouth.

Closed it.

Waited for him to continue.

"He was the one controlling that shell of Prince Alder. I tracked him down by following the energy that creature gave off, and we...talked. It didn't go well."

She considered his words, her eyes jumping from the cut on his jaw, down to the bit of red that had seeped along the side of his shirt. "He did this to you? But he—"

"He's changed."

"Changed?"

"The same tethers that once tied him to me now bind him to the new Death God."

"Such things...transfer? You never told me—"

"Not usually." He ran a hand along his jaw, feeling that cut along it; it felt like it had stopped bleeding at least. "In every other instance I've ever heard of, the servants usually don't survive the death of their god. If they do, then the new god will typically release those servant spirits—by personally killing them, or otherwise. But that apparently didn't happen this time. Not with Caden, at least. *Tara* is dead, but our new Death God decided to keep Caden around, for whatever reasons."

"To use him against us."

Elander nodded.

She hesitated. A storm of feelings flashed across her face—anger, regret, fear, back to anger. She looked to the door. For a moment he thought she might march out of the room, track down her brother that very instant, and demand that he answer for his latest crime. It would not have been entirely out of character for her to ignore the warnings she'd been given about facing him prematurely. He'd seen her do comparatively reckless things... and he'd stopped her from doing worse. He braced himself, ready to intervene again if needed.

But it was unnecessary this time.

Because this time, she stayed.

Her fists clenched. Unclenched. Clenched. She looked back and met his gaze. Took a deep breath. He found himself unconsciously matching that breath, and each one that followed it as she moved closer.

Her hand lifted as she reached him, brushed across his cheek. "I love you," she said softly. "And I'm sorry."

His mouth felt very dry, suddenly.

I love you.

Perhaps the only three words his weary mind could have made sense of just then.

But the ache in her voice had been palpable as she said them, and he hated hearing that pain. It made him want to shake off the ridiculous melancholy that had gripped him...if not for himself, then at least for her sake.

He reached for her hand. Pulled it away from his face, kissed it, and squeezed it tightly for a moment before letting go. He wanted to speak. To say those three words back to her. But they felt inadequate for what he truly felt in that moment.

Without speaking, he took off his belt, his sword, and an assortment of knives, and he laid it all across the foot of his bed. Then he went back to rifling through the wardrobe for more clean clothing.

"You don't have to talk about it if you don't want to," Casia said after a moment of watching him. "I just..."

He glanced over at her. She averted her eyes, nervously rubbing her hand over her arm, and guilt clenched his heart for the second time that night. He had gotten so used to shutting people out—a necessity, given the lies he'd lived for so long during his previous stay in this palace—that sometimes he still did it to her, even when he didn't consciously mean to.

But he could change that habit, couldn't he?

And maybe that was saying *I love you* in a different— and perhaps, more adequate—way.

"It was...brief," he finally began quietly, "our last discussion, before everything that happened at Dawnskeep, I mean. I don't think I even said goodbye to him when we went our separate ways. It didn't seem necessary."

She slowly came closer, each step more cautious than the last—as if she didn't want to startle him into running or going silent again.

"I assumed we'd see each other again soon, because for ages, that's how it went. He argued against my plans all the time, but ultimately, I could always count on him to do what I asked, and to show back up at the end of whatever it was we were dealing with. And there was magic binding us, true—the laws of divine power and everything—but it had always felt like something else tied us together too."

Casia settled on the edge of the bed, listening intently.

"Tara was worse—no goodbyes there either. And I'm not even entirely sure what happened to her, or what she endured in the end, but I *should* have known what was happening. I used to be able to see so much as a god. But everything has narrowed, now, and it feels like things are moving faster because of it."

Casia picked up one of the knives he'd laid on the bed, giving her hands something to absently meddle with. It was the same knife he'd given her months ago when she'd fled Oblivion. Even back then—when they were enemies—he'd wanted to protect her for reasons he hadn't yet understood, and so he'd insisted she take that rare, Death-magic infused blade with her. Caden had been furious when he'd found out.

But he had stayed beside him in spite of that fury, hadn't he?

And the instant they'd realized who Casia truly was, Caden had been the first to insist that he go to her—that he find some way to undo the impossible situation they'd found themselves in.

Elander looked away from the blade, closing his eyes against the memories it stirred. "It's just...strange, the way everything can change so quickly."

"And completely," Casia added.

He cleared his throat, already prepared to move on to the next topic. He *needed* to move on. He felt like he was standing in the middle of a battlefield with neither armor nor weapons, and he could only survive with such vulnerability for so long. "But it's war," he told her. "We're all changing and losing things."

"That doesn't make it any easier," Casia insisted. "They were your family, weren't they?"

He flinched a bit at the word *family*. He'd never liked it. Some words had claws—they dug themselves in. Which made it more painful when those words, and all they represented, were pulled away from you.

But Casia was watching him with a knowing gleam

in her pale eyes, so he didn't bother to deny her assessment.

"The closest thing to it for a long time," he admitted.

She seemed to turn the words over in her mind for several moments. "Family is not always blood, and blood is not always family," she said quietly.

He gave her a curious look.

She shrugged. "It's something Nessa said to me when we were at the High Palace in Sundolia. I've been holding on to it ever since." Her gaze snagged on the cut on his jaw again, and her breath caught. But she redirected her eyes to the frost-coated window pane, and she managed to keep speaking. "Anyway, it was just the two of them, right? I don't think I've ever asked if there were more in the past."

He shook his head. "Most of the Marr only have two or three spirits that serve them, if that," he explained. "It takes too much of their power to create such spirits—much more than the mere essence of power that they sometimes bless a human with at birth. The idea is to delegate without spreading themselves too thin."

"Two or three...so Varen could have other servants aside from Caden? Ones we haven't met yet?"

"Unlikely. Given a bit more time, he might acquire them, but as a newborn god, he won't possess the sort of control to create a new, permanent divine spirit." He lifted his head to the ceiling, losing himself in thought, trying to sort through his complicated memories. "I didn't bring Tara or Caden into my court until I'd been a god for at least a year or two. Though Varen could prove different, I guess. He's surprised us before, hasn't he? And he's managed to trap Caden into his service, obviously—though that was already halfway done for him..."

Casia hugged her knees to her chest and buried her face against them.

A heavy silence passed, and then she finally lifted her head and stared at the frozen window again. "I hate him so much."

She had whispered it...almost as if she was ashamed to admit it. She didn't take her eyes away from the window for a long time afterwards. It was the first time Elander had heard her say it out loud—which was absurd, because if he had been her, he would have shouted it several times by this point.

Blood is not always family...

He could almost see the claws that word—*family*—had hooked into her. The pulling, the wrenching—all the complicated things she was silently wrestling with even as she kept perfectly still on the bed.

"Maybe there's some way we can still save Caden," she said, abruptly, moving the subject away from her brother.

He doubted this. In fact, he could think of dozens of reasons why such a thing would be impossible. But as soon as he met her gaze—as soon as he saw the torment still clearly written all over her face—he decided he didn't want to discuss any of those reasons.

"Maybe there is," he said.

She studied him again, tossing that Death knife nimbly between her hands. "You're humoring me. I know what you're really thinking."

"Do you?"

"I haven't forgotten what you told me, however many months ago it's been now—that *delusion and optimism are the same thing.*"

A small smile curved his lips. "Ah. That does sound like something I would have said."

"Another of those *fond memories* we made the last time we were in this city."

"Well, perhaps I'll be an optimist just this once."

"You might find that you enjoy being one."

He chuckled. "Not likely."

She got to her feet and closed the space between them. "Stranger things have happened."

"They have," he agreed, wrapping an arm around her waist and lifting her up into a kiss.

He'd only meant for it to be a quick, soft kiss. Just enough to chase away the bad taste left in his mouth from the meeting with Caden. But the second his lips touched hers, it happened the way it always seemed to now—he forgot about the meeting, about the clothes he'd been meaning to change into, about everything else he'd been in the middle of doing.

He forgot about everything outside of *her*.

No matter the state of his mind, no matter the number of messy, dark things pressing in, she always seemed to create clarity like this. She didn't make him *forget* about the dark things—she just scattered them and made him feel like there was a chance he could find his way back to the light.

She rose onto her tiptoes and wrapped her arms around his neck, pulling herself more completely into the kiss. It was slow and deliberate, the way she let her arms sink into him, the way her body leaned forward as she steadied herself against him. It somehow made him feel steadier too.

He wrapped his other arm around her, losing himself more completely in the taste of her lips, the warmth of her touch, and the soft little sounds she made whenever he pulled her more tightly against him.

When they separated a minute later, she took hold of his hand. He let her lead him into the washroom, and he didn't protest when she told him to wait there, to sit on the stool next to the sink. He said nothing when she returned with a basket of bandages and salves, or when she insisted on helping him clean away the evidence of Caden's attacks.

"Off with this," she commanded, giving his bloody shirt a tug before turning and busying herself with pumping water into the sink. There was a mirror above it, and he didn't miss the way her gaze traveled over his reflection as he started to undress. He couldn't help but pause long enough to tease her about it.

"Demanding that I get naked again already? Ready for round two, are we?" He grinned, watching her in the mirror for her reaction—a slight blush and a smile that she only half-heartedly tried to fight off. "You're becoming insatiable," he told her.

"Take it off," she repeated, kneeling and digging through a basket of linens beneath the sink.

"Of course, Your Majesty."

She very likely rolled her eyes at that, but he didn't see it as he dragged his shirt over his head. He winced a bit as the rough fabric scraped the open wound on his back.

She turned in time to see that wince, and a brief frown darkened her expression before determination took its place.

She had a damp rag readied a moment later, and she went to work without any hesitation. Her hand was steady for the first swipes. But after wringing out the red-tinted water for the third time, it was shaking as she brought it to his back and traced the edges of the cut between his shoulder blades. It wasn't the intimacy of the space, or their closeness that caused that trembling —the gods knew they'd been far, far more intimate than this.

It was the blood, and all the things it reminded her of.

"I don't need you to do this, you know."

"I know." She narrowed her eyes in renewed determination and went back to dabbing at his skin. "I just want to feel like I'm doing something useful. All the time spent playing queen in this palace is making me a bit stir crazy. I won't lie; a strange part of me was mad that you ran off, mostly because I thought you might be off fighting without me—and you were, weren't you?"

"You weren't missing anything particularly fun."

"Right. Of course not. I'm just finding that I...I think I prefer swinging swords over playing politics, that's all I meant," she muttered. "And sometimes I miss the simple missions. And the *end* of those missions where we could collect our payment and call it a day. There's no end to playing queen. I didn't expect it would be easy, but I'm not used to feeling so...trapped. There are so many things I want to fix, and I'm just *here* and I..." She sighed, and she was quiet for a long moment before she mumbled, "Sorry. I don't know what I'm ranting about—don't tell anyone I said any of this, please."

"You know your secret's safe with me."

She didn't reply. She was too focused now—too determined to finish the task she'd started before her mind became too anxious and her hands grew too unsteady to do the work.

After a few minutes, she seemed satisfied with the look of the wound, so she placed the bloodied cloth in the sink and started to dig through the basket of bandages.

A memory slipped into Elander's mind as he watched her work: The two of them alone in a room outside the city of Belwind. Hurting—as they were now—after a battle that had left them with more questions than answers. He could still picture that night so clearly—it was the first time she'd slept beside him during this lifetime. She'd been stubborn about tending to his wounds that night too. And he'd let her do it, for reasons he hadn't really understood; he'd just known that he wanted her to stay by his side, whatever it took to keep her there.

So much about this moment was similar to that one, and yet...

Strange, the way everything can change so quickly.

"You aren't simply *playing* at being queen, you know."

She angled her face back to him but didn't answer.

"You were meant to wear a crown, and it's obvious to anyone who is paying attention."

She continued her business of searching through the basket for several seconds before she turned around again, ripping a few strips of bandage and winding them around her hand as she did. "You really think so?"

"I think anyone who says otherwise is a fool."

She raised a brow. But again she didn't reply. She

simply slipped around behind him and started wrapping the bandage into place.

"You don't believe me, do you?"

She finished tying it off and washed her hands—scrubbing every last inch of her palms until they were nearly raw, until she finally managed to tuck her hands under her arms and stop the compulsive movements. Then she turned back to him. "I'm just a bit confused."

"About what?"

"Am I a queen or a fugitive tonight? Make up your mind."

A corner of his mouth quirked at her droll tone.

She disappeared back into the room, returning a moment later with one of the clean shirts he'd taken out of the wardrobe.

"Well?" she prompted. "Which is it?"

"I suppose it depends."

She tossed him the shirt, but he didn't put it on.

"On what?" she asked.

"On how you would like me to treat you during round two."

That blush from before was back—brighter this time. "So accommodating."

"I aim to please," he informed her. He continued to ignore the shirt, and instead he reached for her, hooking his fingers into the waistband of her leggings and pulling her to him. She didn't resist. She settled into his lap, draped her arms over his shoulders, and leaned her forehead into his.

"And as long as you're sitting in my lap like this," he added, "I'm even more inclined to be as accommodating as you'd like me to be."

"So I've discovered your weakness."

"As though you didn't already know my weaknesses."

"I wouldn't say I know *all* of them."

His arms circled her waist. He was half serious, half teasing as he said, "It's just you. Only you. I have no other weaknesses."

She laughed. "And here I thought I gave you *strength*."

"You're both my weakness and my strength somehow."

"Ah. I'm multi-talented."

"So very talented. And I suspect I've only just started to learn what you're truly capable of."

She pretended to consider this for a moment before nodding. "You've barely scratched the surface."

"You should stay the night, so I can continue to study you."

She shook her head, smiling. "You never miss an opportunity to invite me to your bed, do you? You're clever."

"And talented. Just like you."

Her smile brightened, and he couldn't resist the urge

to lean up and kiss her. Her smile turned into a soft laugh at the suddenness of the motion, and it was the world's most powerful cure for pain—the feel of that laughter against his lips.

He wrapped her more securely in his arms and stood. It strained the bandages across his body, pulled them uncomfortably against his wounds...but he didn't care, because it made her laugh that breathy, surprised laugh again.

He carried her over to his bed. As he leaned back into the pillows, he brought her with him, resettling her onto his lap. She pressed her lips to his as she sank against him.

The shirt she'd tossed at him was still caught between them, and after a moment she rolled off the bed, taking it with her. She slipped out of her own clothes and helped herself to the clean shirt instead, shrugging it on and not bothering with the buttons on its front. Then she was back, crawling toward him, picking up the kiss where they'd left off. It was several minutes before she leaned away again.

His gaze slid over her as she went, and his hand roamed over her bare leg that was tucked against him. "So I take it you'll stay?"

"Do you really have to ask at this point? I believe it's a given."

He shrugged. "I just like hearing you say it."

The trace of a teasing smirk floated over her face.

"Do you remember when you tried to tell me that you had a black abyss where your heart should be? I didn't believe you then, and I'm sure of it now; you're secretly a hopeless romantic—I think you've been one all along."

"Just say it," he laughed.

She was looking at him the same way she had earlier, her pale eyes softening along with her smile. "Yes. I'll stay."

"Good." He caught a fistful of her shirt—his shirt—and pulled her in for another kiss.

She remained close even as he drew his lips from hers. Their noses brushed together, and her fingers traced patterns across his bare chest—right over the beating of his heart—as she whispered, "I'm here, no matter what happens."

They fell together into a world of soft sheets and softer touches, desire quietly consuming them both. It was different from the desire he'd felt in her room earlier. He still wanted her in that physical, primal way —that was a hunger that was never truly sated—but he wanted her in a far deeper sense too. He wanted this gentle, familiar way she pressed against him, the way she looked at him and answered all his lingering questions without saying another word.

Her eyes were soon fluttering shut. It had been a long night, and longer days were ahead; she needed to rest. So he settled for drawing her against him, molding her more completely against his body. Round two could wait until morning, perhaps.

Quiet settled around them. He tried to focus on something other than his thoughts. He eventually found himself drawn to her heartbeat. It went from pounding rapidly to a slow, regular rhythm, and he thought she had fallen asleep—until she abruptly stirred and then rolled over to face him.

He should have known better than to think she was sleeping; her mind was always racing—and after everything that had happened tonight, it was really no surprise that it hadn't stopped despite how exhausted they both were.

"Something is bothering me," she whispered.

"What is it?"

"That spell that Caden used...I'm assuming he didn't *have* to be so close to us to send that puppet of Prince Alder—because what's the point of such magic, if it doesn't work from a distance?"

"...You're right."

"But he came here personally."

His instinct was to look away—to shut her out again —but he fought against it. He met her gaze, and he braced himself.

"What exactly did he say to you?" she asked. "Why did he come here?"

The truth was perched on the tip of his tongue, ready and eager to drop between them.

He was here to talk to you.

"Elander?"

"I'm not entirely sure. I think...I think he was very confused. We didn't talk much at all, really. We fought, and he ran away after he lost. It was a strange visit—an unfortunate visit—but I wouldn't worry too much about it. We have bigger concerns."

The silence between them grew heavy again.

He was certain she could tell he was keeping things from her.

But if he told her the truth, she would want to go after Caden herself. It would become one more battle she insisted on fighting—one more thing she had to worry about—and she had enough of those things already. So he would deal with this on his own, some-how. And he would keep her safe, no matter what it took.

She was still staring at him expectantly.

He only buried the truth deeper into his heart, kissed her forehead, and drew the blankets up around her. "You should get some sleep," he told her. "It must be almost morning by now."

CHAPTER 10

THE NIGHTMARE CAME FOR CAS SLOWLY THIS TIME, LIKE shadows creeping in with the setting sun.

She was standing on the outer wall that circled the palace grounds, peering out over the wide road that swept into the city of Ciridan. She felt normal—awake, relaxed, alive with the warm breeze that rustled her clothing and played with the loose pieces of her braid.

Then it began to rain.

The drops soaked through to her skin in seconds. She lifted a hand to push the damp strands of her hair aside, and she found the wetness oddly warm to the touch. She pulled her fingers away from her head, studying the beads of liquid that had collected on them.

Blood?

The street below was filled with it—crimson-stained gullies formed along the edges, overflowed, and turned into tumbling rivers that eventually gushed across the center of the street.

Next came the *people*...so many people rising up from the river of red, strands of scarlet and swathes of shadowy magic intertwining to form bodies. And then faces—some of which she *recognized*. They were people she'd lost, people she'd killed, people she had *almost* lost or killed...

They swayed before her, dancing to an awful, silent song.

She was at the mercy of these nightmarish hallucinations. And though she knew they weren't real at first, the longer she stared at them, the more she began to question that knowledge. She couldn't remember the warmth of that earlier breeze, couldn't remember a time before the blood, a time when she was *awake*. The traumatic scene around her had no end, no beginning—it simply *was*, and she was a part of it, so deeply interwoven that she could not separate herself from the madness.

She spotted more familiar figures rising out of the red river—her friends. But they were not marked by blood or made of shadows; they were solid and...normal. Frighteningly normal against the morbid backdrop.

She climbed down from the wall and ran to catch them.

They turned. They saw her...

But they moved away without speaking, leaving her

stranded on the other side as the river between them raged ever higher.

Her lips managed movement then—a single, whispered word.

Impossible.

Her friends would not have left her behind.

She realized then that she was sleeping, and her eyes immediately fluttered open.

But that was as far as she could move.

Paralyzed. *Again.* She couldn't even lift her head from the pillow. Couldn't speak. It was always like this. Night after night after *godsforsaken night*, the nightmares didn't leave even after she woke from them. This was the worst of those nightmares, and it was also becoming the most frequent.

It was one reason she didn't sleep alone anymore.

Elander could usually sense her distress, despite her stillness—and tonight was no different. His hand was already reaching for hers, brushing over her arm. His touch felt faint and far away, but it was unmistakably there.

His fingers threaded in between hers and gave a soft squeeze. She could picture his face, but she couldn't move to meet his gaze. The weight upon her chest and limbs was too great. The hole she'd fallen in was too deep, all the emptiness above her too vast and crushing.

"It's not real," Elander said, voice soft and slurred with sleep.

I know, she tried to reply.

No sound came out.

He squeezed her hand more tightly. "I'm right here. You're safe. We're both safe."

Safe.

She managed a breath.

Months ago, the first time they'd shared a bed in this lifetime, he'd told her the same thing—

You're safe here.

She'd believed him then. She tried to believe him now. It was harder, after all that had happened. She felt like she was still sinking. Like the world was caving in around her. And every time she had this nightmare, she sank a little deeper.

Elander kept squeezing her hand. *One. Two. Three.* She imagined air being squeezed into her lungs with each bit of pressure, and she managed another breath, then another, then another—she was in control of them now.

"Casia?"

Her voice finally managed to escape her. "I'm fine."

She sat up slowly, more control coming back, little by little. The room twisted around her. She drew her knees to her chest and rested her head against them, bracing a hand into the mattress, anchoring herself in place while she waited for the freefalling sensation in her stomach to subside. She was soaked, but not with blood; it was only sweat. She was fine. And Elander…

She lifted her head and tilted it to the left.

There he was. Here *they* were. Together.

His hand was still in hers. In the dark, in the uncertain in-between places, among the wreckage of all of the nightmares and wars they had lived through together... somehow he always found her again, and somehow he always managed to make her feel *safe*—if only for a moment.

She wasn't sure what she would do if there came a day when they couldn't find each other.

If that hole she was sinking in became too deep, and she couldn't reach his hand. If...

No.

She wouldn't think about it anymore.

She rolled out of the bed as quietly as she could. She went to the washroom, splashed cold water on her clammy face, and lifted her pale eyes to the mirror, glaring at herself until her trembling stopped.

She returned to the room, pulled on her leggings and boots, and buttoned up her shirt. She hesitated by the bed for a moment, watching Elander's chest rise and fall with breath, but then she kept moving. The floorboards creaked beneath her—too loudly—and made Elander lift his head from the pillow and blink his eyes open.

"Where are you going?"

She paused. "For a walk."

"Alone?"

"I'm just going to Nessa's room," she said. "I don't

think I'm going to be able to sleep without her magic's help."

His head sank back to the pillow—too tired to formulate more questions or thoughts on the matter. He didn't object to her leaving, though she did feel his gaze upon her back as she went.

Did he know she was lying?

Probably.

She didn't plan to go to Nessa's room, and she didn't plan to go back to sleep. Sleeping felt like a luxury she couldn't afford. Not when so many obligations were waiting for her in the morning. Those nightmares were not real, as Elander said, but then again...

She'd had visions before that *had* turned out to be real.

Yet another facet of her powers. It was the type of magic she had the least control over, and the goddess that might be able to help her harness such things—the Star Goddess—remained aloof. Those visions usually struck when she was tired or otherwise caught off guard...

So she would stay awake and on guard.

Simple as that.

It was almost morning anyway. The hallways had a golden grey tint to them, sunlight leaking through an overcast sky, seeping in through the windows and glowing faintly against every polished and mirrored surface around her. People were beginning to stir, a steady stream of them coming and going in the hallways and chattering amongst themselves.

She set a course for Laurent instead of Nessa. Something told her he would already be awake. After the nasty shock of seeing his brother last night, he probably hadn't slept at all.

She wanted to check on him again, either way.

She stopped by her own room first, where she changed into fresh clothes and grabbed her sword. She'd brought it back to her room after the disturbing meeting with Prince Alder's double, but she could never stand to be away from it for too long; it comforted her to carry it, even while she was just taking a relatively casual stroll through the palace. It made her look more formidable and prepared...and *that* was the image she wanted to project to the many eyes that now watched her every move.

She grabbed the satchel beside Shadowslayer as well —draping it across her body mainly for the sake of carrying more habitual, familiar things—and then she headed toward the large study on the main floor.

Laurent was in here more often than he was in his room lately, and this morning was no exception. He sat beside a dying fire, staring into the glowing embers.

He wasn't alone; Nessa was sitting in the chair beside him, one hand braced against the armrest, the other clutching a cup of something hot and steaming. Laurent was speaking too quietly for Cas to make out his words, but whatever he was saying, Nessa looked distraught about it.

They appeared so engrossed in the conversation that Cas almost decided not to interrupt them. But before she could turn away, Nessa caught a glimpse of her and immediately beckoned her closer.

Cas took a deep breath, shoving down the last thoughts of her paralyzing nightmare, and stepped toward them.

"You're both up early," she commented as she helped herself to the plate of fruit on the table between them. She wasn't hungry, but she popped a handful of tart berries into her mouth all the same. Another habitual, calming motion.

Laurent stood and stretched. "We were preparing to make a quick patrol of the city. Well, *I* was." He nodded toward Nessa. "And someone was just insisting on coming with me."

Cas's heart lifted at the possibility. "I'll go too."

Laurent and Nessa exchanged an uncertain glance, but Cas was quick with an argument.

"Zev swiped a few Mimic crystals from down below —apparently there are entire vaults worth of contraband magic tucked away in the halls that run between the dungeon cells of this palace—and he gifted some of them to me the other day."

She'd put Zev in charge of overseeing those cells— and of trying to get the prisoners within them to cooperate with their plans. He'd won several over with charm, coaxed others with threats of Fire magic, and he continued to work on the rest.

Lord Orbryn, however, still refused to cooperate—no matter how hot the fire or how deadly the threats—and Cas found herself unwillingly picturing his hollow, unsettling eyes as she dug for the crystals in her bag.

Most of her allies wanted her to finish getting rid of the lord. There were whispers that she was afraid of him and his inner circle, she knew. And maybe it made more strategic sense to simply kill him off and put an end to those rumors.

But Lord Orbryn was the oldest, most powerful link to the family she'd been born into in this lifetime. He had firsthand knowledge of that family, and she was still hopeful that she could devise a way to make him talk about it.

Or *write* about it, rather.

She withdrew one of the small chunks of crystalized Mimic magic and held it up to her friends. "It will be fine," she told them. "I'll use this, and no one will even know the queen has left the palace."

They still hesitated.

Cas glanced over her shoulder, making certain there were no guards or servants or anyone else hovering within hearing range. "I have to get out of this palace for a bit, or I am going to lose my mind."

Nessa's gaze turned immediately sympathetic.

Laurent was slower to react, but understanding eventually crossed his face as well. He nodded, and the three of them set off for the city together, pausing at the gatehouse to allow Cas to activate her crystal.

The magic felt almost therapeutic as it warmed a path away from the crystal and over her skin. She closed her eyes and let it flow—it took so little effort compared to her inner magic—and for a brief moment, she again felt nostalgic for simpler days, when using these crystals was the only time she came close to divine power.

They weren't an exact art—not like that inner power of hers—but most believed that these crystals *could* be influenced by anyone with the willpower to do it. Or, in some cases, that the crystal could sense the most powerful desires of the user. Which, in the case of Mimic-kind crystals, meant turning a person into who they *wanted* to be—whether consciously or otherwise.

Knowing this, the reflection of herself in the gatehouse's metal siding made Cas's breath catch.

It had turned her into a vaguely familiar woman. Coils of long, red hair. Golden-green eyes. Sharp cheekbones. It wasn't the first time she'd taken on almost this exact appearance, and as she peered over her shoulder at the palace she was sneaking away from, she allowed herself to question *why* that was.

The dead queen—her mother, Cerin de Solasen—had looked very similar to this.

Cas had ordered all of the portraits of the queen to

be taken down, stowed away in the same wing that she'd closed off. She'd stopped just short of burning them all to ashes.

She didn't *want* to look like Cerin.

She wanted nothing to do with her.

And yet, she couldn't help the morbid curiosity she felt toward that woman and the rest of her family. She didn't want more knowledge of this family, but parts of her *needed* it.

Her friends were staring, concern building in their expressions. She quickly struck up a conversation that had nothing to do with her current appearance or her tumultuous past.

"The palace seemed very peaceful this morning," she told Nessa. "It's beginning to feel like a proper living place—you're doing a great job of keeping things organized and under control."

Nessa beamed. "I am, aren't I? Turns out they weren't all as brainwashed by Varen as we'd feared. Most are becoming more cooperative; I've only had to use magic to calm down a few of them over the past couple of days."

Now, if we can just get the rest of this kingdom—and the kingdoms and realms beyond it—to be just as calm and cooperative, thought Cas. But she smiled back in spite of the concerns nagging her, and she picked up her pace to match Nessa's lighter, more optimistic step.

After a mile or so of chatting about all that Nessa

had accomplished within the palace, Cas's attention slid toward Laurent.

He didn't appear to be listening to their conversation; he was busy narrowing his eyes in the direction of every unusual noise that reached them. She watched him silently, wondering what he might be thinking about those chaotic kingdoms and realms outside of their current one. About his own home realm and the threats Sarith had made.

Not meddling in Mistwilde was not an option; they were already doing it—getting those powerful elves on their side was a vital part of their plans—and now Cas feared the worst for their allies, and *would-be* allies, in that realm.

She was certain that Laurent did too.

Moreth's most revered general, Kolvar Aendryr— and his soldiers—had gone to Mistwilde largely at Laurent's behest, eager for an opportunity to carry out the wishes of their *true* king. If it turned into a bloodbath...

Laurent caught her gaze, and he spoke quickly—as if he knew her worried questions were coming, and he was determined to stop her assault before it started. "This isn't an entirely routine patrol," he informed her. "Our destination is the Edge District."

"...Syndra's place?" she guessed.

He nodded. "She's supposed to meet us with detailed reports of any unrest she's noted in the city.

She's been watching the palace deserters, in particular, as some were organizing and creating pockets of resistance that might interfere with us."

Syndra Talavir had long been a rival of theirs during the days when Cas and her group were running jobs in and around Ciridan, but usually an amicable one. They'd even shared a few drinks together over the years. She and her associates were among those selected few that Cas had entrusted to help her keep order within the capital city. Because Syndra actually had beliefs—they were a touch crooked, maybe, but she had lines she didn't cross.

Laurent cut his eyes toward Cas once more, and the unspoken meaning in his look was clearer than ever. This meeting with Syndra was the *only* thing he intended to focus on this morning.

Months ago, that look would have stopped Cas from prying or pushing, but after everything they'd been through lately, she was no longer content with letting him keep her at a distance. "You didn't sleep last night, I'm guessing?"

He was quiet for several steps, searching the grey sky. "Sleep didn't seem like the most important thing to worry about last night."

"I understand." She considered her next words carefully. "I was thinking a lot last night, myself...and I think we'll need to pay a personal visit to Mistwilde soon. We can't leave General Kolvar to deal with Sarith and her minions alone. And it might win us favor with Mistwilde's leaders too, if we can help them keep the order."

She desperately wanted that favor; beyond her need for bodies for her army, there was also knowledge in the elven realms that she was not finished discovering. The elves had a connection to the divine that most did not. Moreth had been filled with useful information—with books and scholars and stories—things that would have been useful to dive more deeply into, if only she'd had more time there.

"It's probably past time for you to introduce yourself to the rulers of that realm anyway," she concluded.

"Agreed," said Laurent. He lowered his gaze and kept it straight ahead as he spoke, but she could tell he was already making travel plans in his mind.

"And you know we'll deal with it all *together*, right?" she added.

He still didn't look at her, but she thought she saw a begrudging look of acceptance cross his face. "Maybe," he said with a slight nod.

"*Definitely*," Nessa corrected.

"Whether you like it or not," Cas added.

He sighed, but the corners of his mouth twitched upward.

They continued their walk in companionable silence. They had nearly reached the bridge that led into the Edge District when Nessa drifted to the right, and then wandered off the road entirely.

She followed a steep hill down to a dirt path that stretched all the way to a small, currently closed, shop. She finally came to a stop at this establishment, hugged her arms around herself, and studied its faded sign, the peeling paint of its door, the shabby curtains drawn over its windows...

Laurent stayed on the main road, looking characteristically impatient.

But Cas knew why Nessa had stopped in front of this building, so she gave Laurent a shrug and jogged after her.

"This brings back memories, doesn't it?" Nessa said, wistfully, as Cas approached her.

"It does," Cas agreed.

It was the first place the two of them had officially met—on a chilly, somewhat gloomy morning not unlike the one they stood in now. Laurent had encountered Nessa several days before, and extended an invitation for her to meet him—along with Asra and Cas—at this location, to see if she might be interested in helping them with one of their upcoming jobs. An interview of sorts. He hadn't really expected her to show up, and he'd had other business to tend to at the shop, anyway.

But she *had* shown up.

She had waltzed into the place as though she'd been there a million times before, and then she'd used her magic to settle a dispute that had been growing steadily out of control between the shopkeeper and a belligerent customer.

She'd been subtle about it, but it had still been dangerous, given the empire's hostile policies regarding magic. When Laurent asked her what she'd been thinking—to do something so reckless—she had stared at him with a composure that most people did not manage to maintain when being berated by the half-elf. Then she'd shrugged and said, "I was thinking that the shopkeeper needed help."

Cas had immediately taken a liking to her.

Asra had as well, and she had insisted that she stay on as a permanent part of their team soon after.

Laurent joined them a few minutes into their reminiscing. "That Mimic crystal was weak, apparently," he said, frowning as he pointed toward the window.

Cas looked at her reflection, and she mirrored his frown. The strands of her hair were already fading back to their usual grey shade.

It was the quickest she'd ever seen one of the crystals wear off.

Was it possible that she was unconsciously undoing its spell? Her mind was still flooded with thoughts of her true mother, her true past...and she couldn't deny how those things frightened her. Was that fear triggering the protective elements of her inner magic, causing it to push out whatever power the crystal had given her?

A strange, sudden sound in the distance—like a

banner snapping in a sudden gust of wind—drew their attention away from the window.

They turned to see what appeared to be smoke rising from the other side of the bridge. It moved oddly in the still morning air, as though controlled by some unseen force.

Nessa started to reach for the bow strapped to her back, but she clenched her hand into a fist and forced it back to her side.

"Could be trouble," Laurent muttered.

"We should investigate," Cas said.

His gaze traveled over her changing appearance. "You stay back. We'll inspect things more closely."

"If there's trouble, I should be—"

"Hiding," he interrupted. "Given our lack of armed guards." Cas's expression turned indignant, but Laurent paid it no mind. "If anyone spots you, we're likely to end up with *more* trouble. Or at least with more attention... which will likely *lead* to trouble."

She still bristled at the words, but bit back her argument. She knew he was right. "Fine. But if you're not back in ten minutes, I'm coming after you. Be careful," she said, before sinking into the shadows of the shop and out of sight.

She stayed put as Laurent and Nessa headed back up the hill, her gaze alternating between her reflection and the bridge in the distance.

That strange smoke continued to twist around the

bridge. It appeared to be thickening, turning an unnatural shade of blue. It still moved oddly, as though caught in a powerful gust—and there was still no wind pushing the trees or anything else around her.

She lingered by the closed shop for a few more minutes, still carefully watching and assessing, listening for any indication that her friends might have run into trouble.

The shadows around her shortened as the sun fought its way through the clouds. Her gaze was drawn to them as they moved away...and then as they lengthened again. Over and over. Like claws raking over her— or waves crashing upon a shore and then pulling back out to sea, trying to pull her out with them.

Her skin prickled.

As with that smoke in the distance, there was something unnatural at work amongst the shadows, pulling them back and forth in a way that made no sense.

After a moment of focusing on it, she realized...

Magic.

CHAPTER 11

She knew this magical energy.

She'd felt a flicker of it yesterday—right before Elander had disappeared—but she'd been too preoccupied with Laurent and their undead messenger to follow it alongside Elander.

But she followed it now.

She kept the main road within sight. She wouldn't venture far enough that she couldn't hear Laurent and Nessa shouting for her—not if she could help it—but she could no longer sit still and ignore all of the odd things happening around her.

The trail of shadowy energy led her down to an old dock along the Lotheran River; one that stretched adjacent to a small boathouse. Both structures looked equally run-down and abandoned. A pile of lumber was stacked beside the house, rotting and covered with sparkling, dew-laden spiderwebs.

And standing beside this pile was a familiar figure —Caden.

Cas glanced over her shoulder. A sliver of the main road was still visible. She slowly stepped closer to the dock, her eyes narrowing on Caden's right hand. There was something clenched in it; she couldn't tell what it was.

"Hello, Casia."

Her gaze flickered to his face. "You're still in the city. Why?"

He skipped that something in his hand—*a splinter of wood, maybe?*—across the water and then canted his head toward her. "That's not a very friendly greeting."

She almost took it back. Apologized. Because he was just another one of her brother's victims, wasn't he?

But then she thought of the blood that had stained Elander's shirt last night, and she couldn't help it. It might not have been entirely Caden's fault, but her voice still came out flat and cold as she said, "I'm not feeling particularly friendly this morning. My apologies."

He smirked at her tone.

She looked away from that smirk before it could get under her skin.

There was more of that strange, blue-tinted smoke curling in the distant air, winding like a serpent away from the bridge. Following the main road, it looked like.

"Those shadows were yours," Cas thought aloud. "That strange smoke...was that you creating a distraction?"

"Not exactly. But I knew that distraction was coming." He started to close the space between them. "I saw a chance for us to speak alone," he said, "and I decided to take it."

She tensed at the word *alone*. Her gaze shifted once more to the road, and her hand strayed to the sword at her hip.

Caden held up his palms. "I mean you no harm. I only want to give you something. I tried to explain this to Elander last night too—that I come in peace—but he wasn't very cooperative."

"You want to give me something?" She couldn't contain her skepticism. "How nice...but I'm assuming your *gift* comes with conditions?"

He studied her for several seconds past the point of uncomfortable. "Can I ask you a question?"

She kept still, feigning indifference and refusing to let his strange eyes unnerve her.

"Isn't it strange," he continued, "being back in that palace, knowing who you truly are now... and yet knowing so *little* about that truth?"

She couldn't deny it.

He wasn't really asking anyway. The clever gleam in those odd-colored eyes made it obvious that he knew the answer to his own question—he had likely pried it out of her by way of his divine power.

"You've been using your magic to listen to my thoughts," she accused.

"Your mind is very loud this morning. It made you easy to focus on. Easy to track."

Her skin crawled. "You have no business focusing on my mind, whether it's easy or not," she snarled. "What do you really want from me?"

He studied his nails—nails that were extended into claws at the moment.

"Answer me," she commanded, "or we are done talking."

"Your missing memories of the palace, of your real mother and father—the ones that elude you, no matter how many history books you study or how many palace servants you torture information out of..." He trailed off, as if waiting for her to fill in the blanks for herself.

A cold sweat—worse than the one her nightmares had caused—washed over her. "What about them?"

He stopped studying his claws and fixed his eyes on her. "I could show them to you."

Her heart skipped several beats.

"Not just yours either." He reached into the inner pocket of his coat and withdrew a small silver bag tied with a black ribbon.

He offered it to her without further comment.

Cas stared at it but didn't take it. "What is this?"

"A gift, as I told you," said Caden.

"What kind of *gift*?"

"The kind that will make up for all those times you've wondered about the things that took place within the walls of the palace after you'd left."

The moment—the *choice*—stretched before her like a narrow ledge along a steep mountain path. To take it, and possibly slip, could be devastating. To stay, and not see what awaited her on the other side...somehow felt worse.

Her curiosity eventually got the better of her.

She cautiously plucked the bag from his hand, untied it, and peered inside.

It was full of crystals, similar to the contraband kind that she'd used earlier, and countless times in the past... except the ones in this bag were all perfectly formed, with smooth, identical faces; they looked like they had been purposefully *made*, rather than illegally hacked and harvested from the shining veins that criss-crossed the In-Between.

She'd never seen such creations before.

And she immediately didn't trust them.

"They contain Varen's memories," Caden explained. "So you can live out that childhood you missed...at least in some small way."

She delicately pinched one and lifted it, studying it in the dreary morning light. A small dot of red energy pulsed in its center. She thought of her nightmare again, of the red drops soaking her skin, and she shuddered.

"You're welcome."

Cas wrinkled her nose. "I'm still not convinced these are a *gift*."

"Don't you think it could prove useful," Caden said, "to have such intimate knowledge of your brother's mind and memories? Given the...*circumstances*?"

"He only wants to confuse me."

Caden shrugged. "So don't let yourself get confused. You're smart enough to sort through confusing things, aren't you? Strong enough to deal with the pain that sometimes comes with knowledge?"

Cas fought off another shiver. She *knew* what he was doing. What *Varen* was doing.

So why did she find herself tempted by these crystals, even the tiniest bit?

"I wanted to reveal more of your past to you even before this moment, you know."

Her lips parted, but she couldn't seem to make herself speak.

"I could have done it; even in my fallen state, with my limited powers, there were ways I could have drawn your long-lost memories out. Put them into a usable, viewable form for you—just as I've done with Varen's. Perhaps not so cleanly as those crystals you're holding, but I could have managed *something*. I already did it once. How do you think Elander discovered who you truly were in your past life? I'm very good at this sort of magic, and I could have shown you *precisely* how good."

She dropped that smooth, perfectly-formed crystal back with the others and cinched the bag shut.

"But Elander refused to let me."

She snapped her gaze back to Caden, prepared to fire an argument at him.

But she couldn't think of one.

Because it *did* sound like something Elander would have kept Caden from doing—out of a desire to protect her.

And it wasn't right for him to keep such things from her.

But that was an argument for another time, and for the two of them alone—she wasn't going to let Caden twist his way between them.

"You won't turn me against him."

"I didn't expect to," Caden said. "I just thought you should know there were things he kept from you. Things *I* thought you deserved to know."

Her hand tightened around the top of the bag.

"And I could still show them to you."

The sound of shouting in the distance drew her eyes back to the bridge, and she thought of flinging the entire pouch of crystals into the river, turning, and running into the city instead. There was clearly other trouble to deal with—she didn't have time for these games.

But in the end, she stayed where she was.

With a slightly trembling hand, she tucked the small pouch of crystals into the bag at her side.

Caden smiled at the sight. "Good—start with those. They'll be simple to use, and I think you'll be very interested in what they contain. It will be nice to find a bit of firsthand truth amongst all this chaos you've been dealing with, don't you think?"

She didn't reply.

"You don't have to tell me." His smile turned sly as his eyes brightened, and she felt the telltale pressure of his magic pressing against her skull, even as she guarded herself against it. "I already know what you're thinking."

"Then you're aware that I *think* you should go," she said, icily. "Leave this city as Elander told you to do."

The sound of footsteps jogging down the hill interrupted his reply, but neither he nor Cas moved.

Then Laurent's voice rose behind Cas, even colder than her own had been. "Did I just hear her tell you to leave?"

Nessa joined him an instant later. "That's what I heard."

"And yet, you are still standing there," added Laurent, "as though you're too stupid to follow a simple order."

Caden's gaze traveled back and forth over the three of them, assessing.

"...I was going to stay a bit longer," he finally said, "but I've spoken to the queen, which is all I came to do

—so on second thought, I guess I'll be going." His eyes locked once more with Cas's as he said it. He seemed to be daring her to ask him to stay. To speak any of the questions or confused thoughts racing through her mind.

She swallowed every one of her questions down, ignoring the way each hit like a stone in the pit of her stomach.

Laurent stepped in front of her, drawing his bow and readying an arrow as he moved.

It was tempting, the thought of watching that arrow soar toward Caden. She could wrap magic around it, and let Laurent drive it straight into Caden's chest. She was tired of Varen's games, and if Caden was going to become a prominent player in those games...

Her fingertips tingled with electricity.

But she clenched those fingers into her palm, stifled her power, and turned away.

If there was a way to save him, then she was going to find it. She'd promised that to Elander—to *herself*. And if there was a way for Caden's magic to reveal more of her past, then maybe...

She motioned for Laurent to lower his weapon.

"We aren't going to fight you," she said, glancing over her shoulder at Caden. "But you need to go. This city is restless enough without the likes of you running around in it."

A shout rang out in the distance, as if to belabor this point.

Caden's eyes lifted toward the sound, and a strange expression—a cross between amusement and concern—flashed across his face. "You're right. You have other battles to worry about anyway. Other things that are *running around* in your city."

Before she could reply, he was wrapped in shadows that obscured his body entirely. Those shadows tumbled about for a few seconds and then whisked away, taking him as they went. Back to Oblivion, she assumed—or to wherever else Varen had instructed him to go.

She took a deep breath and turned to face her friends.

"What was he doing here?" Nessa asked.

"Just looking to stir up trouble."

Nessa frowned, obviously still confused.

"He's in Varen's service now," Cas explained. "An unusual turn of events, according to Elander. But here we are." She casually reached into the bag at her hip and pushed the magic crystals deeper. Laurent's gaze followed the movement, curious, but he said nothing—another chorus of shouts interrupted them before he could.

"Other battles to worry about..." he began uncertainly, "...what did Caden mean by that?"

"I don't know. What did you two discover when you followed that smoke?"

"Nothing except more smoke," said Nessa, "but we couldn't figure out where it was coming from, and it seemed to be thinning out. So we came back to check in with you."

"And saw that you were not where we'd left you," said Laurent. "To the surprise of absolutely no one at all."

"And we assumed you were off getting into trouble somewhere," Nessa added with a wry grin.

Cas huffed out a humorless laugh. "Why ever would you assume that?"

Laurent started to reply, but his attention was drawn away from her as a cloud of smoke exploded into existence over the bridge.

Nessa gasped and Cas let out a curse.

"...Apparently it isn't actually dissipating like we'd hoped," Laurent said.

Cas pulled the hood of her coat up and fastened it in place, hiding her face and hair as best she could. "We go together from here. If I'm recognized, then so be it," she said, grimly but decisively, as she started up the hill. "Something strange is going on, and I'm going to find out what it is."

CHAPTER 12

THEY FOLLOWED THE TRAIL OF SMOKE.

They were halfway up the hill that led to the main road when the first fireballs became visible—burning, blue and white spheres that twisted wildly in the wind. That wind seemed to have honed in on these fires and nothing else; it whipped the spheres about, gathering them into one large mass and then shifting it this way and that, stretching and pulling—almost as if it was trying to mold the flames into a more defined shape.

"What *is* that?"

The flaming mass shifted direction at the sound of Cas's voice, twisting toward her and *whooshing* down the hill, rapidly gaining speed. It still had no definite shape, but its reckless movement briefly rolled away some of its flames and revealed what looked like a humanoid being buried underneath. Cas thought she saw lashing limbs and bright, alert eyes narrowing on her.

Then its movement slowed. Became more calculated. The fires around it swelled, and whatever lay at the heart of those fires was engulfed once more.

Screams rose to Cas's right—group of townspeople had emerged from the houses lining the river, just in time to see the barrage of flames falling toward them.

It was reflex, at this point, how quickly Cas swept Shadowslayer from its sheathe, and how rapidly her magic rose to fill that metal blade.

She was in front of the screaming group in the next moment, her sword raised before her as strands of turquoise light unraveled from its edges. It was the kind of magic typically used by Sky-kind. She still didn't feel particularly confident about this side of her magic, but it was the kind she *needed* to use. A shield that could absorb this fire would be the safest way to protect the people around her.

And she could handle it—if she could just concentrate on it.

Her eyes found the emblems etched into the base of her blade. They narrowed on the one shaped like a wind-swept cloud—the same emblem that hung from the bracelet given to her by Queen Soryn. As she focused on it, that cloud on her sword pulsed faintly with turquoise light. She imagined it pulsing in time with her own heartbeat.

It grew brighter, steadier.

The wind roared and the fire surged again, but she held her ground.

She heard Nessa and Laurent behind her, shouting orders, trying to direct people to safety. The sound of their voices—and the thought of protecting the people of the city—spurred her on. She dug in her heels and breathed in and out with a purposeful, methodical rhythm. She had plenty of experience breathing her way through harrowing attacks.

And this is no different than fighting off a rising panic.

She swept her sword back and forth, twirling the strands of magic as she did, willing them to fall into place, to stretch wider and protect as much as she could.

Through the barrier she was weaving, she saw the mass of fire begin to change.

It narrowed, growing taller in the center and arching —like an animal puffing itself up, trying to appear larger before its enemy. *Something* was clearly at the center of this inferno, directing it and the strange wind that swirled around it.

But how to get to the heart of it all?

The center column collapsed, pushing fire toward her, striking faster than she could blink.

It slammed into her shield of magic, accompanied by another deafening roar of wind.

The shield buckled and she nearly lost her balance. The sensation rocked through her and rattled her bones, as if she herself had been physically struck—and by something much more solid than wind and flame.

The fire gathered in front of her once more, twisting and swooping taller as though caught in a sudden updraft. It gathered into a tidal wave of rolling flames, and then crashed toward her just as quickly.

The force of this second blast succeeded in knocking her to her knees. Her hood flew back, exposing her face and her Fade-marked hair. There were still people close enough to see her—she could hear them panicking and trying to make sense of what they were seeing.

She no longer cared about hiding her identity, she decided.

She ripped off her coat and the bag she carried, flinging them underneath the porch of the nearest house before turning back to face the inferno behind her.

It had gathered into a column that reached taller than all the buildings around it.

Nessa and Laurent continued to usher the townspeople to safety behind her.

She lifted her sword once more, created another shield, and fought her way back toward the fire. Her shield stopped the embers that rained down, but occasional blasts of burning wind and heat still broke through and scorched the space between her and her target, making her feel as though the skin of her face was blistering and peeling away as she walked.

The Lotheran River gleamed in her peripheral vision,

its grey waves growing increasingly choppy in the unstable air.

A possibility, maybe?

This clearly was not a normal fire raging before her, but there was no reason to think that it wouldn't succumb to water.

She darted to the left, pulling her shield with her. She willed that shield to stretch wider, to curve around the blaze, and then she tried to use it to drive that blaze toward the river.

The column of flames shifted again, throwing her off balance. Another unnatural wind caught it, swirled it into a cyclone of blue flames, and drove it up the hillside.

Retreating?

No—that would be too easy.

At the top of this hill, it stopped and fanned out. Cas once more caught a glimpse of bright eyes burning in its center; it seemed to be assessing her from its higher vantage point.

Seconds later, hot wind rushed through the grass on either side of her. It snaked around her legs and grabbed at her hair and clothing, pulling her forward.

She didn't resist. She made her way up and over the hill, weaving her protective magic and stomping out tufts of burning grass as she went. Her boots soon touched the stone edging of the road. Despite the increasingly suffocating air, she followed the road all the way to the start of the bridge, which was now covered in blue and white fire.

The fire retreated as she stepped toward it.

She fought her way through the superheated air, all the way to the center of the bridge.

The wind finally stopped. It settled abruptly, and a soft sound pierced through the sudden quiet—something akin to purring. It sounded curious. As if whatever was controlling the wind and fire could not understand why someone would *willingly* follow it.

Cas took another step closer.

The flames began to dissipate, save for two columns of fire that rose up on either side of the bridge. It looked like a stage, almost, and something was soon twisting up from the middle of it—a whirlwind of blue fire that flickered and stretched and popped until it had molded into a vague, human-like shape.

A woman?

No, *a giantess*. One that moved with impossibly smooth motions. The way she rose and fell along the stone bridge—there one moment, merely smoke the next...she didn't appear solid. But her eyes did not waver along with the rest of her body; they were clear and fixed upon Cas. Blinking curiously. Intelligent looking, almost.

Could it understand speech?

"What are you doing here?" Cas called. "What do you want?"

A violent puff of wind and smoke was her only reply.

Cas tried to move closer, but the flames erupted and engulfed the bridge once more, concealing the woman in a cloak of smoke and flame that burned blindingly bright.

Cas stumbled back, throwing her arm up to shield her face from the explosion of heat and light. She lifted her sword in her other hand and quickly managed to summon another shield—but not quickly enough. She'd already inhaled too much smoke. Her eyes filled with tears. Her throat was so dry she could barely swallow, and each coughing breath she managed made her feel as if she'd just inhaled a bushel of thorns, but somehow she choked out more words: "Are you a servant of the God of Fire?"

The wind howled louder.

"What do you *want*?"

Another howl, and this time the wind converged toward *her*.

Cas knelt, ducking below the thickest part of the smoke that gust had carried with it. In the relatively clean air, she finally managed a decent breath, which helped settle her swimming vision enough that she could see—

A wave of white fire rushed toward her.

She dropped lower and lifted her sword in front of her once more, weaving a faint wall of magic with the motion. She pictured her friends—*they were still some-*

where behind her—and the magic surged brighter. She remained in a crouched position, her muscles burning almost as badly as her blistering skin.

The onslaught of wind and fire continued, and soon her balance teetered. She dropped to one knee. Then the other came down, hard, against the stone bridge. Her body ached, exhausted by the heat and drenched in sweat, but she willed herself to stay upright. To keep hold of her sword, to keep up her shield...

The assault finally stopped.

Cas tucked her head to her chest and braced her shaking body for a second wave.

None came.

She heard no sound from the being on the other side of her battered barrier. The heat slipped away, little by little, until her sweat-soaked skin was chilled and covered in bumps. The being controlling that heat...it seemed to be moving away from her entirely.

Something had distracted it.

Wincing, Cas lifted her head, and through her watery, burning vision, she started to make out what was happening on the other side of the river.

The wind was sweeping the fire into a shorter, wider form with multiple legs—more beast than human, now—and that beast was slinking off the bridge.

A second beast was racing to meet it.

Golden light trailed behind this second one, as though it was pulling up the sun as it came. It hurtled straight at the flaming mass—then *through* it—and sent fire scattering in all directions.

Light flooded the bridge. Smoke swirled. Fireballs rained into the river on either side, hissing as they struck the waves. Steam rose up and swallowed the bridge. The glow emitted by the newly arrived creature was so bright it cut through the mist, leaving its massive body clearly defined—so when it turned its head toward Cas, she immediately realized what it was.

A wolf.

A familiar wolf.

The same size, the same shape as the shadowy beast that had once haunted her nightmares. But now it was surrounded by light instead of shadows. It was *made* of that light—not solid, like the beast Elander used to shift into, but a powerful projection with limbs of energy and electricity—not unlike the ones Cas had summoned herself in the past, though hers generally took the shape of a tiger.

A moment later, the frame of light collapsed. The magic swirled and rocketed away, called back to its master. As the last glimmers of it faded from sight, Elander materialized among the smoke and the steam, walking toward Cas from the other end of the bridge. His gaze fixed on her and did not flinch, even as the wind stirred and embers flickered threateningly around them once more.

Cas released a slow breath as he reached her. "Thank you."

"My magic stirred me awake—it sensed yours, I think. I could tell something was wrong." He grabbed her arm and helped her to her feet. "It seems you got sidetracked on the way to Nessa's room."

She returned the crooked grin he was giving her. "Just a bit, yes. I—"

"Watch yourself," he interrupted, ducking and pulling her back down to the bridge.

She caught herself against the stone. Twisting, she looked up and saw a whirlwind of fire roaring toward them. She rolled frantically out of its path and then pushed back to her feet.

Elander moved to her side as she rebalanced and adjusted her grip on her sword. They stood back-to-back as flames surrounded them. His hand brushed hers. The simple touch sent a rush of power skipping through her.

His magic had sensed hers.

She no longer felt tired.

She felt invigorated, her magic rising as if on wings, weaving into his with pure, effortless precision.

The shield they summoned together was brighter than anything she'd managed alone.

It wasn't simply protecting them from the fire; it was truly *absorbing* that fire, the way the most powerful Sky spells did. It siphoned off the lashing flames, one by one, until what little remained of the firestorm unraveled and flew away, the pieces of it once more raining down into the water and across the river's banks.

The giantess at the center of the storm had vanished.

An eerie, near-silence followed this dismantling—there were only the isolated sounds of embers falling, hissing into water, of dry grass crackling as it caught stray cinders, of Cas's own pounding heart.

Then she heard Nessa calling her name. After watching a few lingering embers—to make certain they weren't reforming into something more sinister—she raced back down the hill to her friends.

Elander followed behind her, and they quickly found Nessa and Laurent.

Their gazes turned toward the river, watching the last bits of falling fire and the steam that rose up from the wind-swept waves. That steam was fast becoming more like a dense fog, heavy and suffocating and blinding them to the world beyond a few hundred feet. The wind carried it along until it had swallowed the river, the houses, the road, and wrapped them tightly within a grey, unnerving quiet.

"Is it...gone?" wondered Nessa.

"Regrouping, more likely," said Elander.

Cas lifted her hand into the grey. The mark the Storm Goddess had blessed her with flashed upon her wrist, and bolts of lightning snaked out from her veins. It briefly lit the grey around them—allowing her to glimpse landmarks and gather her bearings—but revealed no signs of the creature she'd been battling against.

"*The divine are walking more freely among us.* Isn't this what Nephele warned us about?" Laurent said. "This is some sort of divine beast, is it not?"

"Not just any divine beast," said Elander, "that was Sonas, the lesser-spirit of Wind."

"Sonas?" Cas repeated.

"As in Sonas flames?" Laurent guessed.

Elander nodded.

Cas recalled them now—those blue flames that were commonplace at deathbeds throughout various Kethran realms.

Embers of a similar blue shade began to flicker within the fog.

"I've heard that the ones who believe in those flames pray to Sonas in hopes that she'll grant their loved ones favorable winds in the afterlife," Nessa said, her voice oddly hushed, as though speaking at one of those deathbeds Sonas was believed to watch over. "They pray, and they watch to see which way the wind pushes the flames they've lit in her honor. They know her more completely as the spirit of Fair Winds and Eternal Flames—a benevolent spirit that isn't typically regarded as a being of chaos."

"So why is she here, acting *chaotically?*" Cas wondered.

"She's a servant of the middle-god of Fire, isn't she?" asked Laurent.

"Yes," said Elander, stepping toward an ember as it lit—and continued to burn—uncomfortably close to them. "Sent here to wreak havoc on behalf of that god and the rest of his court, no doubt; she's acting this way because she was commanded to. The Dark God's court is going to try and strike fear into as many hearts as he possibly can in the coming weeks, I suspect. Whatever he can do to make more humans cower and hide and stay out of his way, and undermine leaders like Casia at the same time..."

The ember burned brighter.

Cas summoned another bolt of electricity, lighting a path up the hill and toward the last place she'd seen the lesser-spirit take on a solid shape.

Nothing to see there now.

But she could *sense* that divine creature's power— and it seemed to be building.

More and more tiny flames were popping up in the fog, each fanned into existence by a brief, whistling gust of wind. They were forming a trail that led back to the bridge.

She rolled the tension from her shoulders and started to follow that trail.

"What are you doing?" asked Nessa.

"Not cowering, or hiding, or staying out of the way," said Cas, loudly enough for any lingering townspeople to hear. Laurent and Nessa had managed to drive most of the people away, but a few still whispered nearby. The thick fog caught and amplified their hushed voices. They sounded afraid—and she was determined to fix that.

She paused briefly to glance back at her friends. "This seems like a chance for the people of this city to learn to trust their queen, doesn't it?" she asked, more quietly.

Nessa looked unsure, but Cas had already made up her mind.

If she was truly going to rule over this city, she had to protect it. The fire and wind had pushed her disguise away. The people had seen her. Good. What they *wouldn't* see was the fear that was gripping her own heart and mind.

The fog swirled with a sudden, unmistakably hostile energy.

More embers flickered to life near the bridge, their indigo light diffusing eerily in the murky air.

She took a few more steps forward, braced herself, and sent another burst of lightning through the mists, answering the hostile energy with her own.

Nessa started to speak, but in that same moment, several fiery cyclones spun to life in the distance. Her words became a quiet gasp, instead.

"Keep leading the townspeople away," Cas ordered. "Keep them calm. And let them know their queen is fighting for their safety."

Nessa still hesitated.

But Laurent was already moving, already doing as Cas had asked. He soon doubled back to tell Nessa he needed her help—likely not because he truly felt he needed it, but because he knew it wasn't like Nessa to deny anyone help.

Cas felt a wave of Nessa's warm magic blossoming in the air, wrapping around those lingering onlookers and then following them as they were shepherded away.

Seconds later, the warmth was gone—and Nessa and the others with it—and she and Elander stood alone in the mist.

She continued sending out more lightning. Beacons to distract the spirit and allow the others more time to escape. She kept up a steady stream of these beacons until the spirit answered with a roar of wind so intense that she had no choice but to recoil, throwing up her arms and shielding herself from the sudden onslaught of dust and other debris.

As the roar settled, she peeked through her arms to see controlled gusts sweeping away parts of the fog and creating a path between her and the top of the hill.

Daring her to follow it once more, she thought.

Elander stepped closer to her, and in a clear attempt to cut through the rising tension, he said, "Just once, I want to spend a morning with you that *doesn't* end with us slaying divine beasts and trying to save the world."

"That sounds dreadfully boring."

"Yes, but in the best possible way." He withdrew and readied his sword. "So," he continued, casting a wary glance along that new path that stretched ahead of them, "I assume you're concocting some sort of reckless plan for us?"

"I was hoping *you* had a plan, actually." Her grin was slight and short-lived. The wind swirled again, forcing them to duck for cover and summon another shield around themselves. Dust and fire and small stones whipped about and battered that shield.

Cas's gaze was drawn first to the fire, as before—but now she was beginning to rethink her strategy.

"I thought of dousing it in the river," she told Elander, "but it isn't truly a fire spirit, is it?"

"No. Those flames are one gift from the Marr she serves, but she can become many other things. Anything the wind can carry, I'd guess she can use it."

A whistling wind began to blow. It sounded almost like a high-pitched laugh, and it was followed by spirals of thickening smoke that appeared, seemingly from nowhere, and took on that same giantess shape as before. The spirit swooped wildly about, floated high above them, and then dove...straight into the river.

As if it had heard Cas's plan and was mocking her for it.

Everything went silent and still.

The scent of smoke and dust filled the air.

211

Cas cautiously stepped toward the river to get a closer look.

The trees along the water's edge began to shake and bend in the fresh, cold wind. Leaves were stripped. Limbs broke free. And all of it was spinning as it fell into the water, forming a churning mass of debris that bulged and bubbled at the surface—as if something underneath it was trying to break through.

Becoming something else, just to prove she can?

As soon as the thought crossed her mind, it happened. A beast of water and sticks and mud rose from the river, and Cas fully understood Elander's explanation—the spirit had simply used its wind to shape a new body out of new materials.

She stumbled back a few steps. "How do we fight something that doesn't have *an actual form?*"

"We make it reveal that true form somehow?" Elander suggested.

Before Cas could begin to guess at how they might do this, a rush of wind caught one of the muddy sticks from the spirit's arm and hurled it toward them like a javelin.

Another quickly-summoned shield protected them.

But the javelin had only been a distraction; the bank beneath them was eroding, wind-guided water rushing over the gritty sand and turning it to sparkling mud that nearly ripped Cas off her feet.

She crouched, lowering her center of balance. She

remained upright—somehow—but she was still sliding along with the increasingly watery mud, being dragged toward the river.

She clawed a hand into the bank, and she managed to dig in and jerk to a stop at the very edge of the water.

She kept one hand on her sword while the other grappled for rocks, for wayward roots, for *anything* that she might be able to use to help hoist herself back up the bank. Little by little she managed this, until finally she'd made her way to a solid patch of grass.

She rolled onto her back, muscles burning, and tried to catch her breath as the grey sky tilted and spun above her.

A thick fog rolled over her, blocking out that sky.

For a long, terrifying moment, Cas could neither hear, nor see, nor *feel* anything beyond her own breathing.

Then the mist swirled and the wind howled, pushing and pulling her in every direction, disorienting her further. She felt like she was being tossed about in angry waves—drowning in them—even though she'd managed to escape the river.

Just as before, it was an explosion of light from Elander that eventually came to her aid, drawing the spirit's attention—and its wind—away from her.

As the mist settled, Cas forced herself to breathe calmly, and then she rolled over and pushed herself up to her hands and knees.

Think. Think! What kind of magic reveals the true form of things?

Her fingers clenched into the damp grass and released, clenched and released, over and over. She was grounding herself—but not by counting numbers or breaths, as she usually did. Instead, her racing mind fired names in rapid succession, rattling off all the different gods and their servants, trying to think of a power that could help her. One that she might be able to wield.

What did she have?

Sun, Moon, Star, Sky, Storm.

And the spirits that served them...

Mist, Fortune, Vitality, Prism—

The realization left her in a breath. "Prism-kind magic."

The same power that had once been part of the medicine she'd used to treat Asra's Fading Sickness. It revealed the truth of things—reverted them to their original forms.

She had never met the Prism spirit, but she *had* met the goddess who ruled over that spirit—the Goddess of the Moon—and that was just as good, if not better, wasn't it?

She pictured the Moon Goddess in her mind, focused on the magic that goddess had already granted her and the connection they had forged. The crescent-shaped mark on her sword glowed to life with her next breath, and she lifted the blade and narrowed her gaze toward the last place she'd seen the spirit.

The most powerful gust of wind yet slammed into her. It was supernaturally strong and completely *relentless* as it funneled over her grip—

So relentless that it pried the sword from her hands and sent it spinning toward the river.

CHAPTER 13

Cas didn't think.

She just ran, her gaze zeroed in on her blade as it sank beneath the water.

She thought she heard Elander shouting at her as she reached the river, but it was too late to stop. The ground was growing slick beneath her, so she embraced the impending fall and launched forward with as much control as she could, diving into the grey waves.

The plunge was deeper than she anticipated. She flipped wildly about for several seconds before she managed to right herself and start swimming. She couldn't see much in the turbid water, but she could *feel* —the magic her sword carried was *her* magic, too, and she only needed to make her way toward that familiar feeling.

Following that feeling eventually led her to a pocket

of relative calmness. She dove, squinted through the dark water...and there her sword was, stuck in the riverbed far below her.

She kicked her way down to it, yanked it free, and pushed her way back toward the surface.

But she was in too deep.

She didn't reach the surface.

The waves swirled faster, and she could no longer tell up from down. The water grew darker, murkier. Her lungs burned. She tucked her head toward her chest, focusing, trying to summon the strength to keep swimming, up, down, left, right—it didn't matter, she just had to *swim*.

Where is the closest shore?

Her eyelids cracked open again, and she noticed that the moon-shaped symbol on her sword was still glowing.

Help me.

Her pulse was roaring in her ears—so loud that focusing was becoming impossible—but she would have sworn she heard the voice of the Moon Goddess herself answering the plea, whispering through the wild waters. Cas turned her head from side to side, the movement fueled by a delirious hope of actually *seeing* the goddess again.

There was no divine being in sight, but there *was* a faint thread of light winding its way off to her left.

It might have been nothing more than mad desperation overtaking her, but she kicked her way along that light anyway, and soon one knee struck mud, and then the other, and she hobbled her way forward until she managed to get her feet back underneath her.

She rose out of the river, gasping and shivering and furious, with her sword clenched tightly in her hand.

She spotted the Wind spirit almost immediately.

Elander was on the other side of it, still drawing its attention. A halo of light surrounded him. As Cas stepped from the water, Elander's eyes found hers, and that light shifted and flooded toward her. The same power she'd felt earlier overtook her once more, and warmth surged through her, making her forget about the damp clothing clinging to her chilled skin.

She stepped more confidently up the riverbank.

She squeezed the handle of her sword. The moon symbol on the blade flashed brighter and caught her eye. Calling out to that goddess had worked once, so she tried it again.

Help me!

And she was certain of it this time. She could hear the goddess whispering a reply. One in the Moon-kind language—a rhythmic sequence of words that sent a tingle of possibility rushing through Cas, even if she didn't entirely understand it—a spell. She merely had to repeat the words, and her sword gleamed a brilliant shade of white.

It did not stop with her blade, either; ropes of white

light leapt from her skin and wove together with ones from the blade, crossing over and under one another until they'd formed a large, solid shield—

No, a *net*.

The spirit was caught off guard as this net wrapped around it. It tried to rush away, shedding mud and sticks and water as it went, but the cage that had ensnared it seemed to prevent it from disappearing completely.

It twisted about, a chaotic whirlwind caught in that cage. The Prism magic held tighter, and it soon outlined a clear shape among the chaos—a shape that held, no matter how the winds around it raged, no matter how much of that wind-collected debris fell away.

The newly-revealed shape leapt away from Cas and Elander with catlike grace, landed in a crouch, and then slowly lifted into an upright position.

It was not quite the giant Cas had stared down on the bridge, but it was still at least a foot taller than her with willowy limbs and eyes the color of those flames lit by bedside mourners. Its arms hung like hooks with clawed fingers at their ends. Its back was covered in dark ribbons that shimmered in the breeze. Wisps of blue fire surrounded the lean body, and more ignited and died in the spirit's wake as it moved back toward Cas. Wind stirred wherever it stepped, spinning up dust and making those flames around it fan out, ruffling them like a dress caught in a storm.

Wind howled, louder and louder, around the spirit,

but its solid, true form was still not swept away. Its body only grew brighter, its limbs more defined, and its eyes lost their strange glow and became more human-like as they narrowed on Cas.

These human-like eyes were somehow the most unsettling of its many strange features. Cas could see the depth of emotion in them, and she thought the spirit might start speaking to her as it came closer. That it might try to reason with her...or beg to be spared.

She kept her sword in front of her, kept the strands of the Prism spell glowing and the spirit's true form visible and solid before her—

At least long enough for Elander's sword to pierce the spirit from behind.

He summoned several bolts of Storm magic as his sword plunged through the spirit's back. The net Cas had wrapped around that spirit brightened and tightened around its body, while the Storm magic twisted deeper. Cas braced herself for the messy breaking point, for an explosion of magic and blood—or whatever else filled this divine creature.

It didn't come.

Instead, the spirit let out a painfully high-pitched shriek that made both Cas and Elander flinch.

Then it disappeared similar to how Caden had— dark magical residue wrapping it up and quietly whisking it away. Not dead...just returned to its master.

A gentle breeze continued to blow.

Her sword felt heavier as the rush of battle faded and her muscles began to protest the abuse of the last few minutes. She kept the blade raised until the last scrap of the magical residue had disappeared, and then she let her arms fall to her sides as she heaved for breath.

Elander stepped closer, warily eyeing the windswept piles of tree limbs and other debris as he came. Once the wind finally stilled, his attention shifted fully to Cas. He wiped a smear of mud from her cheek and plucked a broken twig from her hair. "Diving headfirst into a raging river? *Really?*"

"It worked," she said, teeth chattering. "And I got my sword back, didn't I?"

"I would be furious if I wasn't so impressed," he muttered, as he removed his coat and wrapped it around her soaked and shivering body.

Her magic pulsed once more as his arm brushed hers, and the warmth that prickled through her made her think of the moment right before she'd found her way out of the river.

"I think I heard the Moon Goddess's voice in my head while I was in the water," she told Elander. "She showed me the way to the shore when I asked for help, and then gave me the words to summon the magic I needed to reveal Sonas's true form. Is such a thing possible?"

He considered the question for a long moment, and then he said, "It's similar to how the Marr and their servant spirits are connected, even over long distances, I suppose. You and I are more or less members of the Court of the Sun at this point. It's not too farfetched to think we could communicate with them. Or that our combined power—and struggle—caught their attention."

Cas pulled his coat more tightly around herself as she surveyed the destruction around them. "Speaking of gods and their servants...the Fire God is not going to be happy about what we just did."

"No," Elander agreed. "But we'll deal with that when the time comes. I think we should call this a victory for now."

Victory seemed a bit of a stretch, and Cas started to point this out. But he wouldn't listen to her objections; when she tried to argue her point, he simply directed her attention to something behind her.

She turned around.

A humbling sight greeted her—a group of people wandering toward the river's edge, watching her and Elander closely as the hazy air continued to clear. Her friends were among them. Laurent looked relieved. Nessa was beaming, and the fear that had been written all over her face when they'd last seen each other was gone.

The fear was gone from *most* of the faces before her.

An assortment of different feelings had taken its place—hope, awe, confusion; it was difficult to say what the predominant mood of the townspeople was.

But Cas definitely had their *attention*.

Elander pressed a supportive hand against the small of her back. "This part of our habitual morning monster hunt falls under your authority, I believe."

She was not one for speeches. Or for being the center of attention like this. But it was clear that all these people were listening, waiting for her to say something, so she returned Shadowslayer to its sheath and took a step forward.

"The old gods are restless," she said, her voice quiet but strong. "And here is your proof. This will not be the last time they try to wreak havoc in our city. Some of you have your doubts about what has happened with the royal family and the crown—fine. But my brother is no longer here. He ran, and all that he left in his wake is chaos."

She gestured toward the mess the spirit had left behind, and a ribbon of light trailed after her hand, causing a few soft gasps and other intrigued noises.

A faint glow of magic still surrounded her entire body, Cas realized. She had thought it was the rising sunlight bathing her in gold, but no—all her edges continued to glow even as the sun slipped behind the clouds.

No wonder I have their attention.

The Mimic crystal had worn off entirely too. So the crowd was staring, not only at the lingering signs of her inner magic, but at her faded hair, at her pale eyes...at all the things she used to hide. She felt the familiar itch of anxiety, the compulsive desire to find an escape route.

She fought off that itch and stood taller instead. "The chaos doesn't frighten me," she concluded. "And I am not going to run away, no matter what shadows befall this kingdom."

A thick silence fell, and it lasted for nearly a full minute before a few uncertain whispers started to circulate. Soon after this, a woman separated herself from the rest of the crowd. Cas unconsciously held her breath as this woman slowly approached her. She sensed Elander shifting his stance behind her, and Laurent slipped his way to the front of the crowd and narrowed his gaze in Cas's direction—both anticipating trouble.

But the woman simply studied Cas for a long moment, her brow furrowed in judgment and her lips pressed into a thin line. Then she lowered her eyes, bowed her head, and said, "Thank you."

Several others followed her example. Not all. But more than Cas ever would have expected.

She released the breath she'd been holding. The sun seemed to release with it, breaking through the clouds with a swiftness that felt almost supernatural. Its light spilled over the crowd, the sudden brightness and warmth rendering them all silent once more.

And for a moment—however brief—Cas felt like their queen.

CHAPTER 14

With her body aching from her battle, and her identity revealed and more and more crowds converging around her, Cas quickly decided it was safest to return to the palace for the time being.

The glow had faded around her, but her skin was still faintly shivering with the after-effects of magic when they made it back.

As she expected at this point, the closer she drifted to Elander, the more intense that shivering became. She managed to ignore it—mostly—while she briefed a few of her soldiers on what had happened in the city, and while she gave orders that would further secure that city and help prepare it for any lingering unrest.

Soon enough, her commands were all given, and people dispersed in all directions. Laurent and Nessa followed the crowd in charge of making the security preparations—Laurent wanted to further instruct and inform them—which left Cas and Elander to stroll the hallways in relative privacy.

She relaxed a bit once she was out of sight of most of her subjects. But this was a mistake, as it meant letting down the guard that had been keeping the restless magic inside of her under control. The Storm mark on her wrist flashed the instant that guard slipped, and she thought she heard a strange buzzing coming from the sword at her hip. If she had pulled Shadowslayer from its sheath, she suspected she would have seen the symbols on it alight as well.

"Are you okay?" Elander asked.

She nodded, rubbing a hand along her arm, trying to smooth away the little bumps that had risen on it. "It just feels like I'm still in the middle of that battle. On edge. As if my magic is still...*wanting*. It never stops, here lately—it's still reacting to yours. And what we did in the city was our most powerful combination of power yet. It's like it's *awakened* something. Something that won't settle."

He tilted his head toward her as they continued their walk, and something flashed in his eyes—a spark that was a bit curious, a bit mischievous.

He reached a hand toward her arm. Didn't quite *touch* it...but he might as well have. The energy that kindled in the space between them moved over her skin with a certain, solid pressure, once more lifting the little hairs along her arm as it went.

She sucked in a breath. "And that edge becomes especially steep when you do things like *that*."

He fixed his gaze ahead of them once more. "The unending pressure of magic isn't entirely new to me," he told her. "It just feels a bit like it did when I was a god. Too much power to ever settle completely."

"It's distracting."

"You'll get used to it." He gave her a charming, perfectly innocent grin before adding, "Or maybe not, as long as I'm around."

"You're enjoying the effect you're having on me entirely too much."

"Perhaps."

She cleared her throat. "Anyway...I need to see about penning responses to the messages that have arrived for me; that pile of mail is becoming a mountain by this point, no doubt. And you should check in with Zev regarding Orbryn. He believes that lord is close to cracking."

He nodded. "I was planning to."

They came to a divergence at the end of the hallway, and she drew to a stop. Hesitated, and then said, "But perhaps we can discuss this magic more later. In private."

"More experimenting?" He flashed another one of those disarming smiles.

She couldn't help but return it this time.

"I'll be expecting you in my room later this evening," she said, straightening the collar of his shirt, and letting her hand linger against his chest. "And that is an order, Captain."

He lifted her hand and kissed it. He was still smiling when he leaned away. That sly, roguish slant...it would never not make her breath catch and her knees feel weak. It was as devastatingly handsome now as it had been the first time he'd wielded it against her.

She swallowed hard and nodded pointedly at the hall to their left, which eventually led to stairs that wound down to the dungeons. He gave a little bow before turning and strolling down that hall.

"No more getting sidetracked, please," he called without looking back. "I've had my fill of battles for the day."

"We'll see what happens," she called in response, grinning slightly.

She went right while he went left. As she turned around, she was startled to find one of the palace servants quickly approaching her—she had drawn so close that Cas nearly collided with her.

Cas apologized and started to step around her, but the woman remained in her path.

"It's no problem, at all!" This young, mousy-haired woman reminded her a bit of Nessa, with her wide-eyed stare, eager smile. "Is there anything I can do for you, Your Highness?"

The formal address caught Cas off guard; she hadn't heard many use it. But more and more people were apparently warming up to the idea of her as *queen*.

Which is a good thing, she told herself, fiercely, before that familiar feeling of being an imposter could grip her.

"Um, no," she replied. "Not really. I have some correspondence to catch up on, but I'd prefer to see to these letters without any interruptions, so—"

"I'll get a fire started in one of the private, second-floor studies, if you'd like? And I can have your mail carried to you, and perhaps something to eat brought to you as well?"

Cas agreed—it seemed easier than arguing—and a short time later she arrived to the decided-upon room to find a warm oasis awaiting her. A table and chairs had been pulled close to the roaring fire, and, as promised, both her mail and her brunch awaited her on the table.

She stared at the piles of neatly-arranged parchment and envelopes but didn't move to pick up the quill beside them. She didn't eat anything from the silver tray on the other side, either—as tempting as the breads and fruits spread across it were. She *did* have messages to write, and food would be a necessity at some point...

But the truth was that she'd mainly wanted to hole herself up in a room, alone, so that she could more closely inspect those crystals Caden had given her.

They were all she could think about, suddenly.

She waited a few minutes after the servant left, and then she settled down at the table, took the pouch from her satchel, and plucked a few of the crystals from it. She lined up three of those crystals along the table in front of her.

It was foolish, but some part of her wanted to keep them a secret forever. She had so few memories of her early life that it made her feel oddly possessive of the possible revelations waiting within these crystals. Protective of them. She hadn't even wanted to take them at first, but now she was terrified that someone *else* might come and steal them away.

She twisted the ties of the tiny bag that now rested in her lap, trying to think of who she might safely be able to tell.

If she told Elander, he would be upset that she hadn't immediately informed him about her meeting with Caden, and likely furious that she'd taken these crystals with so little hesitation. Rhea and Laurent would be upset too. They might insist she get rid of them, even, that the danger and uncertainty surrounding these magical objects outweighed whatever knowledge she might glean from them. Nessa would support her, but not necessarily because she *agreed* with her...

She peered back into the bag, and she noticed a slip of parchment tucked between the remaining crystals.

The word that would activate the Blood-kind spells was written on it, she presumed. She withdrew it, but immediately folded it over without reading it.

Her gaze drifted toward the fire.

She could drop the piece of parchment into that fire, and that would be that. If she let the flames devour it, then it would be one less thing she had to make a decision about.

She heard footsteps in the hallway.

She swept the three crystals from the table back into the bag. Then, clenching the folded paper in her fist, she casually walked over and leaned against the door until it clicked completely shut. From there she went to the fire, took the paper between her fingertips, and held it out in front of her. Her hand trembled. She took a deep breath, preparing herself...

But she couldn't do it.

Couldn't stand the thought of letting this link to her past simply...*burn*.

She was seconds away from shoving it back into the bag with the crystals when a sudden knock made her jump.

The person who'd knocked let themselves inside a moment later—Zev.

"I didn't say *come in*," Cas said, frowning. "Why bother knocking if you're just going to barge inside anyway?"

He shrugged. "Habit." He glanced around the room,

curious. "What does it matter if I barged in? What are you doing in here by yourself?"

She didn't answer.

"You look guilty," he accused with a grin. "If you're up to no good, the least you could do is include me in your questionable decisions."

She hid that paper more completely in her fist and kept her lips pressed tightly together.

His eyes widened a bit and he moved closer, grabbing the chair she'd been sitting in earlier. He spun it around, straddled it, sank down into the seat, and leaned against its back as he said, "I was joking—but you actually *are* up to no good, aren't you?"

"I'm not *up to* anything," she mumbled. "I was just thinking."

"About?"

She met his gaze. Her fingers unconsciously unfolded the paper again. She folded it back right away, though she wasn't sure why. She trusted Zev with her life—why not with this?

"Did you shut the door completely?" she asked.

He gave her another long, curious look, but slowly rose and went to double-check the latch. As he returned to her, she withdrew one of the crystals and handed it to him.

"A magic crystal?" He lifted it and studied it in the light, just as she'd done by the riverside. "It looks... strange," he concluded, same as she had. "Too clean."

"It isn't the typical, tainted sort that gets hacked out of the In-Between. It came directly from a divine source."

"What do you mean?"

She quickly and quietly recounted the meeting she'd had with Caden.

Once she'd finished, Zev placed the crystal back on the table—as if he wasn't sure he wanted to touch it any longer—and took a deep breath. "These crystals could reveal anything, Cas. And knowing your brother, they're likely not going to be...*pleasant* revelations. Are you sure you want to mess with them? This seems reckless, even for my taste."

Her stomach sank. She'd secretly been hoping for someone else to justify her using these spells, she realized. "I thought you'd be on my side."

"I've never been anywhere else," he replied, draping himself down in the chair once more and studying her with a frown. "I just don't want you to do anything stupid."

"I know it's dangerous, but it might lead to information that could help us."

His nod was slow. Reluctant. "It might."

"And it's not just that." She settled into the chair across from him. "It's so strange for me, being here. I've closed off sections, and I've taken down portraits, and I've done everything else I can think of to erase the family that lived here before, but I can't erase *everything*.

It's like a wound that I keep scraping against all the sharp things scattered throughout this palace. And I can't help feeling like I might be able to actually *heal* that wound, if only I could understand what had caused it. If I could get closure, somehow. Does that sound...wrong?"

He considered her words for a long time before he finally shook his head. "No. I guess not."

The two of them sat in silence. Cas stared into the fire, while Zev's gaze was narrowed suspiciously on the crystal he'd placed on the table. He occasionally poked and prodded it, frowning each time he did.

"Just promise me something," he eventually said.

"What's that?"

"That if you *do* decide to use one of these spells, you won't do it alone. Come find me first. Or Nessa, maybe. Let her use her cuddly magic on you so whatever you see doesn't drive you...you know..."

"Insane?"

"Or worse."

She released a slow, shuddering breath, relieved that he hadn't outright dismissed the idea. "Deal."

He stood and stretched. "Rhea had urgent news for you, by the way. Something about messages received from the Windhaven Realm this morning."

Cas frowned. "And you're just now telling me?"

He nodded toward the crystal. "This was urgent, too, wasn't it? Everything is, these days." He stepped away from the table, nonchalantly waving his hand through the air and summoning a little cluster of flames to it. "Everything is on fire, everything is burning..." He trailed off as a yawn overtook him.

"...Okay, I get your point," said Cas, still frowning. She secured the crystals out of sight once more, and they walked together to the sun-filled room that Rhea had taken as her office.

They parted ways outside the door, and Cas paused to once more check on those crystals she carried, shoving them deeper into her bag. Her fingers twitched against the strap of that bag slung across her shoulder, and she fell briefly into her old habit of tapping, counting out each of her heartbeats, trying to slow them, before she took a deep breath and stepped inside.

Rhea sat in a chair by the window. She appeared lost in thought, her head bowed and balanced upon her clasped hands. Silverfoot was draped in his customary place over one of her shoulders.

As Cas approached them, Rhea lifted her head and offered a smile. The fox jumped onto the table next to the chair and presented his throat to Cas, giving her easier access to scratch it.

"Zev said you had something to tell me," Cas began, her fingers absently massaging Silverfoot's fur. "Something urgent?"

Rhea nodded, pointed to the desk against the opposite wall and said, "Eyes, please, Silver."

The fox dutifully left Cas's scratches behind, moved to the desk, and paced and scanned the letters spread across it. After he'd studied them for a moment, Rhea walked over and plucked one from the pile.

"You recall that negative reply we received from Lord Falone the other day?" she asked, working the chosen letter uncertainly between her hands.

"Yes."

"Well, as of yesterday, we no longer need to be offended by his decision not to grace us with his presence."

"Why's that?"

"Because he's dead."

"...Dead?"

Rhea nodded, solemnly, and handed the letter over to her.

"What happened?"

It was a long time before Rhea answered her. "The rumor...is that assassins sent by the Ciridan Palace were responsible."

The accusation took a long time to settle into Cas's mind—because she didn't want to think about what it meant. She tried scanning the letter Rhea had given her, but all the words simply melted together. "*Me*? They suspect I had a hand in it? Why? Because Falone refused an audience with me?"

Rhea's lips parted, only to press back together in a frown.

"I would never retaliate in such a barbaric way—"

"Ah, but the people of Windhaven don't know that," Rhea interrupted gently. "You're an enigma to them. To *most* of the empire, actually—even the ones that have already pledged allegiance to you. And some are actively working to sabotage your rule before it even truly starts. I've heard from some of our allies in the Kingdom of Ethswen this morning, too...apparently the royal family there is doing nothing to disparage rumors that you are looking to send *more* assassins to Windhaven and the other realms of their kingdom. In fact, it's possible they *started* those rumors. I'm sure they'll claim you intend to attack them next—so they have an excuse to send their armies wherever they like in order to *keep the peace*. It's a common, if cowardly, war tactic."

Indignant heat flooded Cas's body.

"You met the princess of Ethswen while we were in Briarfell."

Cas nodded.

"And that meeting...you two didn't exactly hit it off, did you?"

"Understatement," muttered Cas. She could still vividly remember the meeting she'd observed in one of the gardens of Briarfell. The way that princess had glared at her, the ice in her smile, the poison in her voice...

Rhea attempted a shrug—as if these matters could simply be shrugged off—but her face was full of concern, which made her expression much softer than usual. "Who knew overtaking a throne would be so complicated, hm?"

Cas huffed out a laugh at this half-hearted attempt at humor. "For some reason, I thought it would be easier to get control of the mortal side of things before I attempted to face our divine problems. But I'm beginning to wonder about that."

Rhea inhaled deeply and exhaled slowly, appearing unsure of what to say next. But she kept moving, and she worked with Silver to dig out another letter—this one still tucked into a golden envelope with an impressively large seal holding it together.

"This came from the southern empire," Rhea said. "More *optimistic* correspondence, hopefully? It was hand-delivered by a Sundolian soldier who arrived via an Air portal while you were busy in the city. Not just this letter, but that pile of books with it." She pointed to a stack of ancient-looking tomes resting on a chair in the corner of the room, bound together by a leather belt.

Cas took the letter and studied it, tracing the familiar seal—a black bird and a dragon—with her fingertips.

"From the High King, on Lady Sade's behalf. She's rallied him to your causes regarding the Vitala, it seems. Speaking of *divine problems*."

Some of the fiery indignation in Cas subsided as she scanned the letter, and she calmed further as she walked over and took one of the most promising looking books from the stack. This was more her thing—sorting through dusty pages rather than sifting through war tactics. Books were easier to make sense of than people and politics.

She moved the stack of books to the floor and sank into the chair, her eyes never leaving that tome in her hands as she moved.

Silverfoot followed, winding his way between the chair and her legs and sniffing at the tower of books.

"This is an impressive collection, isn't it?" asked Rhea.

"I never took you to the Black Feather Institute in Rykarra, did I?" Cas asked absently as she flipped through pages. "The scholars there—and the rooms full of knowledge and research that they've built—are some of the most impressive things I've ever seen." She paused mid page flip, and her vision glazed over as a thought seized her. "If I'm still standing—and the throne is still mine—after everything is said and done... then maybe I could create something similar in this city."

"An honorable goal. The world needs more libraries and places of learning."

"Maybe not the most important thing to focus on rebuilding in this empire, but..."

"I think it will be *especially* important after we settle all of our wars," Rhea countered. "People need to know that their existence will live on in some way, don't they? Books matter. Writing things down means we believe there will be a future generation to read them, whatever wars may come—and I think that's important."

A smile eased onto Cas's face. She liked the thought that words and stories and knowledge could persist, regardless of what violent winds might blow. It filled her with warmth—with hope—which was something in desperately short supply around this palace.

The book she held was battered and bent in places, but it had still endured. It was a field guide of sorts, rich with information about the various divine creatures that roamed—or had once roamed—their world. Cas flipped to the index, and was somewhat surprised to find what she was looking for relatively quickly: an actual entry on the Vitala themselves.

It seemed almost too good to be true—how could there be literal books with this knowledge, when she had been ignorant of it all until her meeting with Solatis?

But then she remembered how so much regarding the divine had been erased in this kingdom. The southern empire was a very different place from Kethra... and she felt a surge of gratitude, once again, for the allies she'd managed to forge while in those southern lands.

She scanned the sketch at her fingertips. It looked only somewhat like the image she remembered of

Elander from his moment of rebirth in Dawnskeep; it was only vaguely humanoid, with a face made of unnaturally sharp angles, feather-like hair, and black eyes that appeared bottomless. But its wings—golden and soft and emitting a powerful glow—were familiar, as was the symbol of the Sun Goddess that graced the creature's muscular bicep.

Cas read the annotations in the margin aloud. "Last known sighting of the last known Vitala, circa Year Five-Thirty-Seven, in the Shadowmere region, near the coast of the Glashtyn Sea...a sighting by Meira Alandel, who allegedly hunted and slayed the creature."

Slayed it?

That couldn't be right, could it?

"That name sounds vaguely familiar," Rhea commented.

Cas nodded slowly—it took her only a minute to remember *why*. In the next moment she summoned a servant and sent them off to collect a book from her own library.

She paced the room while she awaited the servant's return. Once they came back, Cas was so anxious that she jerked the book into her possession with unnecessary force. She mumbled a distracted apology at the sight of the servant's shocked face, and then she went to work searching through pages.

These pages were old and yellowed as well, and the ones in the back of the volume remained empty—it was a history book of the royal family, and so some of that story remained unwritten.

Within seconds, she found what she was looking for —a family tree. Silverfoot hopped onto her shoulder, and together they peered at the sprawling image before them.

"Meira eventually married Jon de Solasen, who was the great-grandfather of Varen and...well, *me*," said Cas, dragging her finger along the branches between their names. Her gaze lingered on one of the neatly scripted names closest to the bottom. *Valori de Solasen.*

Someone had tried to scratch it out.

But it was still there.

It had endured, just as the books piled around her had. And it was strange to see her true name written out like this—almost as strange as being referred to as *Your Highness*—but this was her reality, strange or not.

She had endured.

Silverfoot leaned closer to the family tree, pawing at Meira's name and the titles beside it. One of these titles was written in ink the color of blood.

"*Godslayer,*" Rhea read, her tone flat.

"The Vitala were not technically *gods,*" Cas thought aloud.

"No," said Rhea, "but I suppose calling them that made for a better, more impressive story for Meira's subjects. Who wouldn't want to be known as *Godslayer*?"

Cas was quiet for a moment, trying to make all of the facts swirling in her head fit together in a way that made sense. "All of the Vitala died on the shores of Dawnskeep, according to the story Prince Alder told me —it was a massacre at the hands of the Dark God's monsters. That's what led to the creation of the Heart of the Sun. But maybe one survived?" Her gaze slid back to the book with the entry on those guardians that Solatis had created.

Last known sighting of the last known Vitala...

"This one that survived..." Rhea began, uncertainly. "...Elander?"

Cas pinched the bridge of her nose. Her head was beginning to hurt. "Maybe."

"He doesn't remember any of this?"

Cas shook her head.

Rhea was quiet for several moments. "So we don't know the details, but still...it's interesting how your different lifetimes have been woven together, isn't it?" She beckoned, and Silverfoot left the picture of the family tree and leapt into her arms. Rhea turned him toward the window, and the two of them stared out of it together, watching the light rain clouds moving in. "I suppose the next question is how on earth Meira managed to slay one of the Vitala. *If* she truly did. And then what happened after that? Was that somehow what triggered his ascension to the Dark God's court? Perhaps Malaphar saw the last of Solatis's favored warriors at a weak point and decided to take advantage."

It was possible, Cas thought, remembering the story Caden had told her about his own ascension. He had been on the brink of death when Elander had saved him and turned him into a divine being. Maybe something similar had happened to Elander—except a more sinister *rescue* in this case.

"It could all be exaggeration, of course," Rhea added. "There's a good chance she didn't *slay* anything. Wouldn't be the first time the Solasen family told a lie."

"It wouldn't," Cas agreed, picking up the book of her family's history once more.

She could imagine it without much effort—her great-grandmother regaling the people of this kingdom with colorful tales of her battle against one of Solatis's most sacred, chosen guardians.

"I wonder how it happened," Rhea mused, "the shift from the Vitala guarding this royal family to being *hunted* by it?"

Cas shook her head; she didn't even have a guess. All she was certain of was that this royal family she had been born into had clearly been entangled with divine beings—for better or worse—for centuries.

Her heart pounded a little harder at the thought, and the world seemed to shrink to nothing but her fingers as they traced the branches of that printed tree once more.

The names, the titles...this was her *family*. Her past. Or one of her pasts, at least.

She thought again of the crystals Caden had given her, and the things they might reveal. This palace, and all that had happened in it after she'd left...

She needed answers.

And she was going to find them, no matter how painful or dangerous unearthing her buried past might become.

CHAPTER 15

ELANDER WAS NOT IN HER ROOM WHEN CAS FINALLY RETIRED to it that evening—and she was simultaneously disappointed and relieved by his absence.

She wanted to see him, to speak with him about all she'd learned today. He had a way of dissecting political matters, in particular, and making them easier to digest and make sense of.

On the other hand, her desire to use those secret crystals haunted her—and she wasn't ready to have *that* particular conversation.

She hated keeping secrets from him. And the truth was going to come out eventually.

But for the moment, she was glad for the chance to take her time hiding the bag Caden had given her. She tucked it deep in the corner of a cabinet in her washroom—after promising herself that she would decide what to do with its contents first thing tomorrow morning—and then she put it out of her mind.

It was late, likely drawing close to midnight, but she was not tired. Ridding herself of that bag of crystals had made her feel even more awake, as if a great weight had been lifted from her mind, leaving it free to spin new thoughts.

There was movement outside her room—servants.

They insisted on doing something for her, same as that girl in the hallway earlier today. These people referred to her as *Your Highness* too. So she politely asked them to draw her bath...mostly because she knew they would give her privacy while she took it.

She tied her hair into a messy bun on top of her head before sinking down into the warm water, and then she stared at the circular window centered high on the wall in front of her, counting what she could see of the stars.

When this didn't quiet her thoughts the way she'd hoped it would, she closed her eyes and focused on the currents of magic twisting beneath her skin; they were as easy to feel as her heartbeat now, and sometimes they could grow loud enough to drown out everything else— even without her truly *summoning* anything to the surface.

That undercurrent of magic provided the distracting hum she was looking for. It thrummed in her ears, steady at first...until it abruptly skipped for several beats before settling into a much faster, more powerful, rhythm.

She wasn't surprised to hear a knock against the door a few minutes later.

She blinked her eyes open but kept her head partially submerged. Her gaze rose to the window again. She already knew it was Elander in the doorway—who else made her magic and heart beat so furiously?—and she didn't need to lift herself from the warm water to confirm it.

"Rather late, aren't we, Captain?"

She fixed her eyes back on the stars outside, but she could hear the smile in his voice as he said, "A thousand apologies."

"What took you so long?"

"I was with Laurent. Our conversation got...complicated, and I lost track of time."

"Your conversation about...?"

"The situation in Mistwilde."

"I already told him we needed to go deal with it together. Soon."

He hesitated. "Yes, we both agreed that *someone* needs to go. And he intends to go, of course. But...this particular trip is one that doesn't need to include you necessarily."

She snorted, sinking a little lower into the water. "He's convinced you of that, has he?"

"I more or less came to the conclusion on my own."

"Of course."

"But he did make good points. It's a long way to Mistwilde. It's dangerous there, and unpredictable."

"Some of that could also be said of here. Or *anywhere*."

"...True."

Cas thought of her meeting with Rhea—of the rumors that the Ethswenian royalty were stirring up about her. She couldn't dispel those sorts of rumors while hiding in her own palace every damn day, could she?

"I'm going to go to Mistwilde at some point," she said stubbornly.

More hesitation. "At some point, yes."

"I can't expect the elvish king to take me seriously if I won't even have a quick audience with him."

"No, perhaps not."

"I can't ask for him to risk being my ally if *I* won't risk a simple visit."

"I agree."

She lifted her head and cut her eyes toward where he stood with his shoulder leaning against the doorframe. "You don't have to agree with everything I say, you know."

He smiled. "I know. But in my defense, you're at your most persuasive when you're naked."

She let out a soft sigh and sank back into the tub.

"Maybe I'll use this to my advantage at that upcoming summit we're planning."

"I'd rather you didn't."

Desire clenched through her at the dark note of possessiveness in his tone. She glanced over one last time and smiled teasingly at him before slipping even deeper into the water. She closed her eyes and floated in silence for a moment before continuing.

"Never mind diplomatic summits and distant realms," she said, her own voice muffled to her submerged ears. "Talk to me about magic."

The water shifted from the vibration of his footsteps as he came nearer. She kept her eyes closed and followed the sounds of his movement, rising up just enough to hear him more clearly. There was a stool at the nearby sink. He dragged it to the head of the tub and then perched upon it.

She sensed his magic spiraling to life a moment later, little sparks of it snapping in the space above her.

"I felt it again on my way up here," he told her. "Your power calling to mine. Were you doing it on purpose?"

"I was focused on my magic," she said. "Trying to use it to drown out my thoughts. I wasn't really *calling*."

She opened her eyes to a show of little lights floating above the tub. A few of these sparks were spinning down, drifting toward her and the water, which seemed...dangerous. Reckless enough that it briefly took her breath away.

But though the water fizzled and warmed with each spark it swallowed, it didn't hurt; it was as if she was absorbing all of the excess electricity into her body. It made her feel so charged and buoyant that she thought she might be able to float to the water's surface, and then onward up to the window—if only she could relax enough.

Elander stopped this display of magic after a few moments, and his eyes glazed over in thought. "It feels like more and more of my magic is reawakening. Every moment we spend together, every battle we fight together—and even when we're fighting our battles separately. This morning, for example, the surge of power that awakened me was unlike anything I've ever felt. I don't think I could have stayed away from you even if I'd *wanted* to."

She glanced over at him. Her eyes felt a bit misty, her magic a bit lighter, and the same, slightly overwhelming sensation she'd had that night in the throne room overtook her once more. Her confidante, her shelter, this man who had found her across lifetimes...

Her guardian.

"And last night too, when I was fighting with Caden," he continued, "I thought of you—of protecting you—and I managed to summon the most powerful shield of magic I'd summoned up to that point."

"Interesting." It was the only response she could

manage to whisper. Her stomach had flipped at the mention of Caden, and now it wouldn't settle.

She couldn't think of anything else except that secret she was keeping.

Had Laurent mentioned her meeting with Caden to Elander? Had Nessa? They didn't know what had transpired at that meeting, no, but they had seen it happening. They had seen too much, perhaps...

Just tell him, urged a small voice inside of her.

A second, much louder voice, warned her of what might happen if she did. That he might take away those crystals—those memories—that she felt so strangely protective of.

And he had been so upset about Caden becoming their enemy...she didn't want to put him through more of that pain. Not until she had no other choice.

She might not have been a guardian chosen by the gods, but that didn't mean she didn't want to protect him too.

There was a small glass bowl of perfumed flower petals resting on the edge of the tub; one of the servants had left it for her. Cas had not yet tossed any into the water, because they seemed like a superfluous splendor, given the state of things. But she gathered up a handful of them now, her hands needing something to do. She tossed them into the water, one by one, and fixated on the rings that grew from each landing spot.

"I wish I could remember more about the origins of

that magic," said Elander, speaking more to himself than her. "But no matter how much of it awakens, the memories of whatever I was, once upon a time, remain unclear."

It struck her, then, how similar they were—both of them sitting in the shadow of a past that was dangerous and difficult to know, but perhaps *more* dangerous to leave alone.

How could you know where to go next, if you were unsure of where you'd come from?

"There's a stack of books from Sundolia in my room that might interest you," she told him. "From King Emrys. In his letter that accompanied them, he suggested that we not limit our search to the Vitala. They've gone by many different names throughout the ages, he suspects. There's a detailed list of possible names and other things he thought might be relevant— several pages worth of possibly useful terms and other information, in fact. He seemed very interested in giving me a history lesson on the day we met, and that enthusiasm continues."

"Lucky for us."

"Mm-hm."

Elander lifted his eyes to the ceiling, losing himself in thought for a moment. "And you've already gone through each of those pages and books a thousand times, I presume."

"Only two or three times, actually."

"With no break, of course."

"Of course not. Who has time for breaks?"

He exhaled a long, slow breath.

She twisted one of the petals between her fingers. "I'm not the first queen that's ever had a long day, you know."

"No. But out of curiosity, did you remember to *eat* during this long day?"

"You sound like Rhea. Who I was with for most of the afternoon, by the way—so of course I ate. She force fed me. Basically held my mouth open and crammed it full of food."

He laughed softly. "Good."

"I'm fine, really. I wish everyone would stop worrying about me so much."

"And just let you obsess over every single problem we're facing in peace? Completely on your own?"

"Exactly."

He mirrored the small smile she gave him but said nothing else on the matter. He just reached out a hand and brushed it along her cheek, smoothing the few strands of hair that had escaped from her bun. From there, his fingers traveled down her neck and along the curve of her shoulder, massaging away some of the tension she held there. A soft note of contentment escaped her, and he brought his other hand up and repeated the massaging motion on her other shoulder.

It was better than magic, the feel of his fingers

against her skin. Nothing quieted her mind quite like his touch.

Her head tilted back. She reached for one of his hands, laced their fingers together, and pressed it over her chest. She liked the way it felt—the heavy weight of his strong hand resting there. Like it was anchoring her in place, keeping her restless heart from feeling as if it might beat itself out of her body.

His other hand stilled against her shoulder, and he cleared his throat. "Anyway, about that magic..." He trailed off, and Cas waited, but he seemed to have forgotten whatever he'd planned to say.

"I don't believe you're really thinking about magic anymore," she teased. "I think you've gotten distracted."

"Maybe." He moved the hand from her shoulder and braced it against the edge of the tub. Unlacing her fingers from his other hand, he let his touch roam lower along her body, sliding between her breasts and down toward her navel as he rose up, leaned over, and pressed his lips to hers. "Or perhaps I've willingly allowed myself to be led astray," he said, the words a soft whisper against her mouth.

Her head tilted farther back to better angle her mouth against his. He deepened the kiss, and her body arched, drawing her breasts above the water and causing an audible hitch of breath from him.

She grabbed his hand and guided it back toward her chest. He traced his fingers around the peaks of her breasts, which had hardened swiftly from the sudden exposure to air. The droplets of water clinging to those velvet tips were slicked away with rough, precise flicks of his fingers—and then came a sudden, subtle current of electricity, concentrated at the tips of those fingers.

Magic.

He drew his hand back slightly, letting it hover inches away from her body. Her skin continued to tingle as if he was still touching her. It was stimulating from both the outside and inside—his magic, and hers rising to meet it—and she gasped as every nerve ending in the sensitive, stiffened bud of her breast shivered to life.

"Interesting," he mused, echoing her earlier comment.

The pleasant buzzing continued in her chest while he straightened and moved to collect a towel from the hook on the wall.

"Also? If I didn't know any better," he said, as he sauntered back to her, "I'd say *magic* was never really at the forefront of your thoughts either. Admit it—you were hoping I'd find my way up here while you were still naked in that tub. This was clearly a trap."

She took a deep breath. Tossed the rest of the flower petals into the water. Somehow found words among the scorching images and unspoken desires now firing rapidly through her mind. "Catching you... was merely an added bonus," she said, managing a somewhat casual shrug. "But actually, the main reason

I'm in here is that I've found that stripping naked seems to be the best way to get the servants to leave me alone."

"I'm not complaining, for the record."

"I didn't think you would."

He swept an appreciative glance along the length of her body before he stepped closer, and in a voice that was just short of commanding he said, "I think you should get out of the tub."

"I was considering it. But it's much colder out there than in here."

"You won't be cold long, I promise."

Another surge of desire curled through her in response to the low, suggestive tone of the words. Her body seemed to move on its own, following his voice. She still shivered as she stood and stepped from the water; it truly *was* the worst kind of cold, the kind that came after such comforting warmth.

But Elander standing there, ready with a towel outstretched in his hands...helped.

She let him drape that towel around her, and then moved closer so she could huddle against the heat radiating from him. As her water-slicked skin brushed the rough fabric of his shirt, a white-hot dagger of need shot through her and urged her up onto her toes so she could reach his mouth.

He leaned down to her. They picked up where they'd left off a moment ago, with a deep, slow kiss—one that sent her hands fumbling over his body, gripping fistfuls of his clothing as she tried to balance herself.

He slid his hands down, curving them around her hips. Magic shimmered in the sliver of space between them, little flickers of their power colliding, feeding off each other. Her knees buckled as a particularly potent collision sent shockwaves radiating through her. He caught her more completely as her balance swayed, hooking an unyielding arm around her waist. From beneath his touch, electricity began to spread. *More magic.* As before, it didn't hurt; it merely vibrated across her skin, calling her own power to the surface, stimulating her from the inside out.

"That is..." She trailed off, head spinning. She couldn't think of any words that did justice to what he was currently making her feel.

"Just warming you up, as promised," he murmured, one side of his mouth edging upward. "And experimenting, too...as you suggested we do earlier."

"Right." The word escaped on a breath. "That was the plan, wasn't it?"

He nodded, and then went back to that plan with renewed vigor. His eyes closed and his mouth parted slightly in concentration, and the flickers of their combined magic gathered, strengthened into a steady current that ducked and wove around them.

It soon became very deliberate, the path that magic traveled around her...and then *against* her. He was guiding it, occasionally brushing his fingertips along her body to help it along, though this touch was unnecessary—the magic followed his hand even when he briefly pulled it away from her skin, the waves of it vibrating down her arms, sweeping across her breasts, plunging deep into her belly.

She whispered a soft curse as his touch—and their magic—stilled just above the center of her thighs.

His eyes flashed open, darkening as they met her gaze. That look was as intentional as the hand he slid more fully between her legs, and it chased away all thoughts in her mind save for one—

Wanting.

That was the word she had used to describe her magic earlier today, and it was the only word she could think of now as another surge of it spiraled through her.

All she could think about was that wanting. That *need.* Her body burned with it. The very space between them was an affront to her and that desire—she needed to get rid of that space, needed to collide more fully with him in every sense of the word.

She grabbed his shirt once more, yanking him toward her and drawing a deep groan of approval from him as she slid her other hand beneath that shirt and took control of the magic they shared. Warmth blossomed in the tips of her fingers, and she raked it across the hard ridges of his stomach, dragging a tantalizing path along his skin.

And just as it had earlier, a shiver of danger coursed through her. *They* were dangerous. Two lightning bolts intertwining and feeding into the frenzied, hot energy of one another.

He took hold of the hand she still had against his stomach and guided it lower.

Her power surged briefly out of her control.

Part of it manifested as solid and searing sparks in the air around them.

One of those flickers of magic landed with a hiss upon the side of the tub, and Cas paused, her breathing heavy, as she watched it shimmer out of existence. "We're going to set fire to this room if we're not careful."

"This palace has no shortage of rooms," Elander replied, in between trailing kisses along her neck and jawline. "We can set fire to them all if you'd like."

"And burn the entire palace to the ground?"

"We'll build a new one."

She pretended to consider this. "I suppose I had planned on a lot of redecorating anyway."

He laughed with his mouth still against her neck. It was one of her favorite sensations in the world—the feel of that laughter spilling over her skin.

Her fingers moved deftly over the top buttons of his shirt, undoing them, and then over his belt. He drew the shirt over his head and tossed it aside. His pants hung low on his hips. She started to remove them completely, but he stopped her with a kiss that promptly made her forget what her hands—and every other part of her—had been in the middle of doing.

He hooked one strong arm around her thighs and lifted her off her feet, guiding her legs around his waist. His other arm pressed against her back and held her in place. His mouth hardly left hers as he did this, and as his tongue parted her lips, her legs squeezed in automatic response, desperate to pull herself more completely against the firmness of his body.

The closest furniture outside of the washroom was an overstuffed armchair against the wall. Elander sank down into the cushions, pulling her with him. She settled in his lap, straddling him. Her lips collided with his and she gripped the strong curve of his jaw, pushed his head against the chair, momentarily trapping him there with the intensity of her kiss.

As she leaned back, her towel slid down and pooled at the small of her back. Elander slipped his hands beneath it. Their warmth was a heavenly contrast to that cool, damp towel as he followed the curve of her backside, digging his fingers into her flesh and yanking her lower half more fully against him.

Her breasts were level with his gaze, now, and he found one of the hardened tips with his mouth, catching it between his lips in a soft, slow kiss that soon gave way to his tongue tracing patterns that made her body twist and turn at his mercy.

He slid his hand between her legs once more—only

now he wasn't teasing. He was pressing into her with warm fingers; with a confident touch that summoned magic and sent waves of it fluttering through her center.

She rocked back, lifting away from that touch; it felt too good, too close to driving her toward a point she wasn't ready to reach yet.

Her fingers hooked the edge of his pants as she pulled away, and this time he didn't resist her attempts to strip him of the rest of his clothing. His eyes followed her as she did it. It sent heat skipping through her, the way even her simplest movements seemed to mesmerize him. The intensity—the power—that smoldered in his gaze might have been frightening to most...but not to her. He didn't look at anyone else that way. That power belonged to *her*.

She moved back to his lap. No clothing separated them, now. Nothing to keep them from joining completely as she settled back against him, as he guided his hard length into her soft center. Her arms draped around his neck, bracing against his broad shoulders as he lifted his hips and entered her more fully.

Her mouth formed a gentle *o* at the sudden fullness of him filling her. He watched her—mesmerized once more—gazing at her lips as if he hadn't already kissed them a hundred times before. He captured them in a swift kiss.

She returned it eagerly. The harder she kissed him, the harder he pulled her against him. The deeper he pushed inside of her. It became a game of desperate need and escalating bliss, and she wanted it to somehow both go on forever and to crescendo into sweet release.

Then magic began to hum between them again.

His hands traced over the small of her back, along her hips, her thighs...and it was *electric,* just as it had been earlier. A thousand little sparks of power shivering through and stimulating her skin, warming her blood, rattling her bones.

She let out a sound—something between a cry and a gasp—and it caused a...*shift.*

He was normally precise—controlled—in the way he made love to her. Firm, yet careful in the way his touch and his movements commanded her until she was spent and shivering against him.

But she could feel him slipping this time, losing himself in the waves of their magic and the rhythm of their bodies falling and rising against one another's.

There was nothing careful about the way his fingers fisted in her hair and yanked her closer.

Nothing *precise* about the way his mouth took hers and devoured it.

He grabbed her hips and pulled her completely onto him. Pressed a hand against her lower back. Held her still as he took over the work of keeping their rhythm, driving so deeply into her that the rush of pleasure stole her breath and nearly brought her to that release she craved. She caught herself at the last moment, legs trembling against him. Her head dipped toward her chest. Her eyes closed as she searched for balance.

Elander's fingers were beneath her chin a moment later, lifting her face back to his. "Look at me," he commanded.

She did—though her vision had started to blur from ecstasy—and the expression on his face, the dark heat in his gaze, the way he held *her* gaze as he continued to thrust, as he watched her release building...it was her final undoing.

Her body surrendered first, and her mind followed soon after. He caught her face in his hands and pulled her mouth back to his, so that her finishing cries fell against his lips. He seemed to be tasting them, swallowing them, savoring the sound as it filled him and pushed him to the same place she was currently floating within.

He held her tightly against him as he finished, holding her hips against his until every drop of himself was spent, until his raspy breaths calmed and his muscles finally unclenched.

He relaxed into the chair, and she sank down with him as little waves of pleasure continued to throb through her, making her too dizzy to properly sit up.

At least a full minute passed. She still didn't want to separate herself from him. Her heart was still pounding. Her skin was still tingling.

"Warm enough yet?" he asked, cupping her face and pulling her into one last, slow kiss.

She smiled a sleepy, content smile as he trailed his hand up and down her back. She curled into him, and he rested his face against the top of her head, breathing her in and occasionally pressing soft kisses against her hair.

It was a long time before they moved from this position. But eventually it had to happen; they peeled apart and cleaned up in the washroom. Cas pulled on a nightgown and then stumbled toward the bed. Elander followed soon after, wearing only a loose pair of breeches—one of many that had been stashed in the dresser beside the door. He had as many clothes in that dresser as she did, by this point; she wasn't entirely sure why they still bothered with separate rooms. What was hers was his.

But then she remembered...she *did* have something she was keeping to herself in this room, didn't she?

She fought the urge to look toward the washroom, toward that cabinet where she'd hidden the Blood crystals. She was going to wait until morning before she dealt with those crystals—isn't that what she'd told herself?

She crawled under the covers and turned her back to the hiding place.

Soon enough, she managed to fall asleep.

But it was a shallow, fitful slumber; her eyes were constantly fluttering open to make certain Elander was still beside her, her mind jolting awake every time a new, anxious thought fell into it.

He never left the room, but at some point he did move to collect some of those books she'd mentioned earlier. She blinked her eyes open and found him sitting up beside her, studying tattered pages with a distant, somewhat haunted look on his face.

Her hand roamed through the sheets and found its way to his bare chest, coming to rest across his heart. He laced his fingers through hers without taking his eyes away from his book.

She watched him until her eyes grew too heavy to stay open, and she tried not to think about the memories hidden in the room next to them, or about what new disasters tomorrow might bring.

CHAPTER 16

THE NEXT MORNING, CAS JOLTED AWAKE SO VIOLENTLY THAT she nearly toppled over the side of the bed.

She caught herself against the bedside table, but her hand continued to shake, rattling the lamp on that table, shifting the stack of notes upon it and sending a few sheets of parchment drifting to the floor.

Elander was already awake, reclining in the chair by the window with one of the books Emrys had sent open in his lap. He closed it immediately as he caught sight of her. "That same dream again?" he guessed, setting the book aside and starting to his feet.

She took a moment to calm her pounding heart before she tried to reply. "Yes. But it...it ended differently this time."

"How so?"

She concentrated, trying to catch the pieces of it that

were fleeing as her brain continued to wake up. "The blood that flooded the streets, the city, *all* that blood...it disappeared. Everything turned lighter, calmer, and at the end it became almost...pleasant."

He stretched to his full height and ran a hand through his sleep-mussed hair, considering. "That's a good sign, isn't it? If it actually *is* some sort of prophetic magic manifesting, as in the past, then the less bloody, the better, right?"

"Maybe."

He gave her a curious look.

Less bloody *was* better. Of course it was. But the question was *why* it had turned less bloody.

And the only answer she could come up with in that moment was...disturbing.

She bowed her head and continued to focus, hoping she was misremembering the nightmare. It was strange to want the horrific, original version of it back, but at least that was a monster she was intimately familiar with by this point—so it had gotten easier to handle.

But now, instead of watching the end of this dream unfold through her own eyes, as in the past, she had been watching from the bloody streets alongside her friends, staring up at herself. Herself, who had been standing on the outer wall encircling the palace grounds, as always.

Until she'd disappeared.

And when her dream self had disappeared, so had the blood.

The dream had flickered—a blink—and the wall she'd stood upon had suddenly been empty, the sun had emerged, the birds had started to chirp again, the air had turned crisp and clean...

The blood had disappeared.

But only after *she* had disappeared.

The vivid image of herself, there one moment and gone the next, made her stomach churn.

"Casia?"

She lifted her head and found Elander watching her closely, one of his hands braced against the chair he'd started to settle back into.

"It's complicated." She hugged her arms against herself. "But maybe I'm misremembering, and it's nothing to worry about. It's...it's probably nothing."

He frowned, but something else distracted him before he could question her further; his head tilted toward the door and his eyes narrowed in concentration.

Cas let her attention shift toward the world outside of that door too, and she felt a hint of what had likely caught his attention. "I sense powerful magic."

He nodded.

"The goddesses are back?"

"Yes," he said, though uncertainty clung to the word for some reason.

She pushed her dream a little further from her thoughts. "We shouldn't keep them waiting," she said, crawling from the bed and planting her feet firmly on the cold floor.

They agreed to meet downstairs. Elander went to his own room to get ready. Cas changed, cleaned herself up, and then headed out on her own.

She wasn't walking alone for long, however; Nessa caught sight of her only a moment after she'd stepped into the hallway.

"I want to show you something," said Nessa, as she hurried to her side and locked arms with her.

Cas started to protest—she truly *didn't* want to keep those goddesses waiting, or deal with the tantrum that the Storm Goddess would likely throw if she didn't hurry, but Nessa was insistent. So she let herself be dragged down to the second floor, and then to the end of a hallway that led out to a grand, curving balcony.

The chill morning air bit at her nose and cheeks. Cas thought about protesting again—or at least going back for a coat—but Nessa put both hands on her shoulders and steered her toward the edge of the balcony.

"Look," she said, pointing at something below.

Cas looked—it wasn't as though Nessa was giving her a choice not to—and she saw a crowd of people huddled around the main gate to the palace grounds. Her muscles tensed as worst-case scenarios flashed through her mind. But, upon looking closer, they didn't *appear* as if they were here to storm that gate...

"What are they doing?"

Nessa linked their arms once more and gave a little squeeze. "They're hoping for a glimpse of *you*. The Supplanter Queen who did battle with the gods yesterday. It's all anyone is talking about this morning—you and Elander, and the show of magic the two of you put on. Laurent finally managed to have that meeting with Syndra earlier, and she said the city is full of people swapping stories about what they supposedly saw or heard. And it's the same thing here in the palace." She let out a little sigh as she added, "I haven't been able to get anyone to fully focus on the tasks I've assigned them."

"It was a lesser-spirit we did battle with, not a god," Cas pointed out.

"Like that makes that much of a difference to the average person."

Cas tried for a smile in response to the one Nessa was beaming at her. She mostly managed it.

She quickly returned her attention to the people below, and her heart skipped a beat as one of them caught sight of her and pointed. Several other gazes lifted in her direction, and the rising hum of excited chatter could be heard even from where she stood.

It was a stark contrast to the last time she'd used powerful magic in this city. She'd had less control then, and the destruction she'd accidentally caused had been followed by an angry mob arriving at the palace and demanding that Varen make her answer for her crimes —which had led to a chain of events that had ended with Asra's death and all the painful, devastating things that had followed it.

Most of the crowd had spotted her. They were pointing up to the balcony, and a few of them appeared to be attempting to convince the guards to let them inside for a more personal visit.

"I feel a bit like a caged animal on display," Cas mused.

Nessa giggled and leaned her head against Cas's arm.

The sound of paws scampering across the plush hall carpet reached them. Silverfoot wiggled through the partially open balcony door a moment later, and Rhea's relieved voice soon followed. "There you are, Casia."

"Did you see this?" asked Nessa. She held her arms out for Silverfoot, and as soon as he was secured within them, she spun him around and let him get a good look at the crowd by the gate.

Rhea focused only for a moment on the images Silverfoot sent to her, and then she looked to Cas. "Never mind that crowd. There is a far more interesting one awaiting you in my office."

"Yes, I thought I felt a surge of divine energy. Nephele and Inya are back?"

"Not just them."

Cas thought about the uncertainty that had been in Elander's tone earlier, and now a similar feeling flickered through her. Rhea beckoned, and she followed without hesitation. She was eager to escape the crowd that was ogling her anyhow.

"Your latest display of magic has fully caught the attention of not only our city, but also our divine allies, it seems," Rhea told her as they walked.

They reached her office before she had time to explain further, and so she simply opened the door and urged Cas inside with a nod.

Cas stepped into the room. The sunlight streaming through the window was unnaturally bright—blinding, really—and as she uselessly tried to tilt her face away from the light, a feeling of immense magic flooded over her. The only thing she could compare it to was the moment when Solatis had briefly swept her from this world, when that upper-goddess's power had wrapped her in an embrace that had been warm and energizing but still borderline overwhelming. Little bumps erupted across her skin. Her heart fluttered rapidly—a startled bird in a cage.

Her eyes finally adjusted to the abnormally bright sunlight.

She blinked several more times, just to be certain of what she was seeing.

She had been expecting the two familiar goddesses

of her court, but she was rendered speechless by the other two standing beside them. Cas had seen these other two only in books and in works of art, but it was immediately obvious who they were.

The *entire* Court of the Sun had taken up residence in the office, apparently waiting for her arrival.

There was the Goddess of Stars, Cepheid, with her porcelain skin and a body muscular enough that, for a moment, Cas believed the stories that said she had carried the stars across the night sky and hung them by hand. She was dressed in a flowing shirt and pants made of some sort of silky material, the waves of dark blue fabric a bold contrast to her pale complexion. Her eyes were molten lead. Her hair—a soft, rosy white that made Cas think of delicate pearls—was woven through with thin strands of silver that glistened with every movement of her head.

And behind her, studying a small dragon statue on the shelf behind Rhea's desk, was the Goddess of Sky, her true identity heralded by the black staff she casually leaned against. In all of her portrayals in books and otherwise, she was rarely seen without this staff. The swirling cloud shape at its end resembled the one at the center of the thin headpiece she wore.

Indre—most humans called her—though Cas was familiar with her true name, Aendryr, as this was how Elander and Nephele referred to her. She and Nephele had been sisters in their mortal lives, yet the two goddesses looked almost nothing alike. She was shorter, almost dainty compared to the towering Storm Goddess, while the straight locks framing her narrow face were much darker, the color of a starless night sky. She glanced briefly at Cas, and her eyes seemed to sparkle and shift between arresting shades of blue and green, like gentle, rippling reflections of sky against a calm sea. Cas had seen eyes this oddly bright in only one other being before—Queen Soryn of Sadira, who carried the Sky Goddess's mark and magic.

The Goddess of Stars spoke first, her voice deep, almost rough. "Shadowslayer."

Cas automatically reached for the sword that usually rested against her hip, but realized that she'd left her weapon in her room—and that this weapon was not what Cepheid was focused on.

The goddess was calling *her* Shadowslayer.

"*Godkiller*," that goddess continued. "*Sunbringer*. There is no shortage of monikers the people of this city have come up with for their new queen, it seems. I've been listening to them. Watching them."

Something about the way she said *watching* left Cas feeling strangely cold.

"We've *all* been watching your story unfold with great interest," the Moon Goddess put in, her kind voice rewarming the space. "You already knew that Nephele and I were watching and working on your behalf, and you called to me yesterday, didn't you?"

So she hadn't imagined that moment in the river.

"And you answered me."

The goddess smiled. "It didn't require much effort. Your power has grown stronger."

"Though still not strong enough, most likely," the Goddess of Sky commented, her voice distant and her eyes back on that dragon statue on the shelf. Wispy clouds stretched into existence around her as she spoke, similar to the lightning that occasionally accompanied her sister whenever Nephele's moods shifted. The swirls of grey further muted the light in the room.

Nessa moved to the window and pushed the curtains completely open. She moved confidently, though a bit stiffly, as if determined not to let the over-whelming power in the space get to her.

Elander arrived a moment later. He didn't look entirely surprised to see the host of goddesses that awaited him—he had been the first to sense their arrival, after all—but he did visibly tense as his gaze slid over the Goddess of Stars. They had been close once, Cas recalled. But the goddess had turned his back on him soon after his fall from his fully divine status.

Cas wondered what he was thinking—what it felt like, to be reunited after however many years it had been —but now was not the time to discuss it.

She met the Moon Goddess's eyes and pointedly stuck to the matter at hand. "To what do we owe this visit?"

"Our dear Nephele was insistent that we could *all* answer your calls for help more thoroughly," said Inya.

"Annoyingly insistent," added the Goddess of Sky, the clouds around her billowing, growing darker and thicker.

The Storm Goddess looked entirely unrepentant.

Cas nearly smiled; if nothing else, she had to give the tempestuous goddess credit for being stubborn enough to get things done.

"Which is why we've arrived with a concrete plan to help," said Nephele, "as we were just discussing with your Master of Correspondence before she went to fetch you."

Cas gave Rhea a questioning look.

"Weapons, to start with," Rhea told her. "They've come here with a plan to better arm our soldiers."

The Storm Goddess looked pleased with herself, as she so often did. "As we mentioned the last time we were here, a substantial amount of Solatis's magic spilled into this world upon her departure from it, threatening to destabilize things."

"So we have been searching for a way to turn this into our advantage instead," explained the Moon Goddess. "We've gathered up what we could of this wayward magic, and we've nearly perfected a method of concentrating it into something useful." She reached into the inner pocket of her coat and withdrew what appeared to be a long, shimmering thread of silk. Then she took a small dagger from a sheath hidden at her back and held it carefully out in front of her.

Cas and her companions watched, captivated, as the goddess wound the thread around the dagger. Both thread and dagger glowed brightly—separate lines of red and yellow light that soon merged into a single blaze as bold and bright as the rising sun.

"The process isn't much different from the one that allows us to transfer some of our power to chosen human servants." Inya's dagger continued to glow faintly orange as she spoke. "It won't elevate mortal weapons to the level of the blade that Solatis gifted you, Casia, but these Sun-magic infused weapons *will* allow your army to stand more of a chance against whatever atrocities the Dark God and his court decide to unleash upon you."

Cas fought the urge to shift where she stood. It was the word *unleash* that had done it—the heavy acknowledgment of the darkness still to come. To be let loose upon their world. Could even magic-infused weapons stand up to all the terrifying things the Dark God had at his disposal?

She didn't want to admit to this skepticism herself—for fear of seeming ungrateful—but Elander readily voiced it for her.

"Is there a catch to this magic?" he asked.

The Storm Goddess took the dagger from Inya and inspected it, then glanced up at Elander and bared her teeth in a smile. "No catch," she said. "The Court of Solatis has always been home to the most generous of the divine beings. Why should things be any different now that she's gone?"

Inya's gaze circled over each of them in turn, her eyes pleading for cooperation between them all.

Nephele and Elander both fell silent, and Inya quietly said, "No weapon we could create through this method will be enough to stop the Dark God himself, nor any of the Marr who serve him. We're still at a loss regarding how to do that. Not a *catch*—but certainly a downside."

A long pause, and then Nessa surprised Cas by stepping forward and reaching for the dagger Nephele held.

Its glow had mostly faded by this point. The goddess let it go without comment, her indigo eyes sparkling as she watched Nessa turn the magicked weapon this way and that, inspecting it for herself.

"It's better than nothing, isn't it?" Nessa asked, determination hardening her words. "I say we get started making some weapons."

A SHORT TIME LATER, the group of them assembled outside the armory attached to the palace's main training facility. Zev and Laurent had joined them, and there was a lively discussion underway regarding which weapons would be most useful—and the most compatible—with magic.

Cas leaned against the wall a short distance from most of the others, watching them debate and experiment with various blades and bows. The words of the Goddess of the Sun whispered through her thoughts, reminding her again of the task she'd been given.

An alliance of divine beings and mortals unlike anything the realms have ever known...

It was happening, wasn't it?

She should have been excited about the progress they were making. And she was. But she couldn't shake free of all her many questions.

The goddesses were all stunning to look at—nearly impossible to pry her gaze away from—but the Goddess of Stars drew her attention more than any of the others. And every time she caught sight of that goddess, her thoughts circled back to her dream from last night, and then to *all* of the dreams she'd had in the past that had proven prophetic...

Because this goddess presided over such revelatory magic.

Aloof. That was how Elander had described the Star Goddess. It was a miracle that she had graced them with her presence at all. Even now, she seemed determined to keep herself set apart from the rest of her court—she had wandered all the way to the other end of the training ground, and she appeared to be talking to herself, completely indifferent to anything the others were doing.

But she was *here*, wasn't she?

Cas would not miss this opportunity. She steeled herself and made her way toward the goddess with determined steps.

Her nerve faltered a bit as Cepheid's eyes turned her direction, but she kept moving forward. Those eyes blinked rapidly as she drew closer, and for several seconds they turned entirely white—nothing more than pinpricks of light against a pale canvas of flawless skin. Silver swirled into them once more as she asked in a frigid voice, "Is there something that you want from me?"

"Yes." Cas swallowed hard. The words were right on the tip of her tongue, but the goddess's power seemed to swell and push them down every time Cas tried to speak.

The goddess shifted her gaze to the group at the armory door. "You want to know what your recurring dreams mean."

"How...how did you know about my dreams?"

"Because I have been *watching*."

It was the same thing she'd said about the people of the city, and it made Cas just as uncomfortable to hear it a second time. "You've been watching me? Without my knowledge? How—"

"Not *you*, specifically. The stars tied to you."

Cas's gaze lifted automatically to the glass ceiling, though it was still too early for any stars to be visible to her eyes.

The goddess was staring at her when she lowered her gaze. Her expression was not particularly kind, but it was not openly hostile either. Staring into her silver eyes simply made Cas feel like she was staring into an overcast sky on a cold, eerily silent winter's night, when the promise of snow hung in the air; it was somehow both peaceful and foreboding.

"Not the heavenly sort," said the goddess, and then she took a small silver ball from one of the many pouches attached to her belt. She stretched her palm out flat, letting the sphere roll about until it came to rest in the center of her hand. As it settled, the sapphire gems upon its face began to sparkle. The goddess exhaled a slow, purposeful breath, and the sphere unraveled itself, spinning into ribbons of silver that shot into the space directly above them, separating and stretching out until they'd formed a border. Another sigh of breath, and a hundred little points of light blinked to life within that border.

A map of the sky.

Cas remembered something from the conversation she'd had during her last meeting with the Moon and Storm Goddesses. "The Animatir? Isn't that what this is called? The *Map of Souls.*"

Cepheid neither confirmed nor denied the moniker.

"You can see the movements of the divine beings with it, can't you?"

Again, neither a confirmation nor a denial.

Cas pressed on, anyway. "My brother...you told Inya and Nephele that this map revealed he was growing stronger, right?"

"As is the upper-god he serves."

"You mean Malaphar is..."

"Drawing nearer," the goddess said, her gaze narrowing on a large, crimson star. "He's been dwelling in the upper-heavens for these past weeks, but I can see him overtaking the mortal skies soon. A moment of reckoning and retribution is at hand."

Cas tried not to let the words shake her. Elander had told her that this goddess had a tendency to speak in riddles—it seemed to be a trend among the divine—so there was a chance her prediction wasn't as ominous as it sounded.

A *small* chance at least.

Cas cleared her throat. "What about *me*? And those dreams I keep having...do you know what they mean? Can your map explain them?"

"The stars do not explain."

"Yes, but—"

"However, I *do* know when anyone with a great concentration of my magic uses it. The stars that surround these blessed souls have certain patterns, making them like constellations in my own private sky.

And yes—you are one such constellation. Bright. Bold. Demanding my attention." She searched the stars, swiping through them as one flipped through the pages of a book when in search of a certain quote or scene.

Finally, she paused and focused her gaze upon a cluster of faint, purplish-colored lights. Circled her hand around it. The lights swirled and followed her movement, brightening as they did. "And every night for weeks now," she said, "the lights of your cluster have been flickering. I've heard the whispers of your inner mind whenever I listen closely to those lights."

"So those dreams *are* prophetic magic at work?"

"Some parts of them. Maybe not all."

Cas chewed her bottom lip. She had dealt with more than her fair share of divine beings speaking in these riddles. The trick, she'd learned, was to be careful. Precise in your questioning.

"Last night I dreamt that I disappeared from this city," she said. "And when I did, so did all the blood and violent feelings that have been at the center of that recurring nightmare. What does that disappearance mean?"

The goddess kept her eyes on the stars.

Cas pressed on, even though her next question frightened her. "If I disappear, will it lead to less bloodshed? Is that the way to peace in this mortal world?"

"Disappear entirely? Maybe not. It could also be a

sign of a coming sacrifice. Some part of yourself that's destined to be lost."

The little points of light seemed to react to this suggestion, flashing and swirling about. The goddess tilted her head, studying them. "Yes...a great sacrifice that will cause a great shift," she said, more to herself than Cas. "And after that...what appears to be a difficult choice."

This was not particularly surprising to hear—no war was won without sacrifice and hard choices—and Cas had been preparing herself for the worst since the moment she took her sword from Solatis.

But for some reason, hearing this goddess speak of such things unsettled her in a way that made her want to sink to her knees. Her mouth was nearly too dry to speak, but she managed to ask: "What kind of sacrifice?"

Cepheid's eyes widened slightly, and the glow from her map danced upon them like beams of a lighthouse sweeping across a stormy sea. "Ah, now that is the question, isn't it?"

Cas stared at the goddess, refusing to look at her stars and whatever destiny they might have held.

"I don't have all the answers for you, Shadowslayer." The goddess considered her out of the corner of her eye, most of her focus still on the map. "The stars do not explain, as I said. They give guidance, but they do not speak in absolutes."

Then give me guidance.

The goddess considered her more fully for a moment, as though she'd heard that plea.

Maybe she had, same as Inya had heard the plea for help while she was in the river.

"What I *can* tell you," said the goddess, "is that the stars tied to you in this life are the same ones that were tied to you in your past life. You first caught my eye nearly twenty-four years ago, upon your death in that former life. I noticed your stars and all the chaos that surrounded them. A powerful love, a violent death...and a rebirth. A *breaking point*. I've been watching you ever since."

"A breaking point?"

She nodded, and the lights within the Map of Souls scrolled rapidly as she swiped her hand through them once more. Seconds later, she seemed to find what she was looking for. She drew her hand away, clutching it to her chest.

The pinpricks of light tangled and spun together... and then shattered in a silent explosion that sent stardust shimmering in every direction.

"They happen every now and then," said the goddess, her voice hushed, "these points in time during which the stars themselves lose their way, and even *I* cannot guess at what they are trying to reveal."

"And you see another one of these points coming? Do you think my dreams are warning of this?"

Cepheid inhaled deeply. The map grew dark. The

edges of it collapsed and twisted their way back toward her, winding up into the shape of a sphere once more. "I don't keep the stars' secrets for my own amusement, despite what you might have heard about me." She tucked the sphere back into her belt pouch. "I simply don't speak of things I'm not certain of."

"But the end of my previous life was one of these breaking points," Cas thought aloud. "You *are* certain of that much. It changed something in this world—"

"You misunderstand," the goddess interrupted. Her voice had turned reverent and oddly faraway, as if she was holding a conversation with those stars rather than the person standing right in front of her. "My dear...it changed *everything*. Why do you think I've been watching you ever since?"

Cas couldn't think of a good response to that, so she said nothing.

The goddess seemed content to let the conversation drop. She went back to her wandering, mumbling to herself, and Cas watched her for moment before letting her eyes trail back to her friends.

Elander felt her gaze, glanced toward her, and gave her a slight smile. She smiled back, and she hoped that he couldn't see the uncertainty in her eyes from a distance. The world had changed the day they fell in love in that past life.

But was it for better or worse?

What had they really done?

CHAPTER 17

Once the weapons were dealt with, the debate turned, instead, to next moves, to arguments about priorities and possible allies, and it didn't take long before Cas and her group found themselves at an impasse.

"Too many battles in too many different places," Laurent commented, summarizing all their simmering frustrations. "We need to be with our allies in Mistwilde. But we also need to be *here*. And in a host of other realms, solidifying alliances... It's hard enough trying to win support for our new regime. Harder when we have no time to meet allies face-to-face. Meanwhile, the Dark God and his followers can strike essentially anywhere and everywhere in the empire..."

"They *are* striking all over," Rhea corrected. "Another monster sighting in Sadira just this morning—some sort of demonic beast tore its way through the capital city."

Cas's gaze shot toward her in alarm.

"The queen is fine," Rhea added, quickly. "But her advisors are trying to get her to evacuate from Kosrith. That capital city seems to be becoming a bit of a hot spot for divine activity."

"Likely because of Soryn's ties to me," Cas said, quietly.

"Doubt they'll have much luck convincing her to leave," Zev muttered.

There was a murmur of agreement. Soryn would not abandon her city or its soldiers, they were all certain.

Something painful flickered through Cas at the thought; she wanted to see that young queen herself. To make sure she was truly safe. She was so *tired* of not being able to be everywhere she needed to be...

So she was going to do something about it.

Now.

"The Goddess of Sands has a servant that can help mortals with moving more freely, correct?" She looked to Nephele and Inya, who had drifted away from the humans, along with the other two goddesses. "Weren't you two going to pay her another visit, last time we talked?"

"We did pay her another visit," Inya replied, frowning. "She was still not interested in joining us, despite our repeated attempts to sway her."

The other goddesses mirrored her frown, and this

same discouraged look soon overcame her human allies as well.

So Cas made another decision, quick as that: She would sway the Goddess of Time herself.

It was a tangible, fixed goal—not like the shifting uncertainties of the stars—and so she latched on to it with every ounce of focus and energy she had to spare.

"How can I reach her?" Cas demanded.

Three of the four goddesses exchanged uncertain looks; Nephele merely appeared amused as she fisted a hand and rested her tilted head upon it.

"One of you could take me to her, couldn't you?" Cas pressed. "Through the use of your havens' doorways, perhaps? I'll go to her and plead our case myself."

"Of course you will." Nephele laughed. Her tone was not combative for once. There might have been a hint of pride in her bright eyes too—though that was likely wishful thinking on Cas's part.

The rest of the Sun Court still looked considerably less enthusiastic. They were all still frowning, a mixture of worry and disapproval playing across their beautiful faces.

"Oh, why not?" Nephele said, interrupting the uneasy silence that had started to settle. She fixed her eyes on Cas and ignored the beginnings of protests from the rest of her court. "I will take you, Little Queen. It should be an entertaining way to spend the afternoon."

Elander started to speak, but Nephele held up a

slender hand. "I know what you're going to say. But we don't need your input or company on this particular trip. Do you remember the *last* visit you paid to Santi? You may have put that incident out of your mind, but I *doubt* the Goddess of Time has forgotten it."

"What is she talking about?" asked Cas.

"It's a fun story." Nephele's lips curved in that mischievous way that usually came before she started causing chaos. "Shall I tell it?"

"It's not that fun," corrected Elander, "and I still don't think I'm entirely to blame for what happened—but it doesn't really matter at the moment."

"All the same, it's likely better if you stay behind." Nephele arched a brow. "What? Do you not trust me to bring your queen back to you in one piece?"

Elander looked fully prepared to list all of the reasons why he, in fact, did *not* trust her to do this, but Rhea cleared her throat before he could.

"I'll go with her," she volunteered in her familiar peacekeeping tone. It was the same tone she had been using to break up arguments between Cas and Zev for years.

Nephele and Elander are basically squabbling siblings, Cas thought, not for the first time.

Nephele clapped her hands, causing sparks to fly and a noise like thunder to boom through the expansive space. "It's settled, then. One for moral support, one for divine support—that's all we need. But the ceiling in here is stifling me; I'll need a more wide-open space to work with if I'm hauling both of you along." And then she was off, her long, pale blue hair fluttering around her as she began to concentrate her power. She didn't look back to see if they were following her.

Silverfoot was the first to scamper after the goddess, his ears and tail twitching as though he sensed an adventure was about to start.

Rhea followed him after a moment of hesitation.

Elander caught Cas's eye as she turned to follow as well. "Be careful, please."

It sounded like an order, so she gave him a teasing salute which made his jaw relax the tiniest bit—almost enough to give her a smile.

Nephele was already at the training ground's exit, where she had paused and started to focus her power in earnest. Cas could feel the warm shift in the air that always came before a divine being transported themselves.

She jogged to catch up with Rhea and Silverfoot. "The Storm Goddess doesn't frighten me, you know," she quietly told Rhea, "and she's more than proven herself trustworthy at this point, I think. I could go alone."

"I *want* to go with you."

Cas gave her a curious look.

"I owe a lot to the Air spirit and her magic," Rhea explained, nodding to Silverfoot, who still trotted a fair distance ahead of them with his snout lifted, eagerly inhaling the air and occasionally snapping his mouth, as if trying to catch sparks of the Storm Goddess's magic on his tongue. "If she's dwelling in her patron goddess's haven, then I'd like to be the first to meet her...and thank her."

Cas nodded, understanding. She was secretly grateful for the company, anyway...and Rhea likely knew this too, even if she would never point it out.

"Besides," Rhea added, "Zev still talks about the time he spent in the Healing Goddess's haven. It's likely getting old to you by this point, after all the places you've seen, but how many humans ever have a chance to see some of these divine places, hm?"

Cas secretly *did* hope that her days of hopping between realms would soon be over, but she didn't say so. "I guess I hadn't thought about it that way."

"Understandable, given the other things you've had to think about," said Rhea with a shrug.

"Well," said Cas, "as an experienced traveler, I feel the need to warn you—the *getting there* part is not fun."

They would have to travel to the Storm Goddess's haven first. As far as Cas knew, the Marr and their respective servants could travel to their *own* haven from just about anywhere, and most could come and go as they pleased throughout places in the mortal realm that weren't bereft of magic.

Getting into *other* godhavens was not as straightforward, however—so most of them utilized doorways within their own havens that would allow them to travel to those others, so long as the divine being on the other side was receptive to visitors.

Cas was still explaining the nuances of this traveling system to Rhea when Nephele turned to them, wearing that slightly chaotic smile of hers once more.

"Shall we?" The goddess beckoned them closer.

"Brace yourself," Cas told Rhea, taking hold of her hand and giving it a little squeeze.

Nephele's eyes briefly closed, and the air around her crackled with energy that soon engulfed them all.

Silverfoot snapped more viciously at these sparks of energy, which seemed to amuse the goddess; her eyes fluttered open and her expression was softer than usual. She bent and collected the fox in her arms, and once he was secured, she lifted a hand between their small group. Snapped her fingers.

Then came the familiar, uncomfortable pulling in Cas's chest. The sky whirled, the clouds spun, and the ground and everything else *whooshed* away, briefly taking all her senses with it.

They crash landed in a long hall with shiny black floors, their less-than-graceful arrival echoing loudly through the space.

Their time in Stormhaven was brief. Nephele hardly allowed them to catch their breath and massage away their soreness before she was marching them into the haven's room of doorways.

Some of the doors did not appear to be functioning; all of the gateways that led to the divine havens of the Dark God's court—those of the Death, Fire, Ice, and Serpent deities—had symbols that were greyed out, blending in with the weathered grey doors. Most of the others had emblems that glowed in various colors.

Nephele led them to a door that featured one of these glowing emblems—a shimmering, dark gold symbol in the shape of rolling sand dunes.

They stepped through it.

Traveling by way of the doors was not *quite* as disorienting as being pulled along as a passenger of a divine being; the trip lasted only a few seconds, and Cas and Rhea both managed to land on their feet when they emerged into the Sand Goddess's domain. Silverfoot landed lightly, bounced for a few paces, and then started exploring, trotting about with his nose lifted and his ears twitching.

The scent of spice and dry earth was the first thing Cas noticed. The second thing was the strange, gritty ground beneath her, which was solid enough to support her weight and yet still felt thin and unsettled—as if it might shift and collapse at any moment. She couldn't see the ceiling. The space above her simply stretched on and on and on, yawning into a wide, expansive darkness.

Dark was the overall impression she had of this haven. Although the walls and floor occasionally shimmered with golden light, it wasn't enough to illuminate the entire space. It felt as if they were underground—as if they'd descended into a strange abyss where the air was oddly thick and oppressive and absorbing most of the sound and light within it.

Nephele had not landed alongside them. She was *somewhere* within that abyss—Cas could vaguely sense her magic—but she couldn't see her. Panic briefly flickered in her chest at the possibility that this had been a trick, that the goddess had carried them here only to leave them behind. Another *test*, perhaps. She was fond of giving those.

The fear was short-lived; a minute later the Storm Goddess appeared in the distant darkness, the pulses of lightning within her skin heralding her movements as she approached them.

"Seems we've caught her at a bad time," said the goddess.

Cas squinted toward the various illuminated patches around them, searching for signs of the haven's owner. "She's not here?"

"Not all that surprising, is it? Considering she can walk more fluidly than any being between not only realms, but timelines—through the past, the present, some possible futures..." Nephele glanced over her shoulder, eyes narrowing toward an exceptionally bright vein of gold that had just glowed to life on a distant wall, before she leveled her gaze back on Cas. "Wait here," she instructed. "I'll see if one of her servants can summon her."

So Cas and Rhea waited, side-by-side, in the dark. It was difficult to tell how much time was passing. A fragrant wind blew from somewhere up above, and Cas's head slowly tipped back, still searching for the ceiling, for an opening in this cave that might have been letting that spiced breeze waft through.

She still saw nothing except blackness.

But she *felt* as if there was more within that blackness—as if the darkness was somehow...aware. Like something inside of it was staring back at her.

She might have been used to traveling to these havens, but she suspected she would never truly feel like she belonged in these places; they were simply too big, too impossible, too *strange*.

Silverfoot remained at a distance, circling and sniffing. He appeared to catch the trail of something, and he pressed his nose to the ground and kept it there as he loped his way across the space, throwing up little puffs of sparkling dust as he went.

The fox stopped his sniffing just before he reached a wall covered in swirls of gold that were glowing faintly. He settled back on his haunches and stared at those swirls, his tail thumping for a few slow, uncertain beats before quickening to the unmistakable speed of a creature thrilled to see its master.

That master emerged—seemingly from nowhere—seconds later.

"The Air spirit herself," Rhea said in an awed little voice.

Cas felt that same sense of awe blossoming in her chest. She had seen this spirit once before when it had helped her and Zev travel back to the mortal realm from the haven of the Healing Goddess...but it looked different in this place, wrapped in the pure, unbridled energies of its own patron goddess.

She was the same tiny creature—perhaps half Cas's height—with wide eyes, pale skin, and wings folded against her back. But now she was surrounded by green, smoke-like energy. Her wings were not the iridescent, paper-thin extensions that Cas remembered; they were made of thick, golden feathers that ruffled about in her energy and allowed her slender body to hover without any obvious effort. Her movements were as graceful as a dancer's as she moved closer to Silverfoot, knelt, lifted him onto his back paws, and briefly pressed her forehead to his.

The two creatures seemed to be conversing about something. Silverfoot's eyes occasionally brightened, as did the smoky energy surrounding the spirit. The spirit had ribbon-like appendages protruding from her forehead, and they waved about, twirling and snapping in response to Silverfoot's friendly growls and yips.

After a few moments, the fox's head turned toward Rhea. The spirit mirrored the motion. Silverfoot gave a happy little bark and scampered back to Rhea. He circled around her a few times, beckoning her to follow him, and then he led her back to his new acquaintance.

Cas stayed at a distance, allowing Rhea to offer her thanks to that spirit—and whatever else she wanted to say—in private. Meanwhile, she wandered around the space, observing more of the abyss they'd landed in. She didn't intend to go far, but the sound of shifting sand caught her attention and she drifted toward it.

She eventually came upon a wide gateway. On either side of the opening, golden light trailed up and down the stone walls, and falling over these banners of light were waterfalls of sand. As she studied the glowing, cascading curtains of sand, she couldn't help but think of the earth forming and falling away—of Belegor, the upper-god whose hands had supposedly molded their physical world. He was the patron god of this deity they'd come to see.

And now he was gone, just as Solatis was.

Cas still could not wrap her mind fully around the idea that these powerful deities could ever cease to exist.

What would it take to erase the last of those three?

To protect their world from him?

The movements of glistening sand brought to mind

the stars from Cepheid's map too—that conversation with the Star Goddess weighed heavily on her mind even though she was trying not to think about it. The chaos of her own personal stars, the *breaking point*, the past and all the questions she had about it...

What was it that Nephele had just said a few minutes ago, regarding the goddess who dwelled in this dark place? *She can walk between timelines...through the past, the present, some possible futures...*

If that was true, then maybe the Goddess of Time could be helpful to them in more ways than one.

Rhea rejoined her after a few minutes. As they stared at the shifting sands together, a question tumbled from Cas's mouth before she could catch it. "If you had a chance to go back into the past, would you take it?"

Rhea cocked her head. "What for?"

"I don't know. To see things. To understand them better. To...to fix them, maybe."

Rhea considered this for a long time before replying. "I don't think it's that easy to know what needs fixing," she finally said. "Things that happen—the good, the bad—we know so little about life that I think sometimes it's impossible to say what's actually good and what's actually bad."

Cas nodded, even though she wished she could disagree. *It would be easier if things were clearly one way or the other.*

"Although..." Rhea added, after another moment of

thought, "I suppose if I had some way of knowing what was truly good and what was bad, then perhaps I'd change *some* things. Who knows?"

A new sound interrupted their musings—the static crackling of the Storm Goddess and her magic returning to them. She cleared her throat, obviously annoyed that Cas had wandered so far. She said nothing about it, however; she simply motioned for them to follow her.

They made their way into a long, narrow room lined with twisting gold columns that glinted from an internal light source of some kind. The path between these columns led to a grand archway made of stone. More sand was falling on and around this archway, some of it siphoning through intricate grooves upon the structure itself, but far more tumbling down and creating a barrier in the space underneath it.

And beyond the arch, on the other side of this wall of falling sand, Cas could just make out what appeared to be a gilded chair occupied by a large, shadowy figure.

CHAPTER 18

"Santi." Nephele's tone was as close as it ever came to respectful. "Goddess of the Sands of Time and the Vastness of Space—"

"You're here again," came a harsh whisper. "Do you ever stop pestering?"

"I've brought someone new with me this time," Nephele said, somewhat stiffly. "Someone you might like to meet."

Cas did not need the Storm Goddess to speak for her, so she stepped past that goddess and offered a slight bow and an introduction of her own. "My name is Valori de Solasen, Queen of the mortal Kingdom of Melech—"

Santi interrupted her with a loud yawn. "Be quiet. *Both* of you."

A few sparks flew from the goddess behind her, and Cas tensed, anticipating an entire storm.

But there was something to be said for the advantage of *home* perhaps, because Nephele's temper quieted more swiftly than usual now that they were in the Sand Goddess's domain. She merely gave a dismissive sniff, and then she stepped to the side and folded her arms across her chest.

The figure on the other side of the sands leaned forward in her chair, and the air filled with the sound of what might have been jewelry clinking together. Cas still could not see the goddess's features clearly—only a dark outline and glints of gold shimmering in between the lines of falling sand—but she could feel the hard stare that had been fixed upon her.

"You don't need to introduce yourself at this point, do you, dear?" The goddess spoke as though she had just woken from a deep sleep, each of her words in danger of collapsing into a yawn. "Your existence is no secret to anyone who has been paying attention to the happenings on the human plane. You are The Queen That's Come Home. You have taken a mortal crown, and now you seek a divine one to go with it. A crown worthy of commanding not only mortals but the gods themselves. Am I wrong?"

Cas chose her next words very carefully. "I...I do seek your help, if that's what you're asking. But I'm not here to *command* you to give it."

"To plead for it then?"

The question made Cas bristle, but she swallowed

her objections and fought the urge to fix the goddess with a hard stare of her own; if showing humility could win her the favor of this being, then she could manage that.

"Yes," she said.

A contemplative sigh, followed by movement and more clinking of jewelry.

The cascading sand slowed to a trickle, and the goddess stood and stepped through the archway to meet them.

She was beautiful, as Cas was starting to suspect *all* the gods and goddesses were. Her ebony hair was plaited and woven through with threads of gold. More gold dusted her brown skin, and gleaming bangles jingled at her wrists and ankles. She wore an ivory gown that accented her plentiful curves, the waves of its shimmering fabric cinched with a belt. Feathery appendages flanked her head, draping from behind her ears, and sets of similar wings flared from her elbows, her hips, her ankles. They flapped lazily up and down as she stood before them, allowing her to occasionally hover in the same delicate manner as the Air spirit who served her— even though she was at least three times the size of that spirit.

"And why would I answer these pleas?" she asked.

Anxiety started to trace its familiar path through her stomach, so Cas spoke quickly before it could uncoil completely and overwhelm her. "Because the upper-god you once served is now gone, destroyed by the same divine being that I am currently trying to stop, and I thought you might want a hand in stopping him yourself."

The goddess laughed—presumably at the idea of a mortal leading a charge to stop one of the Moraki. The sound was somehow both savage and delicate, and it only fueled Cas's determination.

"You also helped me once before," she continued stubbornly, chancing a step closer, "when I needed to travel from the Oak Goddess's haven back to my allies. You sent the lesser-spirit of Air to take us where we needed to go. I was hoping you might send that spirit back with us today, to serve a similar purpose."

Santi yawned again. She closed her earth-colored eyes, briefly, as though she needed to take a moment to sort out the timeline. "I did help you before, didn't I?" She worked her hands casually in front of herself as she spoke. Sand tumbled and spun between them, drawn up and down by precise, tiny movements of her long nails. "And do you know, I had a feeling then that if I helped you once, you might be back for more. It's why I don't generally answer a mortal's pleas." She pinched two of her fingers together, and the grains of sand froze in mid-air. "You give them something, and they always want more. More answers, more chances, more *time*." She chuckled—a dark sound with more disgust than humor behind it. "Oh, how they *all* want more time."

"Time is...precious to me, it's true," Cas admitted. "We don't have any to spare, and there are countless messages to send and trips to undertake. Which is why we could really use your servant's help."

The goddess studied her for a long moment. "There are risks to moving freely through time and space."

Cas started to reply, but the goddess continued, cutting her off.

"We put limits on you mortals for a reason. It's a dangerous thing, to dwell too much on anything other than one's present condition, on the *current* space you occupy. I've watched many souls consumed by a desire to always be *elsewhere*. By futures that they could not see as clearly as they wanted to. By a past that they could not escape..."

The goddess's gaze narrowed, and Cas had the sudden, alarming feeling that this goddess somehow knew about the Blood-kind crystals she had hidden away.

But how could she know?

It was nothing more than her own guilty conscious making her believe such things, Cas decided. And she refused to wither under this goddess's stare, either way.

"A queen has obligations to fulfill," she said, voice quiet but firm. "One that requires me to be focused on matters that are occurring *elsewhere*, as well as on the past, present, and future—whether such focus is dangerous or not."

The goddess lifted her chin appraisingly.

Cas pressed on. "And if you would like to secure your *own* future, so that you do not go the same way as that Moraki you once served, then I suggest you join me and my allies."

The goddess yawned. "My, we think very highly of our place and purpose in this world and its wars, don't we?"

Cas still refused to cower. She could no longer waste time with such things, so her reply was quick and decisive. "I do. The crown demands as much."

The goddess closed her mouth midway through another yawn. Her stare hardened. The sand at her fingertips began shifting again, funneling down into little piles at her sandaled feet. The air seemed to fall with it, growing heavy and thick and weighing them down; Cas had to fight to keep her chin lifted and her eyes level with the goddess's glinting glare.

Then a hand settled on her arm—Rhea's.

Silverfoot weaved his way between her legs a moment later, his ears flattened and his hackles raised.

Next came a surprising touch—the Goddess of Storms was at her side as well, her hand bracing against her shoulder, steadying her further.

She felt lighter. Unafraid, even as Santi's gold-dusted eyes swept over the group of them before narrowing back on her.

"And if I refuse to aid you?"

Cas inhaled deeply. "Then I will return to this haven every single day until you change your mind. If you think the Goddess of Storms is a pest, wait until you see how annoyingly persistent *I* can be. You are either on our side or against it. And I will not leave you alone until you've agreed to help me."

"Is that so?"

"Try me and see what happens."

Sand swirled around the goddess's feet. The golden lights along the arch behind her brightened, making the full shape and size of her visible for the first time, and Cas recalled an image in a book she'd read about this goddess—how Santi could, and often did, take the form of a winged lioness.

The way she stepped toward them made her appear as though she was only a breath away from slipping into that form. Her many sets of wings had folded to her body and her feet moved firmly upon the ground—yet she made no sound. Powerful but fluid, like a beast stalking through the grass and preparing to pounce.

The goddess did not pounce. She paused before them, and she remained human-like for the moment. Her eyes darted around her dark haven, taking in the glowing bits of gold upon the walls—almost as though she was reading them, studying their patterns.

Finally, she spoke, the single word like a whisper of sand blowing over stone: "*Velia.*"

The Air spirit was there in the next instant, landing

on delicate feet, her wings folding gracefully in behind her. Her head bowed, and the appendages attached to it pressed hard against her elongated skull.

"You may go with them if you wish to help them," said Santi. She waved her hand, and the spirit slowly lifted its head and blinked her large eyes at Cas and her companions.

Velia had a mouth that looked as though it might have been capable of human speech, but she said nothing. She simply bowed her head once more, and then tilted it, studying each of them in turn. Expectant.

Cas fought the urge to exhale a relieved breath—she would not let the Sand Goddess know how anxious she'd felt.

She calmly thanked that goddess. Rhea and Nephele seemed to be in a hurry to leave—perhaps before Santi changed her mind about allowing her servant to help them—and they had already turned and started back toward the more open space they'd initially landed in. Cas hesitated only a moment before jogging to catch up with them.

"We can go directly back to Ciridan with her help, can't we?" Rhea asked once they had put a bit of distance between themselves and Santi.

Nephele nodded. "I'll carry myself back, but the Air spirit should be able to create a smoother path for the three of you." She fixed her eyes on that spirit, appraising it for a moment, and then lifted her hand and started her own transportation spell. "Let's be on our way then."

The appendages on the spirit's head waved as she nodded, and the space around her began to glow with the same smokey-green energy that had surrounded her earlier.

That soft glow was much more alluring than the darkness that permeated most of this haven, and yet, Cas found herself hesitating to step closer to it. Instead, she glanced back toward the last place she'd seen the Time Goddess. She couldn't see her within the shadows, but she had the same sensation she'd had earlier—that something within the darkness was staring back at her.

Expecting her.

"What's wrong, love?" asked Rhea.

"I just need another moment with Santi...there's something I forgot to ask her. Do you mind waiting?"

Rhea frowned uncertainly, and Silverfoot echoed that uncertainty with a soft whine and a worried thump of his tail.

Nephele canted her head, her expression briefly suspicious before becoming something more akin to bored. "Hurry up, Little Queen. If I don't get you safely back to your lover boy soon, I'm never going to hear the end of it."

"I won't be long," Cas promised.

She moved quickly, and before she knew it, she was standing before the goddess's shadowy chair once more.

Santi had retreated back into the shadows of the archway and her waterfalls of sand, but the occasional pulse of gold light from the walls still illuminated parts of her clever face, catching on the curious look in her eyes and glinting off the chalice she was sipping from.

"You're still here." Her voice was almost lost among the whispers of sand.

"I had another question."

Santi paused with the chalice at her lips. "Oh?"

Cas blurted the question out before her courage could fail her. "Does your magic allow you to actually *change* the past? If an occurrence in that past had...*broken* something, for example. And it needed to be fixed?"

A heavy pause. A slowing of sand, a shifting of shadows, a sparkle of a jeweled bracelet as the goddess placed the chalice aside...and then Santi leaned into the darkness between them, her eyes gleaming in the golden light. The movement made Cas think of a snake slowly uncoiling. Sizing her up. Trying to decide whether to strike.

"I am bound by divine laws. I can't change things within the timeline I walk along," said the goddess. "I observe, keep records, and occasionally advise according to those records. Nothing more."

Cas took a deep breath. "But what about a human that's using your magic to travel? Could it be possible for *them* to rewrite things?"

"I'd never allow it. Rewrite time?" She scoffed. "I've never met a human that was deserving of such a gift—or one smart enough to wield such a dangerous thing. And I don't expect I ever will. Though now I *am* curious..." She reclined back in her chair once more and tapped her fingers against her arm, jingling the many gold bracelets encircling it. "What were you hoping to change?"

Cas was not sure how to answer; she hadn't had time to think it all through.

"This *broken* thing that you spoke of—is it within yourself? Something that you personally regret?"

I don't know.

That was the honest answer. She wouldn't know until she used the crystals and otherwise managed to unearth more of her buried past—and maybe not even then. But that sounded weak. Not the sort of answer one gave a goddess.

"I regret nothing," Cas lied. "I simply wondered about how powerful you truly are."

Santi's eyes darkened at the challenge.

All these divine beings are so predictably prideful.

She beckoned Cas forward with a single, ring-laden finger. "Come closer."

The sand stopped falling to permit her clean passage, and Cas cautiously stepped forward. As she approached, Santi curled her finger again, and golden grains of sand swirled around the tip. They twisted and turned, stretched and spun—forming something.

A tiny hourglass.

The goddess procured a golden chain from a pocket hidden amongst the gauzy folds of her dress. She clenched it in her fist along with the hourglass. Grains of gold continued to swirl around her curled fingers. A moment later, she loosened her fist, stretched out her arm, and the chain descended between them. The hourglass was attached to it, swaying between them like the pendulum of a clock.

"...What is this?" asked Cas.

"You are curious about my power, aren't you? So here is a gift for you to take—a small sampling of that power, lest you think I am not willing to share it with humankind. I am on your side, for the record."

Cas hesitated, just as she had when Caden had offered her his *gifts*.

But in the end, she took this one too. Divine gifts were complicated, but so were wars, and she needed all the possible weapons she could gather.

"Keep it close," the goddess told her. "And if you find yourself in a moment where it feels as though time is running out and all is lost, you merely have to break the chain, and a new path will present itself to you."

"A new path?"

Santi nodded. She didn't seem inclined to explain herself further. She was yawning again, looking as though she'd grown weary of the conversation.

Cas decided not to press her luck. For now, she

simply said *thank you* once more, draped the golden chain around her neck, and tucked the hourglass beneath her shirt. It felt much heavier than it looked.

"It won't break unless you truly want it broken," the goddess added, reaching again for her chalice. "You must *want* it with everything in your heart and mind. Remember that."

Cas nodded. Out of the corner of her eye, she caught sight of her waiting companions, and she started to move toward them—but the goddess stopped her with a stare that was impossible to turn away from.

"One more thing." Santi studied her for another long moment before she continued. "If you *do* happen to uncover something in your past that you want to discuss, do pay me another visit. It gets lonely here, sometimes—and I find such conversations fascinating. You humans and all your endless, anxious musings..."

Cas pressed a hand to the hourglass hidden beneath her shirt, unsure of what to make of this invitation.

The goddess didn't seem to need a reply. "Now, run along back to your palace," she said, sinking back into her chair and taking another sip of her drink. "You said yourself that you have much to do. And time is a terrible thing to waste, isn't it?"

CHAPTER 19

Cas and Laurent made a deal.

She would accompany him to Mistwilde...eventually. Soon, even—but not before he, Elander, and a small band of her other, chosen emissaries took a few trips and laid the groundwork for her visit. They could come and go easily enough now that the Air spirit had allied herself with them, which meant that Cas could receive first-hand updates on a daily basis.

Once the preliminary work was done, and the situation in Mistwilde was deemed stable enough, she would travel to that realm herself.

Because of this deal, she found herself waking up alone the morning after her trip to see the Goddess of Time. She vaguely remembered Elander waking up much earlier, and his lips brushing her forehead in a gentle kiss before he left her to sleep and headed down-stairs to meet Laurent.

She suspected they'd left while she was asleep partly because they feared she would go back on their agreement.

But she'd had no plans to insist on accompanying them. Not this time at least. The situation in Mistwilde was deli-cate and important, and it weighed heavily on her heart and mind—but she had other things to deal with this morning.

Her fingers and toes tingled with anticipation as she stepped into the washroom. Sunlight streamed through the window, concentrating in the corner where her target—the locked cabinet—awaited. The light was guiding her toward the crystals she'd stashed inside of that cabinet, she wanted to think.

Dangerous or not, I have to do this.

She quickly retrieved a few of the crystals, tucked them into her pocket, and then quietly made her way to Nessa's room, announcing herself with a soft knock.

Nessa was already awake, poring over lists of supplies and logistical diagrams, preparing for the arrival of all the different leaders they had summoned. It was a confusing jumble of notes and numbers that made Cas's head hurt worse the longer she looked at it. Nessa was entirely engrossed, however, and clearly in her element as she made more notes, crossed out others, and mumbled thoughtfully to herself. Fourteen days remained until the meeting, and Nessa was confident that the turnout would be larger than they expected—in fact, she was planning on it.

Cas sat with her, listening and occasionally offering input when asked for it. She kept mostly still and attentive, but her hands were restless, digging into her pocket and subtly tapping the smooth, warm faces of each crystal she'd tucked away, counting them over and over.

After a few moments, she couldn't hold her question in any longer. "Could I ask you a favor?"

Nessa laid down her pen and arranged some of her notes into a neat stack. "Does it have to do with those gifts that Caden gave you?"

Cas's chest tightened, but she fought through it and calmly said, "Zev told you about them, I'm guessing?"

"Yes," said Nessa. "And he told me to keep an eye out for you doing something stupid with them."

Cas snorted at this, though secretly she was grateful to know that her friends were keeping a close watch over her. "I'm trying *not* to be stupid," she said, getting to her feet.

She paced for a moment before settling in the alcove of one of the room's two bay windows. The cozy benches in these windows were why Nessa had insisted on taking this room for herself—the benches and the view from them, which was of a particularly scenic stretch of the Lotheran River. Some sort of tall purple flower lined the water as far as Cas could see, and a herd of deer grazed among the thick green grass that rolled away from the river's edge, their ears twitching and white tails swishing.

Cas opened the window, breathed in the fragrant scent of the flowers in the box beneath it, and let the cool morning air caress her face. "Which is why I'd like for you to be nearby when I work this magic," she continued. "Just to help keep my mind clear and my own powers calm, so I *don't* end up doing anything foolish."

Nessa joined her on the bench.

"So will you help me?"

"Of course." A reassuring smile accompanied the words, but Nessa's eyes were troubled. She pulled a few weeds from the flower box, tossed them away and watched them flutter down to the grounds below them. Then she quietly asked, "Have you told anyone aside from Zev about those crystals?"

Cas bit her lip. Looked away. Fixed her gaze on one of the deer as its head shot upright. Something had startled it; it bounded toward the river, and the rest of the herd followed, leaping a narrow stretch of water and racing out of sight.

"I'm going to tell the others soon," Cas said. "But for now...I just want as few distractions as possible while I use these things. I want to be able to focus. I don't need everyone and their..."

"Opinions?" Nessa guessed with a sympathetic

smile.

"Exactly. And everyone else has their own missions to worry about. I can handle this in the meantime."

Nessa considered things for another moment before nodding. "We should do this in one of the residential towers," she said. "The taller of the two eastern ones, maybe—no one ever goes up there, even now that I've had it cleaned and organized. Some of the servants claim it's haunted...I wanted to use it for storage space, but they wanted nothing to do with it. Bunch of cowards."

Cas agreed to this spot, and a short time later—after they'd managed to shake free of other obligations and onlookers—they reconvened in the circular room at the top of their chosen tower.

Haunted might have been a stretch, but Cas did feel as if she was ascending into a world apart from the rest of the palace, somehow, as she climbed the seemingly endless steps.

The space they eventually emerged into was eerily quiet—and poorly lit, as two of its three tall and skinny windows were boarded up. It looked as if it might have been a sort of classroom at one point. Faded spaces on the walls suggested large charts had once hung upon them, and the built-in shelves were littered with boxes still containing ink and quills and scraps of parchment. There were two writing tables on either side of the room, and the one next to the only non-boarded-up window had stacks of old books upon it.

Cas gravitated toward this book-laden table. She found the scent of old books comforting, and she inhaled several deep, purposeful breaths as she took out the four crystals she'd grabbed from her room and laid them next to the dusty tomes.

Sunlight glinted off the red-centered crystals, drawing her eyes to the window. A perfect view of the palace's main gate was on the other side of it. She watched a procession of her guards moving through it and fanning out along the outer wall. They were moving unusually quickly.

Was something going on?

No—she was just being paranoid.

"Ready?" Nessa asked, coming closer.

Cas nodded and turned to face her. She tried for an optimistic smile. She must have failed to completely pull it off because Nessa's expression turned sympathetic again, and she gripped Cas's shoulder and sent a wave of warm magic over her skin.

"You can do this," said Nessa. "And I'll be right here when you get back."

Cas felt a surge of confidence. *Or was that simply Nessa's magic?* Either way, she moved quickly before it had a chance to evaporate.

The crystals all looked exceptionally similar. But some, she thought, had more red in them than others. It might have meant nothing at all, but she had theorized that these darker, redder crystals contained longer, more detailed memories. So she reached for the faintest of the group to start off with.

She'd memorized the spell that had been written on the scrap of paper hidden in the bag, and now the Blood-kind words came to her lips with little thought.

The red center pulsed brightly as she spoke...and then it went out like a doused candle, turning to the same smokey shade as the crystal around it.

Nothing happened.

Had she recited the words wrong? Voided or locked up the spell somehow? She closed her eyes against the negative thoughts, and when she opened them again, the room felt even quieter than before. Even her breathing made no sound. She was standing in a circular room as dimly-lit as the one she'd recited the spell in...

But the lack of lighting was not because of boards upon the windows. It was because of a strange fog rolling along the edges of the space.

After a moment of searching through the fog, she realized that Nessa was no longer with her.

Someone was there, however; she could hear voices down below. She stepped closer to the door—which was open, unlike the one in that room she'd apparently left behind. More fog awaited outside, but it rolled away as she stepped forward, eventually revealing a staircase. As she descended, she came to a landing that led to another partially-opened door. She stepped into the light leaking through this door, and the lingering fog rapidly began to clear.

A younger Varen—perhaps around fourteen or fifteen years of age—appeared inside the room before her, his arms folded across his chest as he leaned back in his chair. She saw him through the lens of his own memory, and thus the perception was skewed—as if he was standing in the field of her peripheral vision, but she was unable to fully turn her head to stare at him.

She found that she could move somewhat, though she couldn't go far without the edges of things turning foggy again, and she couldn't feel the ground beneath her feet.

She drew closer to her brother, resisting the urge to reach out and touch him; she suspected her hand would go right through his body. The thought unsettled her.

His eyes were fixed toward the back wall. Two figures stood in front of that wall, one of them giving a lecture that was muffled by more strange fog. As Varen sat up and paid closer attention, the details of the memory slowly came into focus. The voices of the two figures grew louder, and their faces sharper, as the fog thinned...

Anric de Solasen stood on the far side of the room.

His cold expression was remarkably similar to the countless stone sculptures of him that Cas had ordered to be destroyed, or otherwise removed from the palace.

One of his fists held a rolled piece of paper. The other, a small knife.

The figure standing beside Anric fell silent, twisting the wayward strands of his wiry red beard. A stack of notebooks were stuffed under this man's arm, and they looked to have been hastily gathered up and tucked there. His eyes were downcast, shifting occasionally toward his ruler, but never truly *looking* at Anric. Cas got the impression that this old man was the proper teacher, but the King-Emperor was taking over this particular lesson.

"The gods are parasites, is what Lord Brandes means to say," said Anric, his voice hauntingly loud and clear.

Varen shifted slightly in his seat but said nothing.

"They *gift* humans with magic so that the magic might spread, grow, multiply—and then they feed off of the spoils. A self-serving cycle of power. It is what allows them to remain relative and in control of their created world. But if we silence and cut down the marked..." He held up the paper, let it unroll and sway in the air before him. Twisting the knife in his other hand, he flipped the blade out and halved that paper in one expert slice. "...It cuts off the gods' supply chain. It stops their meddling in the affairs of our kingdoms. It stops things like the massacres that their beasts are currently carrying out among so many of our cities."

Cas jumped as Anric slammed the knife into the desk before Varen. The half of the parchment that remained in his hand was crumpled up and tossed at his son a moment later. Varen smoothed it back out, one eye on his father as he did.

"These beasts could not have killed so many if these cities did not have such a concentration of marked people," said Anric. "The gathered energy of the marked invites monsters—like fools who build on the edge of the sea and then cry out when the storms come and the waves crash too high for them to survive."

Varen unrolled the map completely, letting his fingers press out creases and walk between the cities his father mentioned.

And then he said something Cas did not expect.

"I understand..." he began, slowly, as he took his hand away from the map and let the parchment curl back into itself. "But people are *born* with those marks, the same as some people are born in houses by the sea. It's not always easy to move from such circumstances, is it?"

Anric swept around the desk and closed in on his son.

Cas knew they couldn't see her, couldn't touch her, and yet she still found herself backing away, trying to get out of her father's path before he snatched hold of Varen's coat and jerked him to his feet.

She ended up losing her balance as she stumbled away, landing in an awkward crouch. She stared up at her brother—at the uneven edges of him, distorted by memory—while balancing on a bended knee. She again felt as if she was not entirely touching the floor beneath her. This uneasy sensation only grew as the seconds passed, until finally she felt as if she was floating away completely.

The memory was shifting away as well, black spots flickering in while the voices grew softer, less distinct. She wondered if this part of the scene—this violent, tense turn the conversation was taking—was something that Varen had tried to forget. Was that why it was becoming hazy?

Grey fog soon overtook her, and Cas felt like her body was being rocked wildly back and forth in the air. It was nauseating. She closed her eyes and imagined herself back in the eastern tower she'd left behind.

"Are you okay?" Nessa's warm magic flooded into Cas's mind along with the words.

Cas sank into that magic for a moment, let it soothe the ragged edges of the memory away and ground her. She felt the wooden floor beneath her once more, and she slowly opened her eyes.

"Did it work?" Nessa was kneeling in front of her, a hand braced against her arm. "What did you see?"

Slowly, Cas pieced the vision back together and tried to recount it as accurately as she could.

Nessa listened carefully, thoughtfully, then gripped Cas's arm a little more tightly as she said, "You should probably take a break before we try again, shouldn't you? You look exhausted."

Cas didn't want to agree. She wasn't *exhausted* so much as disoriented. Part of her felt as if she still remained in that memory.

As if she *should* have remained in it.

She had started something now, and she needed to go back and finish. She needed to see more. To gather up more of her left-behind pieces, or else she feared she might never feel entirely whole again.

But the concern in Nessa's eyes eventually swayed her, and so they took a break.

They took a late breakfast in one of the smaller, more private palace gardens. Cas sat cross-legged under the shade of a flowering pear tree. She nibbled on wedges of cheese and dried meats, and she nodded along as Nessa told her more of the plans for the upcoming summit, and all that they needed to deal with before the day was finished.

She was trying to pay attention. She felt guilty for *not* paying attention, but her thoughts kept straying to which crystal she might use next.

"Cas? Are you even listening to me?"

Cas gave her head a little shake, blinked, and found Nessa watching her with a frown.

"Sorry, I just..."

They were interrupted by the sight of Zev making his

way toward them. He breathed a sigh of relief as he spotted Cas. "Where in the world have you been?"

He seemed unusually flustered, so now didn't seem like the time to share her memory-diving adventures with him.

"What's wrong?" she asked, instead of answering his question.

He exhaled a long-suffering sigh and sank down between them, grabbing a piece of berry-flecked bread from Nessa's plate as he settled. "There was an attempted dungeon breach early this morning," he said. "I just finished gathering reports from all the witnesses. I've been looking for you for the past twenty minutes, but no one knew where you were. People were starting to worry. First this thing with Lord Orbryn, and then you're missing—"

"Lord Orbryn?" Her entire body tensed. "He escaped?"

"No." Zev took a bite of the bread and chewed it slowly, his brow furrowed as though he was mentally sifting through the reports he'd gathered. "He's dead. Kuma poison, the guards suspect. Don't know if it was slipped into his food or if he took it willingly after someone smuggled it in. Don't guess it matters much either way though. He's gone, along with whatever knowledge he had of this place."

Another reason I need those crystals and their knowledge.

But still, she kept her morning's exploits to herself, despite the questioning look that Nessa shot her way.

"You haven't seen Rhea this morning either, I'm guessing?" asked Zev.

Cas shook her head.

"She had bad news to deliver as well."

"I was actually enjoying this breakfast," said Nessa, her shoulders slumping. "Do you have any *good* news to share with us?"

Zev picked a particularly juicy-looking berry from the bread and popped it into his mouth. "Fresh out of that, I'm afraid."

"It's okay." Cas placed a hand on Nessa's shoulder and gave it a comforting squeeze. "What did Rhea need to tell me?"

"We received word from Soryn's camp this morning. Late last night, the soldiers we'd sent to reinforce her city and help keep her safe were ambushed along the Olan Road. The fighting has settled now, but apparently it raged for most of the night...and their attackers carried the banners of both Moreth and Ethswen."

Cas sucked in a breath. "So Sarith has made allies out of her husband's former enemies."

"Or united them against what they see as a common foe at least. Apparently they're claiming the attack was retaliation for what happened in Riverhill two days prior."

"In Riverhill?"

"An outbreak of Fading Sickness that's already killed at least ten people. There were allegedly monsters of some sort spotted too. The details are murky, but divine magic was definitely involved in the chaos happening there, so they're holding the magic-wielding Queen of Sadira accountable. She's the closest target, I suppose."

Cas suddenly recalled Elander's warning during their battle with the Wind spirit—

He is going to try and strike fear into as many hearts as he possibly can in the coming weeks...whatever he can do to make more humans cower and hide and stay out of his way, and undermine leaders...

This was exactly what was happening; the kingdoms were tearing themselves apart, distracted from the real threat of the Dark God that loomed over them.

That god had to be orchestrating this—attacking places where he thought he could do the most damage to her attempts to build and unite her mortal army. She could picture it: Malaphar sitting before a map of the mortal world, calculating, carefully moving pieces upon his board. Pawns. They were nothing more than pawns in his ultimate, destructive plans.

She set her plate aside. She wasn't hungry all of a sudden. "How many dead on our side?"

"Two dozen at least. The Air spirit's still in Mist-wilde with Laurent and Elander, but once she returns, we could send a team with her to gather more first-hand information. We have a few crystals that we could use too, if you wanted to go before she gets back. But..."

"We should save those for emergencies."

It sent a painful twist through her stomach, to think that two dozen dead did not strike her as an *emergency*. Not these days.

It was official—her entire appetite was gone. She tossed a few scraps of bread and fruit to the birds that had been hopping ever-closer to their picnic, and then she stood, dusted herself off, and hurried to find Rhea.

The bad news continued once she stepped into Rhea's office. Wave after wave of it. New messengers arriving every half-hour, new reports threatening to knock her over just as she finished regaining her footing from the *last* report...

Everything felt as if it was falling apart.

The tower she and Nessa had been in earlier was visible through the window of Rhea's office. Cas glimpsed it once, and she had to fight the urge to keep staring. The urge to excuse herself and get back to that hidden place was strong.

She purposefully positioned herself so that her back was to the window, remembering the warning the Sand Goddess had given her.

I've watched many souls consumed by a desire to always be elsewhere...by a past that they could not escape...

She kept her focus on Rhea. On the messengers and the various advisors that marched in and out of the office. Her chin stayed lifted, her ears kept listening, her words remained calm and collected as she responded to each of the concerns that were brought before her.

She was not elsewhere. She was *here*. She was the queen of this kingdom, and she was here to stay.

Over and over, she reminded herself of this.

But still she felt those blood-tinted keepers of her lost past calling to her, pulling at the corners of her thoughts like the undercurrent of deceptively calm waters, threatening to sweep her off her feet and pull her out to sea.

CHAPTER 20

By the time evening rolled around, Elander and Laurent still had not returned from Mistwilde. The ones who had attempted to break into the palace still had not been captured. There had been no more communication from their allies in Sadira, and everyone feared the worst for them. There was a distinct, melancholic air settling over the palace, suffocating any sense of normalcy or optimism that tried to arise.

And that melancholy extended beyond the palace walls, according to the informants Cas had within the city. The favor that she had won from her battle with the Wind spirit was fickle, as it turned out; her subjects' faith in her was already wavering. The whispers were already starting—whispers of her weaknesses, her failings, and all her many enemies and looming, complicated battles.

Of *cracks*.

The crown she'd unofficially taken was already beginning to fall, people were claiming.

Cas did her best to drown out the noise. To prove her doubters wrong. She had spent the afternoon and evening just as she'd spent the morning—putting out what fires she could, making decision after decision, giving order after order.

But once the seemingly endless stream of people needing her attention finally slowed, she couldn't help herself: She called for Nessa, and they returned together to the eastern tower.

She chose another crystal, recited the spell, and escaped her present hell and traveled, instead, to the past, searching for more information. More answers. Because as stressful as walking through that past was, at least she knew she didn't have to make decisions about it—it was already over and done with.

But it was eerie, the memory she landed in this time, because of how closely it paralleled the present day she'd been having.

Varen was hiding from their father in this vision, pressed against the doorframe of one of the storage closets in the throne room. Anric sat upon his throne, stoic and still, listening to the equally serious-faced advisors that paraded in and out of the room—just as Cas had been doing.

She was witnessing a particularly bad day of news, it seemed.

They told him of demonstrations in the city. Of people calling for his crown. For his death. There were shortages of everything, brought on partly by the harsh demands Anric had imposed on Sadira. They would no longer conduct business with that kingdom to their east, he'd decided, so long as that kingdom continued to let its magic flourish. Sadira had refused to stifle its many divine magic users, and now the two kingdoms had reached a stalemate.

And beyond the typical political struggles, a potentially greater threat loomed on the horizon; a mysterious illness was sweeping its way across the kingdoms, growing ever closer to Anric's own palace.

The Fading Sickness.

Cas's breath caught in her throat at the mention of it.

The talks about that sickness eventually involved a half-dozen other men and women. They continued for what felt like an hour...and yet Cas was certain she had only been inside the spell for a few minutes at most. The scene seemed to accelerate at occasional, random intervals. Skipping around, the way memories often did, highlighting only the most interesting and painful parts.

Once the conversation was finished and the last of the advisors had left the room—and Anric clearly believed himself to be alone—he sank into his chair and buried his face in one hand, raking his fingers through his pale hair.

After a moment, he took the crown from his head and turned it over and around in his hands. More than once, his gaze lifted to a portrait of his deceased queen, which took up the majority of the wall above the main doors.

Cas thought about trying to move closer, but something stopped her. Even though she was invisible, she didn't want to impose on this private struggle—didn't want to get too close to it.

So instead, she stayed hidden, pressed against the wall alongside her brother. She kept her gaze on Anric. It all felt too *real* if she looked at Varen...almost as though they were children exploring the palace together, looking for trouble to get into. And he *was* just a child in this memory; she could tell from a quick glance that he couldn't have been any older than nine.

Anric's head shot up at the sound of boots stepping quickly and purposefully across the marble floors.

A woman was walking toward him. The array of badges across her coat suggested that she was a soldier of great importance. Anric rose to his feet as she approached, and eagerness overtook his features—as if, out of all of his many servants and advisors, this was the person he'd most wanted to see today.

"What news from the northern coast?" he demanded.

The woman bowed her head. "The elves have driven back the last of our forces. We're going to have to pull out entirely, I'm afraid; we've lost too many already. The matter of the Antaeum Point will have to wait."

"It has already *waited*. And for entirely too long." He swept a gaze over the room's many windows, looking paranoid—as though he expected something terrible to swoop through them at any moment. "He is beginning to suspect me, I fear."

"Maybe so." The woman's eyes were hard—unyielding. "But it is folly to continue with our original plan now."

Anric brought his glare back to her. But he said nothing, only shook his head and began to pace before his throne, muttering silently to himself as she continued to speak.

"Dawnskeep is sacred to the Morethian elves," the woman continued, a touch of exasperation in her tone. "We knew this, and we didn't expect them to let us in without a fight. But their numbers were greater than anticipated. We've lost a hundred men just since yesterday—and that's only an estimate. A *low* estimate."

Anric stopped pacing and looked once more at the portrait of his wife before snapping his gaze back to the woman in front of him. "Is there any chance left of sealing it before we retreat? If we could make those damnable elves understand *why* we need to do it..."

The woman inhaled deeply and exhaled slowly. "They don't believe the stories about the Antaeum, you know. They don't want to *understand* anything we're trying to do regarding those points. They see our claims about that concentration of divine power as nothing but more attempts at human trickery, and they think we are merely trying to strip them of their own backwards magic." She hesitated. "Can't say I *blame* them for feeling that way about us, given our history of—"

Anric held up his hand. "That's enough," he said, gruffly.

The woman lifted her chin. "But you understand the situation, I trust."

Anric grumbled something unintelligible in response.

Cas stumbled forward like a starved dog desperate for scraps. For more information. *Dawnskeep...the Morethian elves...*these were familiar things, but suddenly they sounded foreign to her ears. She needed to get closer. To listen more carefully, to understand what she'd missed.

What was this *Antaeum Point*?

And what did Anric mean, *He is beginning to suspect me*?

Was it that god he'd once bargained with making him paranoid?

She tried to find out. But no matter how many steps she took, she never seemed to get any closer to Anric—the limits of seeing a memory through someone else's eyes, once again.

The door behind her creaked.

Varen.

Anric's head snapped toward him. For a fraction of a moment, Cas could not truly read her father's face—too many competing expressions flashed across it. Regret, fear, uncertainty...a dozen different emotions that didn't fit any of the ideas she had of this man.

Then his familiar angry expression stormed back into place, and the entire room seemed to darken as he stalked toward Varen.

Cas spun around as her brother shoved away from the doorframe. Her sight shifted as Varen's did, so that she was no longer seeing the entire throne room—she was searching for an escape route.

Varen stumbled and tripped for a few steps before breaking into a run. Their shared vision veered wildly as he raced along the edges of the room and then out the door, nearly knocking over two different guards as he went. Anric didn't seem to be following, but Cas couldn't be sure; looking behind her only revealed billowing clouds of grey fog giving chase.

The entire memory was quickly swallowed up in this fog, and Cas slipped back into the present with a sharp gasp. Her lungs burned as if she'd truly been running alongside her brother, trying to escape with him.

"That is *terribly* unsettling to watch, just so you know," said Nessa, smoothing a hand through Cas's hair, letting her warming magic bleed through her fingers. "Your eyes turn almost entirely white, and your lips are moving...it's almost like you were reciting a silent spell the entire time."

Cas took a deep breath and swept a harried look around the room, halfway expecting Varen to be hiding somewhere in the shadows. "It *still* kind of feels like I'm in that memory, even now."

"What did you see this time?"

Cas recited all the details she could remember. They puzzled through them together, and both of them kept circling back to the same strange term that Anric had used—the *Antaeum Point*.

"I don't think I've ever heard of such a thing," said Nessa.

Cas frowned. "Me either."

"Maybe something in the libraries here will give us more information? Assuming Anric didn't have that information burned or otherwise destroyed, like he did with so many other divine-related things..."

Cas shook her head. "I don't think this topic is one he would have wanted entirely erased." She couldn't be certain, but whatever this *point* was, it sounded as if

Anric had intended to use it to wage war against the gods.

And she was beginning to think that war of his was even more complicated—and connected to her own battles—than she'd realized.

Now she just had to make sense of it all.

CHAPTER 21

As the days blurred onward, all of them began to follow this same pattern: Cas would wake from what little bit of sleep she'd managed, and she would go immediately to her advising council and get the latest report on the disasters befalling the empire.

They would tell her of battles and uprisings. How many had died, how many sightings of divine creatures there had been, how many monsters were terrorizing how many different cities across Kethra...and how many riots were breaking out in her *own* city.

She would send delegates to concerned rulers in countless realms. Soldiers to stem the bleeding wherever she could. Payment to her associates in Ciridan, convincing them to help her keep order even if it meant offering more than their originally agreed-upon sum—which it increasingly did.

Elander and Laurent returned to Mistwilde almost every day, working tirelessly to try and win over the elven king who was, as it turned out, reluctant to entangle his own problems up with those of the mortal kingdoms, despite their repeated attempts to convince him that they would all ultimately be fighting the same battle in the end.

Once Elander and Laurent were gone and the most pressing of the day's situations were dealt with, a brief quiet often overtook the palace. It was not a peaceful quiet, but one that tingled and teemed with the possibility of the next, imminent disaster.

Whenever this uneasy silence settled, she would walk the halls alone while she had the chance.

Most of the walks eventually led her to the same place.

Time after time, she returned to that room in the eastern tower. Nessa would follow shortly after, and Cas would choose one of the crystals from her hidden stash, and she would slip into the past without much thought.

Some memories she landed in felt insignificant— glimpses of dinners, of lessons, of walks through the gardens or long nights spent in the palace's various libraries.

Some were heavier—arguments with their father that turned violent, tense visits from foreign diplomats, funerals that Varen was expected to attend without question.

All of them were intoxicating.

Even the mundane glimpses of Varen's life clawed themselves into Cas and refused to let go. Because this life, she couldn't help thinking, might have been something like *hers* if things had only gone a bit differently... and the thought was both terrible and captivating.

The memories with the sharpest claws were the ones that actually included her. There had been only a handful of these, so far—Varen had been young when she'd left, after all—but still, he remembered more of her than she ever would have guessed.

There were visions of the two of them playing in a shallow creek, rolling down the hills behind the palace, swiping sweets from silver-plated trays. Of her stretched out on the end of his bed, reading him stories. Of their father telling Varen that she was sick. That she was gone.

After seven days of wading through it all, Cas was no longer able to sleep. She barely ate.

Outwardly, she kept her head high and her voice unwavering as she gave orders and addressed concerns as best she could.

But inwardly, she felt the beginnings of more of the *cracks* that her subjects kept whispering about.

She was being pulled in so many different directions that perhaps it was impossible for her heart and soul to *not* feel as if they were being ripped apart at the seams.

Elander could tell something was wrong during the

brief moments they had together, but it wasn't difficult to convince him that it was nothing more than the deteriorating conditions across the empire taking their toll on her. His own travels and battles were wearing on him, too, and so most conversations they began on any difficult matters were quickly dropped in favor of trying to get some rest.

She was glad to see him actually sleeping—even if she rarely managed to join in. Another justification for not telling him about her memory travels just yet; he needed to focus on sleep.

While he did, she would sit and write notes on the memories she'd collected, trying to make sense of them. Trying to decide what was important and what could be disregarded. She wanted to keep them all—to gather them up into a secret, collected book of lost things—but she could only process so much in such a short time. So she made herself into a soldier collecting helpful information, nothing more, and she did her best to separate her feelings from the facts. She wasn't always successful at this—she just had so many *questions.*

Was her brother actually trying to help her understand their past?

Or was he merely trying to confuse her?

She knew from prior conversations with Elander that Caden's magic could not *alter* memories. So the things she'd seen were true. But she was only seeing what memories Varen gave her to see, so there was always the possibility of lies by omission.

Why had he selected *these* particular images to share?

And what was he still keeping from her?

She was starting to feel like she was going mad, trying to sort the truth from the lies, trying to fill in the blanks and make it all make sense. Her mind was forever turning things over and over. The images of her present and would-be past were beginning to blur.

She could still tell them apart for now, and she told herself she would stop this madness if she ever felt like she *couldn't*. It wasn't going to reach that point. But she would stop if it did. She could always stop.

On the eighth day after using her first crystal, she climbed the stairs of the tower in a daze and found Nessa already waiting at the top.

She wasn't alone.

Zev was standing there as well, and Cas's defenses automatically rose at the sight of him.

"Why are you here?" Lack of sleep and food made the words sharp as they hissed from her lips. She hated the way she sounded, but she couldn't seem to settle her expression into anything softer than a suspicious glare.

Zev was unfazed by her rudeness. "To help stage an intervention."

Cas scoffed and stepped around him, heading for the hidden compartment in the room's built-in shelves.

She'd stashed the bag of crystals there—it had seemed a safer place than in her room, as she had been growing increasingly paranoid of Elander being able to sense the dormant magic in those precious spells.

The bag wasn't there.

She spun around and saw Nessa with her arms hugged around herself. The bag was tucked tightly beneath one of those arms.

"You too?" Cas muttered.

"I just...I think you should stop this," Nessa said, quietly. "Or take a long break, at least. Focus on the problems we have in the present for a while."

"It's all related," Cas reminded her.

"Yes, but you can only spread yourself so thin."

"I can handle this."

"It's a burden, I know, to—"

"I can carry it fine."

"Yes, but just because you *can* carry it doesn't mean you *should*. And it doesn't mean it isn't heavy."

Cas reached for the bag. Nessa let it go without a fight, but that drew a scowl from Zev, who closed the space between them in several quick steps.

"I don't have time to argue about this," Cas growled, angling her body—and the bag—away from him.

Zev pushed even closer, undeterred. "You're taking a break."

"I don't get *breaks*. I have an obligation as queen to—"

"You're not acting like a queen at the moment," he said, stepping so close that his hand brushed her hip. "You're acting like a fucking idiot."

Nessa grabbed his arm and dragged him back, her wide eyes watching Cas's clenched fist, as if anticipating a swing.

Cas might have swung if she hadn't been so exhausted. Her reflexes were slow, her thoughts were sluggish—*everything* was sluggish. So she didn't move to attack him, she only shifted her glare from him to the door. "Get out," she ordered.

He glared right back at her. His chest rose and fell with a deep breath. And another. He took a step back. And another. He narrowed his eyes and frowned his disapproval at her one last time before turning and heading for the door.

Nessa stayed by Cas's side as they watched him leave.

Cas released a shuddering breath. "I just need to see a few more things," she told Nessa, quietly. "I only have a few crystals left to sort through." She heard herself very clearly. Could almost feel the cold fingers of this terrible desire—no, *addiction*—tightening around her throat, choking the words from her mouth.

Stop talking

Stop. Talking.

But it was compulsion, the need to justify what she was doing, even to the most understanding and compassionate of her friends. "I'll only use one more tonight, and then I'll take a break tomorrow, I just..."

"*One more.*" Zev spoke loudly from the doorway—he'd decided not to leave after all. "And then another, and another—and if Caden shows up with *more* of those damn things, what will you do, then?"

She couldn't seem to string enough words together to make a coherent reply.

"You're trying to relive and make sense of an entire lifetime over the course of a single week," Nessa added, softly. "No one is strong enough to do a thing like that—whether they're queen or not. Whether it's *necessary* or not."

Cas automatically scoffed, even though she knew Nessa was right.

"It doesn't matter either way." Zev held up his hand, which was clutching something...*the bag.* He'd swiped it somehow. He smirked at her as he gave it a little shake.

"You *bastard.* Give them—"

"You should have been paying more attention when I tried to teach you my pickpocketing secrets."

Cas let out another curse and started after him, but Nessa stepped in her path. "Let it go. Just for now. Please?"

Zev was already gone—truly out of sight this time.

And somehow it made it easier for Cas to take a deep breath, knowing that those crystals had gone with him.

"Fine," she relented. "I have other things I need to take care of this evening anyway."

Nessa let out a sigh of relief, and after a moment, the two of them headed for the stairs outside of the room. As they wound their way down the tower, Cas found herself calming down enough to speak. Concerns other than the whereabouts of those crystals wove their way into her mind.

"Is Elander back yet?"

Nessa frowned. "They said they'd be gone for a few days this time. Don't you remember?"

Cas nodded quickly, and the lie rolled off her tongue just as swiftly. "Right. Of course—I remember now."

But she didn't actually remember it at all.

What she *did* recall was that Elander had left yesterday evening, and she'd been all too eager to get away from him, to get back to her exploits with those crystals—which was likely why much of her last conversation with him was a blur.

She raked a shaking hand through her hair, wincing a bit as the honest weight of what she had gotten caught up in settled over her.

Her friends were right.

She *knew* they were right.

So why could she not stop searching for Zev every time they rounded a corner? Why was she already devising a way to get that bag back from him? And thinking of the few crystals that *weren't* in that bag, too—because she had a separate hiding place for a handful of her remaining spells...one that even Nessa didn't know about.

"So, where to?" asked Nessa.

Cas blinked.

"You said there were other things you needed to see about this evening?" prompted Nessa.

Cas considered the possibilities. She'd thought about going back to one of the libraries to do more research, or to one of the offices to catch up on reading and responding to any recent messages she'd received. But the thought of going anywhere inside this palace felt suffocating.

"I haven't been into the city for a few days," she said. "I feel like I should make a round and personally speak with Syndra and a few of our other allies."

Nessa looked concerned about this plan, but she didn't outright dismiss it.

"We can arrange for extra protection to accompany us," Cas insisted. "We'll be fine."

"It'll be less stressful than what we've been doing in that tower, I suspect," said Nessa with a somewhat forced smile.

"Exactly."

Cas ducked into her room and grabbed a hooded cloak, a Mimic-kind crystal—just in case—and then sent word for one of her more trusted soldiers to gather a few more armed bodies and meet them outside the main gate.

They were stopped at that gate, however, by several guards who refused to let them pass.

The scene unfolding was borderline chaotic—soldiers funneling in and out of the palace grounds, people scrambling to obtain orders, everyone trying to talk over each other.

Finally, Cas grabbed one of the higher-ranking guards, pulled him off to the side, and demanded an explanation.

"I'm afraid it's not safe for you to head out into the city this evening, Your Highness," said the guard.

"Not safe? What are you talking about?"

"Disturbances in the Market and Edge districts. And the unrest's spilling over into other places—getting too close to the palace. Best you stay behind these walls until everything is settled again."

"Why is this the first I'm hearing of it?" Cas's irritation was more with herself than the guard.

What else had she missed while she was distracted by the past?

The guard fumbled for words. Before he found them, a woman in well-worn armor passed through the gate, caught sight of Cas, and headed over. She gave the guard a pointed look—her hazel eyes sparkling in the setting sunlight—and dismissed him with a nod.

Elayne Caster was her name, and she was one of the

last soldiers Varen had bestowed with the title of *General* before he'd left town. She was the daughter of a revered soldier who had previously served the royal family, though she had little love to spare for the reign of Anric de Solasen—unlike her predecessor, apparently.

Cas didn't know anything about that predecessor, but now that she honestly *looked* at Elayne, at her tall stature, her heavily freckled skin, the waves of light copper hair...

She looked like she could have been the daughter of the woman Cas had seen in one of Varen's memories— the one who had challenged Anric about the Antaeum Points.

Or was it her imagination?

The past bleeding into the present yet again?

She took several deep breaths, picturing each of her inhales pulling that memory down a little farther. She could sort these things out later.

She met General Caster's stern gaze and said, "What is this I'm hearing about riots in the city?"

"Not quite riots yet, Highness. Just some extra unrest. We have it under control at the moment, I assure you."

"Unrest over *what*, though?"

The general glanced over her shoulder, as if she was concerned that unrest might catch up with them as they spoke. "They're uneasy because of the minor earth-quakes that have been plaguing the Bloodstones these past days. One strong enough to cause some damage struck a few hours ago, I'm told. Word is spreading out from the foothills villages that there's something unnatural at work, and they wonder if it's connected to the... well, *unnatural* turn of events we've had at the palace recently."

Nessa made a face. "They believe their new queen is somehow responsible for these disasters?"

"Not exactly. But...the word is that such disasters never happened while Varen was in charge."

"That's absurd," Nessa argued. "*Plenty* of worse things happened while he was in charge. And *everything* has changed now. It isn't Cas's fault if—"

Elayne held up her hand in a gesture for peace. "I agree. But the people are getting scared and confused, and they just want someone to blame."

Nessa still looked disgruntled, but Cas was getting better at letting this sort of blame hit and roll off her. So she simply cleared her throat and asked, "How bad was that latest quake?"

"Early reports suggest no casualties, but..." The general hesitated. "That might change once they start digging things out of the fallen rock. There have been alleged sightings of the Mountain God too." Another pause, heavy with unspoken questions. "I'm not sure I believe it, but..." She trailed off, as if waiting for Cas to confirm that she was right to not believe it.

But Cas stayed silent. Her weary mind had somehow

managed to dig up an older conversation—one from when the Storm and Moon Goddesses had first visited her in this palace—and now she remembered something Elander had said. *The God of the Mountain has long been close to the deities of Fire and Ice. He'll go with them, if forced to pick a side...*

All their fears seemed to be coming true, one disastrous day at a time.

General Caster cleared her throat. "Either way, we'll keep things under control," she assured them. "Once we've established a safe perimeter around the foothills, I'll report back to you myself."

"Establish it tonight," Cas ordered. "And then assemble a guard to accompany me before the morning —because I intend to ride up to the mountains and see the damage for myself. We'll leave at tomorrow's first light."

Surprise briefly registered in the general's eyes, but she dutifully masked it and gave a slight bow of her head. "Of course."

Cas dismissed her, and once she was out of sight, Nessa gave her a sly smile.

"What are you looking at me like that for?"

Nessa shrugged, still grinning. "I'm still getting used to you ordering people around using your *queen* voice."

"I do not have a *queen* voice."

"You do. I like it though."

Cas laughed, and then Nessa proceeded to mimic

that supposed voice, making them both break into even louder laughter and earning them several curious stares.

They quickly stifled their amusement and headed back into the palace.

"Not the circumstances I would prefer, but it will be nice to get outside of the city tomorrow," Cas commented, pausing at the door and glancing back at the gates one last time.

"As long as you're careful," said Nessa, hugging her arms against a sudden gust of cold wind.

"You're in charge while I'm gone, all right?"

"Is that an order from the queen?"

Cas mirrored her crooked smile from earlier. "It is. And you'll follow it, if you know what's good for you."

Nessa pulled the door open and bowed her inside. "As long as you're ordering it in that tone, how could I say no?"

A SHORT TIME LATER, Cas made her way up to her room with plans of going to sleep early. If she was going to be traveling through the mountains in the morning, she needed to at least *attempt* rest.

But once she was alone in that room, the morning seemed...*distant*. A hundred other problems seemed to exist between this moment and the moment she planned to leave—how could she sleep?

She stood by the window, pondering this and

watching all the people scurrying around the palace grounds. The city was too far away to see clearly, but there seemed to be a brighter than normal halo glowing around the vicinity of it. Too many lights still burning. Too many people still awake. And movement... so much movement around the palace grounds between the harried guards, anxious soldiers, curious courtiers...

We have it under control, General Caster had told her.

But did they?

She felt back in control of herself, at least. The break she'd taken from unearthing memories this evening had been for the better. Her mind felt clearer than it had in days—even in spite of her exhaustion—and she felt another surge of gratitude toward her friends for this.

She was still sore about Zev's pickpocketing, however.

Until she reminded herself that he hadn't taken *all* of the crystals.

There were a few of them that radiated a brighter red than the others—those ones that she suspected were more potent. She had stashed those away in a hidden passage just across the hall, with plans to work her way up to using them. The key to that passage was stowed beneath a book that she'd tucked into the smallest, least conspicuous shelf in her room.

She collected the key, and she absently tossed it between her hands, pondering some more.

If she didn't use those most potent crystals now, then when?

If the Mountain God himself was walking freely in her kingdom, it was only a matter of time before worse things followed him. She needed to figure out how to deal with those worse things. And she had been getting closer. Every memory she saw was another piece collected toward the bigger picture. She felt as if she'd been climbing a mountain and getting closer and closer to the summit...and she would be able to see *everything* if she could only keep climbing a little longer.

She only had six days left before those leaders they'd summoned from other realms began to arrive.

She wanted a better plan before then—more knowledge to share, more answers to give her potential allies.

Enough.

She was still so desperate to make sure she was doing *enough*.

So she crept from her room and quietly stole her way across the hall, toward what appeared to be a mere storage closet. Once she pushed past boxes and assorted odds and ends, she came to the smaller door that her key unlocked.

The passage on the other side was dark and smelled of dust and stale, forgotten things. She assumed it had once been utilized by servants to move discreetly in and out of rooms, but now it was closed off after only a few feet.

The crystals were among the boards that blocked the path, tucked away in a box made of special *jobas* wood that further suppressed any energy they might have been giving off.

She plucked two of them from the hiding place and then walked as casually as she could back to her room.

It happened with alarming quickness after that.

One moment she was staring at the closed door of her room. The next, she had locked that door. Then she tiptoed into the washroom. Locked that door too. She took one of the crystals from her pocket and clenched it in her fist, studying the pattern of scarlet swirled over its center.

The justifications came easily; she slipped down into them with trepidation that quickly gave way to relief, like easing into a hot bath.

Elander was still gone, as was Laurent.

Zev was likely still too annoyed to bother with her.

Nessa was busy making plans with Rhea, and it had been Nessa's suggestion that Cas head to bed early, so it was doubtful she would disturb her.

Cas was alone, and as long as she was trapped within the walls of this palace, she was going to make use of her time.

The memory overtook her within seconds of reciting the spell. It was getting easier and easier to fall into them, and it was beginning to feel *good* when she fell— at least, at first. Like coming home after a long trip;

everything seemed fresh yet familiar, and she saw only the good when she first stepped through the door.

This was the youngest version of Varen she had seen yet. Four years old, perhaps, though his still round, babyish face wore an expression that seemed out-of-place on someone so young—it was too somber, too serious.

But why?

The memory was not immediately clear. Grey fog surrounded Varen as he buried his face against his knees. It rolled in and out of the space around him, as though this was a memory he wanted to rid himself of, but—like the waves of a restless sea—it was too powerful to stop.

Finally, Varen lifted his head, and the fog rolled away, revealing a hazy image of the stately parlor he was cowering in. The vision quickly slid, focusing on a wine-colored door that seemed miles away.

And there was Cas herself, standing in the doorway with fear shining in her eyes.

It still was not immediately clear what had frightened either of them. The only thing that *was* clear was... her. Her, with her gangly limbs swinging and her auburn hair flying out behind her as she ran to Varen's side and positioned herself in front of him. Protecting him?

From what?

The memory had been largely muted up until this

point, but now she heard pounding heartbeats. *Felt* them, almost. Varen's? Hers? In the past or present? She couldn't tell.

Then came a growl.

Brother and sister alike lifted their heads toward the sound. The fireplace blazed so brightly it obscured most of the room's details, but the light was soon swallowed up by twisting strands of dark energy.

Those dark shadows...

Horror jolted through Cas's chest as she realized what had just taken place here.

The shadows were forming the outline of a wolf.

The memory skipped before it fully took shape, and then Cas was watching her younger self drop to the floor with her brother, holding her breath as she gathered him up in her arms.

She wanted to look elsewhere. She wanted to escape. But her vision was tied to Varen's, and it wouldn't shift the way she wanted it to. It kept her hostage, holding as tightly as five-year-old Cas held onto her brother.

Varen peeked through her embrace, and in that moment the edges of the memory sharpened again, narrowing on the image that Varen apparently still held clearly in his mind, even eighteen years later—

The queen lay dead on the floor behind her children, her body leached of all color and bent at odd angles.

Leave. You have to leave this memory. Now!

Why was she still here?

She never felt entirely in control of her body during these memory spells, but this was worse—it felt as if someone had wrapped weights around her wrists and ankles to tie her down and keep her here. It was the same sort of paralysis that often gripped her after she woke from her nightmares. She was neither awake nor asleep. She was entirely at the mercy of the images playing out before her, until finally, her mind could make sense of nothing more.

Those images shifted and spun away, and she welcomed the darkness that overtook her.

CHAPTER 22

A LOUD BOOM OF THUNDER JOLTED CAS AWAKE.

Her eyes stayed tightly shut as she curled into herself, her old anxieties surrounding storms resurfacing. Her heart pounded. Her palms itched. Another boom of...*no*.

That wasn't thunder, was it?

The door.

Someone is trying to break through the door.

A moment later, they succeeded. There was a sound of splintering wood and the metallic ping of a lock breaking, and then the door swung open with a loud creak.

Two people stood in the entrance to the washroom. Two blurred figures that Cas didn't recognize right away. They both raced to her side, their identities becoming clearer as they drew closer.

Nessa reached her first.

Elander had made it to within a few feet of her and then paused, distracted by something. Analyzing the scene. Sensing the magical residue that hadn't had time to clear, most likely.

He knelt and picked up something from the floor—something that glittered in the light of the low-burning lantern hanging beside the sink.

"Damn it," Cas heard herself whisper.

Nessa shivered a bit as she looked over Cas's appearance, and her brows knitted together as she summoned magic to help. And the warmth of her magic *did* help—but it wasn't enough to fully erase what Cas had seen. To allow her to fully come back.

Cas struggled to sit up.

Elander's attention had shifted entirely to her now. She didn't mean to lock eyes with him, but that intense, questioning gaze of his was difficult to look away from.

Nessa's touch on her hand made her jump. "Are you okay?"

"Yes," Cas said automatically.

Nessa's gaze traveled, uncertainly, between her and Elander.

"Could you maybe just...just give us a moment alone, please?" Cas asked.

Nessa hesitated, but eventually nodded and backed slowly out of the room.

Cas managed to avoid Elander's gaze this time by

taking in her surroundings instead. A glance at the window told her it was still the middle of the night. There had been a bowl perched on the edge of the tub—another container of perfumed flowers, which the servants seemed determined to make sure she always had on hand whenever she was ready to bathe. She must have hit the bowl while in the throes of memory, because it now lay in pieces on the washroom floor. There were drops of red scattered amongst the shards.

Blood.

She fought the urge to recoil from the sight.

She felt her way along her arms, her neck, and eventually up to her head, where she finally found it—a section of hair that was wet and sticky, and a few strands that were already dried and stiff. The feel of it triggered a wave of nausea. But even more concerning than *this* blood was the blood in the center of the crystal Elander held.

She didn't remember dropping it. But that was clearly what he had picked off the floor, and she thought he might break it, as tightly as he was holding it. A similar tightness took hold of her throat, making her breaths turn shallow and trapping her words inside.

Finally, he broke the silence in a voice that was oddly, unsettlingly calm. "Is this what you've really been doing while I've been away?"

"Among other things." She tried to get to her feet. Her knees buckled. She caught herself against the side of the tub, but she couldn't push herself back upright. Her limbs refused to cooperate. Everything was numb, and she ended up sliding down and landing in an awkward, crumpled position among the blood and broken glass.

Elander was there in the next instant, kneeling beside her and carefully lifting her into his arms.

She wanted to resist, but she still felt too disoriented, so she allowed herself to be carried and laid into her bed. She closed her eyes and waited for the room—and her thoughts—to stop spinning.

"Blood magic." Elander's voice was still calm, but an iciness had crept into the words. "Did you think I wouldn't recognize this for what it was? That I wouldn't be able to feel the lingering energies of the spell you used?"

"You're back earlier than I expected. You weren't supposed to see—"

"Why would you hide this from me?"

The slightest attempt at movement made her head throb. She gritted her teeth against the pain. "Isn't it obvious?"

He didn't reply.

She blinked her eyes open. Took a deep breath before attempting movement again, lifting her head and shifting her gaze toward him. "Caden told me—"

"You spoke with him? Face to face?" She stiffened at his suddenly violent tone, and he made a visible effort to calm himself. "When?"

She sank back against the pillow.

"He came after you? How? *When?*"

"Last week, before the Wind spirit attacked us. I briefly spoke with him while I was in the city."

He was quiet for a long time. So long that she couldn't help but glance back at him, and it was just in time to see something very painful flicker through his eyes.

Her stomach shifted with guilt, and her limbs tingled with numbness once more. She felt heavy, unbalanced—like she might collapse again, even though she was already lying down.

"He didn't hurt me," she reassured him, softer now. "And he didn't *force* me to take these crystals from him. I wanted to take them. To use them. I knew you would worry about it, that it would upset you, but I believed they could help us—"

"Help us?" His gaze shifted to the blood staining the side of her face, and violence edged back into his tone as he asked, "At what cost?"

"It doesn't matter."

"I assure you it absolutely fucking *does*."

She braced herself. Sat up, and *remained* sitting up, even as the room twisted and tried to crash in around her. "The things I've seen are important," she argued. "Things that we can use to help us make decisions about what to do next—things that Caden wanted to show me before now. Things you wouldn't *let* him show me, apparently."

Elander didn't flinch as she flung the accusation at him.

He didn't deny it either.

The silence stretched and stretched until she was fighting off the urge to wince, afraid that quiet might be close to snapping.

She loosed a shaky breath. "So he was telling the truth about that."

Elander fixed his glare on the book resting on her bedside table. "He...suggested it while we were on the road to Moreth, but you had enough to worry about at the time. I didn't think you needed more things to deal with. So yes—I told him to leave the matter alone for the time being."

"I deserved to know these things. To see them and decide for myself what to make of them!"

"Some things are better left buried."

"But not *all* things."

His gaze flicked back to her, and his expression was hard. Stubborn. Unapologetic.

"You don't get it, do you?" Her voice lowered, shaking from her pent-up frustration. "Do you know what it's been like for me, coming back here? Trying to lead this kingdom when half of the servants in this palace know more about my own childhood and family than *I* do? All these people want to know who their new queen is, and what she's capable of, and if she will be enough to lead them, but I don't *know*. Everything in this place feels so foreign to me—and now I've been given a chance to see things that I missed, to try and make sense of them for myself, while *also* gaining insight that could help us fight our wars...and you have the nerve to be *angry* about it?"

"I'm not angry about *that*, I—"

"I knew you'd think I couldn't handle what I might see."

A muscle twitched in his powerful jaw—but again, he didn't protest the accusation.

Cas still felt numb, but she fought through it and planted her feet on the floor beside the bed. Her hands gripped the edge of the mattress. "That's what you're thinking even now. Admit it."

Another beat of quiet.

Venom laced her next words. "Your silence is its own kind of admission, isn't it?"

He exhaled slowly, almost carefully, and shook his head. "What would you like me to say, Casia?"

"I want you to tell me the truth."

His reply still didn't come. She thought he might try to change the subject. Or that he might turn and walk away until he'd calmed down; he'd been known to disappear for hours to do that in the past.

But he didn't leave. He merely shifted his weight to his other foot, and then he met her gaze more fully, sighed and said, "You didn't exactly look like you were *handling it* when I walked into this room. And you barely have it together now—*look* at yourself."

She fought the urge to glance at her reflection in the nearby window.

She didn't want to see it.

Didn't want to give him the satisfaction of making her look.

She clenched the mattress more tightly, trying to keep her hands from shaking. He'd spoken the truth—just as she'd asked him to—but somehow she still had not been prepared for the sharp sting of betrayal the words caused.

"I did what I had to do," she seethed. "You're always saying that lately. Why is this any different?"

"Somebody else could have used that magic on your behalf," he insisted.

"What? Somebody else could have gone digging through the ruins of *my* past?"

"It would have been safer, more objective—"

"I'm tired of just ordering people to do things on my behalf. Tired of sending them off to face the gods only know what, and doing nothing except writing letters and giving orders from behind the palace walls. People are *dying* because of my orders, while I'm losing my mind in here, trying to make it all make sense."

"You aren't—"

"Am I the queen or not?"

He swallowed down whatever he'd been in the middle of saying and took a deep breath. "You are."

"Then why does it feel like nothing is in my control? Like nothing I do is ever enough?" Her voice cracked toward the end despite her best efforts to keep it steady.

He didn't reply right away. The hard lines of his face softened the tiniest bit, and for a moment, it looked as though he might suggest a truce.

But in the end he just shook his head in frustration, averted his eyes, and swallowed his words once more.

"I need to go," Cas mumbled, getting to her feet.

"Go where?"

"Away."

"Casia, wait—"

She tried to step around him, but she was still too disoriented, too slow. He caught her and held her in place without much effort.

"Where are you going?" he asked, again.

"Let go." She tried to jerk free of his powerful grip.

He only held more tightly. "It's the middle of the godforsaken night, you can't just—"

"Yes, I *can*." Magic flared along with her temper this time. Bolts of lightning raced over her arms, leaping over and engulfing him, sizzling so brightly that for a moment his face was lost amongst the glow.

I'm sorry, she thought, immediately.

But she was too frustrated, too angry, too stubborn to say it out loud.

That magic hadn't *physically* hurt him—his own power had merely flashed to life and absorbed hers after a few seconds—but it had clearly stunned him. The shock in his eyes flickered quickly away, but not quickly enough to keep her from seeing it.

Was he thinking about the last time he'd tried to stop her from leaving this way? When they were still enemies, and her magic had lit up the Oblivion Tower he'd tried to keep her in?

Why did it feel like they were back in that awful place with all of their complicated history festering in the space between them?

"Let me go," she said quietly.

He did.

And she stumbled away without looking back because she didn't want him to see the angry tears welling up in her eyes.

CHAPTER 23

Casia had been gone for nearly an entire day.

Elander had spent most of it on his feet, moving through the palace and its grounds, trying to focus on speaking with all the many people he needed to speak to. There were details he needed to catch up on. People he needed to inform about the business he and Laurent had been seeing to in Mistwilde. Questions he needed answered.

Plenty of things to distract himself with.

And yet, he continuously ended up replaying the scene from last night in his mind. The image of Casia's body crumpled beside the tub, all that broken glass and blood around her... He'd seen far more gruesome things throughout his existence. And yet it was *this* that turned his stomach and upset him far more than anything else he could recall at the moment.

It had upset him to the point of stupidity, really, which explained the stupid things he'd said to her.

You barely have it together, look at yourself...

He cringed at the memory of his own voice, and then held in a sigh as he came upon a trio of servants who lowered their eyes—either out of respect or nervousness —as they passed him.

Once they were out of sight, he slipped down a dark hallway and paused for a moment. He leaned against the wall, brought his hand up, summoned little sparks of magic to his fingertips, and waited for the sensation of other magic—*her* magic—to answer. This had worked in the past. Whether it was Dark or Light magic binding them, their connection had always given him a way back to her.

But now he could hardly feel the beat of her magic answering his—and it frightened him. Where had she gone? Was she safe?

He should have gone after her. Should have kept her from leaving in the first place.

And then what?

Locked her up in one of the palace towers and thrown away the key?

This palace already felt like a prison to her; the last thing he wanted to do was make that feeling worse. But what else could he have done?

More importantly, what could he do *now* to make this hellish day without her end?

A drink, he promptly decided, shoving away from the wall. *That's what I could do.*

He made his way to the wine cellar near the main kitchens. He was intimately familiar with this room from his previous time spent living in this palace. It had once been the pride and joy of Anric de Solasen—the king had loved showing it off to any and every guest that came through the doors. That entire family had loved their alcohol, and it was reflected by the size of the cellar.

Vast was an understatement.

Elander's gaze trailed over a row of glass bottles filled with various shades of golden-brown liquid. Brandy. He had once been fond of this mortal concoction; he could hardly stand to drink it anymore because it made him think about past lives, about past servants and other things he'd lost—Tara had once been his favorite drinking companion, and she'd been damn good at discerning what spirits were worth their time, and which ones they should leave on the shelf.

Her death, and the dilemma with Caden...it had all happened so quickly, so strangely, that it didn't feel real. But then little things like these glass bottles kept popping up, reminding him that it *was*. It was the worst part about loss—the way it insisted on lingering in the shadows of your life and catching your eye when you were least prepared for it.

He snatched one of the smaller bottles—hoping it

was one Tara would have approved of—tucked it into the inner pocket of his coat, and grabbed glasses from the shelf by the door.

He moved on through the palace, eventually ending up in one of the small studies that they'd been utilizing as a meeting space. Laurent and Zev were there as well, and both seemed lost in their own thoughts; Zev stared blankly at a letter clutched in his hands, while Laurent sat with his arms folded across his chest and his eyes closed. He looked like he was sleeping at first glance, but his body was too tense, and the occasional twitch of his frown suggested he was well aware of his surroundings.

Silverfoot was here as well, curled up beneath the window in a shrinking patch of the setting sun's light. But there was no sign of Rhea, or Nessa, or any of the countless, familiar courtiers who had started trying to worm their way into Casia's inner circle.

Elander settled into a claw-footed chair at the table across from Zev, thankful for the relative silence of the room, and he poured his drink. He offered to pour the second glass for Zev, and was surprised when the Fire-kind declined and refocused his attention on the letter in his hands; it was the first time Elander recalled him refusing a drink.

It was nearly a full minute before Laurent opened his eyes and looked in Elander's direction. "Still no sign of her?"

Elander shook his head.

"It's not like her to disappear like this." The half-elf's tone was a mixture of concern and impatience. Mostly impatience. Elander knew him well enough by now to suspect he had little tolerance for dramatic storm-offs.

Elander swirled the amber contents of his glass, willing his own patience to hold out a bit longer.

It didn't.

He was already restless.

His gaze lifted to Zev after only a few sips. "How long has she been using those crystals?"

Zev didn't take his eyes from the letter he held.

"How long?" Elander repeated, not bothering to keep his tone civil this time.

"Since the first trip you and Laurent took to Mist-wilde...so eight days or so? Nine? I've lost track."

Elander settled deeper into his chair. The alcohol mingled with his growing irritation, and it was a hot, dangerous, *combustive* combination. He wanted to hit someone. No—he wanted to beat the *shit* out of someone.

He tapped his fingers against his half-empty glass. "So you knew she was doing this, and you didn't stop her?"

Zev peered over the letter at him. "It wasn't that bad in the beginning," he said evenly. "She was in control. And the crystals have shown her useful things, I think.... We told her to stop when it started getting ugly—she didn't listen."

"Of course she didn't listen."

Zev slowly placed the letter on the table, smoothing it out before sitting up straighter and focusing his full attention on Elander. "Is there something else you want to say to me?"

No. I should just shut up.

"You're supposedly her best friend, aren't you?" he asked instead.

A tight smile, and then an even more tense reply. "I am."

"Then you of all people should know that she has a tendency to obsess over things like this."

The Fire-kind leaned forward, and with a curt nod toward the door, he said, "If you want to fight me about this, we can step outside and do that any time you like."

"I'm only collecting information about what happened." Elander remained seated. Took another sip of his drink. "And I have plenty of actual battles to focus on at the moment; I'd rather not waste my time fighting with a child."

Laurent sighed.

That tight, wild smile was still on Zev's face. A tense beat passed. Then another.

He lunged, knocking the second, empty glass to the floor, where it shattered.

Elander's hand shot forward just as quickly, centuries of battle-honed reflexes reacting before he could stop himself. He caught Zev by the collar of his shirt and stood, shoving him down against the table.

Fire magic built in the space between them, the heat so rapid and intense that Elander's eyes immediately began to water.

Laurent was across the room in the next instant, catching Elander by the arm and dragging him back.

Silverfoot sank his teeth into Zev's ankle, wiggling and throwing all his weight into an attempt to hold him back as well.

The fox's owner arrived in the doorway moments later, her voice cracking over them like a whip. *"What in the hells is happening in here?"*

Elander released his grip, shrugged free of Laurent's hold, and sank back into his chair.

Zev shook the fox from his ankle and muttered something in his native Sundolian tongue. Elander was fairly certain most of the words he said were curse words.

"Whatever it is between you two," Rhea snapped, "put it to rest. *Now.*"

Elander massaged the part of his arm where Laurent's fingers had dug in, mildly disappointed that he hadn't thrown a punch. But it was likely for the better. It would do nothing to settle his argument with Casia, for one thing.

And he was angry at himself more than Zev anyway.

At his own stupid self, for not handling things

better. For not being here when Casia needed him, for not realizing what she was doing, for not having the sense to see that *of course* Caden would be persistent in getting his job done.

Zev was not the enemy. He was just very punchable sometimes. *Caden* was the enemy...and suddenly Elander felt like he needed to refill his drink. He rose to his feet instead, and he guided Rhea away from the glass on the floor before kneeling to clean it up.

No blood among *this* broken glass, at least.

"We're *all* worried about Casia, but it's no excuse to act like we've lost our minds." Rhea seemed to be talking to herself as much as to the rest of the room. "She can be stubborn and impulsive, but she isn't completely reckless, and she cares too much about this empire—and about all of you imbeciles—to do anything too foolish. She'll be back soon. And if I know Casia, she'll be stronger when she returns. So why don't we all calm down and stay focused on other problems until then, shall we?"

Mumbles of agreement chorused through the room, and Elander went back to his chair. Back to his drink.

Nessa arrived a few moments later and struck up a conversation with the others. The discussion soon turned—as it so often did lately—to the fast-approaching summit they would be hosting, and then to more general political discussion.

And though he was tired of talking, Elander tried to

answer as many of their questions as he could and to summarize the things that had taken place in Mistwilde —the reasons that he and Laurent had come back so much earlier than planned.

Rising tensions in that elven court had led to them essentially being kicked out of it. King Talos had called them *distractions*—and a host of other less polite things —from his main problems, which were the ever-bolder attacks he was facing from Sarith and her army.

Elander still could not figure out why Sarith was harassing that realm and destroying the long-standing alliance that Moreth had with Mistwilde and its king— especially considering she originally hailed from Mist-wilde herself.

What was she after in that realm?

And why had Varen helped her deliver that message through the dead Prince?

King Talos claimed he had nothing worth starting a war over—that they only wanted to be left alone. But Elander and Laurent had both come to suspect that he was hiding things. Dangerous things. The chances of him turning out to be a threat now seemed as likely as him becoming an ally, and it just seemed as if *everything* was becoming increasingly...well, *fucked.*

There was no other word for it.

He kept trying to come up with more words—better words—to explain the messy situation they'd been wading through in Mistwilde. Laurent was somewhat more articulate on this front, but even he was at a loss when it came to discussing what they should do next.

By the time their conversation reached a breaking point, Elander had had entirely too much to drink. The words had gotten still more difficult to put together. His head was spinning.

And Casia still had not come back.

Why had she not come back?

The others continued to discuss matters. To plan, to argue, to...who knew. He didn't care. The only thing he really cared about was the fact that *she still had not come back.*

Evening eased into night.

He occasionally stood to stretch, to pace the halls, to interrogate servants. But he always found his way back to that room with the others—to that chair—and soon he was drifting off to sleep in it, hoping things might be better when he opened his eyes again.

A COMMOTION AWAKENED him some time later.

He lifted his head from the table and found that he was alone. The room was dark, the lanterns extinguished, and through the curtains he saw a glimpse of a cobalt, pre-dawn sky. He unfolded from his uncomfortable position in the chair, stretched the stiffness from his muscles, and wandered into the hallway.

After a moment of tired confusion, he realized the noise that had stirred him from sleep was the sound of servants hurrying and fussing about—because their queen had returned.

He followed the noise into the main entry hall, where no less than thirty people had already gathered. One of the Air spirit's portals still shimmered in a space between two columns, casting a pale greenish glow over the marble floors.

And there Casia was, standing beside the demure spirit of Air, addressing one of her courtiers with a confident, sharp expression on her face. She didn't look at all like the woman he'd found on the bathroom floor less than a day before.

Of course she didn't. Because she had always been adept at changing her appearance like this—whether by the use of magic or otherwise. Both *fearless and fainthearted* within the span of a few breaths sometimes. He'd told her that once—how it captivated him.

And it *still* captivated him.

But now it worried him too, because he realized how badly he'd misread her over this past week.

What else was she keeping from him?

He wanted to be angry at her. *Furious* at her. For hiding those Blood crystals and everything else, for attacking him earlier, for disappearing without telling him where she was going...

But as he drew closer to the portal—close enough to

hear the steady beat of her heart, to feel the rhythm of her magic change as it reacted to his presence—relief washed over him...such an enormous wave of it that he could focus on nothing else, and there was nothing to do except take her in his arms and pull her against his chest, interrupting the conversation she'd started with the courtier.

The man she'd been speaking to looked somewhat disgruntled, but he swept into a quick bow and then stepped back, affording them some privacy.

Elander smoothed a few strands of hair behind Casia's ear. Blood still stained some of them. "Where were you?"

"I needed to speak to the Goddess of Time about a few things, so I asked her spirit servant to take me to her haven." She absently ran her fingers along the golden chain that goddess had given her, holding it out, twisting it up, releasing it and letting the tiny hourglass at its center spin between them.

He caught the charm in his fist and held it still. He didn't particularly trust the Sand Goddess—or any *gift* she had to give them—but he hadn't been able to talk Casia into getting rid of the necklace.

She glanced up at him from beneath her lashes. "I'm sorry if I worried you."

He dropped the necklace, meeting her gaze, but he found himself unsure of how to reply. He didn't usually feel so...off-balance around her.

"And I'm sorry I ran off in such a hurry." She offered her hand. "Truce?"

As badly as he wanted to put that unbalanced feeling behind him and move on, he still hesitated to take her hand. "What did you need to speak with the Time Goddess about?"

She breathed in slowly. Considered him and their surroundings for a moment before she finally shrugged. "Who better to help make sense of the visions of my past, if not the goddess who can freely walk in that past?"

He waited, but she didn't elaborate.

She swept a discreet gaze over the room and the countless people who had wandered in to greet her. "I don't want to talk about this right now."

"So let's go somewhere private."

She bit her lip. Their unsettled argument was threatening to ignite once more. It most likely *would* have ignited had they not been interrupted by a servant bringing a message that apparently could not wait until later.

"More problems up in the Bloodstones," said the messenger. "The same rumblings as before—I believe you spoke with General Caster about this matter yesterday?"

Casia nodded.

"She's preparing to leave, but she sent me to ask

about you; shall I tell her you've returned? To wait for you?"

"Yes, thank you."

"What sort of rumblings?" Elander asked as the messenger hurried away.

She again avoided his gaze, focusing instead on accepting a letter that someone handed her.

"There have been alleged sightings of the Mountain God," she told him, opening the letter and scanning its contents even as she spoke; she was becoming a queen of multi-tasking, if nothing else. "Along with minor earthquakes, rock slides—that sort of thing. Payback, I'm afraid, for what we did to the servant of the Fire God. You said these two gods have often sided together in the past, correct?"

He nodded, and his chest tightened as images of the deity flashed in his mind. The God of Strength and Turmoil—not one that would be easy to reason with. He could not think of a single pleasant memory he had of that god.

Intaba, the mortals called him. It had been quite some time since Elander had seen him in the mortal realm or otherwise. They'd last met face-to-face at Glathiel—otherwise known as the Dead City—the landing point for souls that stood at the center of their world's three hells. Elander had summoned him there to answer for an influx of dead mortals, caused by the Mountain God losing his temper and making the entire mortal city of Bridgekeep sink into the earth. It had been a breach of the divine laws that bound him, and the Moraki had sent Elander to deal with it—a trial by Intaba's own peer. They'd had a precarious relationship ever since.

"I had planned to ride up to the Bloodstones and inspect things for myself," Casia continued, "and now I'm late—I didn't realize how long I'd been gone. But it seems General Caster is still expecting me, so I should get going."

It was obvious enough why she seemed so eager to *get going*—because here was something else for her to focus on, rather than dealing with all the restless things simmering between them.

She was already turning away, calling for one of the servants to bring her riding gear...but she slowed after taking a few steps away from him. Bowed her head and shook it, as if silently arguing with herself. Then she tilted her face back and quietly called out to him, "Come with me?"

He exhaled a heavy breath. "Of course."

It didn't matter how furious he was; he had no intentions of letting her face whatever was happening in those mountains alone.

CHAPTER 24

THEY WERE ON THE ROAD A SHORT TIME LATER, FLANKED BY two dozen soldiers. General Caster brought up the rear of their company, while Casia led from the front, setting a quick trotting pace. Elander followed closely behind her. They managed not to look at each other for the first several miles, putting their argument behind them for the time being.

It was a quiet ride.

This was just as well. It allowed Elander to focus his senses—to pay attention to any potential threats that might be following or looming ahead of them. The morning was bright, drenched in cheerful sunlight, and warmed by a southern wind that carried the scent of the vast jasmine fields in the distance.

But there was something...*off* about the air.

His horse sensed it too; the creature's ears were

pinned back against its skull, and its flanks shivered with each breeze that stirred its dark mane.

The outer edge of Ciridan was usually bustling by this hour, alive with barking dogs, neighing horses, and chatting people loading up their wares and preparing to bring them to the main market in the city's center.

That was not the case this morning.

And the desolation only increased once they reached Cliffbarrow, the largest of the villages scattered along the base of the Bloodstones. It was approximately an hour's ride from Ciridan, and it was usually lively enough to rival the atmosphere of the capital city, despite being half that city's size.

At the moment, however, it felt a thousand miles away from anything resembling *lively*. The streets were nearly empty. It was silent enough to allow Elander to easily pick out quiet, individual sounds: the wind creaking a nearby gate, the babbling stream that edged the village boundary, the hum of conversations drifting through opened windows—though there weren't many conversations to hear, as several of the houses seemed to have been outright abandoned.

"Some of my informants told me there was a rock slide on one of the south-facing slopes early this morning," Casia told him without glancing in his direction. "It traveled unnaturally far...pushed by divine magic, most are saying. No one within a thirty-mile radius of the Bloodstones believes they're safe at this point."

Elander's gaze trailed along the mountains that sloped up behind the city, fighting off a chill at the thought of how much damage those rocks could do if they came tumbling down.

Casia continued in a grim tone, "The latest activity was up near Roedyn's Pass—part of the traditional route between Cliffbarrow and the villages that are dotted along that southern slope. There's a traveler's camp in the Roedyn Valley midway through that route. I want to speak to the inhabitants there."

He nodded; he'd been to that camp many times in the past. It wasn't particularly deep in the mountains, so hopefully they could wrap up this excursion and make it back to the palace before lunch.

They fell silent for at least another mile. Once they reached rougher terrain, the road narrowed considerably, pushing their horses closer together and making it harder for them to avoid eye contact with one another.

He normally enjoyed the quiet. But this was fast becoming uncomfortable...even for him.

"So," he began, trying to keep his voice light, "did you really think earthquakes and a potential encounter with the Mountain God would be easier than finishing our conversation from your room last night?"

She shot him a glance. Brief. But at least she'd looked at him. "Was that really a *conversation* we were having last night? It felt more like a trial to me."

He took a deep breath. "It wasn't my intention to make you feel guilty."

"I don't feel guilty about it," Casia said in a tone that suggested exactly the opposite. "Because I was only doing what I had to do. But either way," she added, her voice dropping to a near-hiss, "I'm not simply doing this so I can avoid having a stupid conversation with you about...about *all that*. I'm here because it's where the people of this kingdom need me to be. We need to know if the rumors are true. Because if they are..." She didn't seem to want to finish the sentence.

"Then it's a sign things are escalating," he finished for her.

"Exactly. First a spirit harasses the kingdom, and now an actual middle-god..." She trailed off again, pausing to focus on steadying herself in the saddle and clenching her fingers more tightly around the reins.

He watched those fingers for a moment, noting every occasional twitch. She was clearly fighting to keep them still.

Several more minutes of silence passed, and then she softened her voice somewhat and asked, "What *would* a potential encounter with that god be like? For preparation's sake."

Elander tilted his head back and stared at the clear blue sky, trying to decide where to start. "The God of Fire is the one that most pray to during wartime, but Intaba is a close second. He's the god of Strength and

Turmoil and the oldest of all the middle-gods. The magic of the Marr is fluid—in most cases, these divine positions have been held by various souls throughout the history of the world. But the God of the Mountain is the same now as he was in the beginning, allegedly.

"There's a legend that the Moraki he served, Belegor, once tried and failed to replace him, and the battle that ensued between them resulted in untold destruction to *Valla*—the upper-heaven, which is the divine realm where the Moraki once dwelled together. And when that battle spilled out of the heavens and into the mortal world, it reshaped mountains and canyons and the like. The other Moraki eventually had to intervene and help bind up some of Intaba's power. His magic can still—"

A sharp *crack* sounded in the distance, followed by the sound of rocks bouncing and skittering down the mountain face.

Elander pulled his horse's reins sharply to the left, guiding it into an about-face. Casia and the rest of their party did the same, and together they watched the ominous sight of several more rocks breaking free in the distance. As the rocks collided with the road, explosions of dust went up, and the wind slowly carried clouds of it toward them.

Casia swallowed hard. "Can still what?" she prompted quietly.

"...Can still shift the earth. Not living things, but things such as dirt and stone—all the things his upper-god originally helped shape. And he doesn't necessarily even *need* to use magic; his physical strength alone is unmatched."

Their company waited, horses prancing nervously, braced for a full avalanche.

Another minute passed, and no other rocks fell.

Elander's nerves still did not settle. The way those rocks had fallen seemed...unnatural. *Strategic.*

"Blocking our path?" one of their riders guessed, his voice wavering slightly.

"Is that the Mountain God at work?"

"Are we being closed in?"

Casia cut off their questioning before it could grow more frantic. "Never mind," she said loudly. "We carry on to the Roedyn Valley. There are other roads we can take back home from that point, if need be." She resumed her quick pace forward before anyone could argue.

Elander loosed his reins and trusted his horse to follow hers while he spent most of the next mile scanning the road behind and the rocks above them, watching for more unnatural shifting amongst the cliffs.

But the mountains remained perfectly still.

Perfectly quiet.

After two more miles, they came upon another traveling party—a slow-moving caravan of people and carts, and horses overburdened with overfilled bags...a disaster waiting to happen, if the Mountain God and his minions *did* decide to start causing more trouble.

Judging by Casia's frown and the way she anxiously tapped her fingers against the pommel of her saddle, she was thinking the same thing.

"You would think they would turn back once they realized almost no one else was using the mountain roads this morning," Elander commented. "Common sense should have told them there was a reason for the emptiness."

"They're likely hailing from Eldrin. Ciridan is the closest major city, and the goods they're carrying are probably their only means of supporting themselves," Casia countered, her voice clipped. "Not everyone grew up in the halls of kings and gods; some have to work for coin, no matter the danger."

A muscle twitched in Elander's jaw. "Would you like to...*talk* about what you saw in those crystals? About those halls you *didn't* grow up in? We have other problems at the moment, but if you want to—"

Another *crack* of splitting rock echoed in the distance, and one of the horses in their company bolted. Its rider managed to settle and turn it back into line, but several other horses looked ready to copy its escape attempt.

"I'd like to get off this mountain first." Casia started to guide her mare down a steep incline and onto a new path, her focus on that group in the distance. "I'm going to go warn those people that the road ahead of them is likely blocked before they come any farther. If they *are* from Eldrin, we'll pass by their village if we're taking the long way home. They can join our group and return there with us. I'll buy everything they planned to sell today if it will get them to turn around."

He thought about pointing out that this would only make them *all* slow, easy targets for trouble, but he knew the chance of her leaving vulnerable people behind was...slim.

She didn't wait for his input on her plan, anyway, before she kicked her horse into a quicker gait, throwing up clouds of dust as she went.

A few of their group moved to follow her, but Elander sighed and held up his hand. There was no sense in *all* of them rushing down that treacherous narrow path and risking their horses. And most members of the caravan were already bowing as Casia approached. They seemed harmless enough.

He watched carefully for a moment, making certain this initial assessment was correct. They were all trying to speak to her at once, and some were hurriedly taking things from bags and carrying them over to her. Offering gifts, it looked like.

While he waited for Casia, he took a moment to assess the rest of their party. The rear of their company was particularly restless, he noticed—looking frantically around, arguing about something. He narrowed his eyes on each of the riders in turn, and it took him only a moment to realize...

Someone was missing.

He rode quickly to the back of the line. "Where is General Caster?"

"She's disappeared, Sir. She lingered at the last crossroads and never caught back up."

A pang of fear shot through him, but he didn't let it show. "Then why the hell are you all standing around here?" He counted off four riders. "You four—go find her. Stay together."

They bowed their heads and spurred their horses into motion.

Elander paced up and down among the remaining riders, heart pounding, every nerve in his body on fire.

In almost no time at all, he heard the search party calling for help.

He jerked his horse to a stop, causing it to stomp its feet and flick its ears in annoyance.

He hesitated, reluctant to move to where he couldn't see Casia and that group she'd engaged with. But a second series of shouts—louder this time—convinced him that the greater threat was currently in the distance. He ordered four more riders to his side and sent the rest to watch over their queen.

His group followed the shouting, and they soon came upon that search party he'd sent. Three of them were off their horses, gathered around what appeared to be a deep, jagged pit. The fourth was serving as lookout.

Elander leapt from his horse's back and moved to the pit.

Far below, buried beneath several large stones, was General Caster. Her body was bent at a strange angle, and there was a dark...*something* spreading out beside her. It might have been a shadow; it might have been blood. She was not moving, did not appear to be breathing...

Definitely blood.

"I don't see any signs of a rock slide," noted one of the soldiers.

"So how did she end up beneath those stones?" asked another.

"This hole is too clean—it seems unnatural, doesn't it?"

Elander's skin chilled as a possible explanation crossed his mind. He wanted his theory to be wrong. But he had to test it either way—so he borrowed a bow from one of the riders. He concentrated magic into the tip of an arrow as he nocked it, and he aimed at one of the rocks crushing the general's body into the dirt.

The arrow struck and bounced off the largest of those rocks.

And then the slab of stone...*moved*. It rolled off General Caster's body with a terrible, guttural noise— like an ill beast roused from hibernation.

The movement revealed another dark patch—one that was larger, a part of it shimmering in a stray strand of sunlight. More blood. The general was almost certainly dead, and a growing, sickening sense of dread told Elander she would not be the last to meet her end in these mountains today.

He cursed under his breath and took a step back, scanning the cliffs above them, watching for more signs of movement. For makeshift limbs and sparkling crystal eyes.

"Those are not ordinary rocks," he told the others. "They've been brought to life by way of divine magic."

One member of the search party knew the correct term. "Golems?"

Elander nodded. "They're generally weak and slow, but *any* of the rocks around us could be brought to life. And their master can bring down the entire mountain by taking control of a few precise pieces and making them move. We need to get back on the trail. Quickly."

"But General Caster—"

The sound of crunching, shifting earth interrupted him.

A crack split across the ground, zig-zagging toward them. It ran all the way to the edge of the pit they were gathered around, and that edge crumbled, the dirt caving in and cascading down, completing the general's grave.

"*Go!*" Elander shouted.

They went. The air filled with warning cries. The ground shook from the frantic pounding of horse hooves —*or was it from more magic?*

He raced after them, shouting orders for the rest of their company to move. "Ride hard! Spread out! Don't stop until you've reached the valley!"

He didn't think that valley would be entirely safe, but they could at least make themselves more difficult to strike—to completely overwhelm—if they had more space to work with.

As the rest of their party turned up the road to the valley, he galloped for the path Casia had taken earlier. He reached the head of it just in time to see a large rock slipping free from the mountainside high above her, pebbles and dust flooding down behind it.

Elander shouted out a warning.

Another rock slid free, and now the crumbling began in earnest—every shift led to more shifting, and soon the entire side of the mountain was collapsing, a river of rock and dirt pummeling toward Casia and the people around her.

Casia was quicker than the river, thankfully.

She swept Shadowslayer free of its casing, and a shield of blue magic swept into existence with the same motion, protecting not just herself, but the ones around her. The others crouched down beneath her power, their frightened cries muffled by the magic enveloping them.

Elander jumped from his horse and sprinted down

the remainder of the treacherous, uneven path to her, his own magic bleeding out of him and seeking hers as he approached.

With their combined power, that barrier was soon solid enough that she could focus on other things. Rocks and dirt hit and slid harmlessly away, far above them, while she instructed the people around her to leave their heavy carts behind and follow her in an orderly fashion.

One by one, the terrified people obeyed.

She kept magic above their path, protecting them from the stones that continued to fall.

It was an excruciatingly slow, but effective method of moving, and Elander supported it by reinforcing her magic and helping guide her toward that safer route that would soon open up into the Roedyn Valley.

Something slammed into the shield and sent cracks of magic spiderwebbing across it.

That *something* remained stuck in the shield for several seconds, the two conflicting powers twisting and sparking together, creating a blindingly bright flare of energy.

The invading power eventually won out.

The light of the barrier's magic faded, and Elander finally saw what had struck it—an axe made of silver and bone, wrapped in a strange, hazy, grey-colored energy.

He knew that axe.

It dropped to the dirt with a heavy thud as Casia's

barrier flickered completely away, but it didn't remain there; the ground beneath its landing spot rose up, sending it spinning back toward its owner.

Elander twisted around, searching for the one who wielded that familiar weapon.

He didn't have to look far.

A great, hulking beast of a man stood on a nearby peak, axe in hand, silhouetted by the rising sunlight.

No—not a man.

A god.

CHAPTER 25

ELANDER MOVED SWIFTLY TO POSITION HIMSELF BETWEEN Casia and Intaba.

The Mountain God moved forward with calculated steps, surveying the scene before him while nimbly spinning his axe around in his hand.

Casia was still focused on getting people to safety, and Elander could read her well enough to know that *nothing* was going to break that focus.

She caught his eye as he glanced over his shoulder at her. They exchanged a look. It took no more than this to coordinate an understanding. He needed to buy her time.

Elander turned his attention back to the approaching god.

Intaba had a wild appearance, with long, dark hair framing his blocky head and his thick neck. Dirt streaked his tan complexion. His body was massive, with arms and legs twice as big around as a normal man's, and the dull black armor he wore made him appear even bulkier. He was a wall of muscle, rugged and robust—as though he had been cleaved and carved from the very mountains themselves.

Elander was not used to looking up to meet anyone's eyes, and he would have avoided looking up to meet this god's eyes if he could have. They had always unsettled him—there was too much black in them, making him feel like he was staring into bottomless pits.

Pits that now made him think about General Caster, her dead body, and the sparkling blood he'd been staring at just before the dirt had caved in around her.

"The Fallen One himself." Intaba's square, ugly face split with an even uglier grin as he drew closer to Elander.

Elander picked a loose thread from his sleeve. "It's been a while, hasn't it?"

"I'd heard you were fucking around with a human queen. Didn't know whether or not it was true."

"Good to know the rumormongers among the divine courts are still hard at work."

The god's gaze swept over him, appraising, while that unpleasant smile of his tightened. "Do you ever wonder about those rumors? The things they've been saying about you?"

"Been a little too distracted to trouble myself about it, honestly."

Intaba chuckled darkly. "Fool. Traitorous mortal lover. *Weakling.*"

Elander pulled his sword casually from its sheath. "I've been called worse."

"I'm sure." The god tossed his axe up and down, equally casual. Then his gaze drifted toward Casia—following the sudden, distraught wail of one of the people she was trying to protect—and his eyes narrowed as he refocused. "Now, get out of my way. I've been sent here for a purpose, and I don't need you interfering with it."

"Sent by whom?" Elander stepped to the left, blocking the god's view of Casia. "The upper-god you served is gone, is he not?"

Those pit eyes flashed—reminding Elander again of dark, shining blood—and Intaba stopped tossing his axe. "He is. And all power now flows to the Dark God. I go where the power goes. Simple enough."

"Can I give you a word of advice?"

The response was a growl, more animal than human.

This god had never been good at accepting advice.

The ground around Elander's feet shivered—threatening little cracks spreading across it—but he continued all the same. "He's a horrible master to follow. You're better off rebelling while you still can—unless you're too cowardly to do it, of course."

Another low growl. Intaba was fond of shapeshifting, like most of the Marr. He often took the shape of a bear-like creature, and at the moment—between that rumbling in his chest and the way he was flexing his large fingers as though they were claws—he already resembled one.

But he stayed in human form as he rebalanced the axe in his hand and brought it forward, pointing it toward Elander's throat. "You'll shut your mouth if you know what's good for you."

Elander kept talking. "You must have done something to make Malaphar think you deserved this job."

Intaba didn't answer right away. He simply stalked his way around Elander, still holding his axe at a threatening angle as he went.

"What deal did you make?" Elander pressed. "What did he promise you?"

A more intelligent god would have ignored the question.

But Intaba was not known for his intelligence. And he loved to gloat when given the chance, so it was no surprise when he stopped, twisted back around to face Elander, smirked and asked, "Jealous that I've taken your spot, are we?"

"Incredibly so," Elander said, maneuvering back in

front of him. "So how did you do it? Do you have any tips on dealing with that upper-god? I could use them."

The middle-god looked him up and down. Appraising him again. Then he laughed—a grizzled, jagged sound that echoed off the rocks, amplifying to a volume that seemed unnatural. It shook the ground, shifted stone, swayed the trees growing haphazardly from the mountainside.

Elander's gaze swept over the craggy face to their right, where most of the movement was concentrated. He was watching for more of those golem creatures, waiting for them to break themselves from the mountain and launch an attack.

But seconds passed and there was just silence, eerie stillness—

The god shot around him and moved toward Casia with a speed that didn't fit his appearance.

Walking mountains should not be able to move that fast.

Cursing, Elander tore after him, summoning magic as he went. Lightning wove between his fingers and formed a spear. He aimed it at the axe swinging by the god's side. It caught the weapon, snaking around it and then traveling up the god's arm.

The god slammed to a stop and twisted around, the force of his momentum shift digging deep channels in the earth. He roared back toward Elander, his axe still sparking with electricity as he lifted it and prepared to bring it down upon Elander's head

Elander drew his sword quickly enough to parry the swing. Their weapons clashed, locking together for a moment. The god loomed over him and shoved him down toward the earth; he was overpowering him.

Of course he was.

He was not going to win a battle of strength against the actual fucking *god* of it.

He was going to have to be smarter.

The god continued to shove him down. Elander's knees threatened to buckle, so he gave in to the pressure, dropping so abruptly it threw the god off-balance. This gave Elander a few seconds to work with—enough time to summon another spear of lightning and take proper aim.

He aimed for the god's eyes.

Not entirely *smart*, perhaps, but it enraged the god— predictably. And once he'd earned the god's fury, he kept it by throwing more and more bolts of lightning. Like poking a bear with a stick.

The god swung wildly after him, blinded by magic and rage.

Elander led him toward a dead end, to where the mountain shot steeply upward. He paused here for a moment, summoning more magic to make himself an easier target for the blinded god.

Intaba took the bait, and Elander leapt aside at the last instant.

The god's axe struck a wall of rock, sending a thick

crack racing up it. Bits of the mountain began to rumble lose. Elander was fast enough to avoid each piece that fell, and once he was clear of the falling debris, he sent a distracting ball of magic toward the god. It slowed the divine being while more of the mountainside broke free. Several stones pummeled Intaba, but the hulking god shook them off as if they were grains of sand.

He charged after Elander once more.

Elander repeated this trick against another nearby wall. Another reckless slam of the axe, and Elander again managed to slip away as bits of the mountain came raining down. This time, more rocks fell, completely burying the god.

For a moment, at least.

The rocks began to tremble. One by one, they rose as easily as leaves caught in an updraft. Within seconds, the god had flipped them all away. They hit the dusty ground, whereupon some of them kept moving, shifting and forming defined, rocky bodies with powerful legs that propelled them forward. More of those golem beasts, possessed by the god's magic.

Three of them barreled toward Elander.

They were half his size but likely three times his weight, and they moved as fluidly as cats.

The one in front leapt, managing a glancing blow to Elander's shoulder as he leapt out of the way.

Elander landed somewhat gracefully and rolled

aside, narrowly avoiding the second rock as it hurled itself at him.

The third had gotten around behind him and was sizing him up, preparing to leap.

Elander backed toward the second just as it got to his feet and leapt as well. He ducked, causing the two beasts to collide in mid-air and shatter. He remained low, his arm thrown over his head to protect himself from the dust and falling pieces. The last remaining golem hesitated at the sight of the others shattering, showing more intelligence than Elander had thought it capable of. He summoned lightning to the tip of his sword and waved it like a torch, chasing the creature off.

He turned to find Intaba. Through the dust stinging his eyes, he saw a light in the distance, growing bright and brighter—

Casia, reinforcing the shield she'd created.

More of the god's possessed stones raced along the cliffs above her, he realized, and the rocky beasts were knocking boulders—some as big as horses—down upon the humans below.

Casia had stabbed Shadowslayer into the dirt. Magic radiated out from it, casting a protective barrier over the group of people she'd been trying to save. This group was running toward a bend in the mountain path just ahead, while she sprinted in the opposite direction, drawing the attention of the god and his beasts toward her.

Once she'd put considerable distance between herself and that group, she turned and faced the god trailing her.

Intaba was upon her in the next instant, his axe drawn back and radiating terrible amounts of ash-colored energy.

He swung.

Casia threw up a second shield of magic. It was not as bright as the one she'd used to protect the others—and Elander's breath caught as he anticipated it being cut straight through.

But the axe didn't strike her shield.

It hit the ground just in front of the shield instead, making it shake and roll, throwing her backwards. She slammed into a wall of rock, slid down, and landed upon a narrow ledge—one that stretched over a dangerously steep drop. The magic that had surrounded her dissipated as she focused on trying to balance herself.

The last of the caravan disappeared around the bend, beyond the barrier Casia had created for them. Whatever happened to them at this point, happened— Elander no longer cared.

He sprinted to Casia's sword and pulled it from the dirt, wielding it alongside his own. Shadowslayer's grip warmed beneath his palm as he raced toward the Mountain God.

He thought of their theory—that his power grew

stronger whenever he used it to guard Casia—and decided to test it out once more. He clung to that idea as tightly as he clung to the swords in his hand, thinking the same two words over and over—*protect her, protect her, protect her.*

The entire sky came alive with lightning, cracks of white energy to mirror the cracks the middle-god had made in the ground. He swept Shadowslayer downward and it pulled that lightning down as well, forming it into a cage that wrapped around Intaba.

Energy flared out from the middle-god's body—his magic, trying to overpower the storm that had descended over him. The combination of their different powers was so explosive, so intense that it nearly brought Elander to his knees despite the distance between them.

Then it settled, and the middle-god fixed his dead black eyes in Elander's direction.

"That's right," Elander muttered. "Back to me, you big dumb bastard."

The god obliged.

With a roar, he turned and charged.

The earth rattled and the god's shape was lost within rising dust and showering stones, making him seem more a part of the mountain than ever. But even though Elander could not *see* him, he could feel him coming closer with great, thundering steps.

Elander stood his ground. He felt more power unfurling inside of him like sails snagged in a sudden wind, catching so violently it made him feel as though he could have flown off the mountain, maybe taking Casia with him as he went.

Maybe he could overpower the God of Strength after all.

He tossed his own sword aside and took hold of Shadowslayer with both hands, lifting it above him just in time to counter a swing of the god's axe.

They collided as they had earlier, but this time, the Mountain God could not shove him downward. More light energy was wrapping around that god and restraining him, forming a barrier that helped negate his strength.

The middle-god stomped in frustration and more rocks rained down on them, but Elander stayed focused. The Heart of the Sun that was embedded in Casia's sword began to glow. The magic inside of him seemed to rise even further in response. He glanced to his left, saw Casia still precariously perched upon the ledge, and he thought only of making sure she had time to find her way back to solid ground.

The middle-god drew his axe back, took a wild spin to gain momentum, and then attempted to bring the weapon down upon Elander.

Elander swung upward, and a wall of brilliant light overtook Intaba, driving him back just as Malaphar had been driven back that day in Oblivion.

The middle-god stumbled away, his expression shocked. Confused. *Livid.*

Elander smiled, taking a step toward him, sword at the ready.

Then a resounding *crack* echoed through the air, and the middle-god was gone, leaving nothing but a jagged fracture upon the ground where he'd just been standing.

The last of his magic faded as he escaped. The stones his power had brought to life released all at once in a madly chaotic pattern. As they fell they knocked more rocks free. A small landslide started and escalated with terrifying speed.

Casia had still been crouching upon that narrow ledge, chin tucked toward her chest as she focused on breathing and balancing, but now her head snapped up in alarm.

A boulder struck the space directly in front of her, crushing the narrow stretch of rock as though it was nothing more than a bundle of sticks.

Her balance swayed, but she didn't fall.

She *leapt.*

Down and out of sight she went, rocks tumbling after her.

The sound of those rocks bouncing, thudding, *crashing* made Elander's stomach, his heart, his lungs— every vital part of him—clench with dread.

He was too stunned by her leap to move immediately. But he recovered quickly and raced toward the last place he'd seen her, darting between cracked ground, leaping over shifting stones, clamoring for the edge that had collapsed before her. It was all still unstable, crumbling away at an alarming rate—faster than he'd realized from a distance. He caught himself just before he tumbled over and disappeared as she had. He immediately had to shuffle backward to avoid being swallowed up by the caving ground.

He made it back to solid footing, and the earth ceased its shifting a moment later. He moved back to the edge of the drop-off, collapsed to his knees, and peered down into the newly-created chasm. The destruction stretched a hundred feet down. At least. It ended in a pile of broken trees and boulders—a pile that was growing larger as stray rocks continued to roll down and crash upon it.

Casia was nowhere in sight.

He reached out with his magic, trying to find hers, trying to pinpoint the direction he needed to start moving in.

But he couldn't feel her.

At all.

He poured more energy into summoning magic. Light bled from his body, twisted and brightened, forming the familiar shape of a wolf. A beast ready to track her.

He snapped out a command. *"Find her."*

The astral beast dove down and weaved its way

along the shattered mountainside, bouncing from rock to rock. Again and again it slipped into narrow cracks and crevices only to slip back out and continue its search.

But she was nowhere to be found.

CHAPTER 26

THE GROUND AROUND CAS WAS STILL SHAKING.

Or maybe that was her.

She was on her back, one hand braced at her side, the other lifted above her. The entire right side of her body was throbbing, scraped, and bloody.

She had leapt because the alternative had been falling. She'd thought she could land safely, but had misjudged the distance. A pair of wayward trees, growing sideways out of the mountain, had eventually caught her, but she felt like she'd rolled, slid, and bounced for at least a hundred feet before reaching these trees. Maybe more.

A stone face rose sharply up in front of her—impossible to climb back up.

Below her, the mountain quickly curved inward, creating a sheer drop of a dizzying, deadly height.

Rocks had tumbled after her as she fell, and now only a waning shield of her magic stretched between her and those rocks. Even if the impact of them didn't kill her, they would certainly push her down into a deadly free fall if she released them.

Her arms twitched. Her muscles were close to giving out. Her *entire body* felt close to giving out.

She couldn't stay in this position forever.

Her gaze tracked to the right, and she saw possible relief—a shallow cave that had somehow withstood the mountain falling down around it. The path to it was steep and narrow. It barely qualified as a ledge. But more trees like the ones cradling her lined that path, and she thought maybe she could crawl and scamper her way to safety with the help of a few sturdy branches.

She glanced one last time at the shield above her, hoping she could keep it steady while she moved—a much trickier task than holding it in place while she remained still.

She closed her eyes, focusing. The moment she did, she felt warmth surge through her. Her magic somehow felt both lighter and stronger, as though someone else had grabbed a side so they could help her carry it.

Elander?

Maybe it was her imagination, but just the thought of him and his magic reaching out to her was enough to give her the courage she needed.

She opened her eyes.

Took a deep breath.

She clambered toward the cave. She didn't think, she just *moved,* working her way from one tree to the next, her balance wobbling, her boots scraping the bald stone and coming perilously close to slipping out from under her more than once.

Just as she began to feel like she would never reach the cave, she finally found herself within its shadowy mouth. She dove and rolled inside, panting and aching. As soon as she crawled as deep inside her shelter as she could manage, her magic released; she was too tired to keep it up any longer.

The rocks the magic had been holding back began to fall, a trickle of pebbles slipping through the fading shield like water through a cracked dam until it broke completely and triggered another small landslide. The roof of her cave was battered, more and more rocks slamming into it by the second.

A particularly large boulder *thunked* down at the mouth, and Cas watched with wide eyes as the ground beneath it began to sink. Cracks spread through the floor, reaching toward her—too close to her—and she was too slow, too weak to roll farther back to safety.

The floor of her sanctuary caved forward, part of it collapsing completely...and then she was falling again, sliding, careening over the broken ledge, slipping down the steep face of the mountain—

Someone grabbed her hand.

They snatched her in mid-air, and they held her even as rocks continued to pummel her body.

A large chunk of stone hit her shoulder. The pain was excruciating. Disorienting. But she had been saved from tumbling down into almost certain death, and her savior held her until most of the dust and scattering rocks had stopped falling. So that *was* Elander's magic she'd felt a moment ago, she was certain of it now—

But when she found the strength to look up, it wasn't Elander holding her hand.

It was her brother.

Without a word, Varen hauled Cas up and over the crumbling edge and tossed her back onto steady ground —back into a deeper part of the cave.

Trapped.

The word rang like a warning bell in her mind.

She scrambled away from him and tried to make sense of what she was seeing. She no longer heard rocks falling outside, but she couldn't see what was happening out there; the exit was nearly blocked. The opening had been just large enough for them to squeeze through, and now her brother stood in front of it, his body wrapped in shadows that she didn't believe were entirely natural.

Trapped, she thought again.

But as she caught her breath, she didn't feel panic.

She felt...*fury.*

Images of their last meeting raced through her mind.

The blood-soaked battlefield. The dead bodies, the senseless destruction, the sword in Elander's back...

That sword became all she could focus on.

Strength surged through her. She didn't know where it had come from—only that she had to use it to get to her feet. She had to have strength enough for *this*.

She rose onto shaking legs.

And she stumbled forward—*sprinting*, by the end—and swung her fist into Varen's face as hard as she possibly could.

The punch had enough momentum behind it that it sent him stumbling backward, tripping over his feet and landing among the rocks that blocked the exit.

"One could argue that I deserved that, I suppose," he muttered.

She staggered after him and swung again.

He caught her fist less than an inch from his face this time, and rose once more to his feet, shoving her back as he did.

"You deserve far, far worse than that," she snarled, yanking free of his grip and then immediately preparing to attack again. "You obnoxious, *evil*—"

He fended her off as she dove at him again, grabbing her arm and twisting it, throwing her off balance. He pushed her hard against the cave wall. Her breath left her in a rush as her back collided with the stone. Black dots swam in her vision. She let out a groan of pain, and Varen's grip on her loosened somewhat.

His mistake.

She wiggled free enough to slam a knee into his side. As he doubled over, she ripped completely free, rolled around him and started to reach toward the sheath hanging from her hip—until she remembered that Shadowslayer was still somewhere far up above.

Of all the times to not have her damn sword...

She lifted her hand, intending to summon magic, with or without her sword. But it felt like something was wrapping around the strands of that magic and squeezing them, preventing them from expanding.

She clenched her fingers back into a fist and pretended not to be alarmed by her lack of weapons.

She wouldn't show fear.

Not to him.

A few more rocks shifted outside, tumbling down and blocking the cave entrance more completely. Only a narrow band of sunlight managed to keep pressing through, and the dust-filled air made it even more difficult to truly assess her surroundings. She felt like she was walking through yet another one of those foggy, confusing memories Caden had given her.

Varen caught his breath and straightened, still pressing a hand tenderly to his side. "Casia," he began, his usual calm, quiet voice uncomfortably loud in the enclosed space. "It's nice to—"

"Did you send the Mountain God to attack us?" she

demanded, cutting him off. "That god is your ally now, isn't he? The Dark Court and the Court of—"

"That's what it looks like, doesn't it? Or at least I hope so. I *want* him to think we're allies. It will save me some complications."

"What are you talking about? Don't play games with me, Varen. I swear I will rip you apart with my bare hands if I have to—"

"I think you'd be better off calming down and letting me explain."

"Why. Are. You. *Here*?"

"To ask a favor."

She snatched a sharp-edged rock and drew her fist back, preparing to hit him again.

"Also, I believe I've told you this before, but it obviously needs repeating: You are going to have to learn to control that temper if you're going to make any sort of decent queen."

She flung the rock at his head.

He batted it away with inhuman reflexes, slapping it against the wall with enough force to shatter it into several pieces.

She reached for a second rock, but never found it— because the space went entirely dark save for the glow of Varen's eyes. They were no longer the soft earth color she remembered; they had taken on a distinctly pale, golden-red color. A devastating chill permeated the air as those eyes brightened, so cold that it hurt to breathe it in.

Death magic.

And suddenly Cas remembered that this was no longer simply her brother she was dealing with—he was a *god*.

It didn't make her want to punch him any less. But her body felt drained, her limbs impossibly heavy, and as badly as she wanted to fight the sensation off, she couldn't. Her fury had only provided her with so much fuel, and she was more exhausted and beaten up than she wanted to admit.

She sank to one knee with as much control as she could manage.

The darkness scattered. Little pockets of dusty light shimmered around her once more.

Her brother remained half-hidden in shadow as he stepped and knelt in front of her. "I am not here to hurt you, Casia."

Her lungs still felt partially frozen. She couldn't swallow enough air to support a proper response, so she just ended up snarling out a barely intelligible curse, like some feral thing trapped in a too-small cage.

"There is nowhere for you to go anyway," he said. "My magic is stronger than yours. And it's neutralizing both your power *and* the magic that your annoying other half is sending out to try and track you; he can't find you, and you can't change that. At least, for the moment. And so now, for once, you have no choice but to listen to me. *Truly* listen to me."

She swallowed hard to shake off the last bit of Death magic clutching her throat. "No choice? *Really?* How many times have I escaped you at this point? You should know better than to think you can beat me by now. I'll leave if I want to."

"You'd be better off saving your strength in case the Mountain God returns for an encore performance, don't you think?"

No, Cas wanted to snap.

But something made her hold her tongue and kept her still.

It wasn't the fear that she couldn't get away from him. She would have fought her way out—injuries and exhaustion, be damned—if she'd truly thought that was what she needed to do.

But there was something else she needed more in that moment— *answers.*

All the many, many questions she had about the things she'd seen in those Blood crystals...she didn't trust Varen to give her honest answers about any of it, but...

How could she not at least *ask,* now that they had been thrown together like this?

He stood and offered her his hand.

She ignored it, got up on her own, and said in a cool voice, "If you would like me to listen to you, then start by explaining why you decided to become that which you supposedly detested."

"You think I *wanted* to become this?"

"You want power above all else. I know that much."

He looked almost...*disappointed* in this answer. "Come now—I thought you were more clever than that."

She kept her face expressionless. Whatever act he wanted to put on, she would not join it if she could help it.

"I didn't go to Dawnskeep intending to become a god," he continued. "I went there with plans to *slay* one."

Her detached demeanor nearly slipped, but she recovered. "What are you talking about?"

"The Antaeum Points. I made sure my memories of them were transferred to those crystals I sent you, so I presume that you know of what I speak?"

She studied him before nodding slowly, cautiously. "But what *are* they, precisely?"

"*Anchor points*, would be a more simple term for them. Created in the places where the three Moraki first touched down on this mortal plane. One of those points —for example—was in Dawnskeep, under the control of the elves of Moreth. You went to it yourself...that island off the north coast."

She forced another nod as memories of that desolate island flickered through her thoughts. The stone statues that had surrounded her, the way she'd pleaded to them, the desperation she had felt. She had gone there to try and summon Solatis, but...

"But nothing happened once you arrived there, did it?" Varen's tone was smug. He already knew the answer to his own question. "The upper-goddess never entered this mortal realm to help you. She took you *out* of this realm during the battle that followed your visit to that island—but even that was a brief affair, wasn't it?"

Cas's heart skipped several beats. "How do you know all of this?"

"Simple. The reason that Dawnskeep did not react to your magic was because I got there first. The power that was once concentrated there was already neutralized."

"Neutralized?"

"I successfully managed to complete the task that our father couldn't—sealing off that which served as Solatis's anchor point."

Understanding unfurled slowly through Cas's mind. "...You're the reason Solatis can't come back into this mortal realm."

He nodded. "And our father is the reason that the first upper-god—Belegor—was weakened to the point that he could be slayed by another of his order. It was one of Father's final accomplishments before his untimely death; he managed to seal the point in the elven realm of Lightwyn—in the Belaric Empire—which was tied to the Stone God. Belegor made the mistake of trying to come back to this world anyway, and while he was within it and without his full power, he was slaughtered—presumably by the Rook God or one of his servants."

Cas braced a hand against the wall behind her, thinking. "Anchor points...one in Moreth, one in Lightwyn...they're all tied to the elven realms?"

"They are."

"Mistwilde?" she guessed, eyes widening slightly. "Is that where the third anchor point is?"

"You're catching up. Good."

She was not eager to believe anything her brother said. But it made sense. She knew the elves were the first master beings that the Moraki had attempted to create in the mortal realm. It had ended poorly, however, and the elves had been stripped of most of their divine magic as a result. It wasn't a stretch to think that those elves, in their attempts to keep some sort of magic and control, might have done...*something* with these points of concentrated power.

"But how do the Moraki not know about these points?"

Varen shrugged. "Pride? The vanity of the gods is immeasurable, really. The anchor point in Lightwyn was well-guarded and kept secret, as is the Mistwilde one. Dawnskeep was a bit more obvious, but the Rook God wants to believe that Solatis brought about her own end by helping humans. I don't think the possibility of these anchor points existing has ever crossed his mind.

"They aren't entirely natural at this point, after all—these are points that have been corrupted by the elves over the centuries. All of the anti-divine-magic spells and materials that they've developed...it's all derived from their work with these Antaeum Points. It's an entire, complex system of anti-magic, but it's all very clandestine. Our father was one of the only humans with inside knowledge of it."

Cas felt dizzy as she realized just how delicate the situation in Mistwilde truly was.

Did King Talos know what sort of power he had hidden in that realm?

Who *else* knew?

A chilling possible answer to that last question popped almost immediately into her head. "Sarith is harassing Mistwilde. Why?"

Varen sighed. "I was working with her in hopes that she might be the sort of cutthroat ally I needed to get me into Mistwilde. But she's proving less than reliable, unfortunately. I believe she's gotten the idea in her head that she can wield this last anchor point as a political tool, and she's decided she would rather wield it than destroy it. She was not pleased with my destruction of the one at Dawnskeep; she tried to talk me out of it, and it all got very...*messy* toward the end."

Cas felt a rush of exhaustion; she wanted to slump

down to the cave floor and just *crumble* for a while. But she forced her legs to stay straight.

"So what now?" she demanded. "You think *I* will be more useful to you than Sarith? You expect me to just... believe all of this?" She shook her head, exasperated. "After everything you've done, I'm just supposed to accept that you were really trying to be a good person and do the right thing all along...and now you just need help doing it?"

"Good person?" He laughed—a dark, empty sound that turned Cas's insides to ice. "You mistake me for you," he said. "Unlike you, I never set out to be *good*. I set out to do what needed to be done, as did our father before us. You, on the other hand..."

She glared, but he just shook his head at her and kept talking.

"You have been so busy trying to make everyone your ally, trying to protect and please and save *everyone*, and where has that gotten you? Now the world is threatening to break at the hands of a mad god, and I wonder... can you do what must be done to save it all? Because that salvation will take more than *goodness*."

She felt a heaviness growing in her bones again, the desire to slump to the ground becoming more and more intense, but she continued to fight through it.

"A ruler's job isn't to *be* good to people," Varen continued. "It is to *do* good for them—the most good for the most people. It isn't as simple as you want it to be,

Casia. It never was. And it has gotten so much bigger than it was when you and I met all those months ago in my palace."

She stared at what she could see of his face in the dim, dusty light, and she had the thought—again—that this felt like another one of those memory crystals.

Would the fog around him ever fully clear?

Would she ever be able to clearly see and understand him?

"I was researching all of these things well before our fateful reunion, of course," he said. "I knew some of what our father had been up to—though not all of it. He hid many things. Sheltered me from them. So I had a lot of digging to do, and I ran out of time. I had gotten close to a breakthrough before I discovered you were alive, that Elander was not who he seemed, and then...well, things got regrettably *complicated*, didn't they?"

"Why could you not tell me all of this sooner?" she demanded. "If you knew it well before I showed up in the palace?"

"I didn't put most of it together until *after* the business with you and the divine threat became very real. And I *did* reach out a hand to you in Sadira, if you've forgotten. You said—let's see, what were your exact words? That you believed I was a tyrant and a fool, and that my soul was black and beyond repair."

"Because you had just *attacked* that kingdom. And

you killed Soryn's parents a year before that. You sent their hands back to her *in a fucking box*."

"An unfortunate culmination of decades of hostility between our kingdoms—a war that Sadira actually started, for the record. Because Sadira has always had the greatest population of magic users in Kethra. If the old gods are driven away from this mortal realm, the magic will ultimately go with them, and where does that leave Sadira? We've been clashing for decades over this—and the incident at Seap had little to do with me, for what it's worth. It was just another battle in a long string of battles that have been taking place since well before I took the throne. Those hands sent to Soryn were not bloodless, literally or figuratively."

Cas bared her teeth in a sardonic smile. "And you have an excuse for why you tried to kill me and Elander as well, I'm guessing."

"I do, actually."

She stopped smiling.

He was serious, wasn't he?

"It's obvious, isn't it?" said Varen. "The two of you carry an enormous amount of divine power. I don't know what either of you truly are, but my most trusted advisors and scholars warned that you might give Solatis a foothold in this world, even after her anchor point was sealed off." He shrugged. "It looks as if the Sun Goddess is gone. Whether or not she *stays* gone remains to be seen. Hopefully, sealing the point was enough."

"And if something changes, I assume you'll be trying to kill us again. Greatest *good* and all that."

"We'll see if it comes to that." His expression was grim. "But just so we're clear, I don't plan on doing that any time soon if I can help it. If only because I need you to do that favor for me first, as I said."

"You're insane," she hissed. "Why would you come to me thinking I would ally myself with you? After everything you've done?"

"Who do you turn to in desperation, if not your fami—"

"Don't," she warned. "Just...*don't*."

He lifted his gaze to the ceiling of rock that sloped close to their heads, studied a shimmering vein in it for a moment, and then said, "What choice do I have? I can't exactly march into Mistwilde any longer. But *you* can. The Antaeum Point needs to be destroyed if you want any hope of being able to destroy Malaphar. And isn't that your ultimate goal?"

She didn't answer for a long time. *Couldn't* answer.

Finally, she said, "If I decided to go after this last anchor point—*if*—then how would I seal it?"

"I don't know. I didn't get that far—but the method I used at Dawnskeep was not the same as the one our father used in Lightwyn, where that first sealing point was. He had notes started for all three of those points, but what I've found was all incomplete thanks to his, well, *untimely* end."

Cas said nothing. She was not going to think about what had caused that end. Or about different lives, different timelines, or the shifting points that the Star Goddess had mentioned to her. All these things flashed through her mind, but she couldn't let herself focus on them right now. It was too much.

Varen was digging something out of the pocket of the hooded cloak he wore. She tensed, ready for his next trick—but he only pulled out a handful of red-tinted crystals and offered them to her.

"These memories are not mine," he said. "They belonged to Lord Orbryn, who—as you probably know —was our father's closest advisor and confidant."

A realization gripped her, raising the little hairs along the back of her neck. "You killed him."

"He wouldn't willingly part with these memories, unfortunately. Desperate times, desperate measures."

"*Insane*," she repeated.

"Ruthlessly persistent about my goals and the *greater good*," he corrected.

She glared. But one by one she took them, and when Varen produced a small bag of them from his coat, she took that too. It would have been foolish not to. Hadn't they been trying to pry Orbryn's knowledge out of him for weeks?

As she closed the crystals in her fist, yet another

possible complication occurred to her. "You've been doing all of this sneaking around—coordinating the formation of these crystals, and now delivering them—are you not worried that Malaphar is going to find out?"

"Another reason I need your help. That link between us is growing stronger by the day. It's still somewhat tenuous now, but it's only a matter of time before I ascend fully into his power. At which point, of course, I will no longer be able to keep my thoughts and actions separate from him."

And what then?

A sliver of concern shot through her before she could guard herself against it. She quickly shook it off.

Her eyes shifted to the crack in the rocks piled by the entrance. She focused on the sunlight sneaking in, on letting the light inside of herself rise to meet it. Magic tingled across her skin, and she *thought* she felt a spark of power in response—even if Varen's power was supposedly draining it.

It was still fainter than it should have been, but her brother had obviously felt it as well, because he sighed. "My, he's persistent, isn't he?"

"He is. And he won't be as patient with you as I've been."

"I'm terrified," said Varen as he casually drew the hood of his cloak over his head and fastened it into place.

After a final annoyed glance in his direction, Cas

stepped around him and started for the cave's opening. She would dig her way out of this mess, whatever it took.

Varen didn't try to stop her—not physically—but he still managed to bring her to a halt with his words. "I may not be able to meet you like this again," he said. "Not without drawing too much attention and suspicion...but my servant can move a bit more freely."

Caden.

She whirled around, feeling the sudden urge to punch him again. "That servant was never meant to work for you. You've taken him, *tricked* him, and now what will you do with him? You can't just *use* people for whatever insane schemes—"

"It will ultimately be for the good of the world, and Caden will understand this in the end, I suspect. He seems like an intelligent sort."

"He still should have had a say in it! Just because he understands it doesn't mean he would have agreed to it, given the choice."

"And once again, you are boring me with your incessant need for morals and endless ethical discussions. I did what I had to do. He was already tied to the role, which made the process quicker. And in case you haven't realized it, *time is not on our side.*"

She absently reached for the necklace the Sand Goddess had given her. The shining hourglass caught

Varen's eye, and his expression shifted into something...strange.

Concern, almost.

It took Cas a moment to find her voice again. "Why did you agree to become a god?" Her voice was hushed, weighed down by all the uncomfortable, heavy uncertainties that remained between them. "You never really answered my question."

He continued to fiddle with the hood of his cloak as he stepped toward the exit. She thought he was going to ignore the question again. But then he paused and quietly said, "Because the alternative would have been *you* becoming one."

She had no idea how to respond.

"I should go." He studied the rocks piled around the mouth of the cave before turning and reaching back to her. "Can I take you to safety? It's a long way back up the mountain."

She stared at his outstretched hand for what might have been an eternity.

She didn't take it. She didn't trust him. She *couldn't* trust him. Every muscle, from her heart to her fingers to her toes, went numb at the mere thought of it. So she simply averted her gaze and said, "I'll find my own way out."

He sighed, wistfully, as though this was what he'd expected her to say. "I hope we have a chance to talk again before the end."

Cas didn't respond.

The cave became deathly cold once more, and a whisper of sound—like bare tree limbs rattling in the wind—followed a moment later, making her shivering worse.

She finally looked back, expecting to see his eyes once again glowing strangely as his magic manifested.

But he was already gone.

CHAPTER 27

THE WOLF OF LIGHT SLIPPED FREE OF A PILE OF RUBBLE AND shot back to Elander, circled him once, and then bounded back to the pile.

There.

Strength coursed through Elander as he moved to follow the trail of light. He lifted the boulders as if they were mere pebbles, gently tossing them aside, taking care not to trigger any more falling rocks. After what felt like a lifetime of digging, he reached his hand down into a dark crevice and finally saw Casia's hand reaching back.

Their fingertips brushed. He felt another rush of power that gave him the strength to push aside the last stones that remained in her path, and then to grab her arms and heave her back into the daylight.

She collapsed against his chest, and they fell to the

ground together, each trying to clutch the other one more tightly.

After a moment, he bent away and gave a relieved sigh, pressing a hand against the side of her face as he quickly looked her over. She was bruised and scraped, but mostly intact.

"You can't be entirely furious at me this time," she said, somewhat sheepishly, as she leaned into his touch. "I didn't *dive* into anything. I was swallowed up by the earth—not by my own reckless decision."

He tried to laugh. It came out as no more than a shuddering breath; he felt like his chest and lungs were collapsing under the weight of his relief. He swallowed hard and said, "I'm fairly certain I saw you jump."

"Well...yes. But I was trying to jump to safety. I just miscalculated a bit." She coughed—and then winced— as she shook rock dust from her shirt.

"Just a bit?"

She gave him another rueful smile.

"...Anyway, don't worry," he told her, moving to collect Shadowslayer, which he'd set aside before he started digging her out, "I got your sword back."

She smiled at this echo of her words from the last battle they'd fought together. "Thank you."

He watched it glow faintly as she took hold of it, frowning. Thinking. "All of this power connecting us," he mumbled, "and yet it took me what felt like an eternity to find you."

"It's because Varen was using his magic to nullify yours and mine—draining it."

It was a moment before her words fully registered, and even then, Elander thought he'd misheard her. "...Varen?"

She started to her feet, looking slightly shaky. He moved closer and offered a steadying arm as she continued, "And I suppose this, combined with how drained I already was, caused a lapse in our connection for a few minutes."

"He was *here*?"

"Gods come and go as they please lately, don't they?" she muttered.

If he has a message to send to us, he can stop being a fucking coward and bring it himself next time.

That was what he'd told Caden to tell Varen, wasn't it?

Apparently, Varen had taken it seriously—though he was still a coward as far as Elander was concerned, considering he hadn't stuck around to chat with *him*. "What did he want?"

"I'm still trying to figure that out, honestly."

They were interrupted before the conversation got any further as members of their traveling party gathered on the edge of the cliffs high above, peering down and calling out to them in panicked voices.

"I'll explain more once we make it to the Roedyn Valley," Casia promised. "We should get moving."

He agreed, turning to size up the steep paths that led back to their soldiers.

The latest bit of strength that had awakened in him seemed to be there to stay, so climbing back up the destroyed mountainside did not strike him as the daunting task that it would have been to a normal human. He convinced Casia to let him carry her for the sake of time, and then they started up.

He didn't move as easily as he had as a god, but he carried Casia up with enough divine speed and grace that all of the soldiers were staring at him with a mixture of awe and shock by the time he leapt over the last bit of rough terrain and landed lightly on his feet before them.

They had all heard the rumors of who and what he was, of course, but likely didn't fully grasp who they were traveling with. He didn't offer to answer any questions about the matter; they had other things to worry about.

Most of the soldiers were accounted for, and someone had even managed to round up his horse. But several of the other horses were missing—including Casia's—so he ended up carrying her once more, situating her in the saddle in front of him.

She didn't protest this either. The ride was quiet again, but it was not the same prickly silence as before; it was contemplative. And painful, maybe, judging by the way she occasionally clenched her fists and sucked in sharp breaths.

After a few minutes she curled against him and tucked her head toward her chest. He held her gently but securely, taking care not to press against her injuries. Her breathing slowed and she went limp, and he briefly thought the pain had overcome her. But as soon as they were within sight of their destination, her head popped up, and she insisted on walking the rest of the way.

He helped her down, and then he hopped down from the saddle and led his horse on foot. The beast's sides were slicked with sweat and its breathing was getting labored; it needed a break.

The camp at Roedyn Valley was well on its way to being a proper town.

This place had once been mostly tents, fire circles, and crudely-fashioned hitching posts, but there had always been a permanent building to serve as a supply stop, and several other buildings had been erected since the last time Elander had passed through. Most of these new buildings surrounded a small, crystal blue lake in the center of the valley.

A well-kept road—this was new too—wound its way toward this lake. They followed it until they reached a modest hut situated right on the water's edge.

The watery reflection of the surrounding mountains was a serene sight. Casia paused to admire it all, her mouth falling open slightly as her eyes moved over the wind-rippled water, the flower-swept shoreline, the hills of swaying grass that rolled away from the lake.

As they stood there, several members of the caravan approached, all clamoring to know what she needed. She claimed that she was only a bit sore from her ordeal —that she needed nothing from them.

All the same, while she inquired about the leader in charge of the camp, Elander quietly inquired about a healer for her.

That leader arrived a few minutes later—a fragile old man with a distinct scar slashing through his right eyebrow and several braids trailing through his long, grey beard.

"Lord Raevern," he said, offering Casia a leathery hand. "Though I usually prefer not to bother with the *lord* part, as honored as I was to receive the designation. I've lived in this valley for decades—we don't have much use for fancy titles and the like 'round here."

Elander wondered if he had lived in this valley for so long because he lacked the strength to make it back down the mountain; he looked as though one rough gust of wind might snap him in half.

He moved with a surprisingly sprightly step, however, as he led Casia up the rickety steps of that unassuming hut on the water, and then gestured for her to sit on the porch overlooking the lake.

Elander felt restless, so he left them to chat while he

went to take further inventory of their traveling party and to help scout for any suspicious activity that might have followed them into the valley.

He circled back to the lakeside hut some time later, and he found that Casia and Raevern had moved their meeting inside. Raevern was speaking quickly while warming his hands on the fire crackling in the stone hearth.

Elander did not want to interrupt them, so he simply leaned against the wall and waited, his focus alternating between their conversation and what he could see of the lake through the large window beside them.

Between the heady scent of smoke and the cozy warmth permeating the space, it was tempting to close his eyes and nod off. After a few minutes, he felt oddly removed from their trials. He almost relaxed. Almost forgot about the trek back down the mountain that awaited them, and he *did* forget—at least for a moment —that he and Casia had been arguing on their way up that mountain. That argument seemed rather pointless now.

She was safe and warm, she was close to him, and that overcame everything else. He was beginning to think it would *always* overcome everything else.

Always.

That word kept coming to mind whenever he looked at her here lately.

It was...strange. He had lived such an unsteady,

unusual existence that concepts like *forever* and *always* had never held much significance to him.

Not until her.

Her conversation eventually finished. Raevern gave her a little bow, which she returned, and then they parted ways. She spoke briefly with the few other people who had wandered in to see her, and then she turned, spotted Elander, and quickly made her way over.

"We're going to stay for a few hours and join Lord Raevern for lunch," she informed him. "He wants me to speak with a few of the regular inhabitants of the valley. They'll be back soon, and some of our soldiers are still a bit...shaken up after what happened. They probably need another hour or two of rest anyway." She rubbed her arm. Shaken up herself, clearly—though he doubted she would show it in front of anyone other than him. "General Caster, apparently she..."

"I know."

She seemed relieved to not have to repeat the general's fate out loud.

"Fresh air?" he suggested, nodding toward the door.

She agreed, and they moved outside and sat at the edge of one of the many clear little streams that fed into the lake.

The healer he'd sent for still had not arrived, so Elander took it upon himself to take a closer look at the latest injuries she'd acquired.

Her movements were smooth enough; nothing

seemed broken or sprained, at least. There was a faint bruise forming on her forehead—right next to the cut she'd already sustained from her fall in her bathroom. Aside from that, the right side of her body seemed to have borne the brunt of her fall down the mountainside. Her jacket was ripped in several places, and her braid was disheveled.

She glanced at her reflection in the stream, pursed her lips, pulled off the necklace that had gotten tangled in her messy hair, and studied it while Elander wrapped her other wrist with a bandage that one of their soldiers brought him.

"Banged up, but still intact," she commented, rubbing her thumb over the necklace's hourglass charm, which had chipped in one corner.

"Just like you," he murmured distractedly, as he scooped a handful of the cold stream water and washed out the scrapes along her palm.

She sucked in a breath.

"Sorry."

She waved the apology off and went back to studying the chipped hourglass, obviously trying to focus on something other than the pain she was in.

"That little thing...did Santi tell you what it does?"

She arched a brow. "She wouldn't be a divine being if she gave me such straightforward information."

A corner of his mouth hitched up; she wasn't wrong.

"It will open paths for me, she said. But only if I truly *want* it to."

"Hm."

"That sounded like a suspicious *hm*."

He finished cleaning and bandaging her wrist and palm, and then he settled back against a slab of sandy stone, studying the golden chain draped between her fingers. "You don't have to tell me what you spoke to that goddess about while you were there yesterday, but...just be careful with what she gives you. With what she tells you."

"You don't trust her?"

"I don't fully trust any of the divine at this point. Even the ones that are supposedly on our side. This war that's building is unlike anything in our world's history. Who knows what it will lead to? The old alliances and hierarchy of things...I'm not counting on any of it."

Casia's eyes glazed over in thought. "I only went to her because I wanted to ask her about something the Goddess of Stars mentioned."

"Which was what?"

"When she and the rest of the court came to the palace, she showed me the Map of Stars, and she mentioned a *breaking point* that was connected to my own personal stars. I wanted to see if Santi could enlighten me further about that particular point in my past. And I also wondered if her magic might be able to send me back to see some things more clearly. Varen's memories are a starting point, but they're limited to what he saw and understood of certain moments. So I have a lot of questions."

He was quiet for a long time, absorbing what she'd said, trying to stay calm and think it all through. Part of him was still angry at all these things she'd kept from him. But they had to move on and focus on what came next.

So he quietly said, "You were right, by the way."

She blinked and fixed him with a curious look.

"I shouldn't have kept Caden from showing you those things about yourself and your family's past," he told her. "Maybe all of this wouldn't have gotten so complicated if I had helped you start to untangle those past threads before now."

She looked away. Picked at the bandage he'd wrapped around her wrist. Before long she was pulling at it in her typical anxious, rhythmic fashion. "I understand why you kept it from me."

He took her hand and held it still before she ruined that bandaging job. "How many more of those crystals do you have?"

She exhaled a slow breath. "I only had a few left, but Varen gave me more."

A muscle ticked in Elander's jaw. "Is that why he decided to show his cowardly face? Just to bring you those?"

She nodded. "All the previous ones I had were full of his memories. These new ones contain Lord Orbryn's."

He held her hand more tightly, more to steady himself rather than her this time.

"You know I can't ignore them, Elander." Her tone, like his own, no longer contained any trace of the argument between them. It was...*resigned*. "Before I decided to come back to Ciridan," she continued softly, "I tried to tell myself the past didn't matter. But that's just another way of hiding —and I'm tired of hiding. I'm tired of changing my name, my appearance, my story. I've decided to take up this kingdom's crown, and that means taking up *all* of it. All that it was, all that it is, all that it could be. So there are things I need to know, even if they're ugly, confusing things."

She stood, crossing her arms against her chest, and paced the edge of the lake.

Elander watched her without speaking, picking up a smooth pebble and tossing it between his hands.

"I don't want to keep using them. I know what they're doing to me—I know the dangers—I just..." She stopped her pacing, rubbing her arms and averting her gaze in that same uneasy way she'd done in Raevern's hut. "I know the dangers," she repeated, "and believe me, I'm starting to get..." Her gaze trailed to her reflection in the lake's glassy surface. She stared at it for a long time, as if something about it had confused her, before she finished her sentence.

"...Frightened."

"Frightened?"

"Afraid that all these things are going to erase everything I thought I knew. And that I won't recognize myself in the end."

He frowned and tossed the pebble into the lake, watching the rings spreading from where it sank for a moment, and then said, "I will."

"You will what?"

He lifted his gaze to her questioning one. "I'd know you anywhere, I suspect." With a quiet chuckle he added, "And even if I don't recognize you right away...I'll figure it out eventually."

She slowly unfolded her arms and came back to sit beside him. Tucked her legs against her body and rested her chin on them. A quiet minute passed. "In this lifetime and every other?"

"Exactly."

She smiled, and that word pressed against his heart once more.

Always.

He didn't say anything else—only returned the soft smile she was giving him and then went back to tossing rocks into the water.

"Do you want to know what I saw with the help of all of those crystals?"

He inhaled deeply through his nose. *Want* was not the right word. He was as afraid as she was about it all, truthfully. But there was no way of escaping it—so he nodded.

She took a moment to decide where to start. "It's been a lot to sort through, but the things that stood out most to me were the Antaeum Points that I heard the former king talking about."

"Antaeum Points?"

"You've never heard of them, either, I take it."

He shook his head.

"Apparently Anric didn't share the information about them with many people—not even with his own son."

She spent the next several minutes sharing the information she had managed to learn about these points where the Moraki had supposedly first touched the mortal realm, the way their power was tied to them, and the way that power had allegedly been corrupted and changed as the centuries passed.

"A third point still exists," she concluded breathlessly, "and it's *also* tied to the elves—to the ones in Mistwilde, specifically."

Sharp claws of realization raked through him. "And Sarith likely knows about it because of her alliance with Varen."

"Now a strained alliance, supposedly. But yes, that was my first thought as well."

"Does she realize what it actually *is*, though? What it could potentially mean for this mortal realm?"

"She knows at least some of what Varen knows...if not all."

"No wonder she wants to overtake Mistwilde. Imagine the sort of power she could hold if she had control over such a powerful mark..."

"I don't want to imagine it, but I am," Casia said, quietly. "What if she somehow used it as leverage to form an alliance with the Dark God? The two of them would make a terrifying team." Her hand moved to her shoulder, absently slipping beneath the collar of her shirt. Feeling one of the scars that ran along the skin there, he suspected.

His vision blurred around the edges, the way it always did whenever he was reminded of the torture she had suffered at the hands of that elven queen.

A sick part of him was glad it now seemed inevitable that he would cross paths with Sarith again. He was going to make her suffer, along with every member of her court that had participated in what she'd done to Casia.

And he was going to *enjoy* inflicting that suffering.

He forced himself to rein in his murderous thoughts. "We'll just have to beat her to this anchor point," he said. "Though we're going to have to make our way into Mistwilde by force, I'm afraid; its king seems determined to be uncooperative."

Casia considered this for a moment. "The summit we've been planning for is in less than five days. Last I checked with Rhea, we have thirty leaders who have agreed to attend, or at least send delegates. We'll establish more allies at this event, explain things, get them to pledge their help, and then we can march our way into Mistwilde." She took a deep breath. *"Then* we'll find this Antaeum Point, figure out how to seal it off, and save the world from all the mad gods threatening it... Easy, right?"

He huffed out a laugh. "Simple as that."

She sighed and leaned against him. He hooked an arm around her and planted a soft kiss against the side of her head. Together, they stared out over the sun-drenched lake, silently contemplating matters.

Several minutes passed before Casia sat upright again and held out her hand, where the crystals of memory still rested.

"So, we have a plan," she said, dragging one of those gems around in her palm. "And in the meantime, I'll keep searching through these."

He fought the urge to recoil at the faint trace of Caden's magic that he felt emanating from her hand.

What had become of his old friend?

He forced the question out of his mind.

"That lord was Anric's closest advisor," Casia pressed. "I have to find out what he knew."

Elander found another rock, intending to toss it into the lake as well, but just ended up crushing it in his fist instead.

"I won't do it alone. Nessa's magic was helping me, and I was stupid last time to try it without her...I just dove too deep, that's all. I won't make the same mistake again." She fixed him with a stubborn gaze, which he forced himself to hold. "I'm strong enough to do this."

"I know you're strong enough," he said. "That was never the problem."

She'd clearly been halfway to a counterpoint before he'd even spoken, but now she hesitated, tucking her hair behind her ear. Waiting for him to continue.

But he wasn't sure how to put into words what he was thinking in that moment.

He just knew that he wanted to take it away—somehow—all this pain she had to go through...whether it was enduring the cleaning of her wounds, or the dark revelations of her past. He had taken on the role of her guardian, but there were some things he couldn't guard her against, and it made him sick to think about it.

But she was right about this; they needed to see Orbryn's memories.

So he breathed in deep and nodded. "You focus on what you need to find within those crystals, and I'll focus on helping to prepare for this summit." He paused for a beat, forcing his hand to unclench and letting the broken pieces of rock trickle to the ground. "But Casia..."

Her gaze lifted to him.

"Don't hide it from me." He looked away—away from the cut she'd sustained on her forehead and the bruise beside it—so that he could speak his next words more calmly. "Do you know what it was like, to walk into that room and find you lying on the floor like that? I —" He drew in another deep breath. Shook his head. "Don't hide it from me," he repeated. "Any of it. Promise it. Swear it."

Their gazes met once more, and everything seemed to still for a moment—the breeze, the sunlight glinting against the water, the people moving and chattering in the background.

She clutched the crystals in her hand more tightly. "I swear it."

CHAPTER 28

AFTER SPEAKING WITH EVERYONE THEY NEEDED TO, AND following a brief visit from a healer that Elander insisted upon, they returned from the mountains with the help of some borrowed horses and a knowledgeable guide that hailed from Eldrin.

Even with that guide showing them shortcuts and safer paths, the route was long. It was well past midnight before they trudged back through the palace gates.

Once inside, Cas was immediately swarmed by advisors, courtiers, and servants—just as she'd been when she returned from the haven of the Time Goddess—but after a few quick conversations, she managed to slip away and make it to the privacy of her room.

She collapsed onto the bed without really meaning to, drawn to it by some invisible force while on her way to the bath. She only meant to rest her eyes for a few minutes before waking and tending to whatever royal obligations she'd missed while she was away.

But when she woke, it was morning.

She discovered—after a quick chat with the guard by the door—that there had been strict orders not to disturb her. She didn't complain; it was the deepest sleep she remembered having in some time.

She braced herself for the day, quickly washed and dressed, and then headed downstairs. The rapidly approaching summit weighed most heavily on her mind, so she sought out Nessa to see what preparations for it still remained.

She eventually found her in one of the gardens, digging holes and sprinkling seeds into them. Cas watched her for a moment before strolling over.

In spite of her looming obligations and concerns, she felt herself smiling as she drew closer and admired Nessa's work. The walking path that wound through this section of the garden had been cleared of the weeds creeping onto it, and it was lined by dozens of freshly tilled patches where seeds had been planted.

"You've been busy this morning," Cas commented.

Nessa leaned back, balancing on the balls of her feet as she swiped away a smudge of dirt from her cheek. "It's silly, I know, but I found a bunch of seeds and starts in the greenhouse over there." She pointed to a building with foggy glass walls that looked crowded, overgrown

—like someone had tried and failed to take a jungle captive. "I was collecting flowers, trying to put together at least some simple centerpieces for the summit banquet I've been planning...and then I got carried away, I guess."

"It looks like it," Cas said, still smiling.

Nessa picked at a bit of dirt under one of her nails. "I couldn't help but think about the future, and how we might eventually need *more* of this sort of thing. No one's been tending to the greenhouses back here for the better part of the past year, I don't think. They *all* need sorting out. But I'm starting with just the one— just making sure at least *some* of the seeds and such don't go to waste. If there's something else you need me to do right now, I can stop. I know it's silly, like I said—"

"It's not silly," Cas interrupted quietly.

"They might not even bloom in this weather; it's too late in the season for planting. But I thought I could try nurturing them with my magic, and maybe..."

Cas crouched down beside her. "Can I help?"

Nessa nodded, and showed her the proper depth of hole to dig, and how many seeds to scatter, and how to cover them just so. After her instructions were given, she fell quiet, her brow furrowing in concentration.

Ten minutes passed while they worked in tandem, Cas planting on one side of the path while Nessa planted on the other, until Nessa paused and said, "It's overwhelming, isn't it? The scale of it all." She was looking over the stretch of path that still needed to be lined.

But Cas suspected she wasn't just talking about flowers.

"It is," Cas agreed, starting to dig again. "But we'll get there. And it's important to plant things for the future, as you said."

The conversation she'd had that day with Rhea—about her plans to build an institute for learning like the one in Rykarra—surfaced in her mind. She felt the same spark of stubborn hope as she stared at the freshly tilled mounds of dirt around them.

It was easier to think of the future—of *the other side*—when she was with her friends.

There would be a future as long as they kept fighting, wouldn't there? They could get there. To safer cities, newly-built buildings, and rows upon rows of blooming flowers...

The two of them went back to work, and they spent the better part of the next hour digging and planting. No one interrupted them, just as no one had interrupted Cas's sleep. She was beginning to think Elander and the others were running interference, giving her a brief break from her obligations.

Wondering about it made her think of the *last* time her friends had tried to interfere on her behalf, and she found herself fighting off the urge to cringe.

"I owe you an apology, by the way," she told Nessa.

"You and Zev, both. For all that happened with those crystals—I didn't mean to frighten you, or take advantage of you agreeing to help me."

"It's okay." Nessa paused again, staring at her reflection in the dirty metal surface of her spade, her eyes glazed over in thought. "There are no real instructions for any of these things we're trying to do, are there?"

They went back to work. Another section of the path was soon finished, and then Nessa stood, wiped the dirt from her knees, and said, "So, do you have another of those crystals for us?"

Cas did—she had at least a half-dozen in her coat pocket—but she was hesitant to take them out all of a sudden. "Are you sure? You don't have to help if it makes you uncomfortable."

Nessa gripped her spade the way a determined warrior might grip a sword. "You need to deal with them before the summit, right? And the more information you have to present to our potential allies at this summit, the better. So I'm ready when you are."

AFTER CLEANING up their gardening mess, they made their way to a more secluded corner of the grounds—a patch of overgrown yard right up against the forest, dotted with large stones and flanked by several massive rose bushes that further hid them from any prying eyes. They sat on a pair of the stones, and Cas placed the crystals in a line between them.

"Lord Orbryn's memories, this time," she told Nessa, and then she briefly explained her strange meeting with her brother in the mountains before selecting one of the crystals.

The first visions from it were brief—flickers of Lord Orbryn's various undertakings in the name of his king. His meetings, his travels, his countless hours spent studying books and taking notes. Most of what she saw served as confirmation of things she had already discovered, and the things that Varen had mentioned. There was frustratingly little *new* information uncovered, and after the fifth crystal she was almost ready to call it an afternoon.

But then the sixth crystal caught her eye.

She couldn't explain it, but something came over her when she touched this one—a jolt of electricity that made her scalp tingle and her magic feel restless. Eager. Almost as if that magic had just been waiting for her to choose this crystal.

"Last one," she told Nessa.

Nessa nodded, took a deep breath to renew her determination, and put her hand in Cas's. Warmth flowed between them, and Cas relaxed into it, closing her eyes and quietly reciting the necessary spell.

When she opened her eyes again, it was night.

Most of her senses were dulled whenever she

slipped into one of these memories—including her sense of temperature—but this time she could tell that she had fallen into a memory of someplace very, very cold. The sky was clear and pitch dark, and the stars were brighter than she'd ever seen them. The frozen grass crunched under Lord Orbryn's boots as he made his way down a hillside, walking toward a road. A dark carriage, pulled by darker horses, rolled along that bumpy road, the occasional flash of its silver trimmings the only thing that made it somewhat visible.

The carriage lurched to a stop.

Her father emerged from it.

Lord Orbryn turned and glanced back, and Cas's vision moved with his to see a small house that was perched at the top of a hill. It leaned slightly to the left, giving the impression that it could topple down at any moment. A large tree with long, willowy branches stood to the right of it, close enough that even a faint gust of wind likely made those branches tickle the house's windows. Cas could imagine the sound, and it made her shiver.

Something about it was oddly familiar, like a face that she remembered but couldn't quite put a name to.

Time skipped ahead, and they were standing before the house's front door. Lord Orbryn ran his fingers over it, occasionally tapping the patterns that had been carved into the wood.

He never truly knocked, but the door still opened.

He and the king were ushered inside. The distant sound of children echoed toward them. The foyer was dimly lit by a fire roaring in the adjacent room, allowing Orbryn—and therefore Cas—to just make out the shape of the person who had invited them inside. Slender body, teal eyes that sparkled oddly in the light, ears that tapered...

An elf.

"It's all arranged." The elf's shining gaze flickered over the king. "You needn't have come yourself."

"His Majesty likes to put his own personal stamp on important matters such as these," Lord Orbryn said, his voice as cold as the air outside.

The elf was indifferent to the cold. Her gaze stayed narrowed on the king. "She'll be safe here, Your Majesty."

Anric only grunted at this, and then he took something from the leather bag at his side. Papers of some sort, along with a small golden box. Payment and the contractual proof of their *arrangement*, Cas guessed, and her heart jumped into her throat as a realization overtook her.

This place, this awful cold, the sound of children in the background...

This was the orphanage she had vague memories of, and the arrangement was for *her*.

Anric said something in a low voice. She tried to listen closer, but fog rolled in and stifled the sound.

The next thing she knew, they were in the carriage Anric had arrived in, and Lord Orbryn was offering council.

"The elven-kind will be able to suppress her magic in a way we cannot. It's for the greater good."

Those words again. *Greater good.* The same thing Varen had claimed to be so concerned about.

She didn't want to think about it, but her mind raced anyway. She had always assumed that Anric had gotten rid of her out of disdain, not out of...*concern.* But it was concern that clouded his emerald eyes, now.

Then again, of course he was concerned—a king crusading against divine magic couldn't have a *daughter* that wielded powerful, unstable divine magic.

Whether he was worried more about her or his crown...

Maybe she'd never truly know.

She studied her father's tired eyes, trying to see if she could determine the truth. Lord Orbryn was studying him as well, which made the memory exceptionally clear, the King's features sharp and obvious as he looked back at the orphanage. He started to speak, to agree with what Orbryn had said, maybe, but something made him hesitate.

As if he didn't want to let her go. As if he...he wasn't...

No.

He was still a villain. Nothing would change the

horrible things he'd done. He was a villain. Varen was a villain. No matter what *good* they'd set out to do.

"Now we can focus on what needs to be done to protect this empire," Lord Orbryn said.

Anric peeled his gaze away from the orphanage, which was little more than a dark speck in the distance by this point. He nodded.

"We're making progress in Mistwilde; the king is coming around, I believe. And our scholars are convinced they've determined what needs to be done about the Point. They have notes ready to present to you —Master Hamon himself is on his way down from Bellmere to speak to our council, which suggests significant news. He wouldn't personally make the trip, otherwise."

"Let's hope so," muttered Anric, his face turning to stare out of the carriage window once more.

Lord Orbryn followed his ruler's lead, and the memory faded into a darkness that reflected the empty night outside of the carriage. He breathed in deep, and Cas resurfaced into the present as he exhaled—almost as if he'd forced her out with the breath.

She was glad to be back to the feel of Nessa's magic; it was like stepping out of a dark cave into a warm summer day.

"Well?" Nessa prompted. "How'd it go?"

The warmth faded, and Cas steeled herself and recounted the vision. "I saw something...familiar. The orphanage where Lord and Lady Tessur found me. It seems my father left me with the elves that ran it in hopes that they could suppress my magic."

Nessa puzzled over this for a moment before she asked, "Isn't it strange that the Tessurs were able to take you away from that place? If the elves were supposed to be keeping you there, and keeping you safe, on the King's orders?"

"It wouldn't be the first time the elves had broken an agreement with mortals," said Cas with a shrug. "And maybe they weren't able to do what they told the king they could do, so they panicked and decided to get rid of me too. I seem to break things and complicate them wherever I go, don't I?"

Nessa's eyes glistened with sympathy

Cas tried for a laugh, to pretend she'd been joking— because she didn't *want* sympathy. "More importantly," she continued in a rush, "Orbryn spoke of the anchor point in Mistwilde, and a man named Hamon who was preparing to present research on the matter—that name might be a clue we can use to figure out our next step."

"We should check with the library servants," Nessa suggested—though it was clear that she wasn't really thinking about books and scholars; she was more concerned about Cas.

Cas tried again to shrug it off, but everything she thought she knew about herself felt like it was unraveling further even as she sat there, the pieces of her past falling, mixing among the rose petals that surrounded them. She kept thinking of the Star Goddess's words, and that recurring dream she'd asked Cepheid about. Of how she had disappeared, and then...

The bleeding had stopped.

What she had told Nessa was true. She was a complication, a piece that had broken off from the royal family and changed the course of it forever—for better or worse.

"I'm fine." She managed to give Nessa a reassuring smile. "But there's someone I need to go see while I still can."

AFTER TRACKING down the Air spirit and giving her a message to relay, Cas crept up to her room and hid behind a locked door while she awaited the reply. Nessa waited with her, and the two of them passed the time by going over notes about the Kethran leaders who had agreed to attend their summit.

Nearly two hours later, the spirit returned with an invitation from Caden to meet him at the river, near the same spot they'd previously met.

"Are you sure you want to do this?" Nessa asked. "Should we invite the others?"

Cas had considered it, but she was trying to keep this meeting as quick and as simple as possible. Which was also the reason she was currently pulling a Mimic crystal from one of her dresser drawers—she didn't want anyone to recognize her and slow her down this afternoon. "I'll tell them all afterwards," she promised Nessa. "Once I have more information, we can interpret it together."

"How do we know that Malaphar isn't able to listen in on what Caden is doing?"

Cas breathed in deeply, recited the spell to activate the crystal she held, and then turned back to Nessa. "We don't."

Nessa started to voice her objection several times, but never found the words. In the end, she only shook her head and sighed.

Cas went to the mirror to check her newly-magicked appearance. She'd made a point to try and guide the crystal this time so that she didn't end up looking like the dead queen as she had before. And whether because of that willpower or otherwise, she'd been successful; she had transformed into an unrecognizable young woman with ruddy skin and waves of unruly dark hair.

"We know that ascension isn't an immediate process, however," she continued, while trying to wrestle her new hair into a braid of some sort. "When I spoke with Varen, he seemed to think he had a bit more time before his connection to the Dark God was fully established. I assume Caden's connection to Malaphar will follow the same pattern. So we just need to move quickly and hope for the best."

Nessa appeared at her side in the mirror, helping to further tame those locks of hair.

"I know what you're thinking," muttered Cas. "That I'm a fool for believing anything Varen said to me, but..."

Nessa breathed in deeply through her nose. "But we have to believe in something, right?"

"Exactly. *Nothing* is certain or easy at this point."

"I'm coming with you, though. Like it or not." Nessa finished tying off the braid. She tucked it behind Cas's shoulder, letting her hand linger against Cas's shirt afterward.

Cas reached for that hand and gave it a quick squeeze. "Thank you," she said.

After grabbing a few weapons that they could inconspicuously carry, they were off, quietly weaving their way out of the palace and into the city. They brought several armed guards with them as well, but Cas ordered them to trail at a distance—close enough to intervene if required, but far enough away to not draw attention to her.

Once they arrived at the river, Nessa took her aside and summoned a blanket of her magic, letting it wash over them until Cas closed her eyes and visibly relaxed.

"I'll be right here keeping watch," said Nessa. "And keeping them in line too," she added, nodding to the soldiers they'd brought along.

Cas agreed and descended the hill down to the river-bank alone. Once she reached that bank, she didn't have to wait long—a strange shadow was already spilling out from the ramshackle boathouse. Her eyes followed it, watching it shift and stretch and eventually rise into currents of dark energy that quickly took on a recogniz-able shape.

The air around her chilled, and suddenly Caden was there, stepping from the shadows into a solid form and turning to face her.

"Hello Casia." His gaze darted toward the road as he greeted her. Searching the people she'd brought with her—clearly looking for someone in particular, and Cas was certain she knew who that someone was.

"He's not here," she said, "and it's better this way, trust me. Less complicated, so we can take care of this quickly."

"He's still angry with me, isn't he?"

"*Quickly*," she repeated. "I need you to clarify some things for me."

He slowly brought his attention back to her and only her. Rolled the tension from his neck and shoulders. Cleared his throat. "Yes—Varen said you might."

An uncertain chill creeped down her spine at her brother's name.

"So," Caden began, slowly, thoughtfully. "You've seen enough to better understand your father and his legacy by this point, I take it?"

"Understand?" She snorted. "Not exactly. But I've accepted that he was trying to kill the upper-gods, to seal them away, to...to..."

"To save the mortal world."

Another chill down her back—this one made her visibly shudder.

Caden cocked his head to the side, his strange eyes flashing in the high afternoon sun. "Ah. You don't like the way I used the word *save*, do you?"

She averted her gaze. "He was a villain in almost every story I've ever heard about him. In every story I've told myself."

"Plenty of villains started off trying to save the world," Caden said, simply. "He lost sight of why he started, maybe, but I'm certain he didn't think he was a villain."

Cas didn't comment on this. She would likely never understand Anric's true motives; she had already accepted that. And the only villain she needed to worry about now was the Dark God—the one who still needed to be defeated.

The one who might have *already* been defeated, had certain things not...complicated matters.

"What would have happened," she wondered aloud, her gaze still on the river instead of Caden, "if the fallen God of Death had not been sent to kill Anric? If the things leading up to that moment had gone...*differently*? If we'd...chosen differently?"

He didn't reply at first—not until Cas glanced up at him, eyes desperately searching.

"I don't know," he said. "My magic only allows me to see things that were, not alternate timelines that could have been."

Cas's fingers closed over the hourglass that hung from her necklace, absently squeezing it.

When she'd asked that goddess if her magic was capable of changing the past, Cas had not—in that moment—known precisely what she might change. How she might fix the mess she'd found herself surrounded by.

Now she had an idea.

A terrible, *gut-wrenching* idea...

And it wouldn't leave her alone.

"Elander only meant to save me," she said softly. "Not throw off the entire balance of the divine and mortal realms. All of this messiness...can it really be traced back to that other lifetime? To that meeting between us?"

Plenty of villains started off trying to save the world.

Caden didn't repeat his chilling statement, but she could not get it out of her head.

We aren't villains, she wanted to say.

The words caught in her throat.

What came out instead was a quiet, painful thought. "If he hadn't met me, he wouldn't have fallen from the Dark Court. He wouldn't have been tasked with killing Anric. The king might have survived, which means..."

Caden shifted his weight from one foot to the other, but he still didn't speak.

So Cas continued. "Anric could have kept up his work, and maybe he could have sealed away *all* of the Antaeum Points, not just that of the Stone God's. He was so close to achieving that before he died. I saw Lord Orbryn's memory, I—"

"There's no point in thinking about what *could* have happened."

Cas clenched her fists, digging her fingers into her palms. The bite of her nails gave her something to focus on—a sharpness that kept her from escaping, from slipping out of awareness.

"All that's left is to decide what to do about what *has* happened," said Caden. "You summoned me here with specific questions in mind, I presume? We should move quickly through those, as you said."

Cas tried to nod, but she didn't manage it.

She did have specific questions—she'd planned to ask him what he had divined about that Master Hamon she'd heard mentioned, for starters. If perhaps he could give her more information to help her quickly locate that scholar's notes.

But now she knew what she *really* needed to see. What memory she had to unearth if she had any hope of sorting through all these things, any chance of putting the past where it belonged—*behind* her—so that she could focus on the future.

She locked her gaze with Caden's, and she willed herself not to flinch or look away from his unnerving eyes.

"You can show me my own memories, can't you?" she asked, quietly but firmly. "From both this life and every other?"

He hesitated. Then he inhaled deeply, exhaled slowly—bracing himself for her answer before he even asked the question. "What would you like to see?"

CHAPTER 29

They used the small knife Cas had tucked in the sheath at her ankle.

A quick swipe across her palm sent red bubbling across her skin. Cas averted her eyes and forced herself to breathe through it; she still struggled with the sight of blood, and now was not the time to revisit all the traumas it brought to the surface.

She quickly clenched her bleeding hand into a fist as Caden moved on.

It was simple—unsettlingly so—how he was able to take the drops of this blood and work his magic with them. He moved closer to the river's edge. Dipped a blood-coated claw into the water.

He beckoned her forward, and as the toe of her boot met the river, mist rose from the water and engulfed her.

It rolled away just as quickly, and she was shocked by the perfect clarity of her new surroundings.

She was alone, standing at the edge of a dark and restless sea.

Gulls squawked overhead, their cries carried by a steady, humming wind. All of her senses were alive in a way that she usually didn't experience in these memories—she could smell the salty scent of sea spray, could feel the dampness on her skin and the uncomfortable sharpness of a rocky shore beneath bare feet.

A ramshackle cottage stood on a cliff in the distance, its yard hemmed in by a weathered fence and overgrown with flowers in varying shades of purple and white.

As she stared at that cottage, a word—no, a *feeling*—surfaced in her mind.

Home.

This memory belonged to another lifetime, and yet it was the clearest one she'd seen yet. The clearest thing she'd felt. But that was because it was *hers*, wasn't it?

And some things never truly left you, she supposed.

The wind began to die down. The dark sea became a gently rippling mirror beneath the grey sky, and now the reflection within it was clear—that of a young woman with dusky skin and a slightly emaciated frame. Her eyes were wide and a mesmerizingly bright, rich shade of brown, but there were deep circles beneath them that betrayed her exhaustion and made it difficult to guess at her true age. Her long waves of coarse, dark hair were only partially contained in a messy bun. A pale green dress hung from one of her bony shoulders, likely drooping because it had gotten too heavy; it was soaked through all the way up to her waist, as though she had just been wading in the sea.

This woman...

Herself.

Cas *knew* this was who she had been—she'd expected to see her—and yet it was so strange to actually *experience* it. To accept that the soul of this person and her present self were one and the same.

Her past self took a step away from the water and glanced over her shoulder at the distant house.

A strange light flashed around the perimeter of it.

Cas tried to start toward it, curious. But she found it even more difficult to move freely in this memory, compared to others; she felt as if she was actually bound to this past version of herself by unbreakable, invisible threads.

Luckily, that past self did eventually lift her damp skirts and move cautiously toward the house, picking up speed as she drew closer.

Inside, it smelled most strongly of sweet lilac and cooking spices, but there was an undercurrent of something bitter too. The bitterness came from medicinal herbs, Cas realized as the memory wound its way through the small house and reached a dark room in the very back. A figure lay on the bed in the corner of this room, bundled in sheets, unmoving. If not for the occasional rattling breath that interrupted the grave silence, Cas would have thought she was looking at a corpse.

She knew the story of this past life well enough, so she could easily guess who this woman was—her sister.

The memory didn't linger on the sick woman. Whether by Caden's control or otherwise, it was shifting, and Cas found her past self alone in the front room, lighting a fire and casting occasional wary glances toward the window. As the fire kindled to life and warm light flickered over the room, she moved toward that window. Delicately pushed the thin curtains aside. The memory seemed to freeze at this point, and the reason for her wary glances soon became clear.

The God of Death was approaching.

So here it was. The beginning of them. A fateful meeting, the breaking point that balanced on a blade's edge, prepared to twist and change the fate of the very world itself.

Cas was still connected to her past self, but for a brief moment she felt as if she had partially transcended —as if she was watching the scene from above. She could feel the beat of her own heart. She knew she was holding her own breath.

Then that past self did something...*unexpected*. She closed the curtains. Shut the fireplace doors and dimmed all other sources of light in the room, muttering to herself as she did. She stood in the dark for a long moment after, her head bowed. As if she was praying. Or steeling herself, perhaps.

Her eyes went immediately to the window when she finally lifted her head again. She clenched her fists and stalked toward it, covertly peering through a small gap in the closed curtains.

Cas's vision followed hers.

He was *there*. Right there at the edge of the path that led to the front door. Cas tried to move closer but failed once again to separate herself from her prior incarnation —so all she could do was take in the sight of this past version of *him*.

Eyes that glowed slightly, bright orbs of silvery blue in the overcast light. Pale hair. Faint, unnatural shadows moving upon his fair skin. Clearly a god, though his appearance was muted by the airs of the mortal realm. He'd looked very similar to this when he revealed his identity to her in Oblivion—where the divine residue had the opposite effect, and it had enhanced what was left of his godly form.

Those shining and startlingly beautiful eyes swept over the fenced yard, and a corner of his mouth curved upward. Amused, maybe, by the predominant flower among the unkempt jungle of them—*lilies*. It was old superstition, the planting of these flowers that the Death God supposedly favored.

He lifted his gaze from the yard and studied the window instead. Did he sense her watching him? What had brought him here in the first place? It was not normal, during any time period that Cas was aware of, for this god to personally appear and collect the dead.

So why had he come? Why here? Why now?

As the questions swirled in her mind, her surroundings began to churn as well. Another shift in the memory. It skipped ahead to what seemed to be a different day—this one cold and blustery. The flowers swayed in a foreboding sort of dance. The gate creaked and slammed over and over until Elander appeared, caught it, and held it still.

But this time, it was obvious that Elander was aware he was being watched. He looked directly at the window, and Cas felt the shiver that shot through her previous self, the sudden cold of Death magic that seized her and made her gasp.

The shadows upon Elander's skin darkened and lifted, rising around him like mist. With a flick of his wrist, a creature twisted free from these shadows, slinking forward and taking the shape of a four-legged beast. It slipped beneath the gate and raced for the window.

It leapt.

And it struck...*something* that made the air spark with bright power. An invisible barrier. Opposing magic. It stopped the creature, shattering it and sending splinters of shadow fleeing in all directions.

Suddenly, Cas was no longer peering through the

CROWN OF THE GODS

curtains. The memory flickered and moved, and now there was no window separating her from Elander; her past self had become brave enough to open the door. To stare down this god that had come, presumably, to take her sister away.

When their eyes met this time, the other shadows around Elander retreated.

His lips parted in surprise.

Cas felt her past heart thundering, equally surprised —and confused.

She tried to move toward the gate where Elander stood, but again found it nearly impossible to separate her body from the past. And even when that previous self stepped away from the door, *she* was held back as well—pushed back. The same invisible force that had scattered Elander's shadows kept her from drawing too close to him.

The scene wavered. Blurred. Her stomach lurched, and Cas braced herself, expecting another shift in time... but it didn't come.

She heard Caden's voice, distant and echoing, like something in a dream—was it in her mind, or was he truly calling her name?

She had her answer an instant later when she returned to Ciridan with an abruptness that left her dizzy. A concerned Nessa and a confused Blood spirit greeted her.

"What happened? I wasn't done, I—"

Caden shook his clawed hand, as if to relieve it of a cramp. "It was getting unstable for some reason." He studied the tip of the claw that was crusted over with dried blood. "I've never experienced anything like... whatever *that* was."

"Unstable?" Nessa repeated, frowning.

Cas hugged her arms against herself and didn't speak. *Unstable.* Was this more proof that that moment —and her meeting Elander—was truly a breaking point for their world?

The three of them were silent for a long time.

Finally, Caden retracted his claws and said, "An enigma until the very end."

Cas did not like the way he said *end.* Or the way his troubled eyes didn't seem to want to meet hers. Or the way his arm shook as he started to back away.

Before she realized what she was doing, her hand reached out and took hold of that arm and held it—and him—still.

His eyes still did not meet hers. He stared at that grip she'd taken on him. Took a deep breath, and seemed to debate with himself for a moment before he said, "While I have you here, I wanted to warn you: He's rising more quickly, and more *powerfully*, than ever before."

"Varen?"

Caden shook his head. "Malaphar never truly left this mortal realm. He's simply been hiding—aside from that trip he took to Dawnskeep. But that was only a specter of his true self; his actual form has been biding time and gathering strength by the day."

"Gathering strength? How?"

"A side effect, Varen and I believe, of closing off those other two points of divine energy. It's disrupted the flow of magic within this realm—allowed him to create a *funnel* of sorts. The power that already existed here did not fully disappear when the Sun and Stone gods were sealed out of it, and without the other two Moraki here to take in their share, he's absorbing some of it, corrupting it and using it as he likes."

"So what Varen and Anric did only made him stronger?" Nessa asked.

"For the moment, yes. But if you manage to seal *his* point, it won't matter. If he's locked out of this realm as well, you'll have nothing to worry about."

"Easier said than done," Nessa muttered.

"Yes," Caden agreed with a shrug. "So you should probably get moving, shouldn't you? The longer you take, the more powerful he becomes." A strange twitch went through him as he said the words—almost as if he had reached the end of whatever chains bound him, and he had been jerked into silence.

Cas's hand moved subtly, uncertainly, to the dagger she'd hidden against her back.

But Caden quickly slipped free of whatever binding had gripped him. "I need to go," he said, and he didn't wait for their reply before turning and walking away, shadows leaking from his skin and wrapping his body up as he went.

Cas automatically started after him—she wasn't done with their conversation—but Nessa grabbed her hand and held her back. Her gaze was plaintive, her unspoken concern obvious. *We still don't know where his loyalty truly lies.*

And she was right.

Cas knew this, but she couldn't keep from calling after him one last time. "He really *is* sorry, you know."

Caden paused, the shadows billowing around him like a cloak caught in the wind.

"He knows you didn't believe him when he said it. But it's true. I've seen how sorry he is."

Caden's gaze lifted toward the sky. His shadows didn't settle, but he didn't leave.

"And this isn't the end," Cas insisted. "We can fix this. Don't give up yet, and keep fighting for control because it could all still...*change.*"

He angled his gaze back to her. He seemed to be reading her expression. Or her mind, maybe, and possibly understanding her thoughts better than she herself did in that moment. Finally, he said, "Change is tricky, isn't it?"

She opened her mouth, eager to reply—only to realize she had no words.

And he disappeared before she could decide what to say.

THEY RETURNED to the palace grounds—and after Cas reassured Nessa, repeatedly, that she was fine—the two of them parted ways.

Nessa went to speak with the servant she'd put in charge of the banquet menu, but Cas lingered for a moment, studying the dark clouds building on the horizon, before heading for the door. She intended to bandage her hand, and then to go and find Elander and tell him what she'd discovered, as promised.

She had nearly made it inside when it became obvious she was being followed.

"Queen."

She twisted around. The address still hit her ears strangely, but it was even stranger to hear it in this unfamiliar, silvery voice—a voice that belonged to the Air spirit staring up at her.

Cas took a moment to catch her breath. "...You do speak."

The spirit's big eyes blinked. Her antennae floated behind her, nearly scraping the cobblestone path. "Only when my goddess requires it of me."

Cas glanced around for potential eavesdroppers; the closest guards were stationed at one of the palace's grander entrances, at least a hundred feet away. "And she has something to say to me?"

"She sees through my eyes when she wants to. So she knows your questions about the past continue."

"My questions..."

"You once asked her if you were a broken piece."

Cas felt as if the breath had just been ripped from her lungs once more, but she managed to calmly say, "Yes. What of it?"

"Now you have an answer."

"...*Do* I?"

The spirit continued as though Cas hadn't spoken. "So now she can answer your second question."

"My second question?"

The spirit patiently explained. "You wanted to know if she could take you back to that moment." The spirit's antennae waved more enthusiastically, and her head cocked to one side, expectant.

"Does that mean *yes*? That she's open to the idea now?"

The spirit simply bowed.

Cas's heart slammed against her ribcage. Her thoughts splintered into pieces and painful possibilities, each stabbing more viciously than the last.

"I'll keep that in mind," she said, voice barely above a whisper. "Thank you."

And then she turned on her heel and hurried inside.

CHAPTER 30

Hours later, Cas had collected herself enough to walk through the palace with her head held high and an impassive look on her face.

Elander's words from the day before were ringing in her ears, pushing her in his direction even as her nerves tried to overtake her and convince her to run away.

Don't hide it from me.

She'd promised she wouldn't.

So she summoned a bit of magic and let it reach out to find and connect with his.

It eventually led her to the training grounds, where he and Laurent were deeply involved in an exercise with several dozen soldiers. Each of those soldiers was clutching one of the magic-infused weapons that the Sun Court had provided them with.

Cas watched them for several minutes, grateful to

see her old friend and Elander working so well together, and not wanting to interrupt what appeared to be a productive training session.

As she took a seat in an inconspicuous corner, she couldn't help admiring the confident way Elander moved amongst the ranks. She teased him so often about being her *captain* that she sometimes forgot how truly capable he was in the role—that he was in his element when ordering people around like this, taking charge and speaking control into chaotic situations.

He hadn't missed a beat during the tumultuous transformation of this palace. He was still as confident here as ever, whatever his role, and she knew he was equally confident in her role as the new queen. No matter her mistakes, or her weaknesses, or all her doubts and anxieties about it. Despite it all, he still loved her. And she loved him...for that reason and for so many others.

She loved him, she loved him, she *loved* him—

And it didn't seem fair to think that such a love could break a world. Not when it was the very thing that had helped hold her together so many times.

The broken piece.

She closed her eyes and bowed her head, fighting through a sudden wave of nausea.

The Goddess of Stars was wrong.

The Goddess of Time was wrong.

They *had* to be.

She quickly lifted her head again, refusing to reveal this moment of weakness in front of her soldiers and everyone else. She watched the rest of the training with a cold, impassive stare—a queen surveying her army and taking notes on their performance.

As their exercises ended, Elander glanced her direction. His gaze lingered on her face, just for a moment. She thought she'd managed to keep the turmoil in her mind from reaching her expression, but something apparently gave her away—at least to him—something that made the corners of his mouth fall and his brow furrow in concern. After a quick conversation with Laurent, he was striding toward her, studying her more closely as he approached.

"Casia? Is something wrong?"

"No," she lied. "I was just..."

He scanned the space around them, watching Laurent leave with several soldiers, and making certain no one lingered close enough to overhear them. "Hunting through memories again?" he guessed.

She nodded.

"What did you see?"

She tried. She didn't mean to hide. To hesitate. But the walls of the training ground felt like they were closing in around her. Like they might actually try to crush her if she spoke of the rulers that had come before her, or any of the uncertainties she had about taking their place.

"Come on," Elander said, taking her hand and pulling her into motion. "Let's go somewhere more private."

His step was casual as they strolled through the palace. Cas found it easier to mimic his confidence than to summon it for herself. Anybody who glanced at her would never have guessed at the conflicting emotions still tumbling through her.

He stopped by his room to gather some things. She lingered outside, her attention briefly snagged by a courtier who wanted her opinion regarding the menu for that upcoming gathering of leaders—she didn't actually *have* an opinion, but she managed to give a quick, confident answer anyway.

When Elander reemerged, he had a bag slung over his shoulder, and they resumed their walk. He still didn't tell her where they were going, and though she was curious about what he'd packed in that bag, she didn't care enough to ask. They were leaving the confining walls of the palace. He was with her. The outside air was so much easier to breathe...

Nothing else mattered.

Those distant storm clouds had stayed away. The late afternoon air was pleasantly cool, and they walked a mile at least, following the narrow road that wound behind the palace and then out beyond its walls. It was a private path meant only for royalty and those who served them, and it led all the way to the edge of the city, to a tucked-away building where those from the palace could collect goods without dealing with any extra townsfolk.

They didn't go into the city itself; instead, they veered right and made their way up a nearby hillside that was blanketed in lilacs. After a long, steady climb, they finally reached the top, and Cas was treated to a sweeping view of the palace grounds to her right, while the capital city sprawled out to her left.

"Sulah's Hill," Elander informed her as they caught their breath. "Named for the lesser-spirit of Vitality, I believe—that was an old name the people of this kingdom used for that being. And this used to be my favorite spot to come to when I previously lived in the palace." He shrugged the bag from his shoulder and dug out the object taking up the most room in it—a blanket, which he spread across the ground in front of them.

"I even spent the night out here sometimes," he continued, "when things inside the palace got too... suffocating. The air feels cleaner up here, doesn't it? Good for clearing the head. And if you're here at sunset, all the better—when the sun hits the river down there just right, it looks like fire weaving its way through the city."

He settled on the blanket, reached for her hand, and pulled her down to sit beside him. She leaned her head on his shoulder and gazed in the direction he pointed; the sun hung low over the distant hills, and some of its beams were already falling into the River Lotheran and setting it ablaze, just as he'd said. Her gaze followed the trail of fire as it curved down from the distant mountains, cut the city in two, and eventually curved into the woods behind the palace.

Being able to see so much of her world at once brought her a small measure of comfort. All the problems plaguing her city, her palace...they didn't seem to loom so large when she was looking down at these places instead of being swallowed up by them.

"These flowers have been slowly taking over up here," Elander commented, sweeping a hand toward the clump of pinkish-violet blooms that was creeping closest to them. "Which makes sense, I guess, given the spirit whose blessing supposedly resides over this place."

She studied them and quickly concluded that magic *did* seem like a very real possibility; she had never seen such thick clusters of lilac. They were beautiful—though their heady scent did interfere with the clear air he'd mentioned. It made her a bit sleepy. And him too, apparently, because soon he laid down beside her, hands clasped behind his head, and closed his eyes.

She wanted to lay down next to him. To sleep until the stars came out, and to count those stars like lazy lovers indifferent to the rest of the world, thinking of nothing except the simple, wild beauty of all that surrounded them.

Instead, she found herself staring at the palace in the distance. Picking at the bandage over the cut Caden had made. Twisting her hourglass necklace back and forth between her fingers.

And after a few minutes, the question eating away at her heart slipped out. "Do you ever regret it?"

He lifted his head and gave her a curious look.

"Your decision to save me," she breathed, "to try and bring me back and everything...everything that's happened to this world since that moment. Do you ever wonder if we triggered something we shouldn't have?"

He sat up and started to reply, but she cut him off—the words would not stop pouring out of her now that she'd started.

"The Goddess of Stars said that moment changed everything. And some of the things I've uncovered while digging through memories suggest that this...this *shifting* might not have been for the better. So I just wondered if...if maybe you ever thought you'd made a mistake. If you—"

"No." The word came out like a soft scolding. "Casia..." He wrapped his arms around her, his hold gentle but unyielding as he gathered her against his chest.

She fisted her hands tightly into his shirt and pulled herself to him, closing the little bit of space left between them. They stayed like that for several beats, both trying but not quite managing words, until Elander finally continued in a whisper, "My weakness, my strength, my Thorn. My *Queen*." He kissed the top of her hair. "No," he said, his voice growing rough and thick with emotion. "I could never regret you."

She stayed against his chest for a moment longer, gathering strength, before she cleared the thickness from her own throat and said, "I actually went back— Caden took me to the moment you and I met. That's what I saw, to answer your question from earlier."

His face became a wall, guarding against the complicated feelings that must have erupted inside of him.

She didn't try to pry any of those feelings out. She just hurried on, shifting the conversation away from his old companion. "And before that, I saw more of Anric's dealings with the anchor points, and with the elves. I'm more convinced than ever that the path we have to take to defeat the Dark God runs through Mistwilde." She shook her head, frustrated. "But I don't know what becomes of us after that. We carry so much of Solatis's power—what will happen if we seal away all these divine points? And I worry about what will happen to our world in general, if magic fades. It's clearly better than the alternative of letting the gods destroy us, but still... The future is so uncertain, no matter how I try to look at it, and I'm just not sure if we're doing the right things, if..." The tears were back, welling up in her eyes, and this time one escaped and trailed down her cheek.

"It doesn't change what I said." He brushed the

teardrop from her skin. "The past is what it is. And whatever happens next...I don't know that either. But I *am* certain that I want to be beside you in the end."

"It's likely to be a painful end."

"I don't care."

She tried to nod but didn't fully manage it.

"You still don't believe me, do you?"

"I don't know." Her words cut like shards of glass through her dry throat. "I want to. I swear I do. Everything is just so...*messy.*"

He nodded in an understanding sort of way and drew her back to his chest.

They were quiet for a long time, watching the fiery river winding through the world below, listening to the last birdsongs of the day, breathing in the musky sweet scent of the flowers that surrounded them.

"What will it take to make you believe it?" he asked quietly, suddenly.

"I don't know."

"You want proof of how I feel?"

"You've more than proven it."

"A demonstration?"

She smiled a bit, thinking of the outlandish things he might come up with to demonstrate his love.

"A proposal?"

She had started to lean away, to rub her bleary eyes, but now she froze. "Be serious, Elander."

He smiled at the softly chiding tone of her voice.

But he didn't take the suggestion back.

She looked away, fixing her eyes on a nearby patch of particularly bright flowers. Her face felt hot. He was still looking at her; she could sense it.

What was he thinking?

What was *she* thinking?

For all her obsession with her past, she had given relatively little thought to the future. Worrying too much about it was one of the surest ways to get yourself in trouble in the present, Asra used to say.

But something had changed over these past months, and here was the evidence of it. She hadn't completely recoiled when he'd used the word *proposal*. And her heart remained open even as she thought harder about the idea, its beat fluttering about, cautious but hopeful —like a bird discovering its wings for the first time.

She might not have dwelled on it often, but in that moment, she couldn't deny how badly she wanted a future with him.

Their future.

She wanted to say...*yes*. That a proposal was exactly what she wanted from him. She wanted to marry him, to grow old with him, to have a thousand more fights, a thousand more reasons to make up with him, a palace full of children and noise and silly family traditions— she wanted all of it. The good, the bad, the messy in-between. She wanted this to be a love story in the end. A triumph. Not a tragedy.

Gods, how *desperately* she wanted that.

But she was not a fool.

She knew the difficulties that lay ahead. The mess that lay behind. The impossible odds they still faced, despite all they'd already fought their way through. And they were not normal humans, besides—so even if they survived what was to come, she wasn't even certain it was possible for them to have...well, *normal* things. A normal family. A normal happily-ever-after. So before she realized what she was doing, she was already looking back at him and gently shaking her head.

No. The word crashed through her mind, loud and insistent. *No. I can't. I can't. I—*

"I love you," she whispered. "Please don't doubt that. I just..." She trailed off, leaning farther away from him, bracing a hand in the dirt beside their blanket.

"Relax. That was obviously not a proper proposal, so it doesn't need a proper answer." He stood and stretched. "Another time, perhaps."

He was still smiling that easy, comforting smile of his when he looked down at her a moment later.

So she smiled as well, even though her heart felt as if it was cracking, caving in at the thought of not ever being able to tell him what she was truly thinking in that moment—that she wanted that smile for the rest of her days, wanted to see what it might look like when she recited a vow to him, how brightly his eyes might sparkle at the promise of *forever*.

"We should probably start heading—"

"No." The word surprised her as it left her mouth, cutting him off.

He paused midway through another stretch.

She was afraid, but she had made up her mind, so she kept going. "No to what you said a moment ago, I mean. I don't want to save this for another time." She rose slowly to her feet. Steadied herself with a deep breath. "I...I'm not sure how to say this. You know how I am, after all—you know that my mind is constantly racing, my heart is constantly restless, and that I lose the very breath in my lungs sometimes, and I just...I suppose what I mean is..." *Deep inhale. Slow exhale.* "You make it easier to think. To breathe."

He turned to face her more fully.

"And if I am going to be queen of this broken kingdom, then I am going to need help, sometimes, remembering how to breathe. I need you. I want it to be you. Every beat of my restless heart is yours now, and I can't imagine a world—*my* world—without you in it. And I just needed you to know that no matter what happens, as you said, I want to be with you in the end."

As she fell silent, one corner of his mouth lifted in that familiar, crooked smile that still—even after all this time—made her pulse skip.

Again and again it skipped, and the moment stretched until finally she folded her arms across her chest and said, "Don't just stand there grinning at me like that. Say something, you fool."

His smile only brightened. "So what you're telling me is *yes*."

"I'm telling you...*maybe*."

He laughed. "Maybe?"

"You still have to ask me properly."

He hesitated. She thought for a moment that he might have suspected she was joking, that he might start to laugh again—after all, when had they ever done things *properly*?

But he was not laughing anymore. All of a sudden he was looking at her very seriously, and with only the faintest trace of a smile on his handsome face. He started to speak several times. Stopped. Then he glanced away, squinted into the setting sunlight, and said, "I've never told anyone this before, but the very first time I spoke to you in this lifetime, something...changed."

"Changed?"

"It was as if something inside of me woke up. Something was whispering, trying to get my attention.... I could hear it, but I couldn't understand what it was saying. I didn't know what it was—I didn't know who you were—but I couldn't shake the feeling that I needed to listen closer. I could barely think of anything else. I couldn't eat. I couldn't sleep. Not until I made sense of things. Of *you*."

"Is that why you were such an asshole when we first

met?" she asked, grinning. "Because you were hungry and sleep-deprived?"

"Maybe." A flash of a smile, and then the seriousness returned. "But it was also because I was...afraid."

Her grin fell.

He tilted his head back toward her. The sunlight catching on his face made it look like his skin was radiating magic—like he was glowing from the inside out.

"When you spend as much time as I had in the dark, the light starts to seem like an enemy," he said quietly. "*You* seemed like an enemy. Honestly, after I lost you the first time, *everything* seemed like an enemy to me for so long. I just wanted to destroy it all. Gods. Kings. Everything and everyone in between—I told myself I wanted to do whatever I had to do to get back to my god status, but the truth was that I only wanted to cause as much death and destruction as I possibly could, and I knew being a god again would help with that. And if I had managed to become that god again, then it might have been *me* that the world was contending with, now. Not just Malaphar. I still think about that sometimes: how close I came to..." His breath hitched. "To destroying so much."

"It would never have been you," she said without hesitation. "Even if I hadn't shown up."

He took one of her hands, and he absently traced the edges of it with his thumb as he said, "Maybe not. But

I'm glad I came across a light in the darkness, all the same."

She slipped her fingers through his and leaned against his chest, letting the beat of his heart and the deep vibrations of his voice resonate through her.

"And I realize now that the light I felt when I first saw you in *this* lifetime was the same sort of magic I felt when I first came across you in that past life. The same force, reminding me of what I'd been, once upon a time. Dragging me back to the light."

He gently pushed her away from his chest so he could look into her eyes.

Time seemed to slip away, out of existence, and she thought her breath might go with it. That was how it happened in all the stories, wasn't it? Breathless and waiting for those two words she knew he was going to say...

But that was not *their* story; instead, it was just as she'd told him a moment ago: She could breathe again. Every inhale was easier than the last as long as he was there, and for once she didn't feel anxious, or like she needed to escape from the overwhelming feelings bubbling up inside of her.

She remained perfectly calm, even as he leaned in to kiss her.

Even as he took her other hand in his and said, "I love you, Casia. Valori. Thorn—whatever your name, whatever your appearance—I've loved you across lifetimes, through endings and beginnings, with all that I have, all that I've *ever* had. I never *stopped* loving you, even when I thought I'd lost you. I will never stop. Whether as your guardian, your captain, or whatever else. It doesn't really matter to me." He squeezed her hands more tightly.

She felt like she was floating, and she couldn't fight the urge to lift onto her tiptoes, to bring her lips closer to his.

"But I think we should make it more official." He leaned to meet her as she rose up, capturing her mouth in another slow kiss.

And as he drew back, he cupped her face in his hands, and he finally, *finally* whispered those two words she'd been waiting for. "Marry me?"

She couldn't speak right away. So she just nodded. Once. Slowly. Then again, again, again—each motion more fervent than the last—and then she was laughing, stretching taller so she could kiss him once more. He wrapped his arms around her and lifted her fully into that kiss, sweeping her off her feet and spinning her around. They spun and kissed and danced across that hilltop until they were dizzy, until he placed her back on the ground and she collapsed onto the blanket, grabbing his hand and dragging him down with her as she went.

They stretched out, propped partially up and facing each other, and Cas reached to trail a hand across his jaw, tucking a few strands of hair behind his ear.

"Yes," she finally managed to whisper. "Yes."

He pulled her close, and the warmth that rushed through her made her feel as though the sun was shining on them and no one else.

After a few minutes of relaxing against him and replaying the past moments over and over in her head, she smiled and said, "Did you practice that proposal? It was quite good."

He laughed softly. "I've been thinking about it for some time now."

"Lifetimes, I presume."

"Exactly."

She pulled away, restless—but in a *good* way for once; she was simply too happy to sit still, so she sat upright and breathed in deep lungfuls of the flower-scented air, and she fixed her gaze on the world stretching out before them. Even though the sun was nearly set, everything somehow seemed brighter. Clearer.

"What are you thinking?" Elander asked.

She glanced back at him, smiling again. "That I want to see a thousand more of these sunsets with you. At least."

He sat up beside her, moving in that easy, confident way that carried over to his tone. "We will," he promised.

And she hoped with everything in her that he was right.

CHAPTER 31

As NIGHT DESCENDED, THEY MADE THEIR WAY BACK DOWN THE hillside.

Neither of them were ready to return to the palace, so they walked hand-in-hand through the outskirts of the city instead.

Cas kept her hood drawn loosely around her face, but she was only half-heartedly trying to hide her identity. Caution was not a bad idea, but her days of hiding were getting further and further behind her.

A nervous energy teemed in the air—it was becoming a regular feature of this city—but most of the people they passed greeted them warmly enough. Word had spread of the lengths they'd gone to in the mountains, and of the steps they were taking to try and create allies near and far—and these things seemed to have won them some favor.

More and more people were beginning to greet Cas as though she was worthy of a crown.

They wanted to see her, to speak with her. The owner of the city's finest dress shop—who introduced himself as a relative of one of the Eldrin merchants she'd protected—even flagged her down so he could present her with an elegantly wrapped box that he'd been planning to deliver to the palace. Inside, she found a beautifully woven scarf he'd made specifically for her.

The gifts and the attention felt strange, but such things helped her picture it more clearly: A future where she and Elander frequently strolled through the city like this, a king and queen who kept in touch with the needs of their people.

They wandered along with no real destination in mind, and eventually the road curved and led them to the colorful stalls and waving advertisement banners of Market Row.

Most everything was closed by this hour, but the lingering scent of fruits and spices and other goods still hung in the air. The street was narrow, pinched in by countless shops competing for limited space, but the end of it opened into a sweeping view that stretched all the way to the distant palace. It had been a royal decree, decades ago—nothing could be built that would obstruct this view, so that the city's rulers would never be far from the mind of buyers and sellers.

Cas's gaze lifted toward that palace. "If we stay out much later, they're likely to send the army after me."

"No need, is there?" Elander asked, yawning. "I'm worth at least twenty of that army's soldiers."

Cas smiled wryly at the words. "Yes, but I'm not sure Rhea and the others will see it that way."

He didn't argue this point.

"I suppose it isn't going to get any easier to sneak away like this, will it? Once the palace fills up with foreign leaders and such. The preparations for that summit are beginning in earnest tomorrow—Nessa gave me fair warning." Her smile faded a bit as she remembered the conversation.

Nessa was, among other things, arranging a receiving room specifically for the queen and her court to have one-on-one conversations with everyone. Talking with each and every guest was expected—along with dinner and dancing and a hundred other terrible things that Cas had been furiously taking notes about for the past weeks. Her skin itched just thinking about it all.

And that was to say nothing of the terrible threats that they would have to ward off from *outside* the palace.

Caden's warning was still ringing in her ears. She needed to tell Elander *everything* he'd said. They needed to discuss security plans, and so much else…. But she selfishly wanted it all to wait just a bit longer.

Elander's face was contemplative, and she wondered if he was already thinking about those discussions they needed to have.

Probably.

But he didn't mention any of them, thankfully.

Instead, he waited until they were on a quieter street at the edge of town, and then he said, "If it begins tomorrow, then we should make tonight count."

She glanced over her shoulder at him. He had paused beside a small, partially fenced-in sitting area, where stone benches surrounded a small fountain and flowers of at least a dozen different colors dotted the grass.

"Let's make a deal, shall we?" he asked, kneeling and plucking a small bouquet of those flowers.

"A deal?"

The moonlight caught his eyes as he looked up at her, turning them an even more brilliant shade of blue than usual. She shivered. She would have sworn it was more than mere moonlight—that it was his magic glowing, rising to the surface. Either way, it stirred up her own magic and her heartbeat sped up as well, racing to match that pulsing power.

"I'm listening," she said.

"Tomorrow, they will have their queen. But tonight..."

He moved closer. She started to turn to face him, but

he slid one hand against her hip and pressed his body to hers, holding her in place.

Anticipation kindled, hot and fluttering, in her stomach.

His other hand reached around and slid that bouquet of flowers into her grip as he said, "Tonight, you're mine and mine alone." He leaned down, tilted his face into the curve of her neck and shoulder, breathing her in for a moment before he continued in a low voice. "My name is the only one that will be on your lips." He caressed those lips. Parted them. Used a firmer touch to guide her head back against his chest.

She closed her eyes and pressed her cheek even harder against him, drawing closer to his heartbeat.

"And you will think of nothing except the way it feels when I touch you..." His fingers trailed away from her mouth and moved over her exposed throat. "The way it feels when I kiss you..." He planted a soft trail of kisses along her jaw and down the side of her neck, flicked his tongue against her pulse. "The way it feels when I'm inside of you..." His hand moved from her throat and traveled along her body, down over her stomach before pausing, pressing and tapping at the apex of her thighs.

Her back arched slightly and her hand took his, guiding it lower, more completely against that needy center. He buried his face in the side of her neck once more, pulling his hand away as he continued to kiss her.

A little note of protest escaped her at his hand's with-drawal. She felt his lips curve in a smile against her skin.

"Do we have an agreement?" he asked.

She didn't respond immediately, too focused on how good it felt to press against him like this, and on the little sparks that were igniting everywhere their bodies brushed together.

He gripped her arm. Spun her around to face him and pulled her even closer, held her even tighter. Tilted her chin up and lowered his mouth nearly to hers, so that his next words fell upon her lips, sending shivers cascading through her body.

"Do we have an agreement?" he repeated.

"Agreed," she breathed. "No thoughts of crowns or royal duties tonight."

"Good." A wicked smile crossed his face. "So we can be as undignified as we like."

"Yes." She pressed her lips to that smile and kissed him slowly, savoring the way his grip on her tightened each time her tongue teased its way inside. "I expect a complete lack of decency from you tonight, thank you," she murmured when she finally pulled back a minute later.

His lips swept over hers, tasting her one last time, before his hand slid down, grasped hers, and he led her back into motion.

They continued along the moonlit streets, moving like thieves in the night, intent on stealing a few soft moments away from the hard uncertainties that lay ahead.

There was still no clear destination in mind. He asked her where she wanted to go, but she only knew that she didn't want to go back inside the palace—or inside of anywhere else, really. She wanted to feel the night air on her skin, to let the wind caress her hair, to bathe in the light of the exceptionally bright moon.

They ended up wandering toward the palace, but they didn't go inside. Instead, they stole around to the back of it, following the wall that surrounded the grounds until they were a mile away at least, and the rolling lawn gave way to an increasingly dense forest— still within those grounds, but in a part of them that Cas had never ventured to. She could no longer see the palace for all the trees between here and there.

It felt wild, beautifully dark, utterly lost to the rest of the world. She slipped off her boots so she could feel the scratchy leaves and the lush patches of grass that dotted the area. The grey trees glistened in the moonlight. Fireflies danced in the dense canopy of leaves above them, and the night was quiet enough that she could hear the whisper of the Lotheran River in the distance. She walked along that wall that marked off the palace grounds, trailing her fingers over the stone, for a few feet before turning to find Elander watching her in a way that made her insides flutter.

"I've had a lot of fantasies about sneaking off into these woods with you, you know," he told her.

A corner of her lips lifted. "Indecent ones, I hope."

"Wildly indecent, obviously."

"How do they start?" She sauntered back to him, gaze locking with his. Her hand came to rest against his hard stomach, balancing herself as she stretched taller and pressed her lips to his. Her arms soon stretched upward as well, wrapping around his neck so she could pull him deeper into the kiss.

"They start similar to this, usually," he murmured as she finally leaned away.

"And then what happens?"

His fingers trailed over her chest, lifting her hair and moving it behind her shoulder before sliding back to the silver buttons that held her shirt together. He grasped the top one, undoing it with a deft twist of his thumb and forefinger. "Then you undress for me. Slowly."

She held his gaze as she undid the rest of those buttons, as she slipped free of the shirt and everything beneath it. The night was the warmest one they'd had in weeks, but her skin still pebbled and her breath still caught at the sudden exposure.

He mirrored her undressing, and watching his chiseled form emerge from beneath his clothing made her skin prickle for an entirely different reason. The fire that kindled once more in her lower belly made her completely forget about the chill in the night air.

That fire burned hotter still as he brought a thumb up to trace the curve of her breast, circled the stiffened tip, and then dragged his fingers down to tug at the band of her pants. "Keep going," he instructed her.

His eyes roamed over her as she did. He reached for the bag, took the blanket from it and shook it out before spreading it upon the leaf-littered ground—all with one hand, as the other continued to copy her movements, stripping himself of his confining clothing, loosening his belt and trousers and slipping them low enough to allow his full erection to spring free.

He beckoned her closer, caught her hand and guided it to his hardened shaft. His lips parted as she stroked him, and his eyes held hers with an intensity that made her dizzy. It was all she could do to keep her touch steady, to lick her dry lips and manage to speak in a somewhat coherent voice—

"And now?" she prompted.

His mouth pressed to hers, and his tongue followed the path her own had been tracing. She let out a gasp, and his kiss grew rougher, his teeth grazing her lips and softly biting before he caught himself and drew back so he could answer her question: "And now..." He gripped her jaw tightly, forcing her eyes to stay locked with his. "You kneel."

The tone of his voice made her knees so weak that she was already halfway to the ground before he'd finished speaking.

She didn't need instruction beyond this; this was a fantasy they'd played enough that her hands and mouth knew what to do.

The night air felt wild and new against her flushed skin, but the way he eased into her throat was familiar, as was the way his palm remained cupped against her face, his touch turned from commanding to admiring.

From admiration came control—he was at *her* mercy, even as he slid more deeply into her and his fingers pushed through her hair, clutching her head. She drew his gaze down to her level, pulled him deeper into her hold with nothing more than a glance up at him from underneath her lashes.

She wielded that hold over him with increasingly bold movements of her head, her tongue, her lips— hardly coming up for air—until she sensed his knees weakening as hers had moments ago. Then she surfaced from the deep long enough to lean back and teasingly ask, "Are we capturing that fantasy yet?"

"We're getting closer," he said, taking hold of her jaw once more and pulling her upward, guiding her back to her feet. There was a hunger in his eyes that made her knees threaten to buckle again.

Her gaze slid expectantly to the blanket he'd spread out for them.

But his gaze jumped right over that blanket, instead eyeing the stretch of stone wall that cut through the trees behind her.

Then he was stepping her toward that wall, kissing her without restraint, the force of him crowding her all the way up to it. It was cold, but mostly smooth, and not entirely uncomfortable as he shoved her against it. He grabbed one of her legs and lifted it, and she shifted her hips, trying to better angle herself so he could slide more easily inside of her.

But he didn't enter her. Instead, his other hand slipped beneath her other leg, and he made full use of his inhuman strength, lifting her so high, so quick that it made her dizzy. Her back was pressed more completely against the wall, and each of her legs now rested firmly upon one of his shoulders.

Before she could so much as gasp at the...*indecency* of the position, his head was buried between her thighs, and his tongue was moving against her in a way that sent nothing *except* undignified words spilling from her lips.

One hand coaxed a leg farther apart. The other pressed and teased against the places his mouth didn't cover, and she writhed from the pleasure of it, indifferent to the stone scraping against her back.

Some deeply dormant part of her mind reminded her not to cry out—the sound might travel, and this was not *exactly* the way she wanted her royal guards to find her—but that rational thought sank further and further every time he brought his tongue back to her center. Her thighs gripped him more tightly, urging him deeper

*—harder—*and her mouth fell open, anticipating ultimate release.

But it didn't come.

Not yet.

He pulled his lips and tongue away before it could, and then he shifted her roughly from his shoulders, catching her against him as she slid down. "Easy," he growled, crushing her body closer to his. "I'm not finished with you yet."

He wrapped her in a secure embrace, one arm circling around her midsection while his other curled underneath, his hand splayed between her legs and his fingers penetrating mercilessly, even as he carried her away from the wall.

He took her back to the blanket but still didn't lay her upon it; instead he kept her pulled against him, letting the friction between their bodies add to the work his fingers were doing. One of her legs lifted, wrapping around his waist and pulling herself more tightly against him.

He held her in that position, and his fingers slipped out of her and traveled along the small of her back. Then they trailed lower, and when her body tensed in automatic anticipation, he lifted his hand and brought it down in a light, teasing tap against her bottom. It drew a soft note of pleasure from her, which brought his hand back against that same spot—harder this time.

She nearly collapsed against him at the sensation that shivered through her, bringing a smirk to his face.

"I was right before," he said. "You do enjoy a bit of punishment, don't you?"

"I stand by what I said that night—this doesn't exactly feel like *punishment*."

He smiled another of those *indecent* smiles at this. Then he flaunted his god-like strength once more, flipping her easily around and setting her down on her hands and knees. One of his hands caressed between her shoulder blades, pressing the front half of her downward. The other hand cupped between her legs and lifted, properly angling her.

He slid his hardened length over her center, adding to the warm dampness that had collected there. He teased with pressure, but not penetration—and then with his hands, with more of those light taps, now that he'd discovered this apparent weakness of hers.

He'd meant to tease her more than this, she suspected, but her fingers reached between her legs, trailing over both her own softness and his hardness, and her touch drew an aching, needy sound from his lips that brought him crashing into her with an equally needy thrust.

She brought her hands back to the blanket. Clenched it in her fists. Rocked her hips to encourage him deeper, faster.

That rocking grew increasingly less controlled as the

moments passed. It was overwhelming, almost—the chill breeze on her skin, the wild air in her lungs, the fullness of him and the feel of his hands moving over her in that intoxicating blend of new and familiar ways.

Indecent was not the word that came to mind, even if it was the one they'd teasingly agreed on. It felt too perfect for that word. Untamed, maybe, but beautiful and right and *gods,* just...*good.* And soon, too soon, she felt it rising—a need for release that was even more desperate than what she'd felt building while he'd had her pinned against the wall.

Elander drew closer to her, caging her more completely within his warmth and muscle while he continued to drive into her, deeper and slower than before. His hand reached around and cupped between her legs once more, encouraging that release—and it didn't need much more *encouragement* than this.

She buried her face against the blanket to muffle the sound as her body convulsed and then collapsed into contentment. As the lingering waves of her release traveled through her, he leaned back, pulling her with him, arching her against his body and burying his face against her hair so that the sound of his own release was equally muffled.

He held her in that way for several moments after, her body curved against his, his hands roaming over her bare skin.

They finally untangled and faced one another. She

sat partially in his lap, shivering a bit as her sweat-coated skin dried in the crisp air. He drew her closer to his warmth, reached for her discarded coat and wrapped it around her.

Her forehead pressed to his. It stayed there while she regained her balance, while she closed her eyes and let the memories of the evening flood through her. Her fingers absently traveled over his body as her breathing steadied. Over those lines and ridges that were familiar by now, but somehow felt entirely...*new*.

Her warmth, her safe place, her captain, her guardian.

And soon...her *king*.

She had never known a peace quite like what came over her when she pictured the two of them ruling side by side. It seemed absurd—such *peace*—given what she knew it would take to secure that rule. To protect their kingdom and everything beyond it. But it was peace that flooded through her just the same—and for once she didn't question it; she simply breathed it in.

At some point, they dressed and stumbled back into the palace, up to her bedroom—likely drawing more stares and questions than was *decent*, but still too drunk on what they'd done to worry much about it.

They washed the traces of the forest and its fantasies from each other, changed into clean clothing, and contemplated rest. But the night still felt too wild, too infinite to sleep away in the confines of the palace walls, so they moved to the balcony instead, dragging pillows and blankets out with them, creating a makeshift bed so they could comfortably watch the stars.

They ended up falling asleep there, wrapped in each other's arms, piles of blankets draped across their intertwined bodies.

CAS WOKE UP FIRST. Her nightmares had still managed to find her—despite the state of peace she'd fallen asleep in—but she escaped them before they paralyzed her this time.

She slipped out of Elander's embrace, trying hard not to disturb him. Wrapping herself in a blanket, she tiptoed across the cold wooden planks and leaned against the balcony railing. The sun was just peeking over the hills, its light diffused by the early morning mist. She watched it continue to rise, alone with her thoughts, for at least a half hour before she heard movement behind her.

"How is it already morning?" Elander asked with a yawn.

"Time is a thief," she said with a shrug.

"It is," he agreed, with another yawn. "But at least we have a sunrise to appreciate, hm?"

She glanced back at him.

He wasn't looking at the sunrise; he was looking at her.

Her cheeks warmed, and she smiled sleepily and asked, "What are you staring at?"

"The Queen of the Dawn," he informed her, leaning back and framing her with his fingers, as if planning for her royal portrait. "And of everything else."

She laughed, her blush deepening. "Still an incorrigible flirt, I see, even now that you've secured your place as King."

"I don't intend to ever stop," he said, getting to his feet and stretching. "I hope that's not a dealbreaker."

"I'll learn to live with it, I suppose." She turned to face him more fully. Her heart swelled, and that peaceful feeling that had overcome her last night struck her once more. This was what she was meant to wake up to forever, she was certain of it—him, with his hair messy, his smile a bit stupid and sleepy, his features softened by the morning light.

"And what are *you* staring at?" he asked.

"Whatever I like," she told him, arching a brow, "because I am the Queen of the Dawn and everything else."

He laughed and got to his feet. He carried a blanket with him, and he wrapped her up in both his arms and that blanket from behind, hugging her against his bare chest and resting his chin on top of her head.

"I'm glad you're embracing the title," he yawned.

She leaned more fully into his chest. They stood this way for several minutes, until he loosened his hold on her and she shuffled around so they could talk face-to-face.

As the sun rose higher and warmed her back, they passed the time chatting about every possible thing that might lay ahead of them, big and small. She could have stayed there all day with him, talking about everything and nothing at all. But she knew countless obligations were awaiting her inside.

As she started to fully unravel from his arms and the blanket, Elander's smile faded a bit, his attention shifting to something in the distance.

Cas twisted around and followed his gaze, and she saw it for herself—a small company of riders carrying grey and white flags. "Those banners are from the Bywilds Realm, are they not?"

Elander's smile disappeared completely. "They're early. It's still three days until the summit."

So it begins.

She swallowed hard. Forced herself to shift more completely into that hardened side of herself that would help her face those coming obligations. "But they're actually *here*. Which is a good thing."

"True."

"And more will be arriving soon enough; we might as well get started early."

He tilted his face toward her, his gaze slowly taking her in—a final moment of soft admiration before his eyes hardened and he looked back to those approaching riders.

She took his hand and stared out over her city one last time, beyond the riders and toward the mountains, watching the sunlight chase away the last of the shadows.

Queen of the Dawn.

It had a nice ring to it, she thought.

CHAPTER 32

THEY MADE THE DECISION NOT TO TELL ANYBODY ABOUT THE promises they'd made on Sulah's Hill.

Not yet, at least.

A very large part of Cas wanted to tell all of friends her news the instant she stepped back into the palace—and then maybe shout it from the rooftops afterward. But she refrained. She didn't want it to distract from the difficult tasks they had to deal with in the coming days and weeks. Didn't want that happiness she'd felt on the hillside to be tainted by their current realities.

There was another reason as well, if she was being honest with herself. It was just...so much of her felt like it belonged to the people of this palace and the kingdoms beyond. So many things now demanded her attention—and Elander's, as well. But for a short time, at least, they could have something secret, something that belonged to only the two of them.

Over the next three days, more and more of their attention was demanded elsewhere.

The number of arriving guests increased every day, eventually exceeding even their highest expectations. The palace grew cramped in spite of its vastness, and Cas made the decision to open up that former guest wing that she'd previously ordered closed off.

She was there when the servants descended upon the dark hallway. She watched Nessa directing them, the doors to countless rooms opening, light flooding into the space as curtains were thrown open.

And she managed to calmly oversee it all—to separate what had happened from what *could* happen.

So much good could still happen within these walls.

She pressed on. They continued to make plans. Everyone she trusted was now aware of the conversation she'd had with Caden regarding the Dark God and his growing power, and there were endless discussions regarding where their focus needed to be during the coming days.

The one thing they all agreed on was that they were playing with fire, continuing with this gathering.

If that god was going to attack soon, then this would be an opportune time for him to do it. How better to keep the mortal army from expanding, and its morale low, if not by attacking them as they attempted to rally?

But Cas would not cower.

She would not hide, despite the risks.

She pressed on, and so everyone else did, too.

Their security was extensive. Every able-bodied soldier was armed and prepared. The Sky and Moon Goddesses arrived the day before the summit business was to get underway, and they set about creating a complex barrier of magic that stretched for miles around the palace.

The Sky Goddess had only been persuaded into doing this much...and *barely* persuaded, at that. Once she was finished with the task, she made it clear that she intended to leave and let whatever happened, happen.

Cas tried and failed to convince her to stay longer.

It was better than nothing, however—better than the Star Goddess, who had declined to join them and help in any way.

The Storm Goddess would be arriving soon to offer more help, according to her sister. Cas assumed she was waiting until she could make a more dramatic entrance.

The hours raced by in a blur, and in no time at all, another day and a half had passed, and the planned banquet—the inaugural event of their gathering—was upon them.

Cas and her court had managed to barrel through all the doubts and establish a confidence that had infected most of their guests. Those guests were fully embracing their visit to Ciridan as a result, and Cas could hardly believe it—but some of the most powerful men and women in Kethra were mingling in the hallways of her palace, swapping thoughts and ideas, and the air teemed with possibility.

The palace was relatively calm, even though its population had soared. Its grounds were calm. The city beyond it all was calm.

Everything seemed oddly, impossibly calm.

And though Cas knew better than to let down her guard at this point, she felt cautiously optimistic as she slipped away to her room and began to dress for the banquet.

She had chosen a long-sleeved gown of soft, midnight blue fabric for the evening. Crystals lined its bodice, and when she moved, the patterns made her think of moonlight shimmering upon the waves of a dark sea. It hugged high and tight across her front while swooping low across her back, and she paired it with silver flats that were easy to walk in.

She had purposefully selected something elegant, but simple—something that enabled her to move freely, to swing a sword, and to quickly change if need be. Her hair was tied up and out of her way, as well, worked into several intricate, looping braids that were held in place by pins with sparkling crystals that matched those upon her dress.

She still wore the hourglass the Time Goddess had given her, but it was hidden by the dress's high neckline.

Nessa had found a colorful brooch that resembled a sun, and insisted on pinning it to Cas's dress for good luck—and in remembrance of the upper-goddess who had given her a sword and purpose. As Cas ran her fingers over it, the memory of waking up on the balcony, tucked against Elander's chest, surfaced in her mind and filled her with warmth.

The Queen of the Dawn.

Almost as soon as she thought of that moniker Elander had bestowed upon her, she heard a soft knock on her bedroom door, and a servant opened it to reveal him standing on the other side—as if on cue.

The servants bowed their way out of the room and left the two of them alone.

Elander had paused at the sight of her, and he drank her in for a moment longer before crossing the room and reaching for her hand. "You look incredible," he told her, guiding her into a slow twirl, appreciating the seductively low dip of the dress's back.

He kept hold of her hand once they were face-to-face again, and she let her gaze roam over him as well.

His hair was neatly pulled away from his face, with only a few strands free to frame his eyes, which looked exceptionally blue above the navy color of his shirt. He wore a fine jacket with silver fastenings over that shirt, and breeches that fit his form so well that she was certain there must have been some sort of courtly law against it; he was going to disturb the peace they'd been enjoying, walking through the halls looking like that.

She cleared her throat. "And you look like a roguishly handsome captain that I could see myself running away —and getting into trouble—with," she informed him.

"Excellent." He drew her in for a quick kiss. "That's what I was going for."

She couldn't help but return the smile he was giving her.

"Anyway—I wanted to let you know that the Goddess of Storms did decide to grace us with her presence," he said. "She arrived a few minutes ago."

"In dramatic fashion, I presume."

His lips quirked. "She frightened a handful of guards, yes. But it could have been worse."

She exhaled through her nose. "You'll keep her in line tonight, I hope."

"I'll do my best."

"Remind her that our divine allies are not the sole thing on tonight's agenda."

"She keeps trying to convince me to let her put on a display for our guests."

"What sort of display?"

"I didn't ask." He gave her another crooked grin as he offered his arm. "You can't give her ideas that sort of attention, or she'll run away with them."

Cas frowned, but took his arm and walked from the safety of her room—the first steps into the precarious evening that awaited her. She felt eyes following her almost immediately, and she made sure to erase the frown from her face just as quickly.

"It will all be fine," Elander promised as they made their way down the hall. "And I'll be close by if you need me."

He would have stayed by her side in an instant if she'd asked him to, but he didn't care for these stuffy royal affairs. And she felt better about their security anyway, knowing that he was moving freely about and keeping an eye on things—which was why they had planned on him doing this.

They paused at the top of the staircase that wound its way down to the first floor.

That floor below them was already crowded with bodies, with guests sparkling and moving about in all their fineries. The hum of conversation grew louder, and somewhere in the distance, music had started to play.

"I should go inspect our barriers and such outside," Elander said.

"Be careful," she told him.

He nodded, leaned in and brushed his lips across her cheek—the quickest, softest of kisses—and then he was gone.

She paused for a moment longer, alone with the weight of her invisible crown and all she hoped to accomplish tonight. Then she kept moving. She went out onto the balcony at the hallway's end, just for a moment—just long enough to take a few deep breaths of the cool night air.

When she turned back to face the palace, she found Zev approaching, and she couldn't help but smile as she took in his appearance. He was incredibly handsome in a silk, intricately-patterned doublet, well-tailored pants tapered over polished boots, and several glittering rings that he'd almost certainly stolen from somewhere within the palace. He moved toward her with an arrogant stride more befitting of a prince than a commoner.

"Getting a lot of stares in this outfit," he commented. "I'm considering charging people by the minute."

"If I pay extra, can I stare without having to listen to your commentary?"

"That depends," he said, "on how much extra you're willing to pay. It takes a lot to get me to shut my mouth."

"Trust me, I know. I'm willing to pay it, however."

He gave her a charming smile.

She beckoned him closer so she could smooth a crease from his jacket. "I don't believe I'll ever get used to the sight of you all cleaned up and...*civilized* looking."

He brushed a piece of lint from his shoulder and shot her a smirk. "Get used to it. And let's be honest, I was born for this role. I'm pulling all the weight in the *good looks* department for your court."

"I wasn't aware that good looks were necessary for effectively running a kingdom," she said drily.

"Well, you have a lot to learn, Queen Casia."

She snorted. "You're right about that, at least."

He chuckled, and then, in a slightly more serious voice, he said, "So...you ready for tonight?"

"Yes," she replied...and it was mostly true. "I was just taking a moment before it all begins." She balanced against the balcony railing as she spoke, watching the shadows of early evening creep over the palace lawn. She caught sight of Elander in the distance, moving among the guards stationed at one of the gatehouses, giving orders.

"I see you let *him* escape this stifling affair."

"Part of it, yes." She turned and leaned her back against the railing, her eyes narrowing on her best friend. "And by the way...I heard the two of you were fighting while I was gone the other day."

"Nessa told on me, didn't she?"

"Not important who told."

"I'm still vetting him on your behalf, that's all."

She shook her head, her smile wry. "He's battled gods—*several* gods—and essentially changed the entire world on my behalf at this point...what more would you like him to do?"

Zev stepped to her side and leaned against the balcony as well. "I just think he's a bit of a show-off, honestly."

She rolled her eyes, which only made his smile brighten. He put an arm around her, and she rested her head on his shoulder.

"And in my defense," he added after a moment, "I've had to beat up old boyfriends for you in the past."

"Just that one, really." She cringed at the memory. "And I could have beaten him up myself, for the record."

"Maybe."

"*Definitely.*"

He acquiesced with a wave of his hand and another soft laugh.

After a brief hesitation, she quietly said, "This is different."

When she lifted her head and cut her gaze toward him, she found him already looking at her. Curiosity shimmered in his bright eyes, his lips were drawn in an even line, and she thought that perhaps her old friend realized exactly what she meant by *different*—that he somehow knew about Elander's proposal, and her acceptance, even without her saying anything about it.

"You understand, don't you?" she pressed.

His expression relaxed into that easygoing grin once more. "As long as he treats you the way he should, we won't have a problem."

"So no more trying to light him on fire, right?"

"Right." He cleared his throat. "Though just to be clear, I wasn't really *trying* to light him on fire the other day. If I'd been putting any effort into it, I would have succeeded."

She grinned back at him. "Thank you," she said,

before stretching up to plant a kiss on his cheek—which he promptly, teasingly, wiped away.

The sound of the music in the distance grew louder. The few guests who had been mingling on the lawns below began to make their way inside, and Cas absently reached for her necklace; she could feel the hourglass charm through her dress, and tracing the outline of it brought her a sense of calm.

Everything felt as if it was moving very quickly, all of a sudden, and she was struck by a sudden urge to finish clearing the air between her and Zev—just in case they didn't have another chance anytime soon.

"I know these past weeks have been difficult," she told him. "That *I've* been difficult."

"I'm used to you being difficult."

"Can you be quiet for like two seconds?"

He shrugged. "You didn't pay me the agreed upon sum, so you get the commentary, I'm afraid."

She sighed, but she was fighting another smile. "I just wanted to say...I'm glad you're still here with me, that's all."

He arched a brow. "I'm going to have to ask *you* to be quiet now. I'm not drunk enough to start getting so sentimental."

"Oh, deal with it," she said, nudging him in the ribs before spinning him around and marching him toward the door. "And escort me into this *stifling affair*, please. Do your job of making me look better."

"So commanding."

"Get used to it," she said, echoing his words from earlier.

They teased and provoked each other for most of the walk into the palace. Once there, they quickly spotted Laurent and Rhea; a mere glimpse of his sister was enough to make Zev stand up a little straighter and stop his joking around.

Silverfoot met Cas's gaze, and Rhea turned and smiled warmly at her. "Good evening, Your Highness."

CHAPTER 33

Cas fought her usual urge to deny her title while among her friends.

It was easier to crush that urge once she caught sight of herself in the mirrored glass that lined the wall behind Rhea. She barely recognized her own reflection —and she couldn't help thinking that the woman staring back at her actually *did* look like she might pass for royalty.

All of her friends did.

Laurent looked as handsome as Zev, wearing a long, elegant tunic that was more in line with the fashions of his home realm rather than those of Ciridan; he was already drawing the gaze and admiration of several of their guests. If there was any doubt that the true King of Moreth was here among her allies, she had a feeling he would put it to rest tonight.

Rhea looked stunning as well, in a plum-colored dress that seemed to float around her with even the smallest of movements. Silverfoot was draped over her shoulder, a matching purple bowtie around his neck— Nessa's handiwork, most likely.

Nessa herself was nowhere to be seen, but Cas was certain she was whirling about the palace, impeccably dressed and somehow perfectly in command of a hundred different aspects of the evening, making certain that all of it went off according to her intricate planning.

Somewhere along the way, it had happened without Cas paying much attention to it—they had changed right alongside her. From a motley band of mercenaries into a proper royal court who gathered around her now like a shield, fielding all the questions and introductions being fired at her in rapid succession. Like a raft keeping her afloat among the waves of people and expectations she had to meet. She could swim well enough on her own, but they gave her a place to rest when she needed it.

Knowing they were close by gave her the energy and confidence to greet the eager guests, to charm the doubters, to navigate her way through the more tumultuous conversations. She would likely never enjoy these things, but she found herself surprisingly good at it.

There was eventually a lull in people demanding her attention. Rhea went to check in with the kitchens, while Laurent lingered nearby, giving Cas a chance to pull him aside so they could speak in relative privacy. They walked the length of the room together, eventually ending up at the row of windows that overlooked the courtyard.

Laurent frowned as he looked down at the soldiers walking the paths outside, his eyes narrowing in concentration. He seemed to be counting them, making certain they were all where they were supposed to be.

"I know you'd rather be outside, running drills with Elander and the rest of our soldiers."

He didn't disagree.

"But I'm glad you're in here, for what it's worth—I need the true King of Moreth to help win over some of these more skeptical guests."

He cleared his throat.

She gave him a lopsided grin. "If I have to call myself Queen, you have to call yourself King."

He lifted a brow. "Is that how it works?"

"I think there's actually a rule somewhere about only having one disputed ruler per banquet," Zev put in, popping back into the conversation out of seemingly nowhere. Cas wasn't sure where he'd disappeared to, but he'd come back with a plate piled with strawberries arranged around a large slice of frosted cake; her stomach growled at the sight of it.

"If there isn't a rule, there should be," said Laurent, taking a glass of wine from a tray carried by a passing servant. "But I still intend to help with our plans in any way I can, of course," he added, cutting his eyes at Cas. "That's why I'm in here—so you can stop looking at me like that."

"It's her angry queen face," said Zev. "She tried using it on me earlier too."

"Ah, yes, Nessa mentioned she'd adopted a rather harsh royal tone as well."

"Okay, *neither* of those things are true," said Cas.

"I think I hear a hint of that tone now," said Zev.

"It seems Nessa was right," Laurent said, yawning.

"So harsh," Zev agreed.

"I'm going to banish both of you assholes from my kingdom if you keep it up."

"Harsh *and* rude," Zev added.

Cas responded by swiping one of the strawberries from his plate—the one covered in the most frosting. She popped it into her mouth before he could swipe it back.

"Abusing her powers to steal my food now," said Zev, shaking his head. "Fucking tyrant." He looked to Laurent for agreement, but Laurent's attention had already shifted elsewhere.

Cas followed Laurent's gaze, and she saw that Nessa had just appeared at the foot of the stairs on the other side of the room, looking radiant in a dress that shimmered between what seemed to be every possible color of the ocean. Her hair was swept to one side, and her jewelry sparkled in the light of the chandeliers as she laughed with a group that had quickly gravitated toward her.

"Excuse me," said Laurent, handing off his emptied glass to Zev before crossing the room to meet her.

Zev watched him go, a sly smile inching its way across his face. "Is it just me, or are the two of them...?"

"Never mind that," said Cas, hooking her arm with his and steering him toward the opposite side of the room.

"I feel like you don't trust me to be discreet about the matter."

"You're right. I absolutely don't."

He laughed.

"Let them be," she chided.

He finished off the cake, and discarded of his plate and Laurent's glass before weaving back into the thick of the crowd around them, returning to their task of greeting and mingling.

Cas followed, but not before glancing over her shoulder one last time to see Laurent and Nessa walking arm-in-arm together. It gave her another burst of that warmth, thinking of what they were all becoming—and what might *still* become of them once they made it to the other side of all their wars.

"This crowd is bigger every time I turn around," Zev said, pulling her back to the present. He lowered his voice and added, "Do you even recognize half of these people?"

"Not all of them. Very few of them, actually." She sighed. "Don't tell Nessa, though. I'd hate for her to think that all of those notes she made me study were for nothing."

She plastered on a smile and searched through the sea of faces around them, trying to quietly remember and recite names to herself.

Her attention lingered the longest on a man who was standing by the grand piano in one of the corners. Not because she recognized him, but because he seemed to recognize *her*—and not in the casual way that almost everyone in this kingdom did, now. He was looking at her as though they had a personal connection of some sort.

She casually strolled past him so she could study him out of the corner of her eye.

He was young, and undeniably handsome, with dark hair, piercing grey eyes, and a lean figure that was well-suited for the fine silk shirt and tailored pants he wore. His skin was deeply tanned and smooth—flawless. Glowing, almost. The fingers he had wrapped around the stem of his wine glass were adorned with several priceless-looking rings, and more fine jewelry hung from his wrists and neck.

The combination of good looks and obvious wealth had earned him nearly as much attention as Cas and her court, but he hardly seemed aware of the smiling, adoring people around him. He only had eyes for Cas as she walked by.

She couldn't bring herself to go speak with him. And he never approached her. Nearly every other person in the room was clamoring to get closer to her, but though she eventually worked up the nerve to stare directly at this man—to nod hello, even—he only smiled and tilted his head back at her.

It was unnerving.

"That man over by the piano," she whispered, nudging Zev and discreetly pointing. "Do you recognize him? An old client of ours, maybe?"

"I don't think so." Zev studied him for a moment, but he didn't seem nearly as unsettled by the man's gaze as she was.

Before she could question anything else, their attention was torn away from the man by the sudden arrival of a messenger, who insisted on pulling her away from the crowded ballroom and into a more private space.

Zev followed them to a small office and lingered outside the doorway, close enough to listen, but positioned to interfere with anyone else who might have been trying to overhear things.

The messenger gave a quick bow of her head before speaking in a rush. "You were awaiting a response from Queen Soryn?"

Cas nodded eagerly. Earlier that day, they had sent

the Air spirit to personally escort Soryn and any guests she wanted back to Ciridan.

So many other things had distracted Cas this evening that it only now occurred to her that she hadn't seen that young queen yet.

"Unable to come, Your Majesty. She sent the spirit back with the word just a few moments ago. She gave no clear reason."

More unease rippled through Cas, but she didn't let it show. She simply cleared her throat and asked, "She's safe, I hope?"

"As far as we know. The last report from Kosrith declared all was calm."

A hundred more questions came to mind. But Cas uttered nothing except a quick thank you before dismissing the messenger.

Zev wandered into the room once that messenger was out of sight and hearing range. "It's a tricky situation in Sadira at the moment," he offered. "I'm sure she has good reason for not being able to get away—something that wouldn't have been safe to put in a message."

Cas nodded, trying to convince herself of the same thing. But a quiet fear was building in her heart; one that had taken root when she'd spoken to her brother in the mountains the other day. He might not have been telling the truth about everything, but he *was* right to point out how dependent Sadira was on divine magic.

Magic that Cas was soon going to upend in a violent, irreversible manner.

Would Soryn still be her ally once she realized what her ultimate goal had become?

Her thoughts shifted to other rulers. To the empire that lay to the south, which was drenched in even more magic than Sadira. She'd thought of inviting the Sundolian High Queen and King to this summit as well, but had hesitated—it had seemed important for this first meeting to be among Kethran leaders. More focused. She could reach out to Sundolia in the near future, she'd told herself.

But what if it was too late at that point? What if it wasn't enough?

Enough.

That stupid word. She thought she'd managed to banish it from her thoughts, but there it was again.

"You okay?" Zev asked.

She forced a nod.

Those other rulers weren't here. She couldn't focus on them. She had a job to do tonight, and she would not fail at *this*, at least.

She continued through the motions, seeking out faces she hadn't spoken with yet and greeting them personally. Outwardly, she was as eloquent and poised as ever. But inwardly, something had changed since that message. She couldn't deny it. Her sense of unease was growing, which was why her eyes kept darting around, restless and searching, whenever she wasn't speaking with anyone.

And this was why she was able to catch a strange sight through the skylights above them—a sudden flash of light, followed by a puff of smoke that quickly faded from sight.

"Did you see that?" she whispered.

"See what?" Zev asked.

"Something hit the barrier above the roof, I believe."

"A bird?"

She shook her head, her eyes lifting upward once more. "It scattered strangely. Like magical residue of some sort."

Zev studied the skylight for a long moment, but nothing similar occurred. His expression was doubtful when he looked back at her, but he was also clearly growing bored of the festivities, so he volunteered to go take a closer look.

Cas moved to follow him, but he grabbed her arm and held her still, nodding at someone behind her. "I think you're wanted by that group over there."

She glanced over her shoulder and saw several sets of eyes upon her, following the lead of a portly older gentleman who was pointing rather rudely in her direction.

"His name is Lord Aran, by the way," Zev added under his breath.

"Thank you," she whispered back.

She steeled herself, and mentally sifted through the notes Nessa had given her about this man. She wasn't directly addressed by him or any of his circle, but she heard her name being tossed among them, carelessly and continuously, so she made her way over.

"And here she is," declared the lord, wildly brandishing the pewter goblet in his hand.

"Here I am," she said with an agreeable incline of her head.

"I was just over here wondering...what does it take to get the new *queen*'s attention, hm?"

She curved her lips into her practiced smile. "Lord Aran, isn't it?"

He gave a bow so low he nearly lost his balance. A touch mocking, maybe—though it might have simply been the alcohol. His face was quite red.

She greeted the rest of the circle with that same practiced smile.

Just make an appearance. Greet them all, make them feel heard.

That had been her plan for the evening. She could linger for a few minutes, couldn't she?

But the gossip about her continued even as she stood among this particular group. After a moment, Lord Aran's voice rose above them all once more, speaking of her as though he'd forgotten she was mere feet away from him.

"She'll be replacing the king as well, won't she?"

"Beg your pardon?" Cas stiffened, confused and slightly alarmed. She hadn't told anyone about that. So why was Lord Aran looking at her so...*knowingly?*

He took another long swig from his cup—even though Cas was fairly certain it was empty. "I only mean to say—well, what is a *king*dom without a king at its head?"

Oh.

He wasn't somehow aware of her secret engagement.

He was merely being an ignorant ass.

"These are such dangerous times. A little much for such a pretty young lady to handle alone, I believe."

The air around them warmed. Shivered with electricity. Just a few sparks of Storm magic floated around her hand—enough to raise a few hairs on the heads closest to her. The more perceptive members of the circle shuffled where they stood, uncertain—but Cas never lost her smile.

"Are you volunteering, Lord Aran?" she asked. "Because I'm fairly sure you're not my type. And I'm even more certain your wife wouldn't approve."

This elicited a few laughs from the rest of the crowd.

"Heavens, no." He wiped his brow. "I do, however, have a rather dashing young nephew who'd be about right...."

Cas forced her tone to remain as polite as her smile, despite all the less-than-polite responses she wanted to fling at him. "Hardly the most pressing topic of the evening."

"No? Then what would *you* say we should be concerning ourselves with, my dear?"

She could have given him a list.

But drunken pigs were not the sort of allies she was seeking, so she remained coy. "I think finding you another drink should be first on that list of concerns."

A rousing cheer went up, led by Lord Aran, as Cas flagged down a servant and saw to it that they all received full glasses.

She managed to quietly slip away as they drank themselves stupider, and she headed to find a servant to send after Zev. He should have been back by now.

But the Storm Goddess stepped through the door and caught Cas's attention before she found a servant.

It would have been difficult *not* to notice the goddess, given her appearance; she was dazzling in a sleeveless indigo dress with a plunging V-neckline. Her hair floated loosely around her, shimmering as occasional bolts of actual electricity wove through it; her pale locks were nearly the same color as that electricity, so perhaps she'd thought it *subtle* enough. It was the same faint sort of lightning that often lit her dark skin. She was able to hide these glimmers of her power—Cas had seen her do it—but she hadn't bothered to hide anything tonight.

Several people audibly gasped as she passed by them on her way to Cas.

"I sensed someone using my magic," the goddess informed her as she approached, "so I came inside to make certain you weren't blowing anything up."

"Why? Were you hoping to help?"

"That depends entirely on what we're blowing up, of course."

Cas sighed and averted her eyes, annoyed with herself for nearly losing her temper with that lord. She felt the goddess still staring at her, questioning, so she deflected. "Are you even *trying* to blend in?"

"Of course not."

Cas pinched the bridge of her nose and bowed her head, fighting off a sudden throbbing in her temple.

"Lift your head, Little Queen." Nephele's tone was partly commanding, partly concerned, as she cupped Cas's chin and lifted it herself. "People are always watching you now, don't forget."

She hadn't forgotten.

She was getting tired, that was all.

Rhea and Silverfoot had caught sight of the goddess as well. They joined them, and Rhea immediately noticed that exhaustion, even though Cas tried to shake it off before they came close.

Rhea reached to fix one of Cas's hairpins that had slipped loose, letting her hand linger against the side of her head as she quietly asked, "What's wrong, love?"

Cas beckoned them into a more private corner of the room, where she told them of Soryn's message. Of the boorish Lord Aran and his unpleasant insinuations about her position. Of the strange man that had been staring at her earlier, and the stranger shadows that she had sent Zev after.

"I'll find out who that man is before the night is over with," Rhea said, once Cas had finished speaking. Then her fingers scratched Silverfoot's chin, rousing him and prompting him to scan the crowded ballroom—to search out a target. "But I think I'm going to go properly introduce myself to Lord Aran first."

"I'll go with you," said Nephele, looking entirely too eager to get involved.

"We're making allies tonight," Cas reminded them sternly.

"I plan to be perfectly amicable," said Nephele.

"Yes, but are those plans flexible?"

"My plans are *always* flexible."

Cas exhaled slowly. "Don't cause a scene."

"A scene—me?" The goddess *humphed*. She spun around, sending her dress twirling dramatically about her ankles, and then flounced after Rhea, who was already halfway across the room.

Cas watched them go with an odd mixture of gratitude and trepidation.

She didn't have to find a servant to send in search of

Zev, after all; he was already walking toward her, alongside Nessa, when she turned around.

He answered her question before she could even ask it. "I didn't find anything. And I asked around—nobody saw anything to worry about."

Cas still felt uneasy, but she couldn't put into words *why*, so she just thanked him.

He gave a little salute, and then he promptly dismissed himself to go *greet* a blonde-haired woman who had just sauntered by in an eye-catching red dress.

"That's Lady Eletha of Windkeep," said Nessa. "She's very much engaged. Should we tell him?"

Cas shrugged. "He could use a humbling experience."

Nessa laughed, and then quickly moved back into her more formal, directing mode. "Nearly time for everyone to take their seats for dinner, by the way," she informed Cas. And with a grin, she added, "Last chance to run."

"If I can survive multiple battles with divine beings, surely I can survive hosting my first royal dinner."

"Agreed. And you're doing wonderfully so far from what I've heard."

"No major disasters at least."

Nessa's grin brightened, and Cas started to return it —but then another stab of unease drew her gaze to the skylights. She thought she saw a flicker of light, but when she looked closer... No. It was nothing. Just leaves or something falling against their barrier; she was just sensitive to it because of her magic.

But she was still struck by a sudden urge to head outside and check on things herself. To mention her concerns to Elander, maybe.

I'll be close by if you need me, he'd said.

"Cas?"

"I'll be back in one moment," she told Nessa. "I wanted to check in with the guards outside before dinner."

Nessa frowned.

"I have the schedule you gave me memorized," she assured her, already heading for the exit. "I won't be late, I promise!"

ONCE OUTSIDE, she used her magic to seek out Elander, summoning a small storm of lightning and letting it dance upon her skin, then following the distant power she felt pulsing in response.

She found him quickly, leaning on the wall near the main gate, surrounded by a group of soldiers.

As he spotted her, he smiled and stepped away from that group. "I was hoping the queen would grace me with her presence soon."

She returned his smile, but it wilted quickly.

"Is something wrong?"

"No."

He tilted his head to the side, expectant.

"Well, maybe. I saw something earlier...a strange flicker in the barrier above the palace." They walked to a more secluded section of the courtyard, and she hopped onto a low garden wall, taking the opportunity to get off her feet for a moment. "Is everything all right out here?"

He swept a glance toward the palace roofs, squinting into the darkness for a moment before replying. "We haven't noticed anything out of the ordinary."

"Right. It was probably nothing." She hugged her arms against herself. "I think I'm just waiting for something disastrous to happen."

"Understandable, given our history."

She breathed out a humorless laugh.

"But nothing has?"

"No, surprisingly." She decided not to tell him about Lord Aran. She'd almost lost her temper; Elander would be much worse. "But I still needed some air. And I needed to see you." She shrugged. "Well, *wanted*."

He pressed closer, taking her hands in his and squeezing them tightly. The wall lifted her nearly to his height, so he didn't have to lean down to kiss her for once. Her eyes fluttered shut and her skin tingled with another storm of magic as his lips brushed hers.

She managed an earnest smile as he slowly pulled away. "Thank you," she said, blinking her eyes open.

"Any time."

"The banquet is about to begin." She took a deep

breath, preparing to get back on her feet and face the palace once more—

The sound of boots pounding upon pavers made both of their heads jerk toward the main gates as a soldier ran through, followed by several others. He had something tucked under his arm—something large, white, and oblong in shape.

Cas jumped down and took a few steps toward him, before getting a good look at what he was carrying—which made her draw back in alarm. "*What is that?*"

The soldier dropped it at their feet as he heaved for breath.

It was a severed *head.*

The head of a monster—though it wasn't immediately recognizable as such, as most of its facial features were missing. It had no eyes, and only two small slits where its nose should have been.

But Cas had seen this particular monster before. "A void archer?"

She still had nightmares about these creatures and the battle she'd fought against them during her last stay in this city.

"We discovered it trying to break through a distant stretch of the barrier," the soldier panted, giving the head a nudge with his boot, rolling it over. The back of that head—its weak point, where it looked to have been stabbed—was covered in a blackish-red ooze.

"Just this one?" Cas frowned. A single attacker seemed unlikely.

Elander looked equally worried. "They never travel alone."

"We searched all along the barrier," said the soldier, "but found no others."

"A decoy?" Cas wondered. "Or a scout?"

Elander looked to a stretch of that barrier in the distance, uncertainty darkening his features. "Find the Moon Goddess and tell her to do a more thorough examination," he ordered.

The soldier, along with several of the others who lingered close by, gave a quick bow and then hurried off.

Cas and Elander exchanged another worried look as they left.

"You should go back inside," he told her, "and warn the others to be on their guard." He was signaling for more soldiers even as he spoke. "Something's not right."

CHAPTER 34

CASIA HURRIED TO WARN THE GUARDS AND ALLIES INSIDE, AS he'd suggested—and also to grab her sword, Elander suspected.

As he watched her disappear through the palace doors, a shiver of unease went through him. He shook it off and finished firing off orders to his soldiers, sending some to reinforce the palace doors, and others to inspect various areas around the grounds.

Then he looked back to the head at his feet. It was becoming less solid as the seconds ticked by. He was surprised it had remained solid in the first place. Normally they disintegrated quickly once they were dismembered, and that was what it was doing now—transforming into a smoky puff of silver and black. That dark cloud lingered in the air, leaving behind ominous flickers of shadowy energy even as the main mass of it faded away.

These monsters—the *namtar*—were known for their ability to steal and negate power. They were vessels, in a sense—voids that swallowed up and extinguished the energy of whatever their claws and arrows hit. They had originally been created to stand guard at the various mortal afterworlds. To absorb the restless magic and other energies from departed souls and keep the spaces between those afterworlds neutral.

So if *he* was trying to neutralize a barrier of magic, this was the sort of army he would have sent.

Elander forced a deep breath.

It was not an army; it was merely the head of a lone archer. A single breach attempt. It would have taken scores of them to truly break through, so even if it *wasn't* alone...

Another deep breath.

No matter how he tried to rationalize things, the shivers of uncertainty still continued to course through him.

Movement in the nearby bushes.

His hand went to his sword, but it stilled on the pommel as a familiar creature slipped out of the gardens and onto the path before him—the Air spirit.

"Velia," he breathed.

The spirit lowered her gaze, one of the long appendages upon her head stretching toward him as she did. He reached forward, and a vision passed through his mind as that antenna pressed to his palm—a message—showing him a section of the magic barrier they'd erected...and a familiar person waiting expectantly on the other side of it.

Caden.

He blinked away the image of his once friend and ally. It was inevitable that he and Caden would meet again, but it had not been on his list of things he needed —or *wanted*—to take care of tonight. Now that he knew he was close, however, it was just as it had been before...

He couldn't stop thinking about tracking him down.

The soldier he'd sent after the Moon Goddess returned and reported her location to him. He found her in the east gardens in her canine form, inspecting a stretch of the barrier. He hesitated only a moment before he called out to her, asking her to accompany him somewhere else.

After a brief pause and consideration, she swept toward him, lighting the ground with brief prints of glowing dust as she came.

They started toward the spot the Air spirit had revealed, passing through the main gates and the permanent wall that stretched around the palace grounds, and then veering toward a section of that extended barrier the Sky and Moon Goddesses had created.

He didn't plan to run—didn't want to cause his

soldiers to panic just yet—but the uneasiness he felt was getting worse. It pushed him into a jog that didn't slow until he approached the spot in question.

Part of him hoped that the spirit's message had been off somehow. That Caden might have already moved on. But no—he was there, wearing that familiar, clever expression that he so often did.

Elander gripped the pommel of his sword once more, squeezing tightly as he said, "Let me through to him."

Inya lifted her head. Studied him through her strangely luminescent eyes. He heard her soft voice in his head a moment later—either real or imagined, he wasn't sure which.

Are you certain?

He nodded, and she hesitated for only a beat more before she did as he'd asked, breathing pale light onto the barrier and melting away a small section of it.

Elander passed through this opening to meet Caden, but moved no farther than a few steps beyond the barrier. The Moon Goddess lingered over the opening as well, further preventing Caden from passing through to the palace side.

Though he had played out this second reunion over and over in his mind over the past weeks, Elander wasted no time with all of the many questions he'd planned to ask, and he simply demanded: "Why are you here?"

"I came to warn you."

"You've already warned us."

"Yes. But the situation has continued to deteriorate, even since Casia and I last met."

He swallowed down his irritation about that meeting and all the others. Now was not the time to address those things.

"The threat is imminent," Caden informed him quietly.

Elander glanced back at the brightly-lit palace and casually said, "We likely have *several* threats among us tonight. The risk of inviting all these potential allies... they can't all be our friends in the end, can they?"

"I'm not talking about one of the palace guests."

Elander rolled his shoulders, trying to shrug away the tension in them. "You're talking about Malaphar then? He's planning to show himself?"

Caden's gaze followed the path Elander's had, studying the distant palace with a frown. "Soon, I think."

"How do you know this?"

"Varen was...*confronted* by him." Caden's eyes glassed over, as though he was trying to briefly slip away from the memory of that confrontation. Even if he hadn't personally witnessed it, he would have been able to feel at least part of it—*forced* to feel it, to experience it secondhand, even if his link to those gods above him wasn't fully reestablished yet.

"So he's gone and spilled all of the information he was supposedly keeping between us?" Elander muttered.

Varen's *usefulness* to them hadn't lasted very long, had it?

"Not all of it," said Caden. "He withstood the torture well enough."

Elander kept his face impassive, even as an explosion of conflicting feelings blew through him. It would have been a lie to say the thought of Varen being tortured was personally upsetting to him. But if that torture had led to *any* of their potential plans being revealed, it was a problem.

"There were other things I overheard the Dark God inquiring about too," Caden continued, "information that he didn't pry out of me or Varen. So I believe you have a traitor in your midst, as well."

Elander didn't argue this possibility. He was very aware of all the people with questionable loyalties that surrounded them, all the many moving parts and points where traitors could potentially have slipped through. And what he'd told Casia that day in the Roedyn Valley was true as well—he didn't fully trust *any* of the divine at this point.

Including the one standing directly in front of him.

He glanced over his shoulder at the Moon Goddess, who had taken a few steps back toward the palace. Something seemed to have caught her attention.

"So he knows the weak parts of your barrier," Caden went on. "He knows the weak parts of your court. Of your plans. I tried to warn Casia that he was gathering the strength to launch an attack; I didn't think she'd carry on with this summit, given that threat."

"You don't know her very well," Elander said tonelessly.

"Maybe not. But *he* knows her well enough now—and I have a sinking feeling that he is going to put this knowledge to use tonight."

Elander glared at him, his pulse thundering in his ears. What he wouldn't have given for silence. For clarity. For the ability to be able to easily trust what Caden was telling him, just as he once had.

"You know I can't trust that feeling," he said. "Or you. All these ages you've known me, and you still think I would do something so foolish? This is either a trick, or a distraction, or the gods know what else—either way, I don't have time for this conversation. I need to get back to the palace. I never should have left it."

"But you did."

Elander bared his teeth in frustration. He didn't speak, but suddenly he was thinking of that night in his bedroom, and the stubborn way Casia had insisted that there might be a way to save his old friend.

She'd done this to him, he thought, barely able to contain his unamused laughter. He had once been a perfectly content cynic—one who would never have gotten distracted by a need to see Caden and try to make sense of what had happened to him. Not because he didn't care, but because he had seen enough death and loss to know that sometimes you simply needed to let it happen. Holding on caused complications.

He shook his head and started to turn for the palace.

A sudden whistling sound split the night, jerking his attention back around—

An arrow.

Caden moved with inhuman speed in front of Elander, drawing his short sword and knocking that arrow down in mid-air. As it hit the ground, it ignited in a brief show of black flame that scorched a circle of grass no less than five feet wide.

Elander took a step back as he stared at the blackened ground, breathless for a moment, realizing how close he'd come to a very painful wound.

The void archer responsible stood on a hillside in the distance, his pale head and skeletal wings cutting a terrifying image against the darkness. It let out a blood-curdling sound—a screech like a sword scraping over glass—and lifted its bow to take aim once more.

Shadows wrapped up Caden's body just as quickly, carrying him away only to deposit him on the hillside, directly behind the archer.

A swift stab into the back of its head, and that archer was crumpling, tumbling down the hill, black currents of unruly energy bleeding out behind it as it went.

Caden returned to Elander's side on foot, without glancing back. He offered no comment on what he'd done. It all felt so familiar—like just another of the countless, confident kills he'd witnessed Caden make—but Elander still guarded himself against that feeling as best he could.

This could still be a trick.

"You're right, of course." Caden's voice was rigid and cold with determination. "We both know I'm not far from losing my will to that upper-god. But not tonight. Tonight it's just...*me*. So I came to help one last time before the end. So that I might go out in the way I prefer."

Elander swallowed hard, trying again—and failing again—to push that conversation with Casia from his head.

And then he sighed and said, "Maybe it doesn't have to be the end tonight."

Caden averted his gaze. "I intend to go out quickly and cleanly, just so we're clear. No hesitating when that breaking point comes."

Elander studied him for a long moment. "We'll see."

Before Caden could reply to this, another one of the namtar was upon them.

And there was no hesitation now—from either of them.

While Caden drew the monster's attention, Elander drew his sword. He summoned lightning to the tip, and with a slash into the air he sent the magic leaping free, aiming it into the weak point at the back of the namtar's head.

The monster tried and failed to absorb this magic; it was too much, and soon its lanky body was convulsing, stumbling wildly about. It made it to within a few feet of the barrier before collapsing and igniting into darkness, just as that arrow had moments earlier.

The explosion sent a black cloud bursting outward. It collided with the barrier, and as it drifted up and away, it revealed the cracks that it had caused around the goddess-made opening. The dark energy continued to teem within the barrier's magic, and the cracks slowly began to spread. Concern seized Elander, and he started to call for Inya—but she was far in the distance and fully distracted now.

She was racing toward a much bigger problem that was developing.

He passed back through the opening Inya had made and took a few uneven steps after that goddess, his gaze sweeping over her and then up along the barrier she'd been in charge of creating.

More cracks like the ones his latest kill had caused were appearing all over that barrier.

Breaking.

That shield that they'd poured so much power and precision into was shattering, sections of it peeling away, and no less than twenty of the namtar had made their way through the openings. They drifted like ghosts toward the palace, moving in perfect silence until one of the soldiers dared to engage them—at which point more of those awful shrieks rang out, arrows lobbed through the air, and bursts of dark energy began to pop up all across the grounds.

Elander glanced over his shoulder, expecting Caden's smug *I told you so.*

But Caden didn't speak for several seconds. And when he finally did, it was in a hushed, detached tone. "Sooner than I thought, it seems."

Another arrow screamed toward them in the next instant, striking the barrier and sticking into it.

Caden knocked it free before its negating magic could cause more cracks. Then he stepped through the same opening Elander had, coming to stand by his side as he surveyed the developing battlefield in silence.

Elander's wary gaze moved on from Caden and looked to that battlefield as well.

Maybe he should have tried harder to make Caden leave, but another arrow was already flying toward them, so they ended up drawing closer to one another instead, standing back-to-back as they braced themselves for a trio of incoming monsters.

Those monsters shifted their bows—which were actually extensions of their own strange, sinewy bodies —into swords as they came closer.

At first they struck for Elander alone.

Not surprising, as Caden's energy matched that of the Dark God they served. They appeared confused about why Caden was attacking them—which gave him an advantage. He killed two of the three before they even had a chance to raise their weapons against him.

Elander killed the third just as it seemed to realize that Caden was, in fact, its enemy; it stabbed for Caden with incredible swiftness, but Elander's sword was faster, plunging into its skull and shoving it down into the dirt, whereupon he twisted the blade until the tell-tale strands of darkened energy began to leak from the dying body.

He stumbled back as that energy expanded and nearly engulfed him, summoning a quick burst of shielding magic to drive away the last of it.

He had remained untouched thus far, but there were dozens more of those namtar slipping through the increasing cracks in the barrier, converging on a path toward the palace gates.

Caden regrouped, rebalanced his sword, and started after the next closest target.

Elander followed. His questions briefly faded away, and they were allies without complications once more, both aligned toward a single goal. *Get back to the palace.*

Caden swung his sword with the reckless abandon of someone not afraid of whatever ending he was slashing toward.

One last time.

Elander didn't want to think about those words and what Caden had meant by them, so he just kept running for the palace, cutting down monsters as needed.

They made it to the gates where the guards were engaged with five of the namtar.

Elander distracted the void creatures, drawing them in with a blindingly bright display of magic.

The monsters attempted to absorb it just as the one at the barrier previously had, but they were fast overwhelmed by the power, their bodies seized by it, unable to do anything except vibrate violently and wail out a chorus of their terrible shrieks.

Caden sliced his way through the paralyzed row of them. His blade moved so quickly that it was impossible to separate each deadly blow from the next—it *had* to move quickly, as black, dangerous energy began to pour out as soon as that edge cut into them.

As the last of the five was cut down, their seeping energies combined and exploded outward. Elander shoved a guard out of the way and then dropped into a crouch himself, throwing a hand up and summoning a quick shield for that darkness to collide and scatter against.

Once it had finished scattering, Caden appeared, reached for his hand, and pulled him back to his feet

Elander swept an appraising glance over their

surroundings, fighting to catch his breath. A thick haze of that dangerous energy was beginning to settle over everything he could see. "We can't keep this up. Killing them is only going to keep spilling the massive amount of energy they absorb and carry around with them. It's essentially laying out a path to welcome the Dark God inside."

Caden nodded. "You need to contract your forces into a smaller area that's easier to defend."

"A protected center to operate from...and hopefully create a new barrier around it that isn't stretched as thin. One the enemy can't breach."

"Exactly."

Another surge of familiarity made Elander's chest tighten.

He looked away, still refusing to let that feeling sink all the way in, and he focused on shouting new orders to the soldiers who had started flocking toward him.

Caden continued on their march toward the palace, and Elander soon finished giving orders and followed him.

They moved as one, cutting a path toward the doors.

It was eerily quiet inside. The echoes of music and chatter from the banquet had faded, but there were no sounds of chaos, either; Casia had managed to keep order so far, it seemed.

Now he just needed to find her.

He felt it in his bones, in his magic, in that part of his

soul that was forever connected to hers—the darkness was pressing closer, the night felt close to unraveling entirely, and whatever was about to befall this palace...

He just needed to get back to her side.

Quickly.

CHAPTER 35

CAS HAD JUST FINISHED EXCHANGING HER ELEGANT DRESS FOR more casual clothing and boots when she heard the first scream ring out.

She drew her sword from its sheath and hurried to the door, mind racing, preparing to give orders to the guards waiting on her.

But the guards who had accompanied her up to her room...all eight of them...

Dead.

They were drained of all color and strewn across the floor, their bodies at odd angles that suggested a series of swift collapses. There was no blood nor brokenness to suggest that anything other than powerful magic had been responsible.

Their killer had been silent. The dying guards themselves had been silent. The scream she'd heard had come from somewhere in the distance, not right outside her door—she was almost certain of it.

She squeezed her sword and focused on the spell the Moon Goddess had taught her. The crescent emblem on the blade glowed to life, and that personal, reflective shield wrapped around her, hiding her. She should have simply done this to begin with, she realized—but the guards had been insistent about not letting her go to her room alone.

Another scream in the distance.

She willed herself to walk away from her room. To not look back. Her guards were gone, but someone else needed help—and she could still save others. Whatever was happening, she was going to put a stop to it. She just had to *move*.

She scanned the hallway, searching one last time for signs of the guards' killer. Then she sheathed her sword and cautiously broke into a run, her gaze darting about, watching for threats as she wove her way through the halls.

She needed to get back to her friends, to more guards, to Elander and the rest of her divine help.

Another scream.

It sounded almost...*familiar.*

She shook the thought from her mind. It was only paranoia creeping in, making her think that her friends were not safe. She had gone to them first after running back inside, and she had made certain that they knew trouble was possibly starting. They had gathered their guests in the ballroom, and she had poured all the power she could summon into creating barriers to seal off the entrances—just in case.

Just to give her and her guards a chance to investigate.

It had only been a foreboding feeling—a single dead monster that she needed to make sense of. The palace had seemed perfectly calm. Calm enough that she'd chanced that quick trip to her room.

But now...

What was going on?

She ran faster. She was painfully aware of how alone she was. She felt like an easy target, despite her magic making her invisible to most eyes. These halls that had been full of potential allies and promise just hours ago were empty, now, and that emptiness seemed to echo and amplify her growing anxieties.

Faster.

She could still protect the people gathered in that ballroom—they could still be her allies.

Faster.

This was just another chance for her to prove herself, and all the better that she had so many here to witness it firsthand.

Faster.

She ran past one of the libraries, and noted that the door was ajar—

Another scream.

Though she wanted to keep running, she couldn't. Someone was clearly inside that room, crying out for help. She stood in the center of the vacant hall for a moment, chest heaving. Her thumb traced the Heart embedded in Shadowslayer's pommel.

She crept close enough to the library to peer inside.

The space appeared empty at first. A fire was crackling in the hearth. Nothing out of the ordinary—except for the way that fire seemed to be dancing about. Her gaze shot to the window.

It was closed.

There was no breeze.

No other movement in the room, at all.

She was so busy trying to make sense of the flames that it took her a moment to realize the screaming had stopped. She started to back into the hallway.

Then she spotted the woman face down on the floor in the corner.

She thought she saw her twitch—a chance that this woman still lived. Instinct drove Cas to help once more, and she hurried over and knelt by the body. Rolled it over, and barely contained the gag that rose in her.

She had imagined that twitching, apparently.

This woman was just as dead and drained as her guards had been.

Cas didn't linger at her side. She leapt back to her feet and sprinted for the door.

A chill overtook the air, rapid and unrelenting. The flames in the fireplace shifted to a pale shade of blue, catching her attention just long enough to slow her down. A whirlwind of energy—not magic, but something clearly not of the mortal world—roared through the room.

The door to the hallway slammed shut.

Cas went perfectly still. Only her eyes moved, searching for her reflection in the gilded mirror above the fireplace. Her spell was still intact. She was still invisible.

And yet someone clearly knew she was here.

The sound of boots falling upon creaky wood drew her attention to the staircase that led up to the room's second floor. A man was descending that old staircase with unhurried steps—the same man who had been watching her so closely in the ballroom earlier.

She felt her magic unraveling despite her best efforts to hold it steady. The cold in the air penetrated more deeply into her skin, like someone was stripping her of her clothes in the middle of a blizzard.

The man said nothing as the magic peeled away and left her solid and clear before him.

His silence persisted even as she withdrew her sword.

It was so unsettling—that silence—that she broke it herself. "Who are you?" she demanded.

She already knew the answer. Fear had already

gripped her heart and mind and squeezed out all other explanations. And he could *sense* that fear, judging by the way he inhaled deeply, ran his tongue casually over his bottom lip—as if he could taste it in the very air.

She somehow kept her voice from wavering as she asked, "How did you get past our security? Past our barrier?"

How had she—and her divine allies—not felt him approaching?

Why had her magic not reacted to his presence?

He came closer, circling her as the last of her magic slipped away.

She stood her ground, gripping her sword tighter and matching him step for step, refusing to let him behind her—which seemed to amuse him.

Finally, he answered her. "I have walked in this realm since its creation. In all that time, do you *really* think I haven't learned how to move discreetly when necessary?"

"Our barriers—"

"The goddesses who made them are not more powerful than me. And neither are you, for that matter."

There was no denying his identity any longer— because suddenly her magic *was* reacting. It felt like it was trying to turn her body inside out, like it was desperately shrinking away from the enormous amount of power rising around this man.

Power that was opposite of what she carried.

She was life and protection.

He was death and destruction. Chaosbringer. God of the Shade, the too-clever Rook God, the Dark God—

Here.

He was actually *here.*

And he was stepping toward her as casually as one stepped toward an old acquaintance, with his hands clasped behind his back and his gaze traveling over the shelves of books around them. "It's been some time since I visited this palace." His voice was as casual as his gait. Deep, smooth as silk, and entirely *human* sounding.

She took a step away from him, though she didn't know why—there was a bookshelf almost directly behind her, blocking her.

He positioned himself between her and the door, blocking that escape route as well.

Cas sized up the distance between him and the window to her right, wondering if she could be fast enough, if she could break the glass cleanly enough with her magic to make a quick escape. Even with her sword in hand, she didn't like her odds. The room already felt full of his power—and it seemed to be thickening with every breath he took, effortlessly seeping from his being and settling like a shroud of death over the room.

"The last time I was in *this* particular library," he continued, "I was having a chat with your father about a certain deal we'd made."

"The bargain that prevented you from killing him and his descendants..."

"Which was overwritten the moment you accepted my mark during our last little meeting in Oblivion. Surely you realize that? Even though our arrangement was regrettably nullified, it wasn't without its benefits in the end."

She kept one eye on him, the other on the window.

She *had* known that—or suspected it, at least, even though she hadn't come face-to-face with him to test her theory. Not until this moment.

"How things change, hm?"

She focused on drawing magic—a shield of Sky-kind magic—instead of answering him, trying to keep the chill of his power from gripping her too tightly.

"No more bargain. No more protection. And here we are, back at the beginning, in a way."

She still didn't reply.

"I wasn't *quite* ready to make my return to this palace, but I decided the situation was too pressing to ignore." He moved closer to the fireplace, causing the flames to swell to a brighter shade of blue, and leaving the path to the doorway open.

He seemed to be daring her to take that path.

"Because you've been up to no good, haven't you?" he asked, more to the fire than her.

She took a step toward the door.

He didn't attempt to stop her. He simply glanced

over his shoulder and followed her with his pale eyes, waiting until she had nearly reached that door before he said, "You don't deny this, do you?"

She paused. "What should I be denying, precisely?"

How much did he know?

He smiled, and she was again struck by how *human* the expression looked. "Even if I hadn't squeezed the rest of the truth out of your dear brother, I would have gotten it out of someone else."

Her focus shifted farther from the door. He hadn't answered her question—but now a different one clawed its way from her throat before she could stop it. "Where is my brother?"

The god tilted his head. "Why do you care?"

I don't.

But it was a lie, and the cruel, pleased gleam in his eyes told her that he was well aware of this.

"Messy, aren't they? The fragile bonds that you mortals insist on clinging so tightly to." He took a step toward her. "And what a bigger mess *you've* made of everything, just by existing."

She summoned more magic, reinforcing her shield as she grappled for the door's handle without taking her eyes off the god.

Her hand finally closed over it.

The bright blue flames in the fireplace went out.

Everything seemed to have gone out—even the moon and stars that had been shining through the window were extinguished, and with the oppressive dark came a heaviness that made Cas feel as if her body had just tripled in weight. Her wrist wouldn't turn the handle. The hand gripping her sword felt swollen and equally useless, and it took all of her strength to keep herself from dropping it.

Her shield remained around her, but it did nothing to protect her against the sudden tightness that gripped her lungs.

That tightness grew more and more painful as he stepped closer to her. "You've realized, I hope, that this is how it was always going to end for you. That it would have been better if you had never *began* in this lifetime at all. A broken piece that needs fixing. I'm doing the world a favor by getting rid of you—fixing that *mess* you made of the natural order of things."

"The natural order?" She somehow managed to spit the words out despite the pressure squeezing her lungs. "Where gods like you can grow tired of their creations and decide to crush them on a whim?"

"You oversimplify my motives and ambitions. It is more than a mere *whim* that's brought me to this place." He looked ready to elaborate, but Cas interrupted before he could.

"Even if you kill me, the war against you won't end," she coughed out. "I've started something, and the rest of humankind will see it *finished*. You saw the allies I've gathered here tonight—and this is just my first attempt.

There are more in the kingdoms beyond. They will see what you've done—what you're *trying* to do—and they will rise against you."

"Yes." He cracked his neck from side to side, unbothered. "The possibility of that has certainly occurred to me."

The pressure on her body released so abruptly that it was jarring, sending sharp pains shooting through her legs as her balance shifted.

"I never could stand it when you humans attempt to make martyrs of yourselves. It proves again that I was right—that it was a waste of my time, trying to gift you fools with knowledge."

She reached for the door's handle again.

He didn't bother with magic this time. His hand shot forward and closed around her throat and he lifted her, throwing her at the fireplace as if she weighed nothing at all.

Her head slammed against the stone tile of the hearth. Shadowslayer slipped from her hand, clanged against that tile, and spun several feet away from her. She crawled after it, frantically snatched it back, and then she rolled over and fought her way to her knees.

The fireplace still held nothing more than smoke, but there was light streaming through the window once again. She could see a few faint stars from where she knelt.

The Dark God was moving toward her, but she kept her eyes on the stars.

She braced a hand against the floor. Clenched her sword. Pushed through the oppressive magic still veiling the room. Light flooded out from her body and sword, weaving into a shield powerful enough to force the god to stop. To take a step back. Only a small step—but it was a start, and despite her dizziness, she kept pushing.

He abandoned his casual demeanor and lifted a hand toward her.

Her shield crackled with the threat of electricity.

Clusters of shadows rose around his lifted hand. They stretched into spears that stabbed toward her, catching in her hair and clothing and yanking her backward, pinning her to the wall behind her.

A second group of shadows wrapped around her sword and ripped it from her grasp. She struggled, desperately trying to grab it as it flew away, but the movement only aggravated the magic entangling her. The shadows scraped against her like actual blades, the dark magic burning painfully cold against her skin— freezing it off, she feared. She didn't dare look away from the god approaching her to check the actual damage.

"As I was saying," he continued, "that *has* occurred to me. Which is why I intend to do more than just kill you."

She kept trying to narrow her vision, to refocus her magic along with it, but she had little success.

He stepped close enough to touch her.

And she wasn't sure which was worse—the feel of his magic burning over her skin, or the solid, almost careful touch of his fingers curling under her chin, lifting her gaze to his. He smelled of cold earth and dust and something bitterly floral. Like a grave.

"Rest assured that I have a plan to fully *break* you, and when it is all said and done, these allies you've been collecting won't be so willing to rally around your cause. They won't even recognize you."

He gave a casual twist of his other hand.

His magic shifted. Now it felt like hot knives digging into her skin, trying to carve parts of her out with a brutal carelessness.

She stared at the mark Nephele had branded on her skin, and she managed to summon a small storm to surround herself. It was weaker than normal, but it was enough to keep the shadows from settling too long against her, and to make Malaphar briefly draw his hand away from her face.

But the shadows holding her did not abate; they only pulled her more tightly against the wall.

She pushed back, trying to summon more of her own magic to wrap around and repel these ropes. The effort caused a sharp, fiery pain to shoot through her veins, and a cry slipped from her lips, drawing quiet laughter from the god.

She ignored the mocking sound and kept fighting.

He continued to laugh, to taunt her—right up until the door behind him flew open and an arrow struck his shoulder.

Cas watched as the arrow sparked with a light that burned a small hole in the fine silk shirt his human form had donned.

One of the Sun-magic infused weapons, she realized after a dazed moment.

It had distracted him, if nothing else, and his power shifted and scattered enough that Cas managed to shake free of her bindings.

She fell forward, catching herself on her hands and knees. Even before her dizziness subsided, she was diving once more for Shadowslayer, and she secured it in her grip before staggering to her feet and looking toward the door.

Nessa stood in front of that door, a bow still lifted in her hands. Her dress had been tied up, and her heeled boots swapped for more practical ones. She was flanked on either side by Laurent and Zev, who held weapons of their own—swords that were glowing with the same infusion of Sun-derived magic.

Malaphar whirled toward them.

But now that he was distracted, Cas was able to catch her breath and draw her own magic in earnest.

She darted between the god and her friends. The need to protect them brought an enormous amount of lightning surging from her sword and body. It swept across the room, twisting and taking the shape of a familiar beast—a tiger.

The beast opened its jaws, and the room flooded with light.

It heated the space so intensely that her friends were forced to retreat into the hallway. She stumbled out after them, one hand still behind her, directing her magic, while the other urged her friends to keep running.

Zev started to protest the idea of running, but a mass of dark energy—swirled with broken chips of the door and other debris—exploded into the hallway and silenced him.

Cas stopped trying to control her summoned beast. It continued to tumble with the darkness on its own while they turned and raced for the entry hall, where reinforcements waited.

Cas didn't look back, but she *felt* the moment her beast was swallowed up by the dark.

The oppressive cold of Malaphar's magic was biting at their heels a moment later. Shadows closed in on them as they ran, nearly overtaking them more than once.

As they approached the atrium, streaks of lightning hurtled past them, heading in the opposite direction, and collided with those shadows.

Elander and Nephele—the source of that lightning —were waiting for them as they rounded the next corner.

Elander caught Cas as she veered wildly to avoid a collision with the Storm Goddess. He steadied her against him, and she managed to catch her breath and gasp out, "*He's here.*"

He nodded. He already knew—and they had no time for any other exchange before they had to move again, retreating from more approaching shadows.

They made it into the entry hall, and the Moon Goddess—in her humanoid form—swept in behind them as they ran past her, using her magic to close off a shield that she had wrapped around the space.

A small army had been assembled within this protected space, all of them armed with more Sun-infused weapons. Caden stood in the center of them.

Cas's heart squeezed uncertainly at the sight of him, but she didn't have time to question it—she had to keep going, to make sense of a dozen other things.

Rhea was in the sealed-off ballroom behind them, keeping order and preparing to evacuate their guests with the Air spirit's help. Cas sent Nephele to help her as well, and then she, Elander, and the Moon Goddess further reinforced the seals that Cas had put into place to protect that ballroom.

With this job done, Cas turned back to the hallway she'd fled out of. Shadows continued to creep from it, slinking toward them, trying to find a way past their protection. She took a step toward those shadows, the movement an unspoken command to the army of people watching her.

They would hold the line right here.

The Dark God could follow her, fight her if he wanted to, but he would not break his way past this point. Not until those beyond it had gotten away safely.

She started to summon more magic to reinforce the shield that Inya had wrapped around them.

But before she'd woven the first strand of her own power into that shield...it *came*.

An impossible darkness.

So much *darkness*—like an avalanche of despair and death pushing in and suffocating the space, spilling in from every open passage and doorway. It rattled the walls. Extinguished every lantern. Clouded the windows. It absorbed the light being emitted by their shield, and stifled the glow of the Moon Goddess herself, drawing a gasp from her as it overtook her.

Cold grabbed at limbs and throats and sent Cas's army coughing and staggering toward the center of their protected space.

She reached for Shadowslayer. Gripped it tightly and felt it warming, humming to life under her touch.

But even its light could not penetrate this dark that was falling.

That darkness consumed everything in sight, and a moment later, she heard the first body hitting the floor.

CHAPTER 36

A MINUTE PASSED IN COMPLETE AND TERRIFYING DARKNESS—maybe longer.

Then came the sound of a sword being unsheathed.

It echoed in the quiet, nearly swallowed up by the falling darkness that had rendered everything else into silent oblivion. But the sound of that sword—the hum of its magic—was unmistakable, so Elander was not surprised to see flickers of light appearing a moment later, pulling the scene out of complete darkness.

A brighter shield started taking shape before them.

And it flared even *more* brightly as Casia fully withdrew her sword and lifted it in front of her.

A dead soldier lay on the other side of this shield, but the approaching carnage had stopped with him. The barrier Casia had created had wrapped around everyone else before the descending cloud of darkness could overtake them.

Beyond this shield, billowing black clouds obscured everything.

Darker, more powerful tendrils of magic continued to spin to life among those clouds, and to slink around the shield and press against it, searching for a way inside.

Casia kept her sword steady in front of her. The blade glowed, and ribbons of teal magic peeled from both that edge and her own skin, weaving in and healing the places where the darkness had managed to penetrate.

Her light didn't extend far beyond the shield, but enough of it leaked through to reveal a figure who was steadily approaching on the other side—a towering man who moved with smooth steps right up to the illuminated barrier, allowing the glow of it to fully fall upon the sharp angles of his face.

Malaphar.

He appeared human but for his pale eyes, which glowed like lanterns in fog. The air around him was restless, a chaotic whirlwind of shifting shadows and black feathers.

He didn't seem to be commanding any of the chaos.

He stood perfectly still, yet the tendrils of darker power within the clouds grew more numerous, and their attacks became more relentless. The shield wavered as a few of them pierced their way through. They began to spread out once they were on the other side, eating away at the light that Casia and her sword had managed to create. Like blood blossoming in water, darkening it.

Elander moved through the haze and found Casia's hand—just as he had so many times over the past weeks —reaching for her in the night and reminding her that he was beside her.

The nightmare didn't flee, this time, but the light holding it at bay grew bolder, the hum of Shadowslayer's magic grew louder, and the Dark God on the other side of the shield took a step back, pausing to better appraise the scene before him.

Within the growing brightness, Elander noticed a weak-looking part of the shield to Casia's right. He let go of her hand and shifted his focus and magic to that shield. The Moon Goddess did the same with a weakening point on the left. The three of them formed three points of power—pillars to hold the barrier in place.

As the light grew, the soldiers within it became more confident, spreading out, forming ranks, and readying their weapons.

Those weapons wouldn't be enough to destroy the god on the other side. All they could hope to do was drive him away again—to spare lives, to create a chance for them to breathe and regroup.

He had drawn closer again.

The whirlwind of magic and feathers continued to tumble chaotically around him.

No matter how the three of them tried to reinforce the barrier, they never managed to make it entirely solid against his shadows—they were still slipping in, bit by bit.

Could he push his way through?

It didn't matter in the end. He didn't need to push through. He only needed to weaken that barrier enough to see what was on the other side more clearly, to study and calculate his next move...and then he simply...*nodded.*

Elander realized what was happening, but not quickly enough to stop it.

Caden moved so silently, so swiftly that Casia didn't have time to turn around. His hand wrapped around her arm. A dagger was in his other hand, and it sliced across her wrist, causing her to drop Shadowslayer as she instinctively jerked away.

The sound of that sword hitting the ground echoed far more loudly than its unsheathing had.

The entire circle of their soldiers seemed to collapse toward Casia, moving to help—only to draw to an abrupt stop as Caden brought his dagger to her throat.

Everything was still.

Everything was silent.

Then someone cried out—Nessa, it sounded like— and lightning flared around Casia's body in the next instant, wrapping both her and Caden up in a tangled web. They scuffled for a moment until she summoned another bright burst of magic that allowed her to rip her way free of Caden's hold.

She picked up her sword and held it steady despite the blood streaming from her wrist. She staggered a few steps away from him, but she couldn't go far; coils of dark magic had wrapped around her legs to keep her from retreating. She didn't try to shake them. She simply turned to face Caden more completely, dragging the weight of those shadows with her.

In the corner of his vision, Elander saw Nessa starting to run for Casia's side, but Laurent caught her and held her back.

Zev moved in front of them, further blocking Nessa's path. The torn expression on his face as he looked toward Casia mirrored Elander's feelings exactly.

He wanted to rush forward, to snatch her out of harm's way.

But Caden had tossed aside his dagger and drawn his sword instead—and it was entirely too close to Casia. Those ropes of dark magic still held tightly to her legs, preventing her from moving freely. One wrong step might distract her, might give Caden the opening he needed.

He wouldn't need long to take advantage of that opening.

Their shield had weakened further as Casia's attention had been ripped away from it; Elander and the Moon Goddess were forced to focus attention on it or else let it collapse completely. They started to rebuild the weakened spots, but before they could manage it, countless more bands of dark magic had already slipped through.

One of these bands wove itself around Caden's body, lifting and pulling at his limbs and clothing, before sinking into his skin.

His eyes flashed, and he moved again, his sword lifting—

Casia threw her hands out before her. Her palms were still alight with magic, such a solid concentration of lightning that the entire space within their shield was soon buzzing from the power of it.

But she didn't actually *use* it.

It forced those shadows away from Caden—and forced him to a stop—but the searing bolts of it didn't touch him. They merely hovered between them. She glared at him through the electric haze. She never took that glare from him, not even to throw a cursory glance at the upper-god who was watching this all unfold from mere feet away from her.

It was as though there was no one else in the room aside from her and Caden.

"You can fight this," she told him, her voice quiet but clear. "You don't have to do what he says."

Elander had started toward her when he saw Caden's sword move, but now he hesitated.

Because she had brought Caden to a stop.

It seemed impossible that she could overpower whatever controlling magic the Dark God was pressing into Caden's mind—and yet, she *had*.

She had brought him to a stop, and she had dispelled those shadows that surrounded him. Even as the same kind of shadows wrapped more tightly around herself, weighing her down, she stayed on her feet and kept the light burning around them.

But maybe it wasn't *impossible* for her.

She had drawn him out of that Dark God's control, hadn't she?

Maybe she could do it again.

It was no more than a flicker, this hope—like that same flicker of her power that had withstood the invading darkness just minutes ago.

He silently willed it to turn brighter.

A tense moment passed.

"Take a step back," Casia ordered.

And Caden took a step back.

Elander held his breath. The rest of the crowd around them did the same. It was so quiet, and Casia's next words came out in a whisper, but somehow the sound was so powerful that it caused a shiver to trail down Elander's spine—

"You can come back to the light."

Caden blinked.

The tension in his muscles relaxed.

His sword lowered to his side.

Elander almost took a full breath—until another thread of the Dark God's power broke through and wrapped Caden up just as the last one had, whipping around his body, sinking into his limbs and tugging him into motion.

Elander could no longer hold himself back. Because he saw it before it happened—not a *feeling*, but an actual vision that seemed to have been magically planted within his mind—the sight of Caden's sword stabbing into Casia's chest.

He was halfway to Casia before Caden had taken a step.

Casia didn't move. The lightning she'd summoned had dissipated, and she wasn't calling it back. She couldn't—no, *wouldn't*—fight. The cords of dark power wrapped more tightly around her legs, held her in place as Caden swept around her and drew his weapon back, preparing to swing.

It all happened within the span of a few heartbeats.

Elander was at Casia's side, his hand upon her sword. He wrestled it from her grip. Shoved her to the ground.

Caden shifted his course, swinging instead for her fallen body, and Casia's scream rang out—

"STOP!"

Caden didn't stop.

So Elander didn't stop either.

The sword guided itself. Or perhaps it was his magic, the connection between him and Casia, the part of him that knew, deep down, that he could only protect one of them. And if he had to choose, it would always be her, no matter what it took.

Always.

Shadowslayer swept straight through Caden's chest, magic pouring from the blade, burning through his body as easily as if it were made of leaves.

The impact lifted and threw him several feet. He rolled across the marble floor, ending up on his back. Took a single gasping breath. His gaze slid to Elander's for a fraction of a moment. His mouth fell into an easy line, and he gave single, slow blink—a look of contentment, almost—before his eyes glassed over and he went perfectly still.

Quickly and cleanly.

Just as he had insisted it would happen.

Everything went blurry. Elander dropped to one knee, his head swimming.

A soft, pained cry fell from Casia's lips somewhere behind him, and only then did his vision clear—and he realized what he'd done.

It still didn't seem real.

None of this seemed real.

His eyes darted away from Caden's lifeless body just

long enough to see that the middle part of their shield was falling away. Rapidly.

The Dark God smiled as he took a step through that breaking barrier—only to be immediately thrown back by the enormous amount of power radiating around Elander.

Elander had done nothing to summon this power; he wasn't even holding Shadowslayer any longer. He had only risen to his feet to stand between the Dark God and Casia, and the light had exploded up with him, as thick as any of those shadows Malaphar had been throwing against their barrier.

Beasts of light—an entire pack of them—separated themselves from the powerful glow and prowled toward the Dark God.

Malaphar stood his ground, his gaze flickering over those wolf-like beasts as though they were mere nuisances. But the blackness around him had started to thin. The shield was shattering, but it didn't matter—the room remained illuminated.

The god seemed to be weighing his odds for a moment.

He still didn't retreat.

He instead shifted his attention to the shell of Caden's body. Then he lifted a hand toward it. Vines of darkness wrapped around the lifeless form, lifting it briefly from the ground. Like a beast playing with its kill, shaking it until it was bled dry—but instead of blood, it was energy seeping out and curling away from Caden's form.

The room was moving toward darkness again. It was not the same abyss as before, but a chaotic, rippling blackness that pulsed with occasional bolts of grey, as though they were caught in the center of a storm cloud.

Laurent, Nessa, and Zev reached their side, forming a protective half-circle around them while Elander helped Casia to her feet.

"What is happening?" asked Zev.

"The magic that Caden possessed is returning to its higher power," Elander explained, his voice still distant —dazed. "Varen isn't here, so it's flowing to his upper-god instead."

That return grew increasingly tumultuous as the seconds passed, shattering windows, buckling doors, sending little cracks shooting through the walls and floors.

He knew they needed to run.

But as he sought an exit for them, his gaze caught once more on the empty shell of Caden's body. Before he realized what he was doing, he had started toward it. He needed to recover the body—

He felt a sudden weight on his arm, dragging him back.

"We have to go." Casia wrapped herself more securely around him. "He's gone. I'm sorry, but we have to get away from here, away from that power—it's suffocating my magic. I need a chance to—"

Something crashed to the floor nearby—a chandelier—cutting her off. She turned away for a moment to check on the others, and then looked back to him, her eyes pleading.

We have to go.

Another pulse of energy hit another chandelier—closer to them this time. As the pieces of it shattered and rained over them, Casia lifted her hand and managed a weak shield, protecting them both.

His magic automatically flared again as hers did. It sparked something in his mind as well—awareness. He gave his head a shake. Backed away from Caden, and let Casia turn him and pull him further into motion.

Side-by-side, they ran away from all those shattered pieces.

But they didn't get far.

They had nearly reached the main doors when an explosion of power funneled in from behind them. The Moon Goddess managed a shield to partially block it, but the force was still enough to knock them off their feet.

Every window shattered. The walls shook, little chips of plaster and clouds of dust breaking free—and then an entire section of one of those walls collapsed outward. The ceiling started to go with it. The Moon

Goddess redirected her shield, creating a protected, narrow path for them to escape through.

They scrambled up and continued to run. One after the other, they broke out into the night.

But they were only trading one battlefield for another.

The army of namtar had expanded and overtaken the grounds.

They kept moving anyway, trying to organize, but after a moment of shouting orders, Casia seemed to lose her voice. She stumbled to a stop and her head whipped around, searching for him, that same pleading look in her eyes as before.

We have to move.

But where do we go?

Elander wasn't sure how to answer.

And before he could find the words, a wave of darkness rushed out from the palace and overtook them, and the moon and all the stars above them seemed to go out.

CHAPTER 37

Cᴀs ꜰᴇʟʟ ᴛᴏ ʜᴇʀ ᴋɴᴇᴇs ᴀs ᴀ ᴡᴀᴠᴇ ᴏꜰ ᴅᴀʀᴋɴᴇss sᴡᴇᴘᴛ over her.

That dark lifted quickly, but she stayed on the ground. She couldn't find the strength to get up as she peered through the grey haze around her and tried to comprehend the carnage. Her heart was in her throat. Her eyes burned as she counted the dead.

There were so many dead.

So many bodies broken, or in the process of breaking, and for what felt like an eternity she knelt there among the wreckage, trying and failing to catch her breath.

She heard someone shout her name—Nessa—and it was the only reason she tried again to stagger to her feet.

As she finally managed it, one of the namtar

appeared to her right, its cadaverous wings flaring and its bow lifted, aiming a black and burning arrow straight at her heart. She stumbled out of its path, spun wildly, and managed to shoot several bolts of lightning into the back of the monster's head.

Elander emerged from the fog and cut down a second archer as it lunged for her, and then he wrapped an arm around her and pulled her away from the explosion of dark energy that followed the slaying.

She continued to wake up.

More monsters swelled into the space around them. She moved outside of herself, to some place where she couldn't feel pain, her numb body fueled by nothing except rage and grief. Her sword and magic took on a life of their own, slicing and flying out from her until she finally ran out of things to kill.

There were more things in the distance, but she couldn't bring herself to chase them.

She fell against a nearby wall, clutching Shadowslayer to her chest.

The roaring, crashing sound of a collapse rose above the chaotic noise all around her—another section of the palace was falling.

She watched as it crumbled, as dust and dark magic blossomed up into the sky. She started to crumble to the ground as well. But Nessa was there again, shouting her name and running to her side, giving her a reason to stand up.

Nessa had been trying to get her attention *because* of that crumbling bit of palace, it turned out. Even as everything collapsed, she had somehow remained focused, and now her words came out like she was reciting them—like she was checking a plan off yet another list she had carefully composed.

"The office in that section of the palace was still full of people," she said. "They're buried, now, and we can't just leave them—"

Cas shook her head as she looked to the palace. She wanted Nessa to be wrong. But all of her endless diagramming and planning... She likely knew the exact number and the names of everyone that had been buried in that space.

But it didn't matter.

They didn't have enough soldiers to dig them out.

Cas didn't know where to move next, what wound to heal, what fire to extinguish first. She had been so confident of the order of things only hours ago. *How had it gone so wrong, so quickly?*

"We have to focus on the things that are still standing," she told Nessa.

Nessa looked horrified at the thought, but Cas only shook her head again, closed her eyes and tried to make a list of her own. *Find Rhea. Find the Storm Goddess. Evacuate as many as possible. Evacuate ourselves. Live to fight another day.*

She was moving again, shouting these orders before

she realized it, directing soldiers to follow her toward the ballroom. It was still standing. They had sent the Air spirit to help get the people in that room to safety, and she needed to get closer, to make sure the barriers around that room remained intact so the evacuation could be successfully completed.

Elander caught up to her and helped carry out her plan, and for several minutes, it was all Cas focused on.

As they finished reinforcing that barrier, she turned and saw that Nessa had stubbornly made her way toward the pile of rubble and buried people, anyway. She'd been quick; she'd only just been standing at her side—Cas was certain—and now she was at least a hundred feet away.

So quick.

But she was not fast enough to avoid the Dark God as he emerged from that pile of rubble.

Concentrated waves of darkness emerged along with him, and Nessa was thrown to her knees as one of those waves struck her.

It seemed to be reflex for that god, the way he pulled his sword from within those waves. The way he shook it free of the black feathers that encircled it, and then lifted it, angled it toward Nessa. So casual, so *senseless* and random and why, *why* was Nessa still kneeling there—

The god barely even looked at Nessa as he plunged his sword into her side.

And for the second time in a span of an hour, the world seemed to stop.

Cas couldn't move, couldn't breathe, couldn't think anything at first except—

No.

Nothing else that had happened tonight—all the blood, the failure, the wreckage—none of it mattered anymore.

No, no, no, no.

She wanted to scream, to cry, to vomit. She wanted to stop time. To go back, to take Nessa's place somehow.

Like it had in all those memories she'd struggled her way through, the seconds seemed to skip ahead in a way that made no sense. Cas didn't remember moving, but suddenly she was next to Nessa's fallen body, standing face-to-face with the god who had struck her down.

With a furious cry, she slashed her sword toward Malaphar, and the light that flew out from it was as furious as her scream. Waves of it built and built until it had swallowed up everything in sight, turning the night briefly into day—

When the light finally settled, the god had disappeared.

She could still sense him nearby.

Elander was right behind her, picking up her sword as she flung it down and standing guard, continuing to keep their enemy away from her while she dropped to Nessa's side.

Fear should have gripped her at the thought of Elander facing off with that god. She knew this—but she couldn't feel it. She was empty, wrung dry, and everything else faded as Nessa's gaze shifted and attempted to focus on her.

There was blood...*everywhere.*

Cas tried to feel her way over Nessa's stomach, attempting to assess the wound. She gave up quickly, and tried instead to lift her into her arms. But Nessa felt so fragile, and *where would they go* anyway?

How could she possibly take her away from this?

She stopped trying to lift her, to do anything except hold her and force herself not to tremble—as if she might help Nessa's heart and lungs stay steady, if only she could remain steady herself.

"Do me a favor." Nessa's voice was soft but...*strong.* But that had always been her, hadn't it? Clear and steady softness in spite of the pain, the chaos, the *grief.* "Those flowers..."

Cas shook her head, trying to get her to stop talking, but Nessa pressed on—

"Don't let them die. You're terrible with plants, I know, but promise you'll try, hm?" She winced in pain, and her eyes stayed closed. "I don't want all of that work we did to be for nothing."

She was warmth, had always been warmth to go with that softness. But now her cheek felt cold against

Cas's arm, and that chill was worse than any magic the gods had ever conjured against her.

"Tell me again," Cas whispered. "I need you to tell me again how to keep them alive."

Nessa's lips parted, as if to start giving instructions.

But nothing came out.

This couldn't be right.

All of their plans, all of their futures, all of their hopes—

It didn't work if all of them didn't make it to the other side.

It simply didn't *work.*

"Stay awake. We aren't done." Cas's hand trembled. "Stay awake, you have to stay awake and tell me how to do this...*stay...*"

She was still.

Cas was not certain how long she sat with that awful stillness before she managed to lift her head. But when she did, the first person she spotted was Zev, picking his way through the rubble.

He caught sight of them and froze.

Laurent was directly behind him, and his focus was on shouting orders to nearby soldiers—so it took a moment for his gaze to circle around to the sight of Cas curled tightly over Nessa's body, growing damp with her blood.

And when it finally did, a strangled cry unlike

anything Cas had ever heard him utter tore from his throat.

It was the most horrible sound she had ever heard, and for a long moment, it seemed to have destroyed her ability to hear anything else.

But as that silence settled completely around her, a voice was whispering through her mind—the Star Goddess's.

A great sacrifice that will cause a great shift...and after that...what appears to be a difficult choice.

Here they stood at the sacrifice.

It was not her own, Cas realized now, but that of her friends, her followers, the ones who had trusted her to lead them to a better, more unified world.

They had given too much.

They had suffered too much.

Too much.

It was all too much.

As Zev and Laurent fell to Nessa's side, Cas rose and staggered away.

It couldn't end here. She had to keep moving; she had to find a way to fix this. And she already had an idea. It terrified her, but *she had an idea.* She had it figured out—

Now came the *difficult choice.*

She started to sprint away, intending to put space between herself and her friends and that choice she was going to make.

But she only made it a short distance before the Dark God was *there*, blocking her path in a rush of black, unfolding wings and unfurling power.

She stumbled back.

Everything fell away except for his voice, which seemed to cut directly into her mind: "More broken things," he mused, his eyes lifting toward Nessa. "You seem to attract them wherever you go."

She didn't reply.

"You're running toward something, aren't you?" He shook his head at her, soft laughter spilling from his lips. "Where to? You can't save her. You can't fix this world. Accept it. Stop running. Or perhaps I can keep making this night worse for you until we reach an understanding."

She wasn't certain how it could possibly get worse.

He had told her he was going to break her—and he already had. He had broken her so thoroughly that she was not sure how she was still standing, how she was trying to think, trying to formulate a plan to *fix* anything.

But she was.

And broken or not, she could still move.

She swung her sword at him again, but this time she summoned a cage of barrier magic instead of lightning. It wrapped tightly around him.

It didn't hold as dark daggers of his power stabbed through it.

But Elander was there in the next breath, adding his power to that cage she'd started to build.

He was bleeding, Cas noticed. A dark stain covered his shoulder and wound down his arm. She didn't process much beyond that. He was injured, but he was still moving, just as she was—and that would have to be enough for now.

They focused, and together they managed to create a more solid enclosure to slow Malaphar down. The Moon Goddess appeared a moment later, strengthening it further, and she remained behind to hold it while Cas and Elander turned and raced back to Nessa and the others.

Laurent and Zev still appeared too stunned to listen, but Cas spoke anyway. "He's bound, but it isn't going to hold him for long. Find an Air crystal, or the spirit herself, and get Nessa far away from here—away from *him*. Get her to a healer."

Zev's voice was strained. "Cas, it's already too—"

"I'll follow you soon. I can *fix* this. I can still save her." Her voice mirrored Zev's—thin, brittle, *breaking*. "I just need to take care of something first. There's something that I need to do, I won't be long, I just..." She heaved in a breath.

Zev started to argue again, but her next words roared from some desperate place deep inside of her, cutting him off—

"Just *GO!*"

Laurent already had Nessa cradled against his chest. His gaze was distant. Broken. Cas still wasn't certain he'd heard her at all. But then he rose slowly, carefully, and made for the gate that led into the courtyard of the ballroom.

Zev sprinted halfway to that gate himself before hesitating and turning back, his brow furrowed in concern, as if the possible meaning behind her words had only just caught up with him.

Elander hadn't moved since she'd started speaking. He was holding his bleeding shoulder and watching her closely. Suspiciously.

She almost smiled as their eyes met.

Nothing ever got by him, did it?

"You have to trust me," she said quietly.

He took a step toward her.

She took several longer, much quicker steps backward, words tumbling from her mouth as she went: "I love you. Just remember that, even if everything else is gone—even if I've gotten this wrong, and I don't come back—please don't forget that. In this lifetime and in every other. I love you, I love you, *I love you*."

His gaze had fallen to her throat, to the chain of gold that rested against it.

She pulled out the hourglass attached to that chain.

He shook his head, but she moved too fast for him to stop her.

"You'll find me again," she whispered. A question. A

plea. A vow. She didn't know which it was—and she didn't wait for his reply before she jerked the chain. Hard.

It snapped.

And then she was gone.

CHAPTER 38

CAS WOKE TO THE FEELING OF COLD WATER SLIDING OVER HER body.

Her eyes blinked open, and she found herself on the shore of a grey river, its waves lapping at her fingertips.

She sat up. Gazed around. The river ran in a perfectly straight line beside her, and the space around it was as grey as its waves, filled with endless fog that obscured anything else that might have been hiding in this realm.

"Kantrum," came a voice.

It took Cas a moment to realize that she recognized that voice, even though she'd expected to meet her here.

Santi.

The goddess appeared as Cas thought her name, and she reached out her hand, golden bracelets jingling, and pulled Cas to her feet.

"Kantrum?" Cas repeated, still glancing around.

"The realm outside of Time and Space." Santi explained. "And this is the River Drow. All timelines flow out from its waters. While you stand on its shores, you are suspended—both everywhere and nowhere. Inside of every moment, yet out of reach of all."

Cas swiped the flecks of river mud from her clothing. Sucked in a breath at the sight of Nessa's blood still covering her.

"I once suggested this as a place for punishing errant souls," Santi continued, "but even the Dark God thought it too cruel to trap them in this nothingness."

Cas studied the river again. "All timelines flow from its waters?"

Santi nodded.

"So this is..." Cas paced the shore. She could feel the goddess's eyes following her; the stare felt particularly penetrating in this desolate space, with almost nothing to otherwise draw it away. "This is where you go—this is how you move between timelines."

Another nod. "And there is one point in time that *you* are still determined to go to, I believe."

Yes, thought Cas, but the word didn't make it out of her.

"You must speak it," Santi commanded.

Cas took a deep breath.

She peered down, and she thought she saw faces in the water—the faces of all her friends, of all that she had to lose.

She closed her eyes and said, "I want you to take me back to the moment when Elander and I first met. The lifetime that came before my current one."

"You're certain? You must be certain, or the waters won't carry you—they'll drown you."

Cas looked back to the river. The current was gentle. Soothing. Inviting, almost. "And what happens if I die here?"

"Die?" Santi shook her head. "You don't die. You stay beneath the water for eternity, treading the restless current, never able to fully catch your breath."

Cas hesitated, if only for a moment.

But it wasn't the water she feared.

Not being able to fully breathe didn't worry her either.

She was only afraid of failing her friends. Her king. If this did not work, if she had gotten this wrong, it would mean the end of...*everything*. Of the other side she had hoped to reach with them all, of the future they'd been fighting so hard to secure.

That future had seemed so bright ever since that moment on Sulah's Hill. Ever since that morning she'd spent with Nessa tending those flowers. Its light was shining in a hundred other little moments where her friends had held her and carried her through, and she could will herself to see it even now, even among the murky nothingness: A flame inside the fog, leading her onward.

The goddess's soft voice broke the quiet. "You know what you will lose."

Cas nodded. "I know what I have to do."

Santi flicked her bangled wrist, and several grains of glowing sand appeared, floating above her palm. She tossed them into the river, and the waters became rougher. "Then hold your breath, Mortal Queen, and *dive*."

CHAPTER 39

THERE WAS NO THREAD OF LIGHT GUIDING HER FROM THE water as before; the Moon Goddess could not reach her here.

But Cas emerged from this river just as she'd emerged from the one in Ciridan.

Only she was dry this time, and she did not ache, and she was not confused about what to do next. Her gaze lifted to the familiar house on the distant cliff, and she started toward it.

Santi appeared beside her as she walked, her wings fluttering and her feet not quite touching the spiny grass. "So here we are at the breaking point," said the goddess. "I will make this easier for you by offering some instructions."

Cas kept walking, her eyes never leaving the house.

"You know that the Death God trying to spare you—

and then bringing you into the next life—triggered an unfortunate series of events."

"Yes."

"So you must find a way to make certain your past self does not meet the God of Death in the first place."

They reached the fence surrounding the house, and Cas paused with her hand on the creaking gate. "Is that the truth then? That erasing myself is the only way to stop the Dark God from rising in that next lifetime?"

The goddess gave a solemn nod.

Cas narrowed her eyes on the flowers that had over-taken the yard. Not on the lilies, which everyone associated with the Death God, but on the lilacs—the same kind of flowers that covered Sulah's Hill.

"Go inside," urged the goddess. "And find a way to do what you must."

Cas closed the gate and latched it shut.

And then she turned back to face the goddess and said, "Did you think I wouldn't realize what you were trying to do?"

The goddess lifted her chin, appraising.

"You're working for the Dark God."

Santi's lips parted, but no words came out.

"He seemed to think I would be better off erasing myself too," Cas continued. "He even called me a *broken piece*. The exact words I said to you the day we met."

Santi's lips closed back into a smile.

"I wonder where he got those words? This *idea* that I

should erase myself? Perhaps from a goddess who swore she was on our side."

Still smiling.

"He orchestrated all those deaths tonight, all that ruin and chaos—but he wasn't trying to kill me; he was trying to bring me to this moment of desperation. You told him you'd do the rest at this point, I presume."

The goddess inhaled a deep breath.

"*Traitor*," Cas accused—which earned her a slap that was hard enough to send her spinning toward the ground.

"I would stay on that ground, if I were you," the goddess hissed.

Cas staggered back to her feet anyway, spitting blood as she came. "I am a *broken piece*. Isn't that what you wanted me to believe? I have heard that from so many at this point—including *myself*—that you would think I had no choice to believe it, wouldn't you?"

Santi's smile became a snarl, but otherwise she didn't reply.

"You thought you could erase me. But why would you want to do that?"

The goddess had no answer to this, either.

"I think it's because that Dark God you now answer to is afraid of me. Of what my *broken* self is capable of doing. Of what I have already done. Which is why it was not enough for him to simply kill me."

The goddess laughed a cruel, sparkling laugh. "Do tell—what exactly do you think you're capable of?"

Cas wiped more blood from her mouth. "*Broken* doesn't mean I have to stop fighting. It doesn't mean that I need to erase anything."

"My, we believe we have everything figured out, don't we?" Santi mused. "And yet you willingly chose to come back to this point in time. Why would you do such a thing if you knew I only meant to trick you into erasing yourself?"

"I had to."

"*Had* to?"

"All your wisdom of timelines, of past and present and future...and yet you've overlooked something, Goddess."

Santi's smile finally started to fade.

"You bringing me back here to destroy me is what actually *created* me." Cas took a step closer to her.

And the goddess—the master of all those intricacies of space and time—took a step back in what looked suspiciously like alarm. Like *fear*.

"You told me you cannot do anything to alter the past," said Cas. "But *I* can. And I willingly chose to come back so I could make sure it happened. I've seen it happen, and I understand it now. I was meant to be. *We* were meant to be. And you will not erase us. You will not erase *me*."

Santi's beautiful face became marred by irritation and confusion

But Cas was no longer confused—she had never felt more certain of anything.

She was not here to erase her past.

She was here to embrace it.

Because she had realized the truth hidden in that memory Caden had shown her. That barrier that had appeared around the house, that magic that had driven Elander's shadows back. That *instability* Caden had mentioned...

It had been her.

It was this moment, this magic simmering in her veins, ready for her to draw it out and leave a mark that could not, *would* not, be erased.

Here was the difficult choice that the Star Goddess had told her about.

She could choose to stay in the past and forsake her next lifetime, her crown, her empire, her friends and that world that she might ultimately fail to protect.

Or she could choose to live. To keep fighting. To not erase herself, but to *become* herself, in spite of the mess, in spite of the pain, the fear, the uncertainty that lay behind her and ahead of her. She could choose to live.

She would choose to live.

She moved quickly, before the goddess could work out what she was doing.

She made it to the door of the house and then spun

around, magic flying from her palms as she did—several solid ribbons of white weaving together before stretching in a circle around her.

The goddess descended upon her with a furious screech, ripping her from the porch and throwing her away from the house.

Cas hit the fence, scraping the side of her face on the splintered wood. Pain blossomed through her head.

But it didn't matter.

Because through that pain throbbing in her head and blurring her vision, Cas could see her magic fixed in its place, glistening in the pale morning light.

She'd done enough.

A barrier of magic now wrapped around the house. The one that would stop Elander in his tracks. The one that would drive the shadows out, just as the Sun Goddess had told her to do.

"Clever little bitch," said Santi, suddenly looming over her. "But now let me tell you what *you* have overlooked."

Cas fought her way back to her feet, and she willed herself to stay on them even as Santi crowded closer and spoke, in a voice dripping with poison—

"I am still the Goddess of Time and Space, and you are still here with *me*. I brought you here. And how do you think you're going to get back to the ones you left behind? I don't need to alter anything you've done here in the past. I only need to keep you from fully leaving it."

Cas's heart clenched and her breath froze in her lungs, but she stayed on her feet.

"You see, there is no future for you unless I *say* there is a future for you." The goddess held out her hand, and another hourglass like the one she'd given Cas spun into existence above it. "And I say *no*."

She threw the hourglass at Cas's feet.

It shattered, the scenery around them shattering with it—

And then Cas was in the Drow River once more, grey waves churning around her. She tried to swim upward, but she couldn't find the surface. Swimming down got her nowhere either.

It was exactly as Santi had told her. She wasn't drowning, she was merely treading water.

It was cold, at first. Bitterly so. But that cold soon faded, and that was worse—because she *knew* she should have been freezing, but she couldn't feel it. Her senses were fading. The grey waters were growing rougher, throwing her this way and that, and yet she felt nothing at all.

So she closed her eyes, reached for the magic inside of her, and she thought of everything she had to fight for. Her friends. Her empire. Her king.

Find me, she'd told him.

She wasn't certain he'd heard her. If she'd said it loudly enough or clearly enough. But it didn't matter. Somehow, she knew he would find a way back to her.

Across lifetimes, through endings and beginnings. *Always.* There was nowhere she could go that he couldn't find her. They were not finished.

She was not anxious.

She was not afraid.

She was *enough*, and she was focused, summoning every bit of magic she could to try and reach him.

The dark was closing in. It was getting harder to move. To summon her magic. To breathe. To think.

But it wouldn't last.

The light always came back, and this time, it would come back brighter and stronger than ever before. She was certain of it—

And now she only had to wait for the dawn.

Afterword

Thank you for reading! If you enjoyed this book, please consider taking a moment to leave a review to help other readers find and enjoy it :) After you've done that, I hope you'll grab the fifth and final book in the series, The Queen of the Dawn (coming in 2023)!

Also, if you want to connect further, see behind-the-scenes stuff, get the first look at covers, teasers, character art, etc...or just come yell at me for my cliffhanger endings, then you can do all of that in my V.I.P. Reader's Group on Facebook!

Made in the USA
Middletown, DE
21 August 2024

59527977R00380